Tom Sawyer, Avenger

Tom Sawyer, Avenger

T. W. Fuller

Writers Club Press
San Jose New York Lincoln Shanghai

Tom Sawyer, Avenger

Writers Club Press
an imprint of iUniverse.com, Inc.

For information address:
iUniverse.com, Inc.
5220 S 16th, Ste. 200
Lincoln, NE 68512
www.iuniverse.com

ISBN: 0-595-16188-X

Printed in the United States of America

To—The girl with the *mega-grin,* wherever she may be.

CHAPTER I

The news spread throughout St. Petersburg faster than Jimmy Finn could drink a jug full of hard whiskey. It became the biggest news to hit here since the finding of 12,000 dollars in gold a year ago, and flew faster than an eagle from person to person, group to group, family to family; nobody remained left out. Tom Sawyer was no exception.

The boy in question sat upon a decaying log in an open area of St. Petersburg's forest, not far from town. School out for nearly a week, he came here every day, usually to play Robin Hood or pirates, and other childhoods games. Today he had other, more *crucial*, matters to mull over. For the longest time he contemplated in gloomy silence.

Tom looked up. Not a cloud in sight. The sun shined overhead as a flock of birds chattered in the west. It was a beautiful, warm summer day. Tom sighed, yearning for a heavy rainstorm. He believed it wrong for nature to be felicitous when he suffered. With deep sorrow he put his head between his hands and sighed once more.

Two squirrels ran up and down a tree, making a ruckus. Tom captured them in the corner of his eye. Spying a stick near at hand, he picked it up and threw it at the unsuspecting animals. They scurried away and Tom felt glad. He wanted no company, no one to share in his troubles.

"It ain't right!" Tom finally said. "The gang had *no* right to quit. Not the first time, nor when I asked them to rejoin yesterday. I even offered full immunity, and still they turned me down. And not only that but not one of them sapheads tried to revolt or mutiny against me. Why, I consulted all the books on the subject and the only way a body can up and quit is if there's a mutiny. And there warn't even one of *those*."

He rethought the situation for a couple of moments. "Well, I reckon it's just as well! They didn't more know how to be robbers than Sid knows how to lie. And asking all them blame fool questions like—When we going t' kill someone; when's our first ransom and orgy; where were all the A-rabs and elephants? Well, if they'd 'a' read the books on robbers, then they'd 'a' known what to do. And they'd 'a' *seen* the A-rabs!"

Tom fell silent again and observed the dirt. The upper part was soft and powdery. He wrote "BECKY" with his toe. Catching himself, he quickly erased it. This became a recurring habit. Every argument the two became embroiled in, Becky would storm off and neither would see each other for a couple of days. Then, Tom would find himself writing her name on something or other, get fed up, and go seek Becky for reconciliation. This time their argument was over a bonnet Becky bought. Tom, quite fond of Becky's hair, liked it when she wore it down. When Becky put the bonnet on for Tom to admire, he only said it was all right, but that she had a beautiful head of hair and hated to see her hide it under a "silly" bonnet. Becky told him what a meanspirited person he was, then ran off to her home.

"Well, that's just the way of girls. Always frettin' 'bout this and that. I didn't mean no harm. I only meant to say that I like her without she is wearing a bonnet. And for *that* she storms out! And over what? A bonnet!"

As Tom reasoned the situation, he heard a noise, faint at first, but growing louder and closer. Tom vaguely heard it over his speech, for he had gotten into it now, with fists raised high above his head for "style". Finished, he became more aware, putting his ear to the wind and listening. Voices could be heard shouting back and forth, and stampeding of feet. Tom slowly stood and walked toward the noise, which echoed from the direction of town. His feet picked up after hearing a townsman shout, "It's murder!" Entering the forest's mouth, Tom immediately stopped, else he would have been trampled by a steady flow of traffic. All of St. Petersburg was filing down to the river, hoping to board the *Big Missouri* before it filled up. A passerby shouted, "*Murder!*" Other people repeated the statement, equal in tone and pitch and dramatic style.

"He's been murdered! It's murder, murder, murder!"

Tom spotted his bosom friend Joe Harper and hailed him over.

"Say Joe?" Tom asked, getting his friend to one side, away from all the traffic. "What's all the row about?"

"Ain't you *heard!*" Joe spouted wildly. "It's Huck. He's been murdered."

"Huck? No! How'd it happen?"

"I'll tell you on the way down to the dock. Everyone's going out on the *Big Missouri*. They're gonna try to raise Huck's body from the river."

"I can't b'lieve it."

"Huck's pap came in town 'bout a half an hour ago, with a whole crowd of people, yellin' Huck was murdered by robbers who broke into their cabin."

"Poor Huck."

"Judge Thatcher said he might put out a warrant for Huck's pap. His story don't wash too well. Says Huck's pap probably killed Huck his own self while drunk. And when he sobered up, saw what he done and made up the story."

"I reckon he *could* 'a' done it. He had *aim* enough to anyway. Why, many 'a' times I'd see him grab Huck in public and beat him 'thout so much as a thought to anyone watching."

"Everyone figures Huck is in the bottom of the river. They say that's where his body was dragged. And everyone's gettin' ready to shove out and see if they can't bring him up."

Presently they made their way to the river where people were boarding the *Big Missouri*. The Harper's family was aboard, as were Aunt Polly, Sid and Mary. Among the other notables were the Thatchers, Rogers, Widow Douglas, and Jimmy Finn. Joe's mother shouted down for him to hurry before the boat left. Aunt Polly, standing next to Mrs. Harper, did as well for Tom.

An uncomfortable murmur loomed aboard the boat while people mingled with one other. Huck, though having been under the guidance of Widow Douglas once, still was considered a rapscallion by many. The eerie quiet resulted from both a conscious fear of offending Widow Douglas, and offending Huck's spirit. People holding such superstitions would rest easy that night if Huck's body did *not* rise, alive or dead. So why go at all! Even St. Petersburg was not immune to journalism. What a treat it would be to see one's name in the paper so they might brag about it to the unfortunate neighbor who missed boarding the *Big Missouri*.

The cannons roared; holy bread was sent adrift to scour the river in the hope Huck's spirit would rise above the "Big Muddy" with a raging, supernatural hunger for one last meal. And not just any meal, but quality, stately "baker's bread", as it was called. Not the low-cut corn-pone most citizens were used to. In fact, a number of people envied the dead boy for having such a privilege and opportunity only a select few were given on a daily basis. This ritualistic nonsense lasted an hour as the boat circled Jackson's Island; then, with no results, made its way back to dock.

Tom, bored with listening to Aunt Polly and Mary blubbering, and Sid's unsympathetic silence, slipped away. It may not have been proper for family members to part at so solemn an event, but Tom had much on his mind, and he walked about the boat in earnest; for, while boarding, he spied the Thatchers. More importantly, he saw *her*. Walking with encouragement, Tom hoped to reconcile with Becky, and end the day more blissfully. However, he had to halt abruptly after turning a corner, and stumbling into a mob of people. Inching his way inside, Tom saw they were surrounding Jimmy Finn, Judge Thatcher, and Widow Douglas.

Judge Thatcher seemed dismayed, and partly disorientated. He wiped his brow continuously, though the temperature did not warrant it. However, the man did his level best to calm everyone down. Especially Jimmy Finn, who was quite erratic. Tom thought it best to stay back a distance and not "get in the way".

"Looky here, Judge. It don't make no diff'ence a'tall. The boy's deed. So nat'lly the money b'longs to me."

"You won't see *one* penny of that money Jimmy Finn. Not if I can do anything about it."

"You! Think you so high an mighty 'cause you a judge? *I* is the boy's pappy. Now don't that account fer somethin'?"

"As far as the court is concerned, Widow Douglas is a legal custodian over Huckleberry Finn and *all* of his belongings, including his share of the money."

"And don't even think you'll get anything from me you drunkard."

"You hesh up, woman. I'll git that money, Judge. One way or t'other."

"You're a fine example of a father indeed. Your son has been *murdered*, and all you can think about is money. For all we know, it was *you* who murdered Huck for that very reason."

Jimmy's eyes flared. He lunged toward Widow Douglas, clenching his fists around her neck. She fell to the deck, with Jimmy on top of her. It took three people to get him off. His fists were still flying wildly until a passenger knocked him over the head with his cane. He fell to the ground with a thump. Had he been drunk, he might have shaken it off. Judge Thatcher had tried to intervene, but his legs would not budge. Nobody noticed.

Everyone's attention now focused on Widow Douglas, who lay on the floor, quite blue, gasping for breath. People gathered around her.

"Get water, quick!"

"Is the new doctor on board, uh, Ben, Ben Towers?"

"Yes. Somebody get doctor Towers." The word echoed rhythmically. Moments later; "Here he comes."

Passengers made way for doctor Towers who, not used to long strides, or overworking his legs, hurried along as fast as he could. Kneeling down beside Widow Douglas, a bit out off breath himself, he examined her neck. Unfortunately he had not thought to bring his bag aboard. Widow Douglas tried to speak, but found it too difficult.

"Now, there. Take 'er easy. Conserve your strength."

"Will Widow Douglas be all right?" Judge Thatcher asked, still not sure whether anyone had noticed his cowardice..

Doctor Towers flinched. In amazement he asked, "This is Widow Douglas?"

"Why, yes." Judge Thatcher reaffirmed.

For a few brief moment Doctor Towers knelt as a pillar of stone by Widow Douglas' side. Then, springing back to life , he rose, and took Judge Thatcher to one side. "Judge. She may be in bad condition. Her pulse is weak; might be internal damage. I'll have to get her back to her place."

"You mean your *office*, don't you?" Judge Thatcher asked, a bit puzzled.

"No! I mean, no. The thing is, well, let me level with you." His manner was one of apprehension. "I haven't been in this town long, about a week, and, well, my office isn't ready for patients yet. Besides, she's better off in her own bed. More comfortable."

"Yes, I see your point."

Doctor Towers wiped his brow; for his nerves too were tightly bundled. "I'm mighty glad you see it my way."

Judge Thatcher hastily shouted to two men standing nearby. "Graham, Oliver! The boat's docking. Help Widow Douglas off." To another man he said, "You, Gregory. Soon as the boat docks, don't waste any time, but jump right off and round up a wagon. I'll also need escorts to go along with Doctor Towers."

Judge Thatcher was a leader, a doer, a professional organizer. He could handle any situation with the greatest of composure. Commanding a great presence and respectability, most everyone cherished him no end.

Because of his high stature, when the mayor of St. Petersburg died suddenly, quick to be recommended to fill the vacancy until a new mayor could be sworn in was Judge Thatcher. No one else had wanted the position. And enough people agreed he would act superbly as a substitute until one could be found. Some even said it would be well and good to make him mayor permanently. However, reluctantly accepting, he made his intentions clear by saying the role of substitute mayor would only be until another *qualified* candidate, could be found. For the life of him, he wished he had never agreed. The strain, the pressure of being mayor, and always in the public's eyes, and expected to solve every little problem to perfection, steadily took its toll upon the man, and he was beside himself with fear and guilt that soon somebody would realize how inept he really was at politics. His wife knew, and that, perhaps, was worst of all; for she was his biggest critic, and antogonist.

"What'll we do with ol' Jimmy here?" inquired a passenger.

"Somebody fetch a rope to tie him up," Judge Thatcher responded. No sooner had he finished his statement when rope appeared. The people were simple, and unbeknown to Judge Thatcher, had not caught on to his shortcomings.

Jimmy came to as the *Big Missouri* landed. "What! Hey, what you doing with me! I didn't do nothin'. Only protectin' myself."

"Jimmy Finn, you are under arrest for aggravated assault, disturbing the peace, attempted murder, and possible murder."

"You cain't do this to me. Well, you heard what she said. Said I murdered my boy. What was I s'posed to do?"

Judge Thatcher would hear no more. A group of passengers helped carry Widow Douglas off, as another group escorted Judge Thatcher and Jimmy Finn over to the jail.

And what of Tom Sawyer, and *his* role in all this? He merely wanted to find Becky and make up. He now hoped nobody saw him witness this unfortunate circumstance. He had been afraid to testify against Injun Joe. What if Jimmy Finn went to trial, and Tom had to testify again, against him? An idea he relished with one half of his being, the other he feared, as Injun Joe's stolid face startled his vision. He worried about "friends" Injun Joe may have around these parts. Jimmy Finn might have "friends" also.

Tom needn't have worried. As much as one wants to bring forth attention upon ones-self, most people aren't interested in obliging them. And so was true with Tom. No, every-ones attention focused on the scene at hand. Tom eased his mind with this thought, until he felt a stinging in his ear. He quickly jumped up and was ushered with full escort off the boat by his Aunt Polly, Sid, and Mary.

"Honestly, Tom. Don't you know no better? Why, if it hadn't been for Sid, I might never known you was missin.'"

Tom's eyes told Sid he had better watch his back. Sid knew the sign. Tom, apt to glare at Sid all the way home, had his attention diverted when he heard Mrs. Thatcher call after Becky.

"Come *on* Becky. I haven't all day."

"Yes, Ma." Becky gave one look up toward the *Big Missouri*. To her disappointment the glare of the sun blocked her view.

"Hurry along now, quit dragging your feet. You didn't even know the boy. It's not proper you showing him such respect. We didn't get on the boat for sympathy. Our names will be in the paper, and that's all that matters. Come on! We have a social function to get ready for."

They were down below. Tom would have given anything to leap over all the people in front of him and shout out for Becky to wait. He might have done it too, if his Aunt hadn't had a firm grip around his arm. He went home, sadder than before. But still, he held out hope.

CHAPTER 2

At a quarter past eleven that night Tom snuck out of his room and made his way through the alleys and streets until he came across the Thatcher residence and stood under Becky's window. He meowed and Becky quickly stuck her head out.

"Tom? That you?"

"You bet so."

"I been waiting for you, hoping you'd show up."

"Can you get out?"

Becky made use of a lightening rod next to her window. She descended slowly until she hovered four feet from the ground, then let go. She would have slid the whole way down, but Tom told her that a prisoner strapped for time has to make a fast getaway; he doesn't waste time hanging on a lightening rod, but jumps the first chance he gets. He also told her there wasn't a book he ever read where a prisoner had such a luxury. They always had to jump a long ways down, sometimes breaking a leg. Becky "allowed" to meet him half way, and Tom was satisfied. She wore an old, faded dress she kept hidden, and only wore when the two met during the night. Tom, surprised to see her dressed so fast, inquired about it.

"I knew you'd come. As soon as ma left, I slipped in to this dress and waited for you. I didn't want to waste any time. Oh, I knew you'd come

Tom. I saw you on the boat today, and wanted you to catch up to me when we docked. But ma, well she wouldn't have any part of it."

"Becky, I most wanted to catch up to you, but my Aunt Polly she had a grip on me that even Satan couldn't unfasten."

After some reluctance Becky said, "Tom, I'm awful sorry I stormed out."

"Shucks," he said, more relaxed. "I reckon I'm to blame for that."

"No. It *wasn't* right. We should 'a' talked. But look, I've let down my hair now." She twirled around, prompting her hair to dance in the air.

"It's just the way I like it too."

"Oh, Tom," Becky sighed. "I couldn't stay mad at you, no matter what you did. Besides, we're soon to carry out our most secret of missions. Now how could we do that with both of us mad at one another?"

Tom, becoming serious, whispered. "Let's not discuss it here. We might be found out."

Becky's eyes also moved about. She huddled next to Tom as close as she could. "I'm agreed. Same place?" When Tom told her yes, the two slipped off silently into the night.

They made their way down to the river where Tom "borrowed" a small raft. Becky hopped on board while Tom untied the rope. Before pushing off he left a note, or what he referred to as his trademark. He rolled the paper up, fastened it to a stick with some kite string, then stuck it in the ground. It read: *The Black Avenger of the Spanish Main strikes again.*

"One of these days you're gonna get caught and hung Tom Sawyer."

"Not I, my fair maiden. Tis a cunning pirate I am. I shall have us away from this treacherous port in no time."—for they were on the high seas now.

A dog barked in the distance.

"Avenger! Evil King Henry has found us out and called for his royal dogs. Let us away quickly before we are captured and thrown into the dungeon forever and ever."—for Becky liked to join in too.

"Aye. Steady as she goes, but make haste," he called out to the forward oarsmen, which was himself.

"The knights! They come from the north." She pointed to an imaginary space. "By the thousands me thinketh. Oh, brave pirate of the crimson seas, is there hope for us yet? They are gaining. Looketh out yonder."

Tom did "looketh".

"Then so be it. Thinks they can catch up to the Black Avenger, on his own ship even! Make the cannons ready; when they pull up to the stern let 'em have it on the up roll."

"Aye-aye cap'n!" shouted Becky.

"Let it not be said the Black Avenger of the Spanish Main should allow any harm to befall the fair Maiden Marian."

"Actually, I like Guinevere better."

"Then so be it. There'll ne'er be an castle too strong to hold back the Black Avenger; no danger to keep him from his rescue; no princess as beautiful as Maiden, I mean—Guinevere."

And so it went. They fought a harrowing battle, taking many a life, and making out with only imaginary cuts and bruises. In the final climactic scene Tom's vessel began to sink when a cannonball broke the water-line. Becky miraculously spotted land in the nick of time and they fled to safety just as their raft was going under; yet for their purpose it landed safely on sand, where it lay out of *real* harms way. After-all, being stranded for pretend was pure enjoyment and worthy of a stylish fantasy. In reality it would not be looked upon with high regard by either participant.

Their destination, which Tom called "Camelot", or "Sherwood Forest", or "Dead Man's Cove"—he had plenty to choose from—was the famed cave on which Injun Joe had met his doom and Tom and Huck found their glory. And now it became Tom and Becky's secret hideaway.

Tom first brought Becky here months earlier, after Huck's kidnapping, to show her where he and Huck had found the treasure. Becky was apprehensive in the beginning; afraid you might say. It brought back memories of hunger and almost certain death she once faced herself. But Tom recalled to her the good memories; the wall signature "Tom and Becky", the wedding cake, and the moment he saw the light and brought her to freedom.

During the months Huck remained with his father, Tom and Becky came here often; and with each passing visit Becky's enthusiasm for returning grew. Tom had found in Becky an adventurer, an equal that matched both his curiosity and his daringness. Soon the two were best of friends, stealing away to the cave whenever possible to discuss what Tom referred to as "business". Becky learned quickly this "business", and delighted in it. Her strength grew rapidly. Tom liked her independent character, sometimes envied it, but allowed he would take it only so far. It would not do, he thought, to have the damsel in distress save the gaudy heroic pirate.

They made their way up the hill to the entrance only they knew. The sole light they had came from the moon and stars; but Tom and Becky were well aware of the way and could walk it blind folded. Soon they approached a clump of bushes and sat down.

Tom removed his corn-cob pipe with the intent to smoke it, but Becky opposed the idea. "Tom, you ain't gonna smoke are you? The smell can be just awful. If you were to get some *new* tobacco, then it'd be alright. Here, chew on some gum." She took the piece out of her mouth and gave it to Tom, who knew better than to refuse.

"This tobacco *is* gettin' old. I'll have to borrow some from old man Witter soon." He removed the pipe from his mouth for the time being, as he and Becky tried to think of something to talk about. Tom looked at his pipe; Becky looked at Tom looking at his pipe.

"Ain't it awful about Huck, though?" Becky speedily spoke.

"I still can't believe it. Becky, if I told you something, would you swear never to repeat it to anyone, so help you?"

"I swear."

"Honest now?"

"Honest."

"Alright then. I think Huck's pap done him in. I think he did it for the money."

"It's plausible. I heard pa say the same thing. I reckon most of the town thinks that. But why would you want to keep it secret?"

"I seen what he done to Widow Douglas on the boat. She accused him of killing Huck and he went for her. I seen it all, and I wouldn't want to be called as a witness if ever he goes to trial. I been through it once, and once is plenty enough. You won't tell nobody will you?"

"I said I wouldn't, and they could tar and feather me and ride me out on a rail before I'd say anything." That satisfied Tom.

"You know our secret mission? Well, Huck was s'posed to be with me. But then his pa took him, and I gave up on the idea for awhile. I don't reckon I know exactly what it was that made me ask *you*, but, I ain't ever regretted it." Becky sighed in admiration. She knew how close Tom and Huck once were. And she further knew, though he never told her, how difficult it was in asking her to be his partner.

"Huck was a very good friend to you. I never really knew him."

"I know," Tom said with understanding. "With the way the town's talking, they all think Huck's pa murdered him."

"Pa thinks so. Ma, she don't care one way or the other. Mind you, she wants to see him hang, but only for what he did to Widow Douglas." Becky yawned, unexpectedly. Tom was surprised.

"Becky, you tired?"

"Oh, it was that social event mama made me go to. They were supposed to talk about temperance, but they all talked about Widow Douglas instead. I've been going to ever so many of them, since pa was made acting mayor. I've been to them before, of course. But these ones, well, mama has been putting more pressure on me of late. Pa, too. I think she is the only one of us who is happy for pa, and wants to see him be mayor, and not just a substitute. She's changed. She's much more rigid, demanding, temperamental. She used to take the switch to me on occasion. Now, it's every day, practically. I can see how much pa hates being acting mayor. He's changed too. He's much more moody and absent-minded these days. I'm worried for him. When ma and I got home from the social event, pa was in his study muttering loudly to himself. Ma told me to go along to my room, while she went into the study. Oh, did they ever argue."

"'Bout what?"

Becky contemplated. "Well. Tom, I just can't say right now. It's too hard. It's given me nightmares. But don't you tell pa or ma, will you Tom? Ma especially. She'd fill me so full of liquids—the kind that'd warm a person's insides and roast my bowels. Ma thinks highly of those medicines. You won't tell?"

"No. My aunt's the same. But you'll tell *me* 'bout them, won't you?"

"All I remember is waking up in a sweat, with a voice inside my head sayin', 'Let me go, let me go'. Oh—I *do* see myself in a room all alone. I try to open the door but it's locked. I hear laughter on the other side and what sounds like glass being thrown against the door."

"Seems powerful. Is it the same way every night?"

"Yes. D' you reckon there's anything to them?"

"The niggers they swear by dreams. Say they're messages or warnings 'bout things yet to come. But I never took much stock in 'em before."

"Well I hope you're right."

"Course I am. Why looky here, I've had many a dream where I'd catch a ten foot catfish, and I ain't ever caught one larger than three. And then there's dreams about bein' over in England and having the king or queen knight you for being brave enough to fight off the Spanish Armada and saving England from destruction. And dreams 'bout being a pirate and finding all sorts of loot. I reckon dreams are nothing more than things we hope would happen to us in life, but deep down inside we know they won't, so conjure 'em up in our head while asleep to ease the mind."

"I've had those dreams. But nightmares are different. More dreadful."

"Well, now that you've talked about it, they might stop. It's that way with me sometimes."

"I wish you'd 'a' told me that last year, after we made it out of the cave," Becky said solemnly. "I was laid up in bed a long time, and each night I had nightmares. Would've been nice to talk about them with somebody—like you." As Becky talked more about dreams, she watched the way Tom left his pipe to dangle between his teeth. Soon, she fell into its hypnotic swing, recalling the times he had it lit. She wanted to try it, just once, just to watch to smoke curl out, but dared not to; dared not to say a word; she had her reasons, for which she kept to herself.

"Tom, you know what we need?"

"What's that?"

"A secret code. Something, can't nobody but us ever figure out."

Tom removed his pipe in awe. "Becky, I never thought of it before; but it's the best idea yet. That's just the thing. But, what kind of code?"

"I don't know. I've seen people flashing pans at each other once; pa said it was signals. Maybe we could do that."

"Yes. Well, but I'd get skinned alive if I took any of my aunt's pans and lost them."

"True; ma would do the same for me."

"I know! Smoke signals; like the injuns do."

"Oh yes, that's right. They start a great, big fire, and create signals with the smoke."

"Yes, and the smoke represents some kind of a warning or something."

"Oh Tom, but we couldn't start a big fire without getting into trouble."

"No, I don't reckon we could. But here Becky, we could with our pipes; mine and the one I made for you that's down in our secret hideaway."

"Could we see them from a far distance?"

"No. But if we're with the other kids, and then we out with our pipes, we could talk in secret, without the others knowin'."

Becky inwardly agreed, and itched at the chance to draw in the tobacco; allow it to circumference her mouth, then slowly exhale. She hesitated earlier for fear she would accidentally swallow it, knowing first hand the affects. She had seen Emma Lindstrome, a playmate, on a dare, smoke from a pipe. Having no knowledge of pipe smoking but what she saw her pa do, she drew too deeply. Becky, and other girls, watched Emma vomit up pre-digested, and perhaps even digested residue. Months passed before Becky could even look at a pipe. But that was before Tom; before Huck's kidnapping; before Tom showed her the way. She bit her lip.

"Tom, go ahead and light your pipe."

"You mean it?"

"Uh-huh. Let's see if we can't code one word. But give back my chewing gum first. You can't *waste* a precious commodity as this," she said, putting the gum back in her own mouth.

Ecstatic, Tom lit the pipe at once with a "lucifer" match. "Now Becky," he said. "Pay close attention. I'll puff so as to allow the smoke to billow. Watch the pattern." He puffed and soon discharged a pillow that slightly resembled a tree-trunk, spreading itself out into something of a tree. He did it again and again until he perfected it to his liking.

"It's ever so gay, Tom. In fact it's, it's pulchritudinous."

"What's pulchritudinous?" Tom gasped.

"Pa used it once. He said it's a fancy meaning for beautiful and elegant and lovely.

"Well why don't he just *say* elegant and lovely and beautiful? Why's he got to say a word only two people in the whole world might know?"

"I reckon 'cause he's a judge, and has got to use such words, especially around other dignitaries, to fit in with them."

"Well, I can see that. But you won't hear me use such nonsensical words as that. But alright, we'll drop it for now. What'll we use for a code? Something piratical maybe; bloody and dark."

"No!" Becky exclaimed defiantly. "The first code ought to symbolize our strength. We're a team, linked and locked together by unseen restraints. Nobody can separate us."

"I don't hardly see the resemblance in the smoke. Looks more like the trunk of a tree, if even that much."

"We can work around it. It's a tree sure; grows and branches out. What else?"

"Could be an oak, thick and hearty, strong and durable. They live just forever it seems."

"Now we're gettin' somewhere. But by itself, alone in the wilderness, it seems sad and demented. Around other oaks they are much healthier. They ain't nothin' more harmonic than a forest of oaks. Why, you know those two oaks in the forest, near the swimming hole?"

"Course. Been there for hundreds and hundreds of years."

"Yes, and the reason is that they had each other, to keep company with. You know the poem written about them...

From seeds knocked in soft summer air
they converged by fate. But for
a mere subtle glance all was clear,
all was conveyed. They kissed more
often than many might know; their's,
a love everlasting. Then
fortune took a turn, they knew not
why. Whipping winds assailed! Hence,
they kissed no more. From an new spot
now they lay—away; to spend
eternity apart. Down they
sank, in sadness and despair.
Twas eons each thought—so *many* days
weeping, aching under there.
Thus—this throbbing could be contained

no more; with vi'lent fury
exploded from beneath and from
above. No longer blurry,
each rose atop their darkened slum
and behold!—Thund'rous glory.
> Though different now than whence they
> were, sudden remembrance came
> forthwith, wholly without delay.
> Crying out, they asked the same—
> "Come nigh, come nigh, o'er this way."
Each replied, to the sadness
of the other, "My dearest one—
tis not my want I confess
in earnest; these roots are undone
and do wind around with firmness
> so solid, nearer to you I
> cannot come. Forever-more,
> *here*, is where I rest." Twas to die
> a death O so quick that tore
> and tugged at spirits bound to cry
and wail and shout *why me*!; yet,
were resolved they should kiss again;
for a death like Juliet—
and of her beau, Romeo, then
would not answer, nor be met.
> With a mustered might they strained and
> twisted; turned and stretched so high,
> high up in the sky, off the sand,
> reaching to the clouds where fly
> the feathered flocks; and eyed the land
underneath them and exclaimed,
"Goodness me, a way so long we've

come since last recalled. For shame
our thoughts way back when, when believed
it could not be done; but blamed
        and fretted and yearned for death to
        end our woe. Yet, now me-thinks
        with outstretched arm 'cross sky so blue,
        our wait be up—let us link!"
And so their lives began anew
that day, when they endeavored
they should be as one; and with each
year passed, grew an arm levered
and arced just so, over the beach.
Thus, twas vowed, aloud…"Never,
        ever again shall we sever; we're—Together Forever!"

After Becky finished, Tom exclaimed with astonishment, "You mem-orized the whole poem?"

"Why sure! It's the poem I used for examination, if you remember?"

"O' course. Why, the way you stood up and went into it with gusto—,"

"I was sittin' in a chair, Tom," Becky scorned. "And it's not the sort of poem you go into with gusto, but have to be gentle with."

"Oh, confounded—alright, I fell asleep after *my* examination was done. All them others after mine were so dull and boring, I couldn't help but to fall asleep. I would 'a' stayed awake for yours, honest. I wish now I had."

"Well, never mind. It's past. Tom, let's use it for the secret code—*Together Forever.*"

"It ain't exactly pi-ratical or bloody."

"No, but we can think up others that are. This one is symbolic of our friendship; how we've fought over the year and a half to keep it intact. It wasn't until after Huck's kidnapping, really, that our alliance was linked, like it says in the poem. Those two oaks fought long and hard, and won out in the end, and will remain together forever. Let's you and I do the same."

Tom gave it some thought; a kind of thought different to his nature, and one he had never attempted before. Becky watched him with her own interest, and towards the end she knew she had won, and that their first secret code would be *Together Forever*. And it was so! Tom agreed to it, and Becky clasped her hands, and sighed, smiling in her victory.

Around one in the morning they departed. Tom did not intend to stay out too late, else a younger half brother might unexpectedly wake and tell a certain aunt. He told Becky he saw Black Beard and his pirates away off landing on the Island, and that it wouldn't do to hang around because, as he put it, "they weren't up to any good". Becky understood *that* "signal", and the two made a run for it. All and all, Tom got Becky home without any casualties on their side.

As he watched her climb up the lightening he whispered, "Don't forget about tomorrow night; our secret mission."

Becky peered down and winked. "I know," she said, climbing through her window.

Tom had wanted to discuss the secret mission further that night, but could clearly see that Becky was more tired than usual. She was up to it, he knew. And there would be no further need to go over the details. Tom returned to his own home, remarking that the night had been successful after-all.

CHAPTER 3

That night, Tom had haunting nightmares of own. During breakfast he was so jittery, he gulped his coffee rather than sip it, nearly setting his mouth on fire. As a reflex the cup dropped to the floor, spilling in the direction of his aunt, causing her to jump up in a fury of excitement.

"Tom!" she exclaimed in horror. "What *is* the matter with you?"

"I'm sorry," he said, fanning his mouth. "But how am I to know the coffee is scalding?"

"What'd you expect, an icicle? Get down there and clean it up this instant." He obeyed.

"I bet I know why Tom is in such a hurry," Sid gloated.

Tom perked his head up over the table. "I bet you don't, Siddy. And if you know what's good for you, you'll keep it that way."

Mary, who sat in-between the two, and always the level-headed one, spoke up. "Now Sid, Tom lost a good friend yesterday. He's still shaken up by it."

"I don't believe it."

"Sid!" snapped Aunt Polly. "Go upstairs and fetch some more rags out of the closet."

"Yes auntie."

With Sid out of the way, she leaned toward Tom instinctively, motherly, and said, "Tom, is that it?" Pressed for time he told her yes, and that he needed a little space to himself and he would be fine. "Well, I don't say Huck was a model boy. But he was one of the Lord's children. That speaks unto itself. And he *was* coming around under Widow Douglas' guidance before he was—. Now *she's* near death herself." Tears dropped from her eyes. Mary comforted her.

"There, she'll live. She's strong willed; there's not a fragile bone in her body. The Lord is looking down upon her, protecting her."

While they cried in each others arms, Tom snuck away, intent on visiting Widow Douglas. Shortly he crossed paths with Joe Harper.

"Why Joe Harper, you look about as downhearted as ever I see."

"I just come from Widow Douglas' and—,"

"She ain't dead!" Tom bolted, fearing the worst.

"No! That is, I don't know. I never had a chance to see. When I got to her mansion there was a big commotion, lot's of people, all with dogs, up in arms, yelling and running all over; people saying, 'Get your guns and meet back here; don't nobody rest 'til he's found; spread the word!' All sorts of talk I couldn't make out."

"Well that does sound peculiar. But why didn't you *stay* to find out?"

"'Twas the sheriff. He come and grabbed me, and said I ought to go home; said it weren't safe to be out now. I asked him why, but he told me to mind my own affairs. So I left."

"You can bet *I* wouldn't have. I'm on my way now. You with me?"

With conviction Joe shouted, "I bet I am!"

The nearer to the mansion the boys approached, the more strangely people acted. Adults yelled, urging them to find refuge; children poked their heads out, only to be pushed back in abruptly. The increasing amounts of men and dogs amazed both Tom and Joe. Reaching the mansion, trees made for excellent cover; and the two boys slunk in front of one, then another, allowing for a slow, but safe, forward progression. The boys finally slipped, unseen, behind a row of tall bushes against the side of the mansion. Still, the gathering continued.

"Look at all them men and dogs a-standin' out by the porch," Joe said.

"Shh. Sheriff's about talk. Judge Thatcher's up there with him. He looks worried too. Look at the way his hands tremble."

Judge Thatcher appeared a changed man, unlike yesterday. He *was* a changed man. He had had nightmares all night long involving what he considered his cowardice aboard the *Big Missouri*. Frightening, vivid dreams of him standing by while Jimmy strangled Widow Douglas to death, and not doing anything to help. He felt sure somebody would confront him, soon. He wanted to resign, more than anything, but knew he must wait for the new elections. He only hoped he could hold out that long. And not only was his role as acting mayor adding to the stress in his life, but the new sheriff, Cal, as well. Neither man liked the other; neither man trusted the other; and both men knew exactly how the other felt.

When pacing became as irritating for Judge Thatcher as his hatred for Cal, he took him to the side and told him enough men were now present to go ahead with the announcement.

"Look," Judge Thatcher explained to Cal, "the town is already in chaos. I don't need you stirring them up any more than they are."

"You do your job," Cal coldly responded. "I'll do mine. That is, if you can handle your job. You don't look so well."

"Never mind me. I've clout enough in this town yet to force you from office."

"We'll see," Cal smiled.

Judge Thatcher turned away and faced the crowd of men and dogs.

"Rumors have circulated around town about an escaped slave. Miss Watson's slave to be exact. Those rumors, those rumors are factual." The cheers and blasts from guns and rifles riddled the air. "Now, now let's be civil about this. Please." Judge Thatcher's nerves began to show. "Let me finish. There *is* a reward offered of three hundred dollars by Miss Watson." Again, guns fired. "Stop! Stop it! Let me finish. The facts are sketchy right now. He may have escaped with or without help. If he had help, and that individual is apprehended, Miss Watson has said she will add another three hundred dollars to the reward." More guns went off; more shouts from untamed men, and dogs. "Please," Judge Thatcher begged. "Also, a boy, well, as those of you who call St. Petersburg home may know—Huckleberry Finn—has been murdered recently. It is speculated the slave is somehow involved. I don't know if this is true, but I want him brought back alive for questioning. Is that understood? If he is killed, I'll prosecute his killer. Not only may he be innocent, but he may also provide information on Huck's murder." This drew sour remarks from the men; many of whom were in the habit of shooting first and asking questions later; especially where runaway slaves were concerned. They cared nothing for Huck's murder.

Cal, knowing the crowds mentality, intervened with calculating speed and decisive cunning; and, as he has often done, spoke about that to which became Judge Thatcher's primary reason for so mistrusting and loathing the man.

Said Cal, "But that don't mean this nigger can't be roughed up, or shot up some, if need be. Laws on the white man's side where niggers are concerned. And when a nigger runs away from his master he's broke our laws; the very laws our founding fathers fought so hard for in a revolution. This country was, and is, founded on slavery. There's no way out of it, ever. Y' see, our founding fathers wanted it, died for it, and made provisions for it. Men—I believe the Constitution. That it stands for freedom. White freedom. Provisions never were made for niggers. Our founding fathers, being divinely smart, *wanted* slavery as a staple part of our new country. *Wanted* us to own them. And even *God* wanted us to have slavery. For it was Him, after-all, who gave the power and wisdom, and inspiration, to the founding fathers in their quest for independence. Men...let's don't ever forget that, while out on the hunt."

As Judge Thatcher sighed in defeat, disorder irrupted upon the lawn. This is why Judge Thatcher hated Cal. The man's peculiar views of slavery, and the founding fathers, irritated him. Yes, slavery was a staple part of American society, in the south; and though Judge Thatcher himself never condemned it, it was the way in which Cal had manipulated the words of America's founding fathers that so disturbed him. Cal had managed to bring out the worst in the townspeople. But even in a small town such as St. Petersburg, without slavery, and the money and economic security this institution generated, especially through the sale of slaves, the town would be hard pressed without it.

Guns blasted; dogs, and men, howled, filling the air with their stench. Judge Thatcher tried to regain order, but quickly realized he could not, so began a slow descent off the porch. The clout, the respect, he once held, and that he thought he still held, with the townspeople, was quickly eroding, thanks in part to Cal. He feared that any other disaster to befall St. Petersburg might put him over the edge. Within minutes the men and dogs had vanished, and an eerie, foretelling quiet hung over the space they had occupied.

"Something is about to happen," Judge Thatcher said, looking out over the land where he once was proud to be a citizen, and a judge, and now acting mayor. He saw the town moving away from him; perhaps against him. "I pray for a miracle, anything to rid this town of that man for good." An understandable prayer; but one which he might have gladly renounced if he only had knowledge of the future, and things yet to come.

With the men gone, and calm returned to the landscape, Tom and Joe dared to poke their heads up over the bushes. Before either could move an inch, a shadow in that of a human figure approached. They looked up and saw Judge Thatcher.

"Boys," he said calmly, though being somewhat startled. "What brings you here?"

Joe nervously stammered out a few words. "Why, we, that is. Well Widow Douglas, she being sick, we, Tom and me that is." Joe could not go on.

Tom talked for them both. "We hoped to see Widow Douglas. I saw, or rather, *heard* what happened to her. She's always been nice to us. Well, we only came to see how she was." Tom thought to leave the rest out.

Judge Thatcher looked unexpectedly pleased. "Well, that *was* a nice gesture. A shame, a downright travesty, you had to come just when—. Well, I suppose you boys already know what has happened?" Both Tom and Joe nodded. "The whole town will be a buzz with the news by now anyway. But let's come away from the window, away from the mansion, shall we. Lest we be spotted, and accused of something altogether unbecoming."

"Do you think Jim killed Huck, and not his pap, like may people think?" Tom asked, as the three walked down Widow Douglas' winding driveway.

"I don't know. Jim did escape the night of Huck's murder. That's enough for most."

"What would make a nigger do such a thing as to run off in the first place?" Joe asked, innocently. "Don't he know what they do to niggers that run away?"

"Well," Judge Thatcher said, pausing for a brief time. "Indeed, he must. Still—,"

"Joe!" a woman's voice cried out.

"Ma?" Joe replied.

"Joseph Harper!" she yelled out. "I just heard a nigger is loose. You come home with me at once. Oh, oh judge," the woman exclaimed, holding her hand to her chest in sheer exhaustion, as well as a certain amount of fear. "I hope he hasn't been a bother, judge."

"Not at all."

She grabbed Joe's ear. "Thank ye, judge. Joseph Harper!"

"What'd I do?"

"Y' ought to know better 'n to be out right now, with a crazy, murderin' nigger on the run, just waitin' to kill another child." As she hustled her boy down the road, she called out to Tom, "I'll tell Polly you're safe and with the Judge Thatcher. She'll be mighty relieved."

Judge Thatcher watched after the two. "Is this what it comes to?"

"What, what comes to?"

"Hmm? Oh," the man said, stunned; for he had almost forgotten Tom stood beside him. "Nothing. Nothing at all." He scratched his head. "I had something I wanted to discuss with you. I've forgotten it for the moment. But I must go and see if I can't quell an unwarranted fear first." Tom watched him move slowly down the road. He wondered what Judge Thatcher wanted to discuss with him; and had an idea, a sinking feeling, what it was about.

Not wanting to return home yet, instinctively aware his aunt would keep him indoors with an escaped slave on the loose, he walked down to the river, keeping an eye on the myriad of men scavenging up and down the Mississippi. He listened in on their conversations, until one group spotted him and threw an empty jug passed his ear. He moved further down the river, where, surprisingly, he bumped into an old friend.

Cheerfully, Tom exclaimed, "Muff Potter! It *is* you. I thought you left town for good."

As equally cheerful, Muff raised up his hand and said, "Tom Sawyer, yer a welcome sight to come 'pon. Yes, I left, shortly after my trial. Them people kept makin' such a fuss over me. Same ones that called me a murderer. 'Twas guilt, not kindness, I know. So, I left. But, I got home-sick. What's this I hear about an escaped slave? It's all I been hearing all morning."

"Don't you know?"

"Well I only got in town las' night. Been sleeping most of the morning, 'til I was woke by a fury of gun shots, and dawgs barking so horribly loud, it most split my head."

"It's Miss Watson's nigger, he done took off the night Huck was murdered."

"What now? What's this about Huck being murdered?"

"That's what happened. Some say his pa done it. Others say it was Miss Watson's nigger. Nobody knows for sure."

"Well, I'd say it was is pap. But I know the man more than I do the slave."

"Sheriff's got him locked up in the jail, but only b'cause he tried to kill Widow Douglas after she accused him of killing Huck." This revelation surprised Muff more than the other two; and send a cold shiver down the spine of his back. "Why Muff, you look about ready to bust."

"Only tell me, how is she? Will she live?"

"Far's I know she's still alive. Doctor Towers is keepin' a close eye on her."

"Towers?"

"That's right. He's the new town doctor, come up about a week ago." Muff began to turn white. "Muff, you O.K.? You seem awful skittish."

"I'm fine, Tom. Tell me, only tell me—. Oh, would y' look at these hands o' mine shake."

"Tell you what?"

"Hm? Oh. Tell me, is his name *Benjamin* Towers?"

Tom nodded. "You know him?"

"Aye. Once, long ago. Long ago?" Muff sunk his feet into the sand and looked out into the river. "If it's the same man. We was like brothers once."

"What happened?"

"I don't like going into it. But, I'll tell ye, Tom. 'Cause yer 'bout the only one left in this town I can trust. But don't repeat it to nobody."

"I won't."

"Well, has to do with a woman we, Ben and I, both courted a long tome ago."

"Did you ever take her on any adventures, like lookin' for the Fountain of Youth, or maybe the Lost City of 'Lantis?"

"No, no. I was a farmer, and a poor one at that. Spent most of my time tryin' to grow crops to make money for ever we was to get married."

"She ever come to help pass the time?"

"Once. But her folks stopped it. Warn't proper for a southern lady of her stature to work in the fields. I'd low to see the day when it is."

"What caused the feud b'tween you and Doctor Towers?"

"Well, Ben wanted to go into medicine. Studied the books hard, and worked with Mills, the town doctor, a while. I, a struggling farmer, couldn't compete with a promising doctor. Months passed. On the day Clara, thas her name, picked to decide which one of us she'd marry, I lost my farm. Her folks was mighty persistent she choose Ben. But lordly, they alwus was."

"I'd 'a' challenged him to a duel. That's the proper way. You'll see that in any book."

"Almost did. I knew Ben only wanted her money."

"You ever tell her?"

"Told 'er folks. They didn't b'lieve me. Threw me off their property."

"I would've made them believe me or rot. She ever become wise to him?"

Muff shook his head. "Never had time. Not long after they wed, she had an *acc'dental* fall. Died instant."

"Was it proved accidental? I've read about people pushing one another out of a prison tower or somewhere real high, and making it look accidental."

"Nobody ever knew. I accused him of foul play. We fought 'til I knocked him out flat. Licked 'im good that day."

"That's the way. I bet Clara was looking down, and rooting for you."

"Yes, maybe. Well, the whole town banished me. I had nothing except my misery. Took to drinking. I never forgive him, and I don't never wanna see him agin."

"Well, you won't run into him until Widow Douglas is well."

"How's that?"

"He's stayin' at her mansion, and won't leave 'till she's better."

"That so?" Muff returned his gaze to the wide Mississippi.

"Say Muff, Muff?" Tom nudged beginning to worry.

"Hmm? Oh, Tom. Nearly forgot where I was." Muff jumped to his feet. "I beg you Tom, don't tell nobody you saw me. I got to keep low from now on, as long as I'm here. I'll keep in touch with you when I can." He walked off with his head held high; something he hadn't done in years. Tom thought it wise to let the man be by himself for the present. We shall return to him later, when he is more accepting of us delving into his most inner and private of thoughts.

CHAPTER 4

This was to be the night of Tom's and Becky's secret mission. They had talked about it, and planned for it, for months; and they had waited for just the right opportunity to carry out this most "dangerous of missions", as Tom had put it. Huck's murder, and the escape of Miss Watson's Jim, nearly halted their escapade. But each decided to go through with it regardless; neither knowing if another opportunity would ever surface. In reality, each was a trifle scared, and they feared the longer they waited, the more difficult the mission would become.

At half past nine Aunt Polly sent Tom and Sid to bed. At quarter after ten, while Sid slept soundly, Tom slipped out the window; his focus decisively on the mission at hand.

"This is no ordinary caper," Tom explained to Becky, weeks ago. "You know the rumors. We all do. You can't stare at it without itching to go inside. Fear, and the law, keeps everyone out, but you're not afraid?"

"Not me. Not with you. I'm as ready as I'll ever be."

And so there it stood—the Stantan Home, a glorious mansion located atop the highest hill; the most celebrated home in St. Petersburg; the only abandoned home not to be torn down by "unromantic men" searching for buried treasure. For years this mansion, the pride of the founders of St. Petersburg's, and its richest citizens, entertained many noted dignitaries that were, or went on to become, judges, congressmen, and other high officials, Weekend parties, lavish, extravagant weekday gatherings, kept the Stantan Home on the front page of the newspaper.

Their lifestyle, however, took a tragic fate one night. Thieves broke in, stole all they could carry, and then murdered the Stantans, throwing their bodies into the Mississippi. So went the rumors. They were never found. Oddly, Muff Potter had been in the vicinity. Drunk, he could provide little help, aside from claiming he heard multiple gun shots, and saw three or four men, resembling Murrell's Gang, exiting the home. Lawyers presiding over the estate discovered enormous amounts of money, tens of thousands of unaccounted dollars, missing. Immediately, rumors circulated about its whereabouts. Muff Potter spread the first rumor. Drunk one night, he said the Stantans buried it under their mansion.

One man, Senator, everyone called him, and good friend to the Stantans, quickly enacted a law forbidding anyone from coming within one hundred yards the mansion, or digging on the property, out of deep respect, he claimed. With a handful of men he chose himself, Senator had the Stantan Home boarded up tightly. He needn't have fretted. Because the rumor originated from Muff, the town drunk, everybody had a good laugh. That was the extend to the rumor. Due to Senator's immense influence, he had a provision attached to the law preserving the mansion. Though numerous abandoned homes lay scattered across St. Petersburg already, the citizens never objected to one more. They too had deep respect for the Stantans; once thought, and still considered by those who knew them, as pillars of society.

Tom, like every other child in St. Petersburg, knew the vast rumors. He even helped to spread a few of them himself. From childhood he dreamed for a chance to explore the Stantan Home. Yet, conscious of its history, and the fact the Stantan's bodies were never recovered, and knowing the local superstitions about ghosts inhabiting the places where they've been murdered, and all the many other rumors about people going up the long hill that leads to their mansion, but never coming back down, he inwardly feared tackling it alone. Still, his strong-minded curious nature would not waiver. Just when he worked up his nerves to ask Huck to join him, the boy's father took him away. He promptly thought of Becky as a replacement. Becky never failed Tom.

As the two children ascended the hill, they waited for something to occur; something from beyond the realm of the natural.

"Becky, did you remember to make out your will?"

"Uh-huh. And I put it under my pillow, just as you said I ought to do."

"Good. So did I." Half way up the hill, Tom and Becky stopped. "Ain't nothing happened yet, Becky. There's still time to turn around. But once we go beyond the half way mark, there ain't no turning back, no matter what happens. That's what the books say."

"Well," Becky thought. "I reckon we've come this far." That was all she said. It was all she had to say. With a deep breath, Tom and Becky lunged one foot forward over the imaginary half-way line. Once over, they never looked behind them, but kept their eyes peeled to the Stantan Home, waiting…waiting…waiting for something to occur.

"We made it, Becky!" Tom exclaimed, as they reach the top of the hill. "Only a little further."

"Do you reckon others have made it this far?"

"I dunno. All I know is that those that tried to enter the Stantan Home were never seen or heard from again. They say that anybody that's got a lost child or pet will find it in the Stantan Home."

"Susy Harper once told me that if you went up to the Stantan Home, and touched it, you would become rich someday."

"That's how much she knows," Tom scorned. "Why, anybody knows you can't just touch the home, but got to break of a piece of it, and say an incantation, right at midnight, under a full moon. Then you have got to sleep with that piece under your pillow for a whole week; and if don't any spirits come around to claim back that piece of the home after one week, then you know you'll be rich some day. Susy harper! What does *she* know about haunted houses anyway?"

"Well, I was only saying what she said."

The nearer the home the two approached, the more nervous they became. Apprehension, doubt, fear—their minds were swimming in each. When they were within a few yards of the Stantan Home, Tom and Becky again stopped.

"Tom, we made it."

"I wonder how far the others came, who ventured up here. Becky, we must be the only ones to make it this far."

"You think so?"

"Well, maybe. Luck must be on our side." Believing they had made it past harm's way, a newfound courage lifted their inner spirits, and they went in search of a loose plank. Presently, Becky found one.

"Look for a board we can tear down easy."

"There," Becky pointed. "That one, against the window. It's split in half, and cracked."

"Good show! I just knew that by now these boards would be weak and rotted."

Removing the board took no effort. Together, they squeezed inside. Tom lit a candle and waited for something to occur.

"Becky!" Tom gained composure. "They ain't no spirits here."

"Are you sure?"

"They'd 'a' come out by now. Well, but maybe they're only just waiting."

"Waiting?"

"Well, for us to get into the room they was murdered in."

"Which room was that?"

"I dunno. Nobody does. Well, but we're here. And I ain't gonna let local superstitions scare me away from treasure, 'less of course I see one of 'em flying right towards me."

On their guard, Tom and Becky entered the nearest room, and began patting the walls with their fists, and stamping the floor boards with their feet for the next fifteen minutes..

"I'm not having any luck. What about you, Tom?"

"No. Course it won't be out in the open. I never heard of a secret passageway that was."

"I reckon not. What about behind this bookcase?"

"Let's see. Come stand by me and push."

"It's not budging. Too heavy. Are you there would be a secret passage, and that is where the treasure is?"

"Course I am. That's what all the books say. And every mansion has at least one secret passage somewhere. Most often they has got more." Tom pushed with all his might, but the bookcase still would not budge. "If only there were books on the shelves, all we'd have to do is find the right one, pull it out, and *swoosh*, open comes the bookcase. Feel around against the walls; check behind any pictures or mirrors. Sometimes there's a wall candle that's really a lever. When you push it the right way a secret panel opens. But don't push it the wrong way, else you'll open a false trap in the floor where you're standing, which leads to a moat with alligators and snakes. Sometimes it's a bottomless pit. That's what the books say."

"How am I to know if I push it the wrong way?"

"If you do, you'll know."

"Thanks!" Coming upon one picture, Becky exclaimed, "Tom, is that the Stantans?"

Tom looked up at the picture with interest, then said, "I reckon so. It *was* the Stantans, anyhow. Wasn't they something, though, Becky? I always wondered what they looked like."

"They were beautiful people in life," Becky remarked, solemnly, respectfully.

"We'd best not stare too long, Becky. Lest their spirits might take offense."

"Tom, if their spirits are around here, do you think they'd let us find the treasure?"

"Well, spirits are a funny sort of bunch. Sometimes they'll trip you up, and keep you from ever finding treasure upon their property. Other times they'll wait for just the right person, or persons, to come along who they *want* to find the treasure."

"Then, if *we* find it, they must have wanted us to."

"P'rhaps. But the books say it generally takes hundreds of years."

"If we do find the treasure, we ought to use part of it for a memorial to the Stantans."

"That ain't no bad idea, Becky. 'Cause the nicer you are to their spirits, the nicer and kinder and friendlier they are to you. And the friendlier they were in life most often dictates how they will be in death. Everyone I hear tell says the Stantans were the nicest people you could know and associate with and be proud to have shook hands with, if you got the chance."

"I wish we could have—." A sudden disturbance interrupted Becky's thought. Tom heard it too. "Sounds like somebody, or some *thing* is trying to get inside. It's their spirits sure, making all that racket. Oh, Tom, what do you think they'll do to us?"

"In the books they generally do awful things." Becky blew out the candle and clung to Tom. "That won't make no difference. They can us in the pitchest and blackest dark."

"Maybe so. But if they are to do awful things to us, I don't want to see it."

The front door swung upon with great force, echoing throughout the home. Tom and Becky stayed close together, and waited for their imminent doom to befall them. There was quiet for about ten seconds; then both children saw a dim light. "Spirits" they both thought; knowing that ghosts often emit light. Then strange voices were heard; voices not characteristic of ghosts. Tom and Becky listened. It was all they could do. Said one voice,

"Ain't much Sim, but it'll do fer us, fer what we got t' do."

"We'll have real good times here," the other voice said. "Jed, make it lighter."

"If I make it any lighter, the whole town'll see. You want that?"

"No. I warn't thinkin'. Less look around some. Upstairs maybe."

"Tom," Becky dared to whisper, "Those aren't ghosts."

"No," Tom said in bewilderment. To himself, he wondered how two, living human beings could make it all the way into the Stantan Home without harm befalling them. Especially these two, whom Tom could clearly see were up to know good.

"No," said the first voice in defiance. "We ain't goin' t' go upstairs, or anywhere.

"But Jed, how come?"

"'Cause I don't want t' fool round here longer than I got to. I heard tell of a murder right here in this house years ago."

"Shucks. That never bothered you b'fore."

"You shush or I'll make you."

"Okay, Jed. Don't do somethin' you may regret."

"Well, this'll be a fine hideout fer the *first* job. There's still someone up to Jack's Isle. I saw smoke again."

"D' you reckon it's that runaway nigger we been hearing' s' much about?"

"I don't k'yer. Three hundred dollar ain't worth nothin' to what we're gonna get. That's what *he* said. *Shh*! I heard somethin'."

"It's speerits Jed. I bet you that's what it is. Comin' to get us fer disturbin' their rest."

"Sometimes Sim, you go too fer."

"I hear it agin."

"Oh my god! *Becky*!" Tom said hoarsely. "What's wrong?" He felt Becky rattling, and shaking tremendously, violently, irrationally. He held on to the girl for dear life, and instantly thought she had been possessed by one the Stantan's spirits "What is it, Becky?"

"Just hold on tight. It'll go away. Just hold on."

Said a voice, "Sim, yer alwus hearin' things. I don't hear nothin'."

"Well, but I thought I did."

"Yeah," the other voice said with disdain. "Alright. We found out what we needed to. Let's go." Tom and Becky heard the reverberation of footsteps, and then the slamming of a door.

Within a minute Becky had calmed; and after another five minutes they felt it safe enough to venture out of the room.

"I'm so sorry, Tom," Becky nearly cried. "Oh, why did that happen?"

"Well, it was only nerves is all. But you're fine now."

"No! No, not nerves. Something worse made me tremble. I don't know what, but it ain't the first time. It's happened before too; the shaking. And always unexpectedly."

"I thought maybe you was being possessed."

"I am, in a way. Something taking over my body, for a brief time. It first started about a month ago. I shake uncontrollable for a minute. then it goes away."

"Then it warn't because of the voices?"

"No. I don't believe so. Tom, those weren't spirits. They were men."

"Yes," Tom agreed. "I b'lieve so, now. And they talked about a job."

"What do you think it could be?"

"I dunno. Likely nothing. Maybe hunting or fishing. Maybe they're lookin' for Jim, and figured he might be hiding out in here somewhere."

"Not the way they talked. Something awful is gonna happen in this house. I know it. I don't want to be here when it does. Should we tell?"

"You know we can't. We ain't s'posed to be here ourselves. Why, we could be arrested."

"We'll, alright. I hope you're right, about them only hunting or fishing. And I suppose your right about not telling anyone. If ma found out where I was, she'd really skin me good. She's getting more and more impatient with me all the time. I can't ever get on her good side anymore, since pa became acting mayor. I told you she whips me most everyday now, for what amounts to little offenses, but what she calls immoral practices not to be done by those of us in high society."

A thought occurred to Tom. One in which he did not like.

"Becky, it can only be me who is to blame for you being whipped so much."

"No! You're not the problem. Ma is. She *won't* put a wedge between us! Our friendship is too important. She can whip me 'til doomsday if she wants. I've come along too far. Pa likes me this way, and *I* like me this way. And if I had this much gumption and determination when we were lost in the cave, I might not have acted so terribly negative."

"Why, you only acted like anybody would."

"No. Not everyone. You didn't act that way, Tom."

"Well, but I—,"

"Don't make excuses for the way I once was. I'm changed now. I won't go back." Tom did not know what else to say. He knew Becky had changed. And he was glad to have seen the transformation. After several minutes of listening to each others breathing, Becky finally said, "Well, we'd better leave now, before the real spirits come. Anyway, I think ma checks in on me once in a while, to make sure I'm in my bed at night. I don't want her to find me away."

"Becky, maybe we ought to stop sneaking out together nights. I don't want to get you into trouble with your ma. I never thought about it before. I always used to sneak out with Huck, but he didn't ever have anyone to tell him not to go."

"I know," Becky said with trepidation.

When the talk began to wane, they agreed to meet the next morning, at a more respectful hour. Tom followed Becky home, making sure she got inside alright, but also fearing her mother would be waiting for her, as his Aunt Polly often has a habit of doing. She wasn't. And he didn't know what he would, or could do, if Becky's mother had actually been there. He gave it no further thought that night, finding the answers that popped inside his head disturbing.

CHAPTER 5

Today would be Jimmy's hearing. Fifteen minutes beforehand, and on his way to meet up with Becky, Tom passed by the office of doctor Towers. Seeing a shadow within, the boy's spirit brightened; for he hoped to find out Widow Douglas' condition. However, when he went to open the door, he found to his consternation it was locked. Tom rapped his hand against the door, to obtain the doctor's attention. But this action only caused further dismay, as the shadow within made a violent jerk, then disappeared altogether. Tom gave up, shrugging his shoulders as he walked away, with this thought on his mind—"Why should the door be locked when the doctor is inside?" Meeting Becky near the docks, this thought was buried for the meantime; for the discussion of finding buried treasure in the Stantan Home took all his concentration.

All manner and construction of boats, rafts, and skiffs passed by them, either going upstream, or down, to their destination. It seemed to Tom there were more people out on the river, than in all of St. Petersburg. Most often he would come down to the river by himself to plan out his future, his escape, as he called it, for when he would leave here for good. Today, he was with Becky, and escape was the furthest thing from his mind.

"Could there really be treasure buried in the Stantan Home?"

"Of course, Becky. Why, St. Petersburg may be a one horse town, 'thought more'n a few hundred people, and that's counting the slaves too; and it may not be England or France, but they's been pirates and robbers here a plenty *sure* over the years. St. Petersburg is a perfect place for pirates anyhow, being located right off the Mississippi River and all. And don't everyone know about Murrell's Gang? They ain't no more famous gang around these parts than them."

"Yes, I've heard about them as well."

"Course! Ain't a body within a hundred miles of here that hasn't. And naturally there's been pirates roaming the waters of the Mississippi River, for hundreds of years, p'rhaps. Now, just you look at the Stantan Home, Becky. It's so big, and so easy to see, settin' there off the river, on the highest of all the hills in St. Petersburg. The best of *all* the hills in this town. See it settin' there, overlooking the Mississippi? It's like a castle. It *is* a castle, in some ways. And the river boats use is as a marker, so they know where they are. 'Specially at night, and when it's foggy. And the Stantan's were the richest townspeople ever to inhabit St. Petersburg; they had just slathers of money. More than Widow Douglas has got now. Ain't it so?"

"Yes, I suppose."

"Well now. If we know how rich the Stantans was, don't you reckon all the robbers and pirates would have heard about them too, and all their money?"

"I suppose."

"Course they did. It's in their line of business to know all that, else they'd never know who to rob. Why, if they didn't know no better who to rob, they might end up robbing a drunk or a vagrant, or somebody that ain't got a penny to their name. And how would *that* look, if it ever got around? Why, Becky! They'd be laughing stocks. They'd be disgraced as robbers and pirates and have to quit and become clergymen or some other low profession."

"I never thought of it that way."

"Not many people do. But I do, 'cause I read all the books on robbers and pirates, and so o' course know just everything about them, and their ways, and how they conduct their business. And look at Murrell's Gang. Didn't *they* murder the Stantans?"

"That's what all the rumors about them say."

"They's facts. And wasn't they the most famous gang of outlaws in these parts, west of the Mississippi? Not more'n ten years ago?"

"Yes."

"Sure they were. They're been other rich families living here on and off too. I bet they've been robbed. Course they have. Most rich people get robbed. And most often the robbers hide the loot, as the books say. And they think they'll come back for it later. But they never do. 'Cause they either are killed, or plum forget where in tarnation they hid it. Well, this town ain't more'n three, four miles long, and not much wider. And the Stantan treasure ain't been found anywhere. I ought to know, I've looked for it most all around, everywhere I could think to look. But ain't nobody looked for it *in* the Stantan Home, 'cause it was all boarded up right after they was murdered. And of course they passed a law to protect the home for a hundred years."

"Pa said some lawyers found their record books, and saw that thousands of dollars were missing and unaccounted for; and nobody knows what happened to the money."

"See. Now, why would anybody do that, 'less they was something inside the home? Something like treasure. Becky, I just knows there's treasure in there. And like as not who ever passed that law and sealed off the home done so *knowing* they was treasure in there, and only biding their time 'til the rumors quieted down and were forgotten about. Then they could go right in there 'thought any trouble or hassle and find the treasure for themselves. Well, I been itching to get in there for a long time. And always sweating, and hoping didn't nobody get in there before me and find the treasure. I might-a had it by now too."

"You mean, if Huck hadn't been taken away by his pa?"

"I don't know what I would-a done 'thought you, Becky?"

"Me?"

"Why, I couldn't go in on a thing like this alone. I'd be too a-feared. They're ghosts are around sure, somewhere in the home, or by the river where they was thrown. That's what the superstitions say. And o' course they're true, because the niggers talk about them mostly, and *they* more'n anybody know the way of ghosts and witches and such. I near gave up on the whole idea, after Huck was gone. But then you popped in my head. And I knew you'd be willing."

"I do so enjoy your adventures, Tom. I can't imagine what my life would be like if I'd never have met you. Dull, perhaps. Boring, maybe. Well, yes. 'Cause I just know my ma would have made me into what she is. And now that I see that, I'm so happy I'm more strong-headed. Pa likes me this way too, 'cause he knows ma's ways, and he don't want me to be like ma when I grow up. He won't tell her that though. And it's all owed to you, Tom. That much he did tell me. He really likes you, Tom." Tom inwardly smiled; for it pleased him immeasurably to hear this news. "He told me in confidence you have been an inspiration to me; that you've helped me grow, in some ways. I'm stronger now, he says, than before I met you. Then, I mostly stayed in doors, or close to home, and didn't do much in the way of fun. There aren't many children to play with in Constantinople. And I could only play with the children, and only the girls, whose parents were in the same class as us, and that wasn't too many. You know, I've had more fun with you, in the year and a half I've known you, than in all the rest of my life? And I never thought that possible before. And now, to be with you, looking for buried treasure. I never would have dreamed of it, before meeting you. I never would have wanted to, probably, if I'd never known you. I'd be like ma, and say it was silly and childish, and a waste of time. Oh, Tom!" Becky suddenly squealed. "I hope there's treasure."

"Did you see that side door, on the outside of the house I mean, that's boarded up?"

"Yes."

"Well, we never got a chance to look at what that side door led to, 'cause, of course, them men came. Becky, I'll *bet* that's where the secret passage is. I hope so, because a house ain't worth two cents that don't got a secret passage. All them castles has got 'em, in those far away lands. Wouldn't it be just something to visit one of those lands, and go inside the castles that has been standing there for hundreds and hundreds of years?"

"You mean in England and France. Those lands? I think it would be romantic."

"It's the history I enjoy. That's why I read all those books, 'bout far away places. It's so dull and boring here, in this one-horse town. It's so downright lifeless, a body could starve and die from lack of anything interesting. And everybody knows just everybody; and everybody knows what everyone else is doing all the blame time; and if I get into a scrape, why, my Aunt Polly she knows about it before I even get home. It ain't like that over in England or France."

"No?"

"No. They's so many people in them countries if you lived two hundred years you could meet a thousand different people everyday, and never come acrost the same ones again, so long as you lived. And the castles! Why, just one of them castles, Becky, is larger than two of these towns puts together. Becky, the first chance I get I'm leaving this town for something better."

"I don't know, Tom. I like it here. I like knowing everybody. Constantinople is small too, but larger than it is here. And when I lived there, I didn't get a chance to know everyone, 'cause ma wouldn't let me talk to most people. She said they was below us in class."

"That's the one thing about small towns like St. Petersburg. Most everyone is the same here. 'Cept for Widow Douglas; but she's true. She don't let class say who she converses with."

A group of men approached Tom and Becky, interrupting their conversation. Drunk, tired, worn out and dirty from hunting for Jim, they cussed into their whiskey flasks.

"Hey!" one man shouted. "Don't sit so close t' our rafts. We've had considerable trouble what with thieves stealing 'em and leaving notes."

"That's it." said another man. "Kinder funny ones too. Black Avenger or something; and sayin' they struck agin.'"

"You kids get away from my raft. There's a runaway nigger I'm gonna catch," he boasted. "I don't want nobody touching it." He looked at Tom. "That means you." He looked at Becky. "And that means you too little girl."

Immediately the "little girl" fumed.

"Who do you think you are, to say we can't sit here? We ain't doing anything. We can be here long's we want. So these are your rafts; move them if you're scared they'll get stolen. But don't get mad at *us*, 'cause you haven't the ingenuity for lookin' after them yourself."

Tom heard gumption and solidarity in Becky's speech. Partly his doing, he knew. The men however, exploded in drunken laughter.

"Well, a girl who speaks up. Don't you know that ain't polite?"

"You tell her Johnny," a man said. "Don't you let her sass you." He clenched his fists, though he never dreamed of physically participating.

The only sober man in the crowd said, "Never mind. We got a nigger to catch."

"He's right; Josh's right." the clench fisted man said. "You listen to Josh." He had a habit of agreeing with everyone.

The men gone, Tom relaxed. Becky didn't.

"Tom, I don't mind them shaking their fingers at me; I don't care if they call me *little girl*; but they won't tell me where I can sit, and how I should talk. They *won't*!"

"Becky, they're drunk. They didn't know what they were saying."

"It doesn't matter," Becky huffed. "Look at 'em out there on the river. I'd like to get even. That's the one thing about this town I don't like...all the riffraff."

The courthouse bell rang throughout the town. "That's for Jimmy's hearing."

"I hope pa is up to it."

"Why shouldn't he be?"

"He's been acting strange. Mumbling to himself, forgetting things. He's been have nightmares too, Tom. And walking in his sleep. I'm worried about him, but he won't let on that's anything's wrong. Ma yells at him a lot, more often than she used to, since he agreed to be mayor until the town could find someone else. Tom, he hates it. I can hear him pacing back and forth for hours in his study. He hates being mayor; he hates the sheriff, and now he's worried about Huck's pa. He's been stirrin' up trouble for pa since he came back to town."

"He wants Huck's money. And now that's he dead, thinks he's got a legal right to it. But he won't never get it. Not after he tried to kill Widow Douglas."

"That's what pa says. Tom, he's scared of him, Huck's pa. Of what he might do. After they put him in jail, he hasn't stopped ranting and storming about what he would do to pa when he got out. I'm afraid for pa. He tries to pretend it ain't anything, but I know better." The court bells sounded again. "Oh," Becky pouted. "You got to go, don't you?"

"Becky, I wish I didn't," Tom lamented.

"I know. You want to be there; to see if you'll have to be called as a witness."

"I don't know what will happen."

The two reluctantly bade farewell. Inside the courtroom, Tom took a seat near the entrance. While waiting for Jimmy to be brought in, he listened to the surrounding talk.

"He'll hang sure," a man said.

"Ah, take away his whiskey and let the fool drown in his own clear-headedness," said another man. It sparked laughter.

"Anybody up for a lynching?"

"Oh, go jump in the river. You couldn't lynch a fly."

"Hey, maybe we'll get us a second chance now."

A dark shadow now cast itself upon Tom. He looked up and saw two strange men standing right beside him. The same strange men Tom had seen around town of late. Mostly along the river, or wherever whiskey was being sold. He thought he saw them with Jimmy Finn once, but upon straining his memory, he could not be absolutely sure if he had or not.

Each man was dressed in the shabbiest, dirtiest, cast-off clothes imaginable. All things considered, even Huck's attire was more fashionable that anything these two men were wearing. The clothes concealed most of their bodies; tattered gloves did for their hands, and cone shaped straw hats, pushed way down below their forehead, hid most of their faces; an expanse of dirt and mud did the rest. Tom returned his focus to the floor, fearing what might happen if the men spotted him looking at them. One man, the smaller of the two, smoked a corn-cob pipe. Their speech sent shivers down Tom's spine; not so much because of what they said, but because he recognized their voices as the same he and Becky heard the night before at the Stantan Home.

"Jack's Isle t'weren't but a deed end. Taint the place t' go."

"Ain't it out'n the way, with caverns t' hide. Thas what *he* said."

"*He* don't know nut'n. He got hisself killed. Well, we'll be long gone by the time it's found out."

"But we got t' come back here fer the *second* job."

"I know that."

A man rushed in shouting, "Hey, Jimmy's coming! They're bringin' him over now.."

Two armed guards escorted Jimmy Finn inside. His hands were tied with rope, his feet shackled in irons. And when Tom looked up in their direction, he noticed the two strange man had disappeared. Jimmy waddled like a penguin to the front, where he was abruptly pushed down into a seat. He let off a grunt, then stayed quiet; but only for the moment.

Judge Thatcher now swaggered in to cheers and hand clapping. He didn't hear any of it, however. The townsmen did not notice Judge Thatcher straining to keep his composure. He showed no outward signs; but internal doubts warred viciously. The onset of a terrible disease afflicted his mind. He did his level best to hide it.

Pounding a gavel, he called the room to order. "The prisoner will rise," he commanded.

Jimmy, his eyes full of rage, rose swiftly. "What you think yer up to Thatcher, treatin' me like a nigger? Why am I shackled an' brought in here on d'splay? I ain't no nigger at an auction."

Judge Thatcher ignored him. "Jimmy Finn, in order to speed this preliminary hearing I will get right to the point. You have been charged with the attempted murder of Ms. Douglas."

"Thas a lie!"

"You are also charged in connection with the murder of Huckleberry Finn, your son."

"I ain't got nothin' to do with it I tell you."

"How do you wish to plead?"

"I don't plead nothin'. I wanna lawyer."

"You waived your right to a lawyer earlier. However, you may retain one, *at* your trial."

"You think you so high an' mighty. I'll whittle you down b'fore *I'm* through with you."

Five men in the front row jumped up. One man held a rope. "Let's hang 'im!"

Jimmy cringed with terror. "Judge, you cain't let 'em. You got t' protect me. Ain't that the law! Don't let 'em hang me like I was a nigger."

Pounding on his gavel, Judge Thatcher recalled order. "I *will* have order." Sweat dripped from his forehead. "Do you hear! Disruptions will not be tolerated. You men, sit down."

Tom noticed trepidation in Judge Thatcher's speech, and wondered what could be bothering him. "He's never acted this way before," Tom noted.

"Well, Jimmy? What is your plea?

"I ain't pleadin' nothin'. But you watch your back judge, an' you give me that money of Huck's, that's rightfully mine, an' I'll git me a lawyer an' I'll sue thish'yhere whole town."

"As you wish. The trial will be set for Tuesday. Those of you who are to be called as witnesses will receive a summons at your home by Monday. Jimmy, you will remain in jail until the trial. I find you a great threat to society, and—,"

"Threat t' soci'ty! You cain't get away with this. I low I'll make you suffer fer humiliatin' me, an' paradin' me 'round like a nigger at an auction. I'll revenge you judge."

Judge Thatcher banged his gavel. "This hearing is adjourned."

As the guards led Jimmy out he turned his head and shouted, "You watch out judge. I ain't forgettin' this. You can't treat a man like a nigger, and think he won't fight back. Just you put your ear to the wind. You're gonna hear somethin' soon."

Judge Thatcher slumped wearily into his seat after thinking everyone had filed out. He did not see Tom sitting in the back row; did not discern his presence, until the shuffling of feet, growing nearer to him, attracted his attention. He looked up. An immediate surprise overtook him, and he sat up.

"Tom! I, I wasn't expecting to see you."

Tom, somewhat shocked to find himself standing before Judge Thatcher, when his entire being pressed and urged him to leave and let the man be, said, "I was only wanting to see the hearing. I know what Jimmy Finn did to Widow Douglas, on the boat."

"And you were naturally curious to see what would happen to the man." Judge Thatcher composed himself, and found that in Tom's presence he could relax, if even for a little bit.

"I reckon."

"Hmm. Well, I'm glad we have this moment together, anyhow. There's—something I've been meaning to discuss with you, regarding my daughter."

The uneasiness Tom felt when Judge Thatcher first mentioned a discussion, returned; this time with more force.

"Mrs. Thatcher found fresh footprints outside Becky's window the other day. Becky admitted going out in the night. Something about Huck's murder keeping her awake. Mrs. Thatcher found other footprints also. Becky refused to say whose, so her mother promptly whipped her. I wanted to bring it up with you earlier, but there was so much confusion and pandemonium going on at the time, and I had so much to preoccupy myself with, it slipped my mind for the present. I'm afraid I'm partly to blame for all her whippings these past few months. Since I became acting mayor, it's put more stress upon Mrs. Thatcher than it has on me. I don't believe in whippings, but I can't convince ma; she being raised on her own mother's whippings. The reason I am telling *you* is that I feel you have a right to know. Becky may deserve a whipping, but certainly she is not alone. Isn't that so?"

Tom felt sick all over. "I reckon I'm to blame. I didn't mean for her to get whipped. It ain't right she was. Them's my footprints. I'm the one who should get the punishment, not her."

"Tom, I'm glad you confessed. I had a feeling about it. And I *know* you would take Becky's punishment in a heartbeat." He rested his hand atop the boy's shoulder, lightly. "You proved that once before, you recall, when you took the whipping rightfully belonging to Becky after she tore out a page of the school master's book." He admired Tom; and Tom, in turn, secretly looked up to him as the father he never had. "However, just what were the two of you doing out that night, so late?"

"Well, only making up. We had another disagreement. I came to patch things up, and we did. I didn't mean for her to get whipped."

"I see." A relief came over the man. "I'm not saying what you did was *right*. But I won't hold it against you. She has told me of these—fights; and I know them to be petty. I *don't* believe you would do, nor would you allow, any *harm* to befall Becky. No, of course not."

"And I wouldn't. Will you tell Mrs. Thatcher?"

"No. Mrs. Thatcher might—. Well, but I don't think she would understand. She's been a changed person ever since I accepted this infernal post of acting mayor. I've…changed, myself. Law is my life, not politics. I can't make head or tail of it. But that's between you and me, Tom. It won't be too long until the new elections are held; and I count the days with a passion, when I will be rid of this curse. Ah, but I am babbling, I can see. Tom, let me just say I've the utmost faith and trust in you, and confidence, where my daughter is concerned. However, when Mrs. Thatcher has got her mind set on something, there usually isn't anyone who can persuade her otherwise. Becky is much more headstrong now than she has ever been. And just as you took her whipping, she has taken whippings for you too. But you did not know that, did you?"

Tom shook his head. "Becky never told me."

"No. I dare say not. You see? You've created something of a nobleness within Becky. She is willing to take the whole of a punishment in which she really ought to receive half."

"I'll go to Mrs. Thatcher right away, if it'll help."

"No. That would be unnecessary. *I'll* do my level best in getting Mrs. Thatcher to ease off the whippings. But you must do your part too, Tom. Do come around earlier in the day to see Becky, won't you? Do it for Becky's sake. Do it for mine as well. I do not believe in whippings, and cannot bear to hear my Becky being whipped for anything."

Tom began to choke up, but held back the tears. When Becky told him of her whippings she all but brushed them off as being nothing.

However, hearing it explained from her father's point of view, he saw the whole situation in a different light. Judge Thatcher let him leave; and as he walked out the building, he made a mental note to himself that, for Becky's sake, he would be more conscious of their late night escapades. His heart sagged so low, he hardly had any spirit left within him to visit Widow Douglas. Still, feeling obligated, he knew he must.

CHAPTER 6

"Yes?" asked Ginny; Miss Watson's slave girl. She opened the door a crack and, timidly, poked her nose through.

Tom had not time to identify himself when he heard a man's voice from within the mansion call out rather disdainfully, "Who is at the door? Is it that nosey reporter?" Footsteps approached. The door rudely swung open, and Ginny quickly hid behind it. The voice belonged to doctor Towers; and before he could focus his eyes squarely on Tom, he said coldly "I thought I told you not—. Oh," he relaxed, now seeing that it was only a boy, and not a reporter. "Forgive me. I thought perhaps you were that nosey reporter, come to pester Brit—. Widow Douglas."

"No sir," Tom explained. "It's only me, Tom Sawyer. I came to see how she was doing."

"You weren't just outside her parlor room window by chance, were you?"

"No sir. I only just got here."

"Oh? Could have sworn I—. Well, it's nothing." He tried to smile. "Again, forgive me. I haven't had much sleep, and my mind is on other matters. You're the fifth or six person today. I expect others will be dropping by throughout the afternoon."

"How is Widow Douglas?"

"Better. Better. She's resting now."

"I thought I could see her, if she was feeling alright."

"Very thoughtful indeed. However, as I've had to tell the others, it is not recommended. Not yet. But don't you worry. She has told me about St. Petersburg's annual town picnic, to be held tomorrow. By then she will be up to venturing out."

Another of Miss Watson's slave's, Ruth, entered. "Doctor, de Widow she axwin' fer y' to come." Spotting Ginny still hiding behind the door she shook her head and said, scornfully, "Ginny, come out f'm b'hind dat door. Y' know dat ain' polite."

"Tell Widow Douglas I'll be right there, Ruth. And don't worry about Ginny. This is still all a new experience for her."

"I keep tellin' her dat if she don' start b'havin' an' actin' more 'spectful she gonna git it good f'm Miss Watson. I alwus afeared for Ginny, dat Miss Watson gwin-a try sellin' her down river, like she tried wid Jim. But Lord, Ginny so young, she don' understand nuthin'." Ruth took hold of Ginny's hand and guided her away.

Looking back toward Tom, doctor Towers said, apologetically, "I must go tend to my patient. But I'll be sure to let her know you stopped by." Strangely, he closed the door on Tom before the boy could ask him if he even remembered his name. Tom had a mind to knock on the door again, but thought better of it. Then he heard a peculiar sound; kind of like a whippoorwill, only more sickly. He turned his head, out of a common reflex and natural curiosity.

"Muff?" Tom exclaimed is surprise."

"Shh!" Muff whispered forcefully. He beckoned Tom over to a group of tall standing bushes where he had kept himself hidden. Tom entered, and scrunched down beside him.

Talking softly, the boy said, "What are you doing here?"

"I couldn't keep away. Not after you told me what happened to Widow Douglas. I been on pins and needles, as they say, ever since. Tom, it's awful, 'pon my word, powerful awful, what that man is doing to her."

"You mean doctor Towers?"

"I *do*. I been up in that tree out yonder that sets just in front of her parlor room window, keepin' watch. It ain't no easy task either, tryin' to keep your balance on them branches. Then Ben he opened the window, so I slunk down hoping I could hear what was a-goin' on in there. Oh, *Tom*! 'Twas awful, awful."

"You been spying?"

"I reckon maybe thas what it amounts to. But I got to. I know he's up t' no good with her, and I got to catch him in the act. I told you what he done to Clara."

"The woman you was gonna marry?"

Muff nodded. "He killed her sure as I am settin' here. I couldn't prove it though. Don't reckon I ever could. Been over twenty years. I only wanna do right by Widow Douglas. 'Specially after all she done for me when I was rotting over in the jail awaitin' my trial." This was news to Tom, and he promptly inquired about it. "I would 'a' been lynched but for her. She heard a group of men was comin' to get me. She stopped 'em. Stood right in front of my cell and gave a speech about American law, and how I was innocent until proven guilty; how the preservation of that law must be maintained at all costs." Now Tom had heard nothing of this, and when he asked Muff about it, he was shocked to learn that this had transpired the week he and his comrades, Joe, the "Terror of the Seas", and Huck, the "Red-Handed", were off pirating. "After the trail, she continued being nice to me. Even let me eat dinner in her home the night I was freed. I owe Widow Douglas plenty."

"What d'you think the doctor is going to do to her?"

"He's already doing it. Sweet talkin' her; cozy-in' up to her; bein' friendly, and so much more. Tom, he ain't left her side a'tall, not once."

"Well, but he did, 'leastways once," Tom said, remembering his visit to Doctor Towers office. "He was in his office earlier today."

"No," Muff said, shaking his head. "No, he 'tweren't."

"Well, but I saw him. I saw his shadow, anyway."

"Couldn't 'a' been him. 'Cause I been here all day, and I had my eye on him most always. And didn't he nor anybody else leave the mansion in that time."

"Well," Tom reflected, "maybe I only *thought* I saw a shadow."

"Likely so," Muff agreed. "Could 'a' been the sun casting a shadow on a branch."

"I reckon so. The door was locked anyhow. So of course, it weren't any but the sun." Tom put the subject out of his mind; for the idea occurred to him he had been bewitched somehow, and that his mind was playing tricks in him. He knew well the ways of witches, from all the accounts given by the slaves, and how they liked to have their fun with mortals.

"Well," Muff went on, "I got to stay right here now 'til it gets dark. Then I can slink over to them trees on the side of the mansion. They's all around, and 'll give me plenty of cover, fer what I need to do."

"Muff, I could keep an eye out for Widow Douglas too."

"No. Oh, no. They's no tellin' what that man 'd do if he found you out. I cain't chance it, you gettin' into trouble on my account."

Tom persisted. "Maybe if I could get inside sometime, and visit with Widow Douglas."

"Well," Muff thought. "I don't reckon thas so bad, 'cause other people have been stoppin' by too. I heard tell Ben sayin' she'd be up to company soon."

"He'll be with her at tomorrow's picnic, so that ain't a good time."

"Is that so? Well, just you be careful for when you do see her. And don't go giving yourself away."

"Why Muff, I know everything they is to know. All I got to do is what the books say."

"Books? Tom, ne'ermind books. Jus' try and find out what you can about Ben from Widow Douglas, 'thought making her suspicious." The two shook on it, and Tom left.

CHAPTER 7

"Tom! Wake up! Hurry!" Tom opened his eyes and looked around the room, dazed. He did not know if it was dream or reality. Sid stood over him, terrified. "Tom! Are you awake?"

"I am now. Sid, it can't be three yet. What's it all about?"

"Don't you hear all that ruckus outside?"

Tom listened. Hearing nothing he said, "You're dreaming. Probably just old Hays throwing rocks at a cat." He laid back on his pillow. Distant rumblings prompted Tom to sit up. They soon became more distinct. "I hear it now. You don't s'pose the town's being invaded by pirates do you?"

"There aren't pirates within one thousand miles of here."

"Well, go find Auntie and ask her what it's all about."

"You come with."

"Shucks. You ain't scared are you?"

"No. Maybe you might want to sneak out and see what the trouble is."

"And get myself killed? I don't reckon I'll be anywhere but here."

A slight pause. "Okay." Sid hesitated until Tom waved his arm at him to go. Within a minute Tom had dressed and gone out the window.

He crept cautiously, avoiding windows or doors where his aunt might pop out and say "Boo". Away off into the night Tom caught glimpses of torches seemingly floating by themselves until they neared, displaying human figures underneath. Tom sweated to know what brought these men out of doors this late at night. He spotted Joe Harper down the street.

"Joe, over hear! What's going on?"

"It's the most 'mazing thing yet."

"Well, what is it? You might let someone else know."

"An escape, down to the jail."

"An escape! You mean Huck's pap?"

"Yep."

"When? Do you know?"

"Nobody's sure. But at least two hours ago. My pa is out with the other men. I snuck out as soon as I could."

"He must be long gone by now."

"Deep in Illinois territory right this minute?"

Tom shook his head. "No. He wouldn't head to Illinois. If he was caught, likely jurisdiction would allow for his return. He must be heading south, towards Mexico. That's what I'd do, if I was him."

"Do you reckon he'd take the river, or go cross country?"

"I dunno. The river would slow him up. But if he went horse-back, there 'd be tracks sure, and that'd give him away dead to rights."

A lone, torch-less man came hustling up the street and approached the boys. He stopped within a few feet, exhausted and out of breath.

"Who goes there?" he asked between breaths.

"Tom Sawyer."

"And Joe Harper."

"What are you boys doing out this time of night?"

"Same as most I reckon," said Tom."

"It's dangerous times," the man said.

"We know. Tom and I heard 'bout the escape."

"Do you know how Jimmy escaped?" Tom asked the man. "Didn't he have two guards laying shotgun on him?"

"Yeah. But those no accounts fell asleep, drunk. When they came to, both of them were tied and gagged."

"Jimmy did all that?" Tom questioned.

"No. His accomplices."

Two pairs of eyes broadened and glowed under the moonlight.

"Accomplices?"

"How many?"

"Nobody knows. Somebody came by and saw them guards layin' there. He untied them, and they went straightaway to Judge Thatcher's. He gave orders to round up as many men as we could, quick."

"Any ideas as to the whereabouts?" asked Joe.

"Wish I knew."

"Joe and me figured he might head for Mexico; but couldn't decide whether he'd take the river or go cross country."

"Well, that's smart of you boys. I'll pass it along—oh, say, here comes someone now."

"Timothy, that you?" asked the new arrival.

"Yeah."

"Well, come on. We got a lead."

"You don't say."

"Yeah. 'Pears two fellas were whooping it up last night and earlier today down near the ferry landing 'bout how they were gonna break Jimmy out. Nobody b'lieved them. They were drunk. But when they see the torches, and all the men, they wanted to know about it. You should have seen them turn green,"

"Two fellers you say? Suspicious looking?"

"I'd never seen 'em. Figured they come up looking for the nigger."

"I saw two fellers yesterday, outside the drugstore. Heard 'em say something about heading for Goshen, then Canada. You suppose they were the same ones you saw?"

"Could be. Could be."

A group of men approached, their torches blazing a golden light so intense the whole side of one street illuminated every tree, house, and unlucky alley cat.

"Come on!" they shouted. "We're hot on their trail."

Timothy rose. "Found tracks did you?"

"Three sets. One of 'em is Jimmy's. Nobody but he has that nail-cross in the left boot heel. Looks as though they're headed for the river."

"By gosh, Timothy, you reckon those two are the same ones?"

"Sammy, if it is, I just bet there to Goshen right now."

"Quick, if we hurry we might catch up to them before they're clean away."

The men "made tracks". The boys envied them.

An idea struck Joe. "Let's go down to the jail and check it out. We might find a clue, anything to help capture Jimmy."

Tom's curiosity immediately burst wide open. He made a mental note to curse himself later for not thinking of the idea first. They wasting no time.

In another part of town the Stantan Home, vacant for years, until Tom and Becky explored it, now sheltered three new lives. A perfect locale, it provided a grand view of all the men who carried torches. Seeing them head north, Jimmy Finn knew his plan had worked.

"Look at 'em boys! Headin' fer Goshen."

The "boys", Jed and Sim, did not as of yet share Jimmy's enthusiasm.

"That don't mean we're out 'a' the woods yet," Jed complained.

Sim agreed. "They might come back b'fore we can leave."

Jimmy laughed. "Not *him*. He'll keep at it, never knowing how close we is. He'll head up to Canada to find us. You did leave the false clues?"

"Sim and me done everything you told us. We spread ourselves around town so we'd be noticed. Made sure they all knew we'd be headin' for Goshen, then up to Canada."

Jimmy looked through a space in-between a flat board originally used to cover a broken window. "Alright. We're safe."

Jed scratched his beard. "Can we get these dern clothes off then?"

"Can we Jimmy? We had real good times in 'em, but now they is gettin' a might oncomfortable. I'd like to get shed of 'em."

"They served their purpose. Get 'em off."

Jed and Sim quickly threw off their outer clothes; the beards came off too, exposing reddish faces. Dressed in frontiersman attire, down to their moccasins, belts decorated with knives, arrowheads, and one scalp apiece, they felt whole again. The removal of their hats allowed a river of oily, black, musky hair to flow down to their shoulders.

"Thatcher treated me like I was a nigger. I'll get even with him for that, mark my words." Jimmy gleamed with evil pleasure. Turning to his accomplices, he bellowed, "*Now* you look like half breeds. Hide them clothes in that closet over yonder. Won't nobody find 'em for a hundred years, maybe."

"Jimmy?" Jed questioned seriously. "How long we got t' wait for the second job? The job with the big payoff, that we was to do before you got yourself jailed."

Jimmy angered. "Don't talk that way t' me! Tomorrow night, or the night after. D'pends. We got to make sure he's far away."

"Tell us again how much money there is? Jed and me want to know."

"Thousands. More, if I can make him squirm, which I can. Is the place up on Jackson's Island fixed up?"

"No."

"No! Why? You two doin' more loafin' than work?"

"They's someone up there. We saw smoke t'other night an this'n."

"Damnation! Well, there's a small, two story cabin-house, up a mile or so on the Illinois side. It's hid real good. Nobody 'll ever find us there. Hate to use it, it's so unstable. I'd prefer Jackson's Island, but I ain't sharing it with others. Well, I'm starved. Who brought food?"

Jed shrugged his shoulder's. "I didn't."

"Neither did I."

"No food! I got to starve 'til tomorrow? They don't hardly feed a body at that jail. Nothing but molded bread and dirty crick water when they do. You brothers 'll both be the death of me yet. I hoped to eat before we started out. Well, when those men are far enough away, we'll slip down to Scott's Wharf, get a canoe, some jugs of whiskey, and head out."

"Thas real good times!"

In the opposite part of town, Tom and Joe entered the empty jail which Jimmy occupied hours earlier. Tom lit a candle.

"Look at it, Tom. Ain't it right out of a book?"

"I'd druther a hundred times more be here, than *read* it in a book."

Each boy beheld this spectacular event, breathing in its historical significance. The jail door, kicked in violently, swung loosely, back and forth. Rank weeds, upturned and flattened, showed chaos. Scattered footprints impacted soft dirt; Jimmy's infamous nail-cross unmistakably preserved. Rope lay in pieces; the same used to tie up the guards.

While Joe explored one area of the jail, Tom stooped down near the cot. Overturned on its side, Tom thought Jimmy might have attempted digging a tunnel underneath. He found no such evidence to indicate Jimmy had. However, an object glittering near the cot caught Tom's eye. He looked towards Joe. The boy had his back to him. Tom quickly pocketed the object. Joe whirled.

"Tom! Did you hear that?" Joe, frightened, froze.

"No. What was is?"

"Sounded like footsteps."

"Might only be your heart."

"Well it is racing. No! There it is again."

"I heard it too. That ain't your heart. Let's go out and see."

Stepping out of the jail, a man's voice boomed into their ears.

"Hey! Who's there?"

"It's one of the guards, Tom," Joe whispered. "Quick, the candle."

Tom extinguished the candle, and both boys ran away to their respected homes before they could be identified by the guard.

Climbing through his window, Tom felt his body being sucked in on somebody else's power. A lantern lit, he faced his Aunt Polly. Sid, having told her of Tom's absence, waited patiently to catch him returning.

"Auntie!" a surprised Tom exclaimed.

"Didn't expect me, did you?"

"I, no."

"What were you doing out there this time of night? Getting into some kind of trouble? Come now, tell me. What devilment has occupied your time?"

"No, Auntie. No devilment."

"No! Tom Sawyer, I know you. You tell me what you were doing out there. Off pirating again? Sneaking around graveyards? Come now, what's your story this time?"

"I only wanted to find out what was going on outside. Well, I was curious. Sid woke me, and told me he heard noises. I heard them too. Curiosity grabbed hold of me. Turns out Jimmy Finn escaped, and there's men all around after him. Well, I apologize, Auntie, if I scared you."

Aunt Polly thought she could catch Tom off guard in one of his lies. Tom, instead, caught her off guard by telling the truth.

"Apolo—. Tom, I. And here I thought you'd make up some lie to cover yourself, and I'd catch you in it." She blushed. "Tom, sometimes you can surprise me. Of course you were curious. You're a boy. It's your nature, I reckon. Well, it's over. Off to bed with ye; the both of you." She left the room, much to Sid's disappointment, not at all displeased with Tom.

CHAPTER 8

Confusion reigned over the town this night. Lack of organization played a key role. Groups of men, out hunting Miss Watson's Jim, had to be found and convinced Jimmy Finn's apprehension meant a great deal more to the town. Some men quickly agreed; other, hot-tempered men, refused. Adding to the night's disarray, groups of men from neighboring towns, and from across the river, roamed St. Petersburg, also looking for Miss Watson's Jim. They did not enjoy being stopped and harassed by townsmen, and having to constantly explain their business. Some were jumped even before they could. Fights often broke out. One such fight began this way, when a group of men spotted a suspicious character roaming the woods...

Shouted the leader, "Ay, you! Stop."

The man kept walking, ignoring the men.

"You there, state your business, or I'll let you have it." The leader drew his rifle.

The man turned in their direction. Clouds obscured the their vision, but they all saw him walking towards them. From a distance he looked small. As he neared, the clouds lifted. They saw the outline of his size.

"A mountain he is," one man in the group gasped.

"Solid rock too," another man whispered. "Must weigh over 300 pounds."

"Good God, look at his face, You could hit it with a steamboat and it wouldn't phase him. Not one inch."

The lead man, seeing his enormous size, began to shake.

"Put down that rifle, now," the man bellowed.

"Did you hear that voice? Deeper than a bottomless pit I tell you."

"You best do as he says, and put down the rifle."

"I'll not."

"Do you hear, put that rifle down? I've dealt with worse riffraff than you in my time."

"Get ready with the rope, Bob," ordered the lead man. "Looks like we got ourselves a live one."

The man eyed the rope without moving his head. He kept walking.

"On my signal, ready." The rope hovered and twirled above Bob's head. If anyone could snare his victim with a rope Bob could. He won many rope throwing contests and loved to brag about them every chance he got. "Now!"

The man walked on, his eyes squarely on the rifle; his ears attentively on the rope as it sped through the air. About to lasso him, he struck out his hand, caught it, and tugged with great force, throwing Bob to the ground.

"Shoot him," they yelled.

The lead man shook with fear. He could not pull the trigger. The man, upon him, grabbed hold of his hand.

"Oooh!" the lead man cried in great pain as the man squeezed his hand until he heard the bones crack. Then he ripped the rifle away and smashed it to pieces against a tree.

Anger overflowed. Humiliated, the men cried revenge. They circled this strange man.

"On the count of three, men, we rush him."

"Eagerly they dug into the dirt with the tops of their shoes; their feet, if they went barefoot.

"One! Two! THREE!"

Late that same morning, waves of tired, dirty, hungry, men returned home to tell their wives and children they failed to capture Jimmy. Nobody sensed more defeat than Judge Thatcher. He blamed himself for the escape; not even his wife could convince him differently, and strongly opposed him going back out in search of Jimmy.

"Nonsense," she said. "You'll stay right here, where you belong. Let the sheriff go out after him. That's what he's paid for. There are plenty of men looking for him already. You have higher duties here. Well, look at yourself. You haven't slept in thirty hours. You're so tired. What if someone came to the door to see you."

"I know ma. The sheriff is out, on the Illinois side, hunting Miss Watson's slave. He doesn't know yet."

Judge Thatcher wanted Cal back also. Before Jimmy's escape, he welcomed his departure, believing the longer Cal stayed away from St. Petersburg, the better for the town. This sudden turn of events shook Judge Thatcher. He took Jimmy's threats to heart, and feared for the safety of his family. With Cal away, however, finding Jimmy became *his* priority.

"Follow him into Mexico!" Judge Thatcher lashed out, unknowingly.

"Follow who into Mexico dear?"

"What?"

"You said, 'Follow him into Mexico'. Follow who?"

"I said nothing of the kind." Judge Thatcher angered.

"Yes you did, dear."

"Absurd! Don't tell me what I said. I should know what I say, and what I don't say. I don't need you to tell me differently."

"Don't you raise your voice to me like that. You said something, and I inquired about it."

"Nothing." Judge Thatcher pounding his fists onto the table.

"There now," Mrs. Thatcher cried out. "You've spilt coffee on my cloth. That belonged to my mother, and her mother before that, and her mother too."

"Well then, I'd say it's high time we bought a new one." He did not realize what he said any longer. Tormented with hunger, desperate lack of sleep, fear and guilt, a mounting sense of insanity slowly embedded itself inside Judge Thatcher's mind, waiting, waiting, waiting...

Mrs. Thatcher, deeply wounded, set her husband's breakfast by his side.

"Here," she scorned. "Eat it, then go back out; if Becky nor I mean anything to you anymore." She ran from the kitchen.

"Ma!" Judge Thatcher called after her. She did not hear him. "You don't understand. You don't—,"

His family meant everything. Jimmy must be apprehended soon. The threats made in the courthouse against Judge Thatcher were idle ones when rope bound his hands, and irons shackled his legs and feet. Without restraints, Jimmy's threats loomed more dangerous, more *real*.

"What's the matter with ma?" a voice inside his head asked him. No, not inside his head. He looked up.

"Becky?" Yes, Becky."

"Why is ma crying?"

"Oh, Becky. Go to her, please. Help her through this, will you?"

"Help her through what?" Becky, having slept soundly through the night, did not know yet of Jimmy's escape. "Pa! Just look at you. What ever did you do to your clothes? They're in ruins?"

"I know. Go to ma. Make her understand."

"Understand what, pa?"

"Why I've been out looking all night. That I have to keep looking. He must be found before he harms anyone."

"The runaway nigger?"

"No! Jimmy Finny!"

"What!" The truth now dawned for Becky.

"Jimmy Finn, Jimmy Finn. He escaped last night. Didn't you know?"

"Know? No. I slept all night."

"Oh, child. I'm sorry. I didn't mean to tell you in this way. I thought you already knew."

"I, I didn't."

"We'll find those men, and we'll bring them back under heavy guard, so they can't ever harm anyone."

"They? They who?"

"Jimmy had help. Two men."

"Two men? Who?"

"Well, we're not certain. It might be two men who have been hanging around town the past few days."

Sudden guilt racked Becky's conscience. She asked herself, "Could they be the same men Tom and I overheard at the Stantan Home talking about a job?" Becky thought to keep silent until she knew for sure.

"Becky. You're sweating."

"Am I?"

"Yes, child. You are."

"It's intolerably warm inside. I'll go check on ma now."

"Yes, do that won't you? And tell her I'm very, very sorry for everything. Tell her I'll be back tonight, as soon as I can."

"Yes, pa."

Judge Thatcher, constrained, none-the-less managed to smile. His daughter gone, that smile evaporated. An extended amount of time must pass, before Judge Thatcher's strength ever permitted him to smile again.

All over town, families woke up to the news of Jimmy Finn's escape, and grappled with whether or not to cancel today's picnic. As well, in the Sawyer household, downcast faces pondered the issues.

"It's just terrible what's been going on the past week," Mary said. "Jimmy's escape gave me nightmares I still can't rid my mind of."

Sid said, "I dreamt I was walking in the Garden of Eden alongside Adam and Eve. Did you ever have such dreams, Tom?"

Tom gritted his teeth. "Never you mind, Sid."

Aunt Polly, entering the kitchen, used her authority to put an end to this family bickering.

"I'm back now. You three behave."

"Who came to the door?" Sid asked.

"The Simmons boy. He's going around town, on Widow Douglas' instructions, telling everyone the picnic will not be canceled. The Simmons boy says Widow Douglas will be there too, to show support for the picnic. Now Tom, I reckon you'll go whether I tell you, you can or not. So you be good, and don't get into mischief. And stay close by the picnic. I don't reckon Jimmy Finn'll be anywhere near there, but it's better to be in a crowd, than by yourself. Mary and me is a-goin' down to see a new neighbor, Judith Loftus. She and her husband just come up here, and I want to welcome her in, and make her comfortable."

Pleaded Sid, "Mightn't I come along too?"

"I reckon, if you'd rather not go to the picnic."

"No. The other kids pick on me, 'cause they're jealous I'm so good."

Tom knew better than to say anything.

CHAPTER 9

At noon precisely, under august skies, near an open field of grass along the Mississippi River, the picnic officially began. About half the town's menfolk were absent, still out looking for Jimmy. However, enough of a gathering was produced to call the picnic a success. Most came just to see Widow Douglas for the first time since her run in with Jimmy. Her voice returned, and almost fully healed, she thanked everyone who came out to the picnic in defiance of Jimmy Finn, and to celebrate one of St. Petersburg's most joyous, yearly, occasions. Parents and their children frolicked and socialized with one another. Cricket and horseshoes topped the adult list of favorites, while the children enjoyed tag and marbles.

Tom and Becky did not partake in any activities. They arrived at the picnic separately; but neither were apart long. Each had something to tell the other. Together they slipped behind a large tree and talked privately. Their hearts raced.

"Becky! I know who busted out Jimmy. At least, I'm sure I know."

"So do I. The two men from the Stantan Home." Tom glared at Becky, amazed she also thought of the two men. "We could be in a lot of trouble, if it *is* them. We'd be accomplices for not telling anyone."

"I thought as much too, Becky. *If* it is them. We only heard them mention a job. They never said *what* job."

Something occurred to Becky. Her hands dropped limply to her lap, and her face paled. "Tom! The Stantan Home!"

"What? What about the Stantan Home?"

"Don't you remember? The men; the Stantan Home. Don't you see? I told you something was going to happen in the Stantan Home. And it did."

"Sure," Tom realized. "That must 'a' been the first job they talked about. We should 'a' known. *I* should 'a' known. But, they mentioned a second job. Becky, they might be there yet."

Tom and Becky both knew what had to be done. Neither relished the idea, but each discerned the importance of finding out for sure; then they would go to Judge Thatcher and tell him what they had seen.

For twenty minutes they hid in a thicket of bushes, thirty yards from the Stantan Home, unsure what, or who, might be on the inside.

"Tom, somebody has been here. That front window was boarded up solid before. It's busted in half now. An animal couldn't have done that."

"Becky, do you reckon they are still in there?"

"Oh, Tom. I hate to admit it, but there's only one way to find out."

They both walked cautiously up to the mansion, each waiting, and half expecting, somebody to poke their head out a window.

At the door, Tom said, "Now, Becky, if there is anyone in there, you don't wait for me, but run as fast as you can. I'll hold the door shut long's I can."

"No!" Becky opposed. "I won't leave you here. You close the door and we'll both run."

Becky would not waiver. Tom reluctantly agreed, then slowly pushed the door open. They waited for something to happen. When nothing did, their courage rebounded and they stepped inside.

"Ain't anybody here," Tom said, after some hesitation.

Becky moved her eyes around. The outside light that poured inside the mansion was all there was to see by. Tom had candles, but dared not light any; not yet, not until he was sure it would be safe.

"No, it don't appear that way," Becky said. Her eyes fell upon a closet. "Tom, look," she immediately said. "That door wasn't open when we were here."

"No. I don't b'lieve it was. Well, it could 'a' been, but now I don't remember. Let's go see."

In unison they walked toward the closet. When they peered down at what lay bunched up on the floor, they at first thought their eyes deceived them.

"Becky? Do you know what these is?"

"I've seen those clothes before."

"Everyone has." Tom and Becky each picked up several articles of clothing to examine them. "These are the clothes those two strangers were wearing. They must 'a' been in disguise!"

"Here. Look at these. Fake beards."

"That explains it."

"Explains what?"

"Well, I only assumed before. But now, what with these beards—Becky, they're injuns."

"Injuns! How do you know?"

"I saw their skin up close. It's red. And there's something else. Something I found the night of Jimmy's escape, in the jail."

"You were there?"

Tom nodded, while he slowly removed an object from his pocket. "Look at this, Becky."

"Tom, it, it looks to be an *arrow-head*."

"Not looks. Is! Ain't it dandy? One of Jimmy's accomplices must 'a' dropped it by accident, helping him escape."

"Tom, what'll we do?"

"Ain't nothing we can do. That first job was to break Jimmy out. That's done. Likely the second job was to find somewhere's to hide out. They came here alright. These clothes prove it. I reckon the worst is over now. They're long gone."

"I hope so."

"Why else would they remain in town?" Tom's courage returned to him. "Becky, we was scared for nothing. But don't you see, everything's fine now. They ain't no need to panic."

Becky, too, began to see the light. "No. Not any longer."

"You know what this means?"

"What?"

"We can look for the treasure, 'thought any worry at all."

"Tom, have you still got the Stantan treasure on your mind?"

"I always have. Becky, there's that side door out yonder. It's boarded up good, and probably locked. I'll go home and get a crowbar that's in my aunt's shed, and as many candles as I can pocket. You go home and get candles too, as many as you can. We'll meet back here in half an hour, by them bushes we hid behind." It was agreed.

And while Tom and Becky go for supplies, we shall take this opportunity to see what else is occurring in the "sleepy little village" of St. Petersburg.

The picnic was become a roaring success, even with Jimmy's escape looming over the townspeople's heads. But nobody believed he would return to mar their fun; and as the hours passed, the people grew safer in that belief. They were all too overjoyed to see Widow Douglas out and about, and healthy once more, to concern themselves with anything else. All day people came up to wish her well. Though she thanked each and every one of them, she vaguely heard their remarks. Muff's fears were being recognized, and Widow Douglas was falling under the spell of doctor Towers; he was all she could think about. But for fifteen minutes, while he went to check his office, she was never without him. And when he returned to her side, she was contented and pleased.

"Is everything in order?," she asked. "You seemed most insistent, anxious as it were, to check your office."

"I had a shipment of medicine come in. I didn't want to leave it at the post office."

"Oh. Ben. Dine with me tonight?"

"Haven't I dined with you every night?"

He doesn't understand! "Well, well yes, you have. Ben, I, what I meant was—will you dine *with* me."

"Oh." It began to sink in. "I'm ten years older than you."

Widow Douglas blushed. "I know. My husband, my *late* husband, God rest his soul, would be your age."

"I didn't—. Brittany, there's so much you don't know about me."

"There's so much you don't know about *me*."

"I may not be what you hope for."

"Do you know what it is I hope *for*?"

"I wouldn't want to hurt you."

"I've been hurt before. I lost my husband before I was thirty. He left me a mansion. He left me with more money than I'll ever know what to do with. But he left me. And I've been alone all these years, waiting for another, another *him*. Another like him. Moral, upstanding, forthright, unselfish—,"

"Does such a man exist? Am I such a man, in your eyes?"

"Have dinner with me tonight. We'll find out."

Doctor Towers said, reluctantly, "Alright."

Crouched behind a row of short evergreens, up on a high hill overlooking the picnic, Muff Potter nervously stole glances at every opportunity. He would have given anything to know what they were saying. Still, he had ideas. The way they looked at one another, smiled, laughed, Muff knew what was going on, and he cursed to high heaven. He had spent years trying to forget the pain doctor Towers had caused him. Whiskey, any hard liquor, helped. Eternally convinced Clara's death was no accident, and fearful Doctor Towers might levy serious harm against Widow Douglas, Muff pushed himself to stay sober. Her well being meant a great deal to him. He owed Widow Douglas. Muff owed another person too. He thought of him regularly.

Muff shrieked. "Ben, 'pon my honor, if you harm Widow Douglas like you did Clara!"

Not everyone attended the picnic. The town sheriff, Cal, had just returned to his office, after a long stay over on the Illinois side in his desperate search for Miss Watson's Jim. It is evident, from his staggering, how tired he is. Twisting the doorknob took effort, as his hands jittered excitedly. A townsman, happening upon the sheriff, told him about Jimmy's escape.

"What of it!" Cal coldly responded "I got my own worries. Don't you know that runaway nigger has got to be caught? Don't you know what his running away means to the country? Well, he's only taken our Constitution and ripped it to shreds. Founding fathers fought and died for that Constitution. It's up to us to see they didn't die in vain."

This strange belief of Cal's plagued him his entire life. His own father used to beat those words into him every day; and remind Cal how his grandfather had fought and died in the Revolutionary War. His father's voice haunted him constantly; his and his grandfather's ghost were ever present, all around him, circling him, hounding him, condemning him.

Cal pushed the man aside and entered his office. He tried several times to light a match, but his nervous fingers kept extinguishing the flame. After four attempts, the office burst forth with illumination; but not by Cal's doing.

Scared, and hallucinating, Cal jumped back against a wall. "Who's there?"

A shadow lurked from behind the desk. Cal saw a man's face coming into the light. Recognizing the man immediately, he doubled over.

"Cy!"

Without concern, Cy said, "You're an abomination."

"What are you doing here?"

"Business."

"Oh, god, no! No! I don't want any more of your business. I, Cy, please now. It's been years."

"Don't you act that way with me. You know what I can do. I already whipped five men within an inch of their lives. Damn fools tried to jump me last night."

"Oh," Cal moaned wearily. "Let me sleep awhile. I been awake near forty hours."

"Do you think that means anything to me? I'm here to find a runaway nigger worth three hundred dollars. That's my business, you understand."

"I thought you were a bounty hunter."

"I am. Don't get smart with me. I am many things; but I am first and foremost a southern patriot. You will have a few hours rest, then our hunt will begin. We'll begin on the upper side of town. It's forested. He could be pinned down under any number of trees. We'll also try Jackson's Island, later on. That's the next best place for a runaway nigger to hide. Plenty of caves; and it's close to the Illinois border."

"You know this town well, better'n me."

"Yes. I've been here once before, years ago, on business. But that's none of your concern, you understand. Now get your sleep. I'll return in a few hours time. I don't want to waste any time, you understand."

CHAPTER 10

As planned, Tom and Becky met back at the Stantan Home; and, with crowbar and an ample supply of candles, took aim at the side door. They made fast work of the boards; but when they came to the door itself they found that it was locked."

"I just knew it would be too," Tom said.

"How will we ever get in there *now*?" Becky asked.

"Well, look at the door. It's old and rotting. I'll bet with a little bit of work we can pry it open in no time."

Tom's optimism, and Becky's faith in him, paid off. With a few hard tugs the old wood gave way, and the door was thrust open for the first time in many years. However, the hinges attached to the door were so rusty they created a hideous echo.

"Well," Tom contemplated, "I'll see about getting some grease, sometime. But I won't bother with it 'less it's worth our while. Let's see what's in there."

Their hearts fluttered as they entered. Before Tom closed the door, he lit a candle; then they were on their way.

"We're descending, Becky. Can you feel it?"

"Yes."

"'Pears to veer to the right here. It goes down *under* the Stantan Home. Why Becky, it's a cellar. The Stantans must 'a' kept food and liquor down here. It's *perfect*, Becky. Everybody knows there ain't no better place to put a secret passage but in a cellar.

Tom and Becky came upon steps, and counted twelve of them as they descended its length; then they walked down a long corridor, until embarking upon a large open room, with stone walls and a dirt floor. Except for ten or so boxes up against one wall, the room contained nothing; least of all anything that might "lead to their imaginations".

Tom said in disgust, "This can't be all there is!"

Becky, her fantasy shattered, lethargically sank to the ground, in a worse condition than Tom. "It was all for nothing. Tom, I was so sure. Even if there was nothing inside, it would have been worthwhile. For the first time in my life I enjoyed the idea of finding a secret passageway. I enjoyed the adventure of it. I wouldn't have given anything to have the moment taken away. But now, I don't know, Tom. It seems so dreamlike."

Suddenly Becky began to shake. Her quivering body forced the candle from Tom's hand. He fell backwards against the boxes. Pitch dark!

"Becky, where are you!"

"He-here. Here. T-Tom. T-Tom!"

"You're shaking again!"

"I'll be all right in a minute. Just hold me until it's over." Becky shook for two minutes; slightly longer than the one before. "There, it's gone now. I don't understand it. It appears without any warning, and leaves the same way. It lasts a few moments longer each time."

Tom quickly lit another match. Becky saw something behind the boxes. She pointed her finger and exclaimed, "Tom. Look. There. See?"

"What? The boxes? What about them?

"No! What's behind the boxes."

They both turned their bodies.

"Wood planks, Becky. Everywhere else there's stone, but here. One, two, three—five planks."

"They're loose too, Tom."

At once the planks were brutally yanked, exposing an opening.

"Who'll go in first?" Becky spoke hoarsely.

"Becky, y-you go." Tom spoke with trepidation.

"Oh *thank you*, Tom!" Becky hugged Tom, knowing how hard a decision it was for him to make.

"Here." Tom handed his candle to Becky. "How is it in there?"

"Small. Not much room to crawl." Becky poked her head out. It dead ends. Nothing but dirt."

"Dirt? Let me have a look."

"Be careful." She waited a few minutes before she heard anything.

"Becky. You know what this means?"

"What?"

Tom came out. "It's a pile up."

"Then, then we'll not *ever* find the treasure."

"Sure we will. Why, all we got to do is move the dirt."

"Move the dirt! A fine thing indeed. And how long will that take?"

"Wouldn't you like to find out?" Becky could not say no. She did not want to say no.

One at a time Tom and Becky crawled in and, using their hands, dug into the dirt, placing it, for the time being into the empty boxes until all of them were filled.

Tom said, "We'll stop for now. It must be late. Help me push these boxes up against the hole, to hide it."

Finished, they rejoined the outside world, just in time to witness one of nature's most awesome of spectacles. The sun, beginning its descent, cast a marvelous orange-like hue upon the sky and clouds. Tom and Becky watched it in all its splendor. Only one thing remained for Becky, to make this day among the most cherished in all her life.

"Tom, before we leave there's, there's something I'd like to, that is there's something I *want* to do. I *must* do. Please don't think it strange."

"What?"

Becky bit her lip. "S-smoke, on your pipe. Oh, I know I was afraid, and I still am, sometimes. I've seen what can happen when it's smoked the wrong way. But now I want to try for myself."

Tom hadn't any objections. He took out his pipe, applied *new* tobacco, which he wouldn't use even for himself, and with the last remaining match, combined the two, creating a hailstorm of combustion within the bowl that released a pleasant, heavy-scented aroma.

"Here." Tom handed the pipe to Becky. "Draw in slowly. Let it roll around inside your mouth 'til you get a taste. Be careful not to inhale. I learned the hard way how to smoke a pipe."

For five minutes Becky smoked from Tom's pipe, savoring every second, until the fire naturally extinguished; not once did she inhale or choke, or turn away in disgust.

"I reckon it'll take some doing before I can keep it going longer. Here's your pipe back."

"Becky, I got something for you, to hold on to." Tom rummaged through his vest pocket.

"The arrow-head!"

"I'm afraid I'll loose it. I'd feel safer if it was with you."

"Me?" Becky gently, lovingly, caressed it. Tom I, I don't know what to say, but—thank you." She engulfed the boy with another hug.

"I knew you'd like it."

"I'll treasure it for as long as I have it with me."

"Here. You didn't notice before, but look. I've made a hole in it, and I've got some string. You can wear it as a necklace."

"I will. And it'll make a fine necklace. I *had* better keep it hid. If ma ever found it on me, she'd take it away. And probably whip me for having it. I'll keep it under my dress."

"Becky, I —. Becky, about your ma whippin' you. Well, I'm awful sorry for it, 'cause I know it's on account of me she's doin' it."

"No! No, now Tom, you listen, haven't I told you—,"

"'Yes, yes you *have* told me. But you and I both know that if you warn't spending so much time with me, well, you wouldn't be getting into trouble."

Becky put her hands on her hips. "Now Thomas Sawyer, how often have I got to tell you I don't want to hear that kind of talk from you? Tom," Becky pleaded. "I've had more fun in the year and a half I've known you, and in the past three of four months especially, than all the years I've been alive. I don't like ma whippin' me. I *don't*. But Tom, you got to believe me when I say she'd whip me anyway. That's her nature. Her ma whipped her 'til she left home, and likely ma will whip me 'til *I* leave home. Well, I might as well *earn* those whippings. Now," Becky warmed, "we'll meet again late tonight. I want to find the treasure *too*, Tom. And we will. We will find the treasure, and everything will be alright. Oh, Tom, but I am so excited. I'm as alive as I have ever been. And it's owed all to you. I can't *wait* to know what the future will hold."

Tom brightened. He admired Becky, and her grit. "I'll bring shovels. Digging out dirt with your hands is fine if you're a prisoner, but it's time consuming. And since we ain't prisoners, it's within our rights to use anything we choose."

"Tom," Becky sweetly smiled. "I don't care *what* we use to dig out the dirt. Just so long as we dig it out together."

Becky skipped home in high spirits, as excited as Tom, and hoping she could remember every minute detail of this day, to record in her diary. Home, she stumbled upon her mother preparing supper.

"Hello ma," Becky said gaily.

The woman turned around, and without warning she screamed; a pitch shrilling enough to break glass. Indeed, glass did break. Mrs. Thatcher, holding a very dear and precious plate, handed down to her from her mother, and her mother before her, all the way back into times long forgotten, held that plate no more. It smashed to pieces in front of her and Becky.

"Rebecca Thatcher! What have you done to your dress!"

"My dress?" It seemed a silly question to ask. Unfortunately, Becky hadn't realized the state her clothes were in. Looking down, she instantly became aware. The high spirits upon her earlier, dissipated.

"Young lady!" Her lips curled; her hair stood on end. She leaned down and grabbed Becky's dress. "Where *did* all this dirt come from? Answer!"

Speechless and horrified, knowing the impending doom to be brought forth upon her, tears trickled down Becky's cheeks. No explanation would satisfy her mother, be it truth or lie.

"Mama, I—," was all Becky could say. Her mouth gaped open. She tried desperately to say something to halt her mother's rage.

"It's that boy. When pa returns and sees these clothes, perhaps then he will be more receptive of my opinions. I've told you a hundred times, I *won't* have you acting improperly. Well, there's ways of getting to the bottom of matters. Come on!" She dragged Becky up to her room, taking one of her husband's belt's with her. It would be made very useful.

"No mama, *please!*" Becky cried. Her mother shut the down behind them.

When Tom arrived home, he slipped up the lighting rod to his room and changed into cleaner clothes. Lucky for him; for when he ventured downstairs, he saw that his Aunt Polly was not alone in the kitchen. Seated next to her was Judith Loftus, newly arrived to St. Petersburg. Aunt Polly always enjoyed welcoming in new guests.

Shaking her head, Aunt Polly scorned, "'Bout time you decided to show up. Well, say hello to Mrs. Loftus. She just come up from Sincton, with her husband."

"Hello."

"Well," Judith sighed. "So this is your Tom Sawyer. She's told me much about you, and your adventurous ways. Polly, he's just as you described. Husband and I always wanted children, but with him away all the time, well—laws! but there jus' warn't any time."

"What's he do?" Tom asked.

"Husband is a bounty hunter."

"Oh, there," Aunt Polly gasped, waving her hands. "Now you've done it."

She was right; for now Tom was as attentive as he had ever been, and wanted to know just everything about this man.

"At the moment, husband is on the track of that runaway nigger. If anybody can find him, husband can. Cain't nobody elude husband."

"A shame he don't spend more time with you," Aunt Polly said.

"Oh, now, if you knew husband, well, you'd understand him better. I ain't got no complaints agin him. Why, he's everything a woman could want in a man." Looking to Tom, Judith said, "Your Aunt Polly has been telling me about this town, what's been going on. She mentioned an Injun Joe, which is when I stopped her, 'cause that's when I said, in amazement, 'Why husband once had a run in with him, about two year back."

"What happened?" Tom asked, eager to know every last detail.

"Well, I'll tell you. 'Twas back in Sincton. Husband was a-going into town to see the sheriff about a vigilante. At that particular moment the bank was bein' robbed. Husband darted out of the sheriff's office jus' in time to see three men run out of the bank. One man he recognized as Injun Joe. As a habit, husband ran after the men. Laws, he ain't afeared of nothin'. The men all jumped on their horses and fled away. Husband got one shot off, but that was all. He didn't have no horse, and they wasn't much he could do, but watch 'em all get away. My, but was he sore. 'Cause he wanted to go after them. But he had other obligations—other men to hunt down, you see. Well, it ate at him for months, until we all heard the news Injun Joe was dead. Starved to death right around these parts, in a cave, as Polly tells me."

Tom remembered vividly that scene, when the door to the cave was opened, and there, only inches away "Injun Joe lay stretched upon the ground, dead".

When Tom was excused for bed, Aunt Polly turned to Judith and said, "Oh, but I am sorry for Tom's ways. he can be tiring at times, but he means well. There ain't any harm in him."

"Why I should say not, Polly. Don't you ever be sorry for him, or his ways. He's a blessing." Then, rather sullenly, she added, "Be all the more glad you got him."

CHAPTER 11

Night had come. Thick, puffy, dark, ominous looking clouds loomed high above the town, foreshadowing violent weather soon to arrive. Tom, in bed, counting the seconds drearily tick away, thought nothing of it. His mind, absorbed with deep, diabolical images of what lay beyond the dirt, distracted him from everything else.

Becky thought nothing of the weather either; nor the treasure. She lay in bed, on her stomach, the only *bearable* way to sleep. Mrs. Thatcher sat near her in a chair; the belt laying casually upon her lap in case the need to use it again arose. She watched Becky rest, still wearing her dirty dress, wanting her husband to view Becky in the same way she had. Then maybe he would not mind so much, Becky's whippings.

Ten o'clock approached. "Where *is* pa?" Mrs. Thatcher wondered. Since dark, no noise presented itself within the house. The dead of night set her on edge. She became skittish; thought she heard noises; thought she heard the front door creak open. "Pa?" She turned her head. Another noise.

Determined to *find* the source of that noise, she left Becky's room. Standing on the top step, she leaned her head. "*The door is open!*" Mrs. Thatcher went down to investigate. "The wind. It's only the wind," she reassured herself. "Pa?" she uttered once more, to make sure. No response. Her hand upon the knob, in the process of closing the door, something cold, oily perhaps, fell atop her wrist. "What!" she screamed.

Turning, she saw a hazy shadow. "Pa?" The door slammed. "*Oh my god!*" A hand muffled her voice. She bit it, hard.

There came a shout. "Ooooh! That done it." Mrs. Thatcher recognized the voice. Her mouth was pried open, and a handkerchief crammed inside, along with another to gag her, she could not scream out to Becky. Judge Thatcher's belt dropped loosely from her hands.

The intruder picked it up. "Well now," an enthusiastic voice gleefully pondered. Mrs. Thatcher felt her body turn and squeeze against the door; her hands being tied tightly behind her back with the belt. Seconds later she sat near the staircase. She tried to make noises, anything to wake Becky, hoping somehow the girl would find a way to escape.

"Git the girl," the voice ordered.

Two men ascended the staircase and searched the rooms. Jeff, as a custom every summer, left for Constantinople only a day ago, so his room was vacant. Becky had begged her pa to let her remain. When the two men entered her room, they found Becky sound asleep.

"We'll make quick work of it," one man said.

"I got the sack right here," said the other man.

Before Becky could wake, her hands and feet were tied, and her mouth gagged. Unkindly, they placed her inside a large sack, with only a few holes, no larger than the width of Becky's fingers.

"Ma?" Becky groggily whispered. "Is this another nightmare? *Dream*," Becky said. "Strange, I said dream. Normally, every other nightmare I've had, I always woke up after saying the word *dream*, in a deep, devilish, demonic-like voice. I didn't do that this time."

"She's heavier than I thought," Becky heard somebody say.

"Oh, goodness!" Becky realized. "This isn't a dream!"

"We got 'er," Becky heard the same person say.

"Another voice said, "Good." This voice, Becky easily recognized. "Thatcher lady, you tell that no 'count husband-judge of yourn I got his daughter. If he wants her back, he can give me what's rightfully mine, and ought to b'long to me anyhow, without I got to go to all this trouble gettin' it. Nod if you understand." She nodded. "Don't tell nobody else about this. If words leaks, and I see a posse', I'll kill her. I'll get in touch in my own way, on my own time."

Thirty seconds later Mrs, Thatcher was all alone. An hour passed. Finally Judge Thatcher walked in. His lantern hit upon something at the edge of the staircase. Tired, he nearly stumbled over his wife.

"Good god! I, wh-what is the meaning of this? What has become of you!"

Mrs. Thatcher jerked violently. Her husband lifted the gag. Restrained for an hour, she contemplated Becky's kidnapping. Now, unstrained, she let her feelings run wild.

"I told you we should have sent Becky back to Constantinople with Jeff. I told you! But she was determined to stay. You were determined to *have* her stay. This is what I get for listening to you. This is what you get for not doing your proper duty. You should have been more demanding. You should have been more stern. Then none of this would have happened. You should have—,"

"What are you talking about?" His body tensed. Sweat began to pour fluently. "Where is our daughter!"

"Oh, they took her! They took our daughter! She's gone; gone; *gone!*"

"What? Who did this? Who was it?"

"*Jimmy Finn!*" Mrs. Thatcher slipped away.

CHAPTER 12

Just before midnight, Tom stood under Becky's window. Now knowing a storm imminent, as long as he and Becky could make it to the Stantan Home in time, he didn't mind how hard the rain poured.

"Meow,"

Nothing.

"Meow," a little louder.

Still nothing.

"What's with her? She wouldn't fall asleep?" Impatient, he climbed up the lightening rod, and into her room. Becky's pillow looked to be her head. Tom discovered otherwise. "Not here?" In his disbelief, he hadn't seen a light growing brighter behind him.

"Thomas Sawyer!" two bellowing, surprised voices exclaimed. Tom turned around and faced Mr. and Mrs. Thatcher. *Caught!*

An uneasy moment of silence transpired. Nobody could find the right words to say. Judge Thatcher looked to Mrs. Thatcher; Mrs. Thatcher looked to Judge Thatcher; Tom looked to both of them; both looked to Tom.

Tom spoke first. "I. Becky. Becky and I—."

Hearing her daughter's name, Mrs. Thatcher fell to the floor, where she broke down and cried uncontrollably. Judge Thatcher picked her up and set her upon Becky's bed. She clung to the pillow, the sheets, anything of Becky's.

"Come with me, Tom." His voice was weak; he was weak; too weak, perhaps, to lash out at Tom, if he desired. Tom followed him downstairs, growing ever more nervous.

They entered Judge Thatcher's study. The room lay in shambles. A bureau, an antique over one-hundred years old, destroyed; chairs, broken to bits, possibly against the wall, where gaping holes stood out; papers, all over the floor, in no particular order; paintings, ripped and hanging loosely from corners of tables and night stands; a chandelier once hung in the center of the room atop the ceiling; it's shape grossly distorted, it now occupied the floor just beneath. Only the desk remained intact.

"Becky's not, not *ill* is she?" Tom asked, innocently.

"Please, Tom. Just listen, please." Judge Thatcher paced around the debris, looking for the right words to say. Tom waited. "Tom, no, Becky, she isn't ill. She's not here. Becky, my Becky is not here, Tom." He broke down. "Tom. Becky's, Becky's been—*kidnapped*."

Tom's knees buckled. He fainted, in the same spot he fainted when he learned Judge Thatcher sealed the entrance to the cave, with Injun Joe inside. Judge Thatcher revived him; Then, against Jimmy's wishes, he told Tom everything, without mentioning names. Tom asked, but in vain.

"I tell you, I can't say. And I don't want you to tell anybody about this. Nobody! It's bad I told you, but—."

A thought occurred to Tom. "'Twas Jimmy Finn."

Judge Thatcher bolted up wildly. "Good god, how could you know!"

Tom's heart stopped. Mrs. Thatcher entered, disillusioned, completely out of her mind. She seemed relaxed, but only on the outside.

"Becky's fine now, pa. I put her down. Her fever's gone down. I took her temperature." She elapsed back to a time when Becky had the fever.

"Woman, get hold of yourself. Snap out of it."

"Becky's fine, pa. But I'll stay with her tonight in case she needs me. Is that her now, pa? I think she needs me. Pa, I'm going to make her some socks so her feet don't get cold when winter comes. Isn't she just the most precious child. I love her so."

"Oh, *ma*." He watched his wife sink into depths of deception and illusion. He could do nothing for her; he was also headed in that direction. Mrs. Thatcher left, thinking she heard Becky cry.

"*I* am to blame for all of this!" Judge Thatcher announced.

Tom loathed to watch the man tear himself apart. Especially for something Tom believed entirely his fault. He knew what he had to do.

"You ain't to blame." A long hesitation. "I am."

Judge Thatcher looked at Tom; not in disbelief, or anger; for it seemed to him an impossibility. The statement itself puzzled him.

"Now why would you think *you're* to blame?"

Tom told Judge Thatcher he overheard the two strangers in the courtroom, planning two "jobs". He didn't know what they were, but once Jimmy escaped, guessed that had been one job.

"I never expected they'd kidnap Becky. Honest! If I'd 'a' known, I swear upon my soul I would 'a' told." In his confession, he left Becky's role out. "So you see, Mr. Thatcher, I *am* to blame for all of this. Not you. If I came to you sooner, Jimmy would be in jail yet; and Becky would be here now. I reckon I'll be held as an accomplice to Jimmy's escape. I know they'll hang me. Just make sure Aunt Polly, and Sid and Mary, are well taken care of. Tell them I love them all and wish them the best."

Judge Thatcher mumbled. "Tom. How *could* you know what they were up to? No, I am solely to blame. Ma warned me to stay home. She warned me about quite a lot. I'm taking her back to Constantinople shortly. She's better off with her relatives. If anyone asks, Becky went *with* her mother. Again, keep this to yourself. You go now, alright. There's nothing you can do. I know what Jimmy wants, and as soon as I hear from him, I'll give it to him." Judge Thatcher paused in the middle of the room, where he remained motionless. Tom left. He didn't want to, but he could see Judge Thatcher needed to be alone.

Thunder vigorously exploded. The winds ferociously wisped across the landscape. Lightening engulfed St. Petersburg, and other regions.

Tom ran. Half way home, the clouds opened up; rain drenched the boy with cold water. The next morning he woke with a high fever. Aunt Polly confined him to bed, where she could administer her "remedies". Tom remained delirious for a week, mumbling, "All my fault". Aunt Polly didn't know what to make of it just then.

CHAPTER 13

The rains did not disturb Jimmy. The clouds were just forming when he landed on the Illinois side, and guided Jed and Sim up to the cabin-house he told them about.

Inside, Jimmy removed Becky and untied her restraints. "Jed, throw her in t'other room over there," he pointed. "And lock the door."

"Come on girlie girl, git movin'."

Jed pushed Becky into a small room, nearly five feet lower than the rest of the cabin. Becky landed in a fetal position on a dirt flooring. Nobody heard, or cared about, her cries.

Sim anxiously asked, "Now can we out with the whiskey, and have real good times?" He concerned himself with nothing else.

"Hold on!" Jimmy angrily pulled the jug from between Sim's hands. "So you both know, that room upstairs, with the bed, it's mine. Don't neither of you two go up there. You both sleep down here; keep watch over the girl."

"How come you git the room with a bed?" Jed argued.

"'Cause they ain't but one."

Sim, apathetic, said, "I don't k'yer. Jus' so I git my whiskey. I'll sleep on the floor."

Into the early morning all three men drank without stop. In their intoxicated state, they did not hear the rain, or the thunder. Becky heard it. With nothing else to do to pass the time, she walked the length of her dungeon, as she called it, to find out its size.

Hours after the rain's inception, water seeped in, soaking the dirt around the walls, until it turned to mud, then slush. Becky's feet were bare. The sharpness of cold rainwater made its presence known. She banged away on the door with her fists.

"Let me out, *please*! There's water in here!" Empty whiskey jugs, tossed against the door, were Becky's answers. Realizing the futility of her pleas, she sank to the ground, where water had not yet reached, and cried.

How could they not let me out? They laugh! They silence me with jugs tossed against the door!

Becky shook violently. This time, Tom could not be there to hold her. She had to comfort herself, which she did. Eventually Becky fell asleep, with the assumption the whole town already knew what had happened.

About mid-morning, Jimmy awoke. He never made it upstairs. Jugs, broken in many pieces and various sizes, covered the floor and table, and stuck to greasy hair and clothing. Jimmy kicked his two partners.

"Git up. We got work t' do." They opened their eyes, stretched, and proposed, by a two to zero vote, to go back to sleep. Jimmy overruled the vote. "Don't sass me. Jed, check on the girl."

"She's asleep," Jed replied.

"Good. Let's go scare up some food." Jimmy opened the door. "Ahhh! What in thunderin' tarnation!"

"What is it?" Jed and Sim rushed to the door and peered out. They saw the Mississippi at its most violent. Whitecaps foamed and frothed; waves bounced, turned and eddied; trees recently uprooted, swiftly bobbed up and down, passed the cabin. They saw a handful of cabins skid down river also.

"Damn!" Jimmy shouted, slamming his fist against the door. "How am I gonna get back to town *now*! How we gonna deliver the ransom note?"

"We best go, 'fore the river takes this cabin," Jed warned.

"Thas right. Let the li'l girl go, and then let's *us* go."

"You both panic too much. The river won't rise much higher. And we ain't lettin' go of the girl. I mean to make her pa squirm. Well, come on. We got food to scare up."

Hearing the men leave, Becky sat up. She had only pretended to be asleep when Jed checked on her.

"Oh! My dress. My body. Everywhere, covered in mud. Becky stood. "I shall never ever be set free." She sighed, wringing as much water from her dress as she could. "I am meant to *die* hear." Her hand struck upon something. She removed it. "Ah! The arrow-head. Mama hadn't caught sight of it when she whipped me. What would *Tom* do in my place? Have a jolly good adventure of it. It is hard, so very hard, but I must remain calm. That much I know. If I learned anything from being lost in that cave—there is always some amount of hope." A tear descended. "No. Won't cry. Won't give in. Yes, if Tom were here he'd know what to do. He's not. So, it's up to I—Guinevere, Joan of Arc, Juliet—no, not Juliet. Tom says she was weak, and so she was. Well, the other two, any-how. Or, is it just up to *me*?"

Becky plotted her escape. She would not wait to be released. A year and a half ago she might have. Not any longer. Not ever again. Becky worked one scheme after another, not stopping even when her abduc-tors returned.

"Jimmy, you should 'a' *seen* the look 'pon yer face."

"I tol' you, *quiet!*" Jimmy shook a fist at Sim.

Jed came to his brother's aide. "Oh, Sim warn't meanin' no harm."

"Falling in the river ain't nothin' t' laugh at. Could 'a' drowned. I swears, you brothers 'll both be the death of me yet."

"We got food hasn't we?" Jed held up a large catfish.

"Well, what of it? We ain't got dry matches to start a fire with, now." Sim worried. "Not a one?"

"Thas right. We got a big fish alright. But without we ain't got matches to start a fire, to cook it, it ain't any use t' us *raw*. And they ain't no fireplace either. Ain't no dry sticks anywhere to be found."

Jed lashed out at Sim. "You see what you done Sim! I ought-a lam you."

"I'd like t' see you try!"

"Well, I've lammed you good b'fore. I reckon I can do it agin."

"Yes, and I lammed you good in the past too, don't you forget."

"Will you two hesh!" Jimmy pushed Jed one way, and Sim the other, so that each bounced off a separate wall.

"That warn't necessary, Jimmy."

"Yeah, Jimmy. 'Twas all talk, anyhow. Jed and me—,"

"Talk nothing! You two want to kill each other, do it *after* we git the money. We're stuck here, fer now. What we gonna do with a raw fish? Well, this storm cain't last much longer. T'night we'll sneak over to Megan's farm, and borrow some of his crops"

"*I* is hungry now Jimmy," Jed protested.

"Oh? Well, eat the fish."

"Don't you do it, Jed. It's Pi'son. Don't you do it."

"We can't starve to death, Jimmy. Neither can we let the girlie girl starve to death. We got to feed her."

"If *we* c'n go without food, so c'n she. Let Thatcher's girl fend for herself. They's bound to be things crawling in that room."

"Hey, give 'r the fish to eat."

Sim applauded. "Now *thas* real good times."

"Real good times indeed," Becky moaned. She heard their every word. Unfortunately, she heard them mention food. Her stomach growled emphatically for sustenance now.

"I must put food out of my mind. They'll feed me. They have to. Remember—the *cave*? Have strength, Becky. Have strength." As the hours wore on, however, she slowly came to the conclusion they *wouldn't* feed her.

Nowhere to go, the men spent all day confined inside, getting on one another's nerves. They, like Becky, were prisoners in the cabin too.

Jed whined. "Jimmy, it ain't no use. We got t' have food. *I* got t' have food. I don't k'yer 'bout *you*."

"Hesh, numbskull," Jimmy whispered, himself ravished with hunger.

"Who you callin' numbskull! I am tired of you callin' me names. Yer mad 'cause things ain't goin' how you planned."

"What've I told you 'bout sassin' me?"

"Well, go an' kill me then. If you got the strength."

"Don't you do it, Jimmy," Sim intervened.

After a brief silence, Jimmy, in desperation, announced he would cross the river, storm or no storm.

Jed exclaimed, "You said the river would stop rising by now. Well, it ain't. Pretty soon we'll be up to our necks in Mississippi mud."

"I said hesh!" Jimmy glared at the catfish. It had been lying undisturbed upon the table for hours. "Don't stare at me. Don't you laugh, just 'cause I can't eat you."

"He's out-a his mind, Sim."

"It's so."

"Damn that rain! Maybe I'll eat Thatcher's girl. Ha!"

"Hunger has claimed him sure, Sim."

"Boys, it ain't no use. We're stuck here, temporarily. But I'd just as soon be drunk through the most of it. Jimmy flipped the fish onto the floor, to make room for whiskey jugs.

With an idea in mind, Sim picked it up. "Hey li'l girl, you hungry?" Becky looked up, into the light, just as Sim threw the catfish at her. She caught it, involuntarily. "That ought t' tide you over li'l girl."

Before Becky could protest, Sim shut the door.

"A very fine joke indeed. Do they really expect me to *eat* this? Raw, and who knows *how* rotten and *how* infested with diseases." Yet, temptation drew the fish closer to her mouth; the smell hovered around her nostrils, putrid and strong. "Anyway, I couldn't eat it; not with all these scales." The arrow-head popped into her head. She had to capitulate. "It's sharp enough to scrape away scales, drat it. Now I haven't a reason in the world not to eat this fish. Kill me! So will starvation. I'll not go without a fight." Settled, Becky held her "dinner" in one arm, and applied the arrow-head to a portion, scraping away at it until she could feel the meat.

"I don't know whether to be thankful for the dark or not. Not that I *want* to see what it is I'm sinking my teeth into, but I'd surely like to *know* what my lips shall press against." The preparations were finalized. "A small bit; a sliver, that's all. Don't chew if you can help it. Swallow, and hope it don't come in contact with anything; and hope it digests *fast*." Her face grimaced. "Awful. Poo-pooey. Oh, but I must. It's food. It's, *something*."

Becky consumed a good portion of the fish. She felt as though a hundred pounds of it had weighed and lined and fattened her stomach.

"There. I think I have eaten worse, but if I have I've forgotten" She resumed eating, until her stomach began to feel awkward. "Oh!" Becky gasped. "How much *did* I eat? Wow! That's not a good feeling I—. Oh! Let me sit down. Oh, water everywhere. Well, I haven't a choice. They were right, drat them. It's poison."

The feeling in the pit of her stomach continued to grow for over an hour. However, Becky hadn't been poisoned, as she would discover later on. During this ordeal, and as it "passed", Becky gratefully welcomed the privacy, and encouraged the notion they would forget about her for the time being.

"At least, until this indisposition is over," Becky grunted in pain. "I'll not complain. I'll not regret eating it. No matter what," Oh! No, no matter what. I made a judgement call. One that's making me move my bowels like I never before have. But I'm alive, for the time being. That's the best I can hope for, until I can find a way out. Not too many people would go through what *I'm* going through, to save their lives. A year and a half ago I—oh, *pooh* a year and a half ago. Times are different now."

While Becky squatted against a far wall in discomfort, a much different scene took place yards away. Now fully inebriated, the men celebrated. They no longer felt hunger. In their state, they felt nothing. *Bother Becky! Becky who? Was there a girl in the other room? What other room?*

Into the early morning the drinking persisted. Wild, vulgar stories flourished—that is, they *began* with zest and intent, but very rarely were ever finished or carried half way through before something interrupted the teller's thoughts; usually how the story ended. But story telling did not last the whole night. Uneasiness, aggravation and contempt settled in. Unbalanced equilibriums stirred and inflamed tempers, sparking brawls.

Sim started. "Hey, don' you take *that* jug; thas *my* whiskey, Jed!"

"Tain't yourn neither. *I'll* be drinking f'm this'n."

"No! I set that p'ticular jug down on the table not two minute ago, 'cause this'n in my hand 's pert near empty. Now you set it back."

"I low I'd like to see you make me."

"Hesh you two, stop the bickerin'. I has had it up to here with it." Jimmy pointed above his head to indicate his frustration.

"I ain't, 'til Jed give me back my whiskey." Sim grabbed for the jug when his brother had his head turned. A clumsy effort, Sim fell on his face. Consequently, Jed irrupted in hysterics.

"Ha! Maybe *that'll* learn ya. Try an' steal *my* whiskey will you. You'd do better t' stay down there on the floor, amongst the rats and sech."

"You take that back, Jed. I'll kill ya deed!"

"Oh, sure, sure ya will. You jus' try."

"Knock off boys! They's plenty of whiskey. No sense 'n fightin' o'er—." Jimmy stopped, in order to polish off the remainder of *his* jug. By the time he came up for air, he'd forgotten what he said.

Sim hadn't. "I want *that*'n, by golly." He stood, then lunged for Jed. This time, his determination paid off. He hit Jed square in the face.

"Hey! You ornery devil." He swung at Sim, and hit him in the chest. Sim fell back in his chair. Jed stole another "swig" from the jug, irritating Sim all the more. Now they wanted blood, and took turns hitting one another.

Jimmy had enough. He stood, irate. "I done said t' *quit*! How many time I got t' tell you?"

"No way, Jimmy. This thing b'tween me and Jed has got to be settled." Sim pushed his brother against the wall.

"Thas right," said Jed, shaking it off. "You jus' stand back a-ways. so's you won't be in the way." Jed swung at Sim's jaw.

"Ah! Why'd you go an hit me so hard?" He fell down, clutching his wounded chin. Blood discharged. "I'll *git* you fer that one." He rushed his brother, sending him sprawling over the table.

"Thas *enough*!" Jimmy screamed. "I don' want no more fightin'. You've tempered my patience more'n I c'n—. We got a ransom t' c'llect. I said stop! Sim don' do—. Sim! Jed! Set down, both you! No! Now listen I—."

Neither Jed nor Sim paid attention to Jimmy who, with a new jug, sucked in more than he could handle.

"I got y' licked *now*, Sim."

"Oh you think so do you?" He eyed Jimmy's rifle leaning up against the door. He made a grab for it.

Jimmy put out his hand. "You hear, I—. " Suddenly, Jimmy began to choke, violently. He turned and hunched over.

"Put down that rifle, Sim!" Jed demanded.

"Make me."

Jed did try to make him. "When I get this away f'm you—." Both men struggled to gain a firm hold on the rifle. They pushed and shoved, twisting and turning the rifle in every direction. Jimmy continued to gasp for breath.

By now, Becky's bowels were healthy again. She listened attentively to the scuffle, hearing many coarse words, threats, Jimmy's violent hacking. She *felt* the vibrations as the brothers flung each other against every wall. Then just as Jed and Sim seemed to quiet down—for they tightly clenched their teeth, and firmly pressed their lips together, making speech impossible—the most hideous, quite possibly the most wicked noise Becky ever heard rang through her ears, and buzzed inside her head for over five minutes.

"Jed, what'd you *do*!"

"What'd *I* do! 'Twas *you* that done it."

"Weren't neither. Jimmy, 'twas I-"

"Where'd he go? Was here a second ago."

"Jed! Oh Jed, look yonder down there on the floor." He pointed to the man lying face down, sprawled against the ground.

"Jimmy! Jimmy!" They bent down, one on either side of Jimmy.

"Jed! Blood!"

"Jimmy!" They poked and prodded the fallen man for two minutes.

"He ain't comin' 'round, Jed."

"You know what I think? I think he's *deed*."

"*Deed*? Jimmy? It ain't *possible*. It *jus'* ain't possible."

"He ain't movin' none. Push him on his back."

"No! I don't wanna see his face. Was scary enough when he was alive."

"What're we gonna do now?"

"I dunno. But I don't wanna stay 'round here, where a man's been killed. Oh it's awful. I cain't bear t' look at 'im."

"Well, he alwus wanted to sleep upstairs, in that bed. I reckon now he'll git his chance." Jed picked up Jimmy's body and carried him upstairs.

When Becky's hearing returned, she promptly pounded on the door; not out of curiosity, but because cracks in the sloped ceiling, so small a short while ago, had widened, creating a waterfall.

"Hey! Please! There's water in here. You've *got* to let me out!" Jed and Sim heard nothing. They both slept soundly at the table. "Please!" She pleaded for a few more minutes then stopped.

"I must conserve my voice. Don't wanna end up like Sabrina. She was in the same predicament as I; but *she* whooped 'til she had no voice. They made her walk the plank 'cause she couldn't answer where the secret map was buried; and them pirates had no more use for her. Wish I'd 'a' finished that story, to see what ever became of the treasure. Oh, well, can't worry about that right now. I must remain strong. Can't show weakness.'

"Live as Joan of Arc lived. Let me draw strength from her life. She feared nothing. Course, she heard voices; thought they were angels. I don't know whether or not that's true, and I sure don't want to start hearing voices myself; but Joan of Arc *was* courageous; and if one girl can demonstrate such perseverance in face of defeat, then so too can another—I hope."

CHAPTER 14

Noon. The rain slowed to a drizzle. A small patch in the sky allowed for one or two rays to sneak by, filter through the cabin's only window, and hit Sim in his left eye.

"Oh!" Sim muttered. "You awake, Jed?" He shoved his brother.

"I am now. What'd y' push me onto the ground fer?"

"T' see if you was awake."

"If I didn't have sech a split head, I'd lam you."

"Not if Jimmy were here."

"Jimmy! Where is he?"

"Dunno. Jimmy!" Sim called out. Ji—. Oh, Jed, look, on the floor."

"Wh—. Blood! Oh, now it's comin' back," moaned Jed. Jimmy's deed. He's deed."

"Thas right. *You* killed him."

"*I* did? Don't start that agin.

"Well, what're we to do?"

"I wish he might be alive two seconds, thas all."

"Thas all what?"

"Thas all it'd take t' kill him, fer dying on us. He had no right."

"We still got the li'l girl too."

"Girl? Oh. Well we *are* in a fix. And Jimmy, deed and no worries. We got t' think of a way out of here."

"Thas it. We'll let the girl go, and high tail it up to Canadar."

"What! Not likely."

"But Jed, Jimmy's deed. We can't jus'—,"

"She's our only security. Long's we got her, ain't nobody gonna touch us. But once we let her go, we is deed just as sure as Jimmy. And they'll kill us in cold blood too, 'thout any worry of goin' to jail."

"You know what's best. But we can't stay *here*."

"Not much longer. Look, Sim; look at that river. It's crested on *this* side. Couldn't be t'other. Won't be long b'fore it reaches the cabin."

"Let's go to Jack's Isle. People or not, it's high off the ground."

"We still got some time. I noticed some berries up stream yesterday. Looked mighty appetizing. Let's you and me check 'em out."

"They *could* be pi'son."

"I thought of that. We'll let the girl have the first taste."

Becky vaguely heard those remarks. An earlier idea inspired her. With the arrow-head, she bobbed in and out of the water, chipping away at the wood near the ground. She needed to chip a hole to drain the water, or she would drown. Holding her breath, Becky made plunge after plunge until—*Eureka!* A small hole. Becky worked another twenty minutes, widening it.

"It's working! I *feel* the water slowly receding. I owe you Tom, for the arrow-head. What a lifesaver it has become." Becky smiled. "Joan of Arc couldn't have done any better."

The water did not recede very fast. Becky had to create more holes. If discovered, she could blame them on rats. Finally, Becky succeeded in creating enough holes to drain the water, which, when receded, left a muddy surface. Fatigued, Becky leaned up against the wall directly under the door, where she promptly fell asleep.

"Hey girlie girl! Hey! Wake up!" Becky opened her eyes.

"What? What's going on?" She looked up. Jed and Sim stood over her.

"Sim and me thought you might like some berries."

"Berries?"

"I'm awful sorry 'bout that fish," Sim apologized. "We thought these 'd make up fer it." Sim handed Becky a pale filled with berries.

Becky instantly recognized them as quality. More importantly they were ripe. She chose one and placed it in her mouth.

"She's eatin' it Jed," Sim whispered.

"Hold on. Pi'son might take a spell to work." But after a cautious ten minutes of observing Becky indulge herself, Jed, satisfied, conceded. He took the pale away and refilled it for her. "You make those last. Don't think you'll be gettin' any more, anytime soon."

The door closed and locked, Becky said, "You're all *heart*." If Jed heard her, he did not make trouble for her, yet. "Well, they may have me locked in a tiny, unlit room; they may treat me like an animal, and make me live as one, but I shan't become one. I'll not go insane. And I won't wind up like a character in a book. Remember Rachel? Weak, Rachel. Captive only a week, *she* went stark mad. Her wicked, younger sister kept her in a dungeon, deep below the castle. Everyday she came to torture Rachel. Poor, weak, Rachel. Chained to a wall. At least I can walk around. And the food they fed her! Rotten, moldy meat and bread. I know what that fish did to me. I can *imagine* what Rachel went through. Worse, no doubt. There was no outhouse for Rachel. Not one for me either. And her younger sister, doing this to her, just to gain the crown. Ah, but that's only a book. Only a book. Too bad for me this is not also—oh, I'll not go insane. Promise yourself Becky—*don't go insane!*"

CHAPTER 15

After a week of merciless, unrelenting rain, the heavens softened and took pity upon St. Petersburg, leaving in its wake a light, spotty shower. Sid, finished dressing for breakfast, became horrified when Tom bolted upright. His senses regained, he had to know about Becky.

"Tom! What's the matter? You need anything? I'll fetch Aunt Polly."

"Aunt Polly! What ever for?"

"The way you jumped, I thought maybe, maybe the devil got hold of you, and you were about to die."

"Devil your granny. I'm fine, Sid."

"Oh, well, Auntie will be happy to hear it."

Sid ran downstairs in a flash to tell Aunt Polly all about it. Peter, the cat, in Sid's path, scurried away to find a more hospitable refuge. Aunt Polly had not time to rise from her chair to verify Sid's claim, before Tom, already dressed, stood in front of her.

"Well, Tom. You've saved me a trip. Sid *said* you was better, and I was just on my way to check you out."

"Ain't no need. I feel fine."

A knock at the door. "Somebody's at the door, Aunt Polly."

"I see, Mary. Looks to be Judge Thatcher." She went to the door and peered out through the drapery. "And so it is. He don't look well either. Aunt Polly opened the door. "Judge! Welcome. Come in and set down."

Judge Thatcher nervously entered. Stuttering, he said, "I c-can't stay long. No I, here c-can I sit down a minute. I won't take up too, too much time."

"Nonsense. You're welcome anytime." Judge Thatcher stumbled. "Here, Mary, help him to a chair. He don't look well at all."

"Th-thank you."

"You Tom, and you too Sid, stand up; let him set his feet on the chair."

"No, ho-honestly. I don't want, wouldn't think of intruding. But please, let m-me explain why I'm, I'm here." Judge Thatcher clenched his fists every time he stuttered, grinding his fingernails into the palms of his hands. "I h-haven't stuttered in th-thirty years."

Tom, worried over the way Judge Thatcher acted, suspected the worst.

"Perhaps some coffee?"

"No, P-Polly. I, no." He looked towards Tom. "Tom, have you told?"

"No. I—."

"Tom's been sick with fever all week," Aunt Polly explained. "Tom? Were you supposed to tell me something?"

"No."

"No," Judge Thatcher reaffirmed. "No." "I asked him not to. B-But, I, I c-can't k-keep it secret. Oh! Why m-must I s-stutter so!"

"Mr. Thatcher, do you want me to tell her?"

"Tom, I, y-yes, you had b-better. Then I'll explain why I, I h-have come."

"What's going on, Tom?"

The words were hard for Tom to say. Trying to say them, he stuttered like Judge Thatcher. "B-Becky's been, been k-kidnapped."

Three astonished voices had just enough energy to gasp, "What!"

"Judge, is it true?"

"Y-yes, Polly. P-Please ask me no m-more. I've s-said too much. B-But she, m-my Becky, I haven't h-heard anything. No w-word. No ransom note. I, I've b-been on edge all w-week. What w-with the storms, the r-rising river waters, I c-can only f-fear the *w-w-worst!*"

Aunt Polly sobbed. "Oh, now, there's always hope. You must believe it. How do you come you know all about it, Tom?"

"I, I found out is all."

"Now I reckon all that mumblin' you been doin' makes sense."

"Polly, T-Tom's done no wrong." Judge Thatcher slumped over the table, but picked himself back up.

"You need rest."

"P-Polly, I m-must search f-for her. Alone. That's w-why I came h-here. I d-don't know if sh-she's, sh-she's, if anything's—. I need you, all of y-you, to help k-keep an eye on f-for her. T-Tom, when I'm g-gone, tell them everything; why th-they must k-keep it too th-themselves."

"You can't leave in your condition."

Judge Thatcher rose unsteadily. "I d-don't have a ch-choice. It's m-my fault. Sh-she's m-my daughter."

Aunt Polly begged Judge Thatcher to stay, and rest. He, however, stumbled out the door, and down the street. After which, Tom did just as Judge Thatcher asked, and told everything he knew about Becky's kidnapping, and why they must not tell anyone else.

"Poor girl," Aunt Polly sobbed again. Mary and Sid took turns consoling her. Tom snuck away, to attend to "matters". Aunt Polly spotted him out the corner of a teary eye. "Well," she thought, "the boy's been cooped up a week with fever. The devil himself couldn't hold him here."

CHAPTER 16

Many citizens took sick during the storm. Doctor Towers, throughout, hustled and bustled back and forth between Widow Douglas' mansion and where ever his duty called him. Finally, it looked like things would settle down.

As Widow Douglas descended her grand staircase, Doctor Towers entered the mansion. This was not a coincidence. She saw him from a window upstairs, and planned the encounter.

Widow Douglas, pretending to be surprised, said, "Oh, you're back."

"Ah-choo!" Doctor Towers responded.

"Bless you. Sounds like you need a doctor," she joked.

"No. No, they think they know it all. They're too highly opinionated," he joked back. "Ah-choo!"

"At least the storm is over now. Maybe you won't have to keep running out at all hours of the day and night. Come, let me take you to the parlor. I'll have Ginny bring us some tea. She's been just an angel, since Ruth took sick with fever. Poor woman. So young. Will she live? Oh, what a terrible thing to say. I'm sorry I said it, Ben. I was, I—,"

"She'll live. But she'll have to remain in her quarters, in quarantine. Just a few more days, I think."

"Sometimes I want to go in there, and be of help."

"Brittany!" Doctor Towers froze. "Oh, no. No, the best help you can be to Ruth is to let her be. *I'll* tend to her."

"Of course. That is, if you think you—know it all."

"Madam," the doctor smiled. "You're in too high of spirits this day."

In the parlor room their talk continued.

"You know, Brittany, I can't get over the way the town talks about you. Every home I go to, they all ask the same thing. 'How is Widow Douglas? Is she getting along?' They care about you, Brittany. Deeply."

"They have always been friendly towards me. Back when my husband died, I can remember all the town coming to his funeral, to pay their respects."

"A fine man?"

"Outstanding! Oh, but I don't mean to embarrass you."

"Nonsense! He was a lucky man. He certainly had no difficulties providing for you."

"No. He inherited a sizeable portion of wealth from his family. But most of it came from business dealings in land surveying and speculation for the government. I, I remember how he and Robert always worked together in our study. They had such entertaining times."

"Robert? I don't believe I've ever heard mention of a Robert."

"Oh? Oh, no I suppose not. I, well, Robert, Robert is, *was*, one of our best friends here. He and his wife, Marribelle. Robert and Marribelle *Stantan*. I haven't spoken their names in, well, not in a long, long while."

"Tell me about them, if you don't mind. I don't mean to intrude—,"

"No. No, you're not. I'd like to talk about them. I haven't, for many years. I, there never was reason to. Well, where to begin!"

"Where ever it makes you feel most comfortable."

"We were very good friends with the Stantans, my husband and I. They came to our parties, and we to theirs." Widow Douglas choked.

"Brittany, what is it? I've made you uncomfortable."

"No. No. Ben, it's just hard, even after all these years, to tell you my best, my closest, my dearest friends in all the world, no longer share a place *in* this world."

"No longer share a place?"

"They were murdered."

"Murdered!" Ben took out a handkerchief, with which he used to dry Widow Douglas' tears. "That's just terrible. Just terrible."

"There mansion still stands, proudly. Well, you can see it, from any place in St. Petersburg. Thank goodness Senator had foresight enough to preserve it. He passed a law, making it a landmark."

"Senator?"

"Yes. I haven't seen him since after my husband's funeral."

"It must be hard, at times."

"What makes it more difficult is how closely their deaths came. Within a week of each other. First the Stantans. Then—my husband."

Suddenly, a frantic, angered, Miss Watson burst into the parlor; red in the face, puffy eyed. "It's gone! It's gone!" Miss Watson squealed.

"Sis! Heavens!" Doctor Towers and Widow Douglas repositioned themselves. "What is gone? My goodness. Something has happened."

"I'll say it has. My diamond necklace, the one Mr. Johansson gave me. You of *course* remember? The man who was courting me."

Doctor Towers lifted his eyes towards Miss Watson, with vexed interest.

"The man who was called off to Texas?"

"That's the *one*! The *only* one. I, it's been in my dresser under lock and key all this time. I only took it out earlier this morning, to put it on for—well, never mind *why*. I admit I carelessly forgot to replace it back in my drawer. Something came up. When I returned to my room—*oh!*" Miss Watson collapsed on the sofa and buried her face in her hands.

"There, Miss Watson." Doctor Towers tried to comfort her.

Miss Watson saw his hand approach her. "Don't you touch me!"

Doctor Towers instantly returned his arm his own lap.

"Sis! That was uncalled for. He's trying to be a friend."

"Who asked him? I don't need his friendship. I don't need any man's friendship. Not ever again."

Widow Douglas, perturbed at her sister's rudeness, asked, "Well, what *did* you come in here for?"

"What? My necklace was stolen. Somebody in this home stole it. I hoped to be consoled."

"Well isn't that what Ben was—,"

"I told you I don't need a man."

Doctor Towers, feeling uncomfortable, stood. "Would it be better if I left? I don't want to come between two sisters."

"Yes!" Miss Watson agreed.

"No!" Widow Douglas objected. "Sis, how can you act this way? I love you. But I," she stared at doctor Towers, then back at her sister. "But I won't have you act unkindly towards Ben. He's a good man."

"Oh!" Miss Watson rose stiffly. "How could you be so cruel to your own sister!" She ran from the room.

"Sis! Sis, I—." Widow Douglas wrung her hands. "Ben, I—. She had no right to act that way to you. I apologize for her."

"It's not your fault. I've seemed to create a wedge between you two."

"No. Oh, no. Please, you mustn't think that. She wasn't always like this. That necklace meant more to her than anything. It is very precious to her. But that is no reason to take it out on you."

"This, Johnson, I gather gave her the necklace."

"*Johansson*. Yes. He and sis were to be married. But he received word from his relations in Texas a week prior. Some kind of trouble with the Mexicans. One of his brother's was killed. He told sis he would return just as soon as he was able to settle the dispute. That was almost ten years ago."

"Ten years!"

"Mr. Johansson wrote letters whenever he could. Sis never touched them in my presence. Each letter was more heartbreaking than the last. The dispute intensified rapidly. Sis waited, however, all those lonely years. The last letter to arrive was perhaps the most crushing and morose of them all. It seems the dispute was to turn to war. A group of men had barricaded themselves inside an abandoned church called the Alamo."

"I heard about that. Remember it distinctly."

"Then I needn't go into details as to it's outcome?"

"No." He bowed his head to the floor.

"We, sis, never heard from Mr. Johansson again. Word of the Alamo spread quickly. She cried for weeks without stop, privately, in her room. She doesn't know I often stood by the door, listening to her sob. It sounded as though she tried to muffle her tears into her pillow. Sis never liked me to see her cry. Not even as girls.

Doctor Towers sighed. "Terrible."

"I've looked after her, both I and my husband, until his death. It's only been recently she's moved in permanently. So you see, it's hard at times, dealing with sis. I love her with all my heart. But I don't feel she has ever gotten over Mr. Johansson. I don't think she ever will."

"I see, now, the importance of the necklace. I do hope, I *know*, she'll find it. Likely it fell behind the dresser. Happens all the time."

"If sis thought it was lost forever, well, a price could never be put upon it. It's all sis has left to remind her of Mr. Johansson; the only man to ever show her any interest. Very gentlemanly and chivalrous, very patient and caring towards her. His leaving nearly destroyed sis. In some ways, it did."

"That settles it! I'll look myself. When she is away."

"I'd like that. And I know sis would appreciate it too, even if she never comes out and says so. I like to hope so."

"I know so."

Ginny ran into the room. "Miss Douglas, you got more company." She no longer hid behind doors when company stopped by. Ruth had made it very clear to her what might happen if she did not behave herself.

"Oh," Widow Douglas sighed. "I'm not really in the mood to see anyone right now. I'm talking with Ben—doctor Towers."

"No, no," the man said, speaking right up. "I must check up on Ruth any way. The company will do you good."

After doctor Towers left, Widow Douglas allowed her guest to appear. Expecting another of St. Petersburg's "ladies", she was surprised, pleasantly so, to be wrong.

"Tom Sawyer! Well, come, sit. It's *good* to see you again."

"Thank you."

Tom, here to uphold his vow to Muff, desired to do so quickly. Not that he wished to back out. On the contrary, Tom did not want doctor Towers, or anyone else, to do the woman harm. But now he had Becky to worry about also.

"How are you, Tom? How's Polly, and all the rest?"

"She,-"

"I'll have to call on them soon." Widow Douglas rambled. "Ben— doctor *Towers*—has done wonders for me. My voice has never been better. He doesn't like to admit it. Pride, you know. You know, I used to take snuff. I threw it away. Unhealthy, doctor Towers says."

"Yes, but—,"

"That *was* a terrible storm. The thunder and lightening. The lightening especially. It plays tricks on a person. Makes those trees out in the back appear like people. I've seen them move. It's my imagination, of course."

"Is the doctor in?" Tom tried to ask. Widow Douglas, did not hear him. For the moment, she could only concentrate on doctor Towers.

"But those trees *did* move. I know what doctor—,"

"Widow Douglas!" Widow Douglas halted.

"Why Tom, I forgot you were there. You should have said something. I've been rambling. I'm sorry. You must think strangely of me. I haven't stopped talking all day. I've stopped, now. Now, Tom. What is it you want?"

Tom took a deep breath. "Is doctor Towers still here?"

"Why, yes. Are you sick?"

"No. That is, I was, but I'm fine now. But I wanted to know if doctor Towers was still here, what with you being well again."

"Yes. Yes, he'll stay on a while longer. Longer, I hope. I mean, Ruth, one of our slaves, is ill. B——. Doctor Towers says it will be at least another week. But you didn't come all this way just to talk about Ben?"

Of course Tom did. Now he must gather his thoughts.

"No," Tom stammered. "I came by to see *you*. I feel awful about what Huck's pap did to you. He could've killed you, if the other passengers hadn't grabbed hold and knocked him—,"

"Why Tom Sawyer! Did you *see* what Jimmy Finn did to me?"

"No, I, well, sort of. I was hid behind some of the other people on board. I warn't meaning to spy. I only just stumbled across the confrontation is all. It happened so fast."

"What a shock it must have been. And this is why you've been wanting to see me?"

"Well, I felt bad. I *had* to see you. I'm awful glad you're well, now."

"That's B——. Uh, doctor Towers doing."

"Do you know much about him?"

"Well, that depends. What is it you would like to know?"

"Oh——." Tom's mind blanked. He didn't think he would get this far. But he overcame this obstacle, and his nerves strengthened. "Well, where did he work before coming here?"

"Oh, well. My, you should have come right out. Of course I know. And I'll be only too happy to tell you."

"I'm much obliged. Could you start with where he came from?"

"He came up from Mission. There's an awful feud going on down there, he says. The patient load exceeded his capabilities. But what really upset him was seeing the same people come in with gunshot wounds week after week. Then, a small boy came in, with a serious gunshot wound to his abdomen. When he died on the table, before doctor Towers could look at him, he had had enough. Hearing St. Petersburg was looking for a new doctor, he gladly handed his practice over to his partner, then left on the first boat he could get passage on."

"And he left on the first boat he could get passage on. That's what she told me, Muff."

Tom, having learned something about doctor Towers, sought out Muff down by the stables, where he told Tom he had bargained for living quarters.

"Mission?" Muff scratched his chin. "That's a *ways* south. By foot."

"I reckon. Widow Douglas didn't say how far."

"Well, you did good work, Tom. I'm mighty obliged. Was there anything else, anything? Nothin' more 'bout Ben? Yer sure now?"

"She did mention a missing bracelet. She told me 'cause she wanted to know if my Aunt Polly had ever lost any jewelry, and later found it wedged between the dresser and wall."

"Ah! *That's* something! Yes, course it was stolen. I jus' need proof."

"Proof?" Muff leapt off the hay. "Muff! Muff, where you headed to?"

"I'll be back, Tom!" Muff jumped upon a horse, and rode off.

"Muff!" Tom fell back against the hay. "Well, I reckon he knows what he doing. Course he does. Never know'd him to ride a horse, though."

CHAPTER 17

Throughout the day, light sprinkles continued to shower St, Petersburg. They were the least of Tom's troubles. The Mississippi River, when Tom investigated it up close, ran insane with fury. The *Natchez*, at top speed, could not surpass the torrent of the river.

"How will I ever make it to the cave *now*?" Tom questioned, misery stricken.

Everything Tom needed lay inside the secret hideaway. Everything he believed he needed, for rescuing Becky. This is the idea which bolted Tom upright in his bed. He must find a way in to the cave, even if it meant riding against the heavy current. Against his own will, Tom left the river, for the time being, and pressed on into the forest, his special place of contemplation, where he could "think matters out". Sitting upon the same log he always used when in deep mental concentration, and requiring nothing short of absolute privacy, Tom collected his thoughts.

"I don't care nothing for what Judge Thatcher says about it, *I'm* to blame for Becky's kidnapping. Was I who knew about them men. I should 'a' said something. Leastways I should 'a' told Judge Thatcher I knew they busted out Jimmy, even if I couldn't actually prove it. I should 'a' said *some*thing. I got to get her back. I just got to. I couldn't live with myself, knowing I was to blame. I couldn't live with her thinking I didn't try to rescue her. I don't blame her at all, for what she must think about me right now. She's got to despise me just awfully. Well, don't I deserve her hatred!"

Returned to the river, Tom inspected it. He toyed with the idea the river's swiftness was only a mirage. Anything, any idea, no matter how trivial, so long as it helped to ease his tensions.

"I just got to get to the cave." Tom paced back and forth. "Never mind the river. No gaudy heroic pirate, nor any knight in shining armor, ever worries about danger. He don't sweat over it one bit. No! 'Thout ever batting an eye *he*'d welcome danger, and not be a-scared."

Standing stolidly at the bank of the river, Tom determined to risk the current—for chivalry. For Becky! Now, he needed transportation. He saw plenty of rafts, canoes, skiffs, and other vessels floating down river. Unfortunately, they never were in reaching distance. For half an hour Tom impatiently waited to grab hold of *any*thing. He detected something, distantly up river. More importantly, on the Missouri side. As it neared, Tom identified it. A canoe!

For some time, Tom intently watched its movements, hoping it would stay within an easy grasp. It wobbled, repeatedly, to and fro, into the banks, then out into the river. Tom, understandingly agitated, did not wait for the canoe to come to him. He ran up river, to the canoe. But he misjudged the river's speed, and the canoe rushed passed him. Undaunted, Tom ran after it, until he caught up. His spirits were high, when the canoe pushed closer to the banks. His spirits lowered as it pushed away.

Growing braver, or perhaps more frustrated, Tom attempted several times to catch it. With each try his fingers inched closer. Nicking a part of the canoe gave Tom the added courage he needed to journey on. Now he got a hand on it. He struggled with the river's current to pull the canoe ashore. One of these two forces had to give up. And after all the many grunts and groans, countless slips, Tom, bruised on both arms and legs, dragged the canoe out of the river, up on the sand, where he fell along side it.

"I'll rest. But not long." Tom breathed uncomfortably, while watching meddlesome debris "scoot" down river. "Won't be easy. No. But, Becky. What I do is for Becky. And 'cause it's the right thing *to* do," Whether he truly convinced himself, Tom earnestly believed, deep down in his heart, he ought to do everything possible to rescue Becky. "Treasure! Secret passages! I don't give a dern for any 'a' *them*. Not without Becky. Not without she returns, safe and sound. Who knows what condition she's in! What vile tortures they are inflicting upon her this very minute!" Tom's strength regained, he rose steadfastly, decidedly, resolved he should not let happen to Becky what his imagination only perceived might be her fate. "What I need is at the cave!"

Shouts rang loudly, and coarsely, behind Tom. He turned. Three men hastily approached him. The same men that had accosted Becky and him days earlier. The lead man raised his arm.

"Hey! You, boy!" the man shouted vigorously.

"Stop thar!" a second man, panting his tongue, yelled.

A third man. lagging behind, screamed, "Don't go out in that canoe!"

The men surrounded Tom in a triangle formation. For a fleeting moment, Tom thought they were out for revenge against him.

"You wasn't planning to go out on the river, with that canoe?"

Tom shook. "What if I was?"

The lead man laughed. "What if he was! Thinks he's mighty *smart.*"

"You had better change your mind about that, and fast."

"Thas right, you listen to Josh," the laggard said.

Explaining, the lead man said, "Rains kept up all week. We been trapped here, while that nigger roams free; freer than we. We is aimin' to find him, ain't we men? And we got a real good idea where he's held up."

"Where might that be?"

"One place ain't nobody has tried—Jackson's Island."

"So why tell *me* about it?"

"Why tell him about it he says. Yes'r, a mighty smart boy at that. 'Cause we is going out there *now*. And seeing how there ain't but this here transportation, well—. Do we need to spell it out?"

"See here," Tom protested. "This canoe's mine, fair and square. *I* went to all the trouble of fetching it out of the water. It belongs to me."

"Oh, boy! That is a mighty fine story. A mighty fine story indeed. And we all here is mighty impressed."

"Thas right, you tell 'im Billy. Mighty impressed."

"Don't bother with the boy" the second man stated, quite aggravated. "We need not waste our time with him."

"Well, boy. You heard it. What's it gonna be?"

Their scouring faces told Tom they meant business, and were duly intent on *taking* the canoe. But Tom, duly intent on *keeping* it, held his ground.

"Why can't you go find another canoe? What do you want with this one? Why, it *is* rather small. It couldn't accommodate the three of you."

"We appreciate your concern, boy, really. But we'll fit just fine."

"Thas right Josh, you tell 'im."

"Are we to stand here all day diddle-dallying?" said the impatient one.

"Time's a-wasting boy. We've been good up 'til now, but my patience is dwindling. What's it gonna be? Either you git out of our way, or else."

Tom stood still.

"Alright boy, we didn't want to have to do it the hard way. As I said to Bill here, when we first laid eyes upon you and the canoe, I said, Bill, we'll go easy on him; he'll be fair. Well, you proved me wrong. You proved me wrong, and what's more you did so in front of my pals. That don't set well with me. You think I want it gettin' round I let a *boy* git the better of me? And this one here 'd blab it all over. Then I'd never hear the end of it."

"Thas right Josh, you tell him."

"Shush. Well, you've forced our hand."

The lead man picked Tom up and dumped him ten feet away.

"Come on. We got the canoe."

Climbing in, the three men had to admit a tight fit. Tom, helpless to do anything but sit and watch them ride away with his canoe, scorned them. He cursed them, privately; lest they might hear him, and make him recant.

Tom averted his eyes; his hatred of the men was too great. Picking himself up, with what little of his dignity remained, he slowly walked off, wondering just how he would make it to the cave.

And so it was, less than fifty feet from the river, Tom heard those shrilling screams, and terrifying yells; at least, that is the way it sounded. His mind, abuzz with fury, he thought quite possibly it might have been him. He turned around, towards the river, only to satisfy his curiosity.

What Tom saw, or rather did not see, were the men. He saw the canoe, traveling down river—but upside down. He scanned the length and width of the Mississippi, trying in vain to locate the men, who were no where in sight.

"Where *could* they be?" Tom returned to the river's edge for a better look. "Nowhere in sight. I wonder what—." A frightening thought occurred to Tom. A horrifying assumption. One he refused to believe. One he did not want to *make* himself believe. Yet, what else could have happened?

"They made it to the other side. Yes, that's it. It's bound to be so. They're over on the Illinois side, trapped. Yes, of course. Of course it's so. Goodness, it *must* be so."

CHAPTER 18

Tom spent the next three days looking all over town for any signs of Becky; any clues to her whereabouts, He had little else to do. The river never slowed to a congenial speed. Tom would not idly sit back, twiddle his thumbs as it were, and only *hope* for Becky's safe return.

At last!—The mighty Mississippi River, once a natural force brimming with hostile animosity, now "labored" and "sweated" to push its way downstream, and had the most trouble in navigating its own waters, which were become lethargic and calm. Logs, trees, cabins, and other debris still floated down stream. But by no means at any particularly dangerous speed.

Tom wasted no time. One unlucky man's floorboards became his life savor, and he jumped aboard, using a large, thick branch he found lying up on the sand for a paddle. Now—on to the cave!

There, Tom lit a candle, though he could walk the way blindfolded, and had once, with Becky behind him, as a safeguard. He missed her immensely.

Tom stopped near where the ground sloped downward. Originally a clay walkway, wooden planks, extending deep into the passage, provided an easy trek. These planks were set over a two week period by Tom and Becky, who "borrowed" them from old slaughter houses and tanneries, and anywhere wood seemed to them to stick out like a sore thumb. The two had constructed it during the night, the wee hours, when few people were about town; and those that were, generally did not notice them, or take an interest in their enterprises. It had been tedious work. Tom and Becky, with considerable might, pushed each plank into the clay to prevent popping or sliding. The work paid off, and they contrived a safe, soil-free walkway,—Standing at the rock, the one "with the cross", Tom breathed a sigh of remembrance for when he first showed it to Becky. *Here* is where Becky began her metamorphosis. Watching him push away the clay, then the wood, exposing a hole leading to the chasm where he and Huck found the treasure Injun Joe hid, something fantastic happened to Becky. Her senses had filled with a newfound freedom. The shackles of conformity most others in town had succumbed living to, and that she, unknowingly, would have, broke free.

Tom, traversing along the winding corridors, reminisced Becky's total make-over, her 180 turnabout. He hung his head remorsefully, and trudged hither and thither until he crouched in front of a "snug little cavern", decorated with childhood riches. Becky had made her contributions also; and except for bowing his head respectfully in front of hers, Tom paid no attention to the other "rubbish". What he really wanted lay only feet away.

Tom marveled. "There it is, Injun Joe's rifle." Huck, long ago, had shown Tom how to properly load this rifle. Tom went to it, reliving, in his mind, the dream he had three days earlier. In it, Tom, first killing the two strangers, marched on Jimmy. The two fought a harrowing war, with swords that appeared out of nowhere. After many grueling attempts, Tom struck the fatal blow sending Jimmy to his knees. As he breathed his last, Becky manifested. She embraced Tom and cried on his shoulder, calling him a brave and noble hero. Giving him a light kiss, the scene changed. They boarded a ship loaded with treasure, and sailed off to be—together forever.

The one draw back to Tom's dream—reality? Tom would have to "go it alone". He gladly excepted this responsibility in his dream. In reality, he preferred back up. With the rifle loaded, Tom set it aside, and contemplated.

"Why did I ever come here? I haven't the slightest idea, really I don't. I know nothing; nothing; nothing! I am cursed with ignorance. How *can* I rescue Becky? Alone? I don't even know where she is. Why is it only now I realize this?"

Tom caught a glimpse of the pipe he made for Becky long ago, on her insistence. It rested comfortably in a box, undisturbed since its entombment.

"You dreamed of us one day lying under a tree together, near a pond, in the sunlight, smoking freely, and talking of the peacefulness and tranquility and felicity that pipe smoking brought."

Removing it, Tom held Becky's pipe gently to his heart, then placed it inside his vest pocket, next to his own. He departed, taking the rifle with.

Out on the river, Tom thought of Jackson's Island, the one place yet to be searched for Becky. Instantly he propelled the raft upstream, against the current. Even in these calm waters, Tom "sweated".

Stepping on dry land a shot rang out, nicking the raft. Tom, shocked, jumped back onto the raft and paddled furiously to town, before the echo ceased. Whoever shot at Tom did not want company. Tom obliged, happily.

Ten minutes passed. The wind wisped against some shrubbery atop a hill near an opening to a small cavern. No, not wind. A *man*! He emerged hesitantly, with rifle in hand.

"Alright. We's safe. He'll never step a foot 'pon this island agin."

"D' ya reckon he got a good look at us?"

"Naw. Heard the shot and took off 'thout so much as an up'ards glance."

"You don't reckon he'll come back, with others?"

"In a day or two, I won't k'yer. We'll be off by then."

"The sooner the better. If we stay here longer, we might see the cabin float by. And *him*, on top a-waving and smilin' at us. His *ghost*, anyway. *Oh!* That ain't real good times."

"You talk too much. Didn't I go to all the trouble to carry him upstairs to his bed? The one he boasted and gloated over, but never once slept in? Well, he's sleepin' in it now. Likely fer all eternity."

"He did envy that bed."

"He didn't envy it. Only taunted us with it, 'cause we hadn't one. He never would 'a' used it *himself*. Jus' made sure neither of us used it."

"When y' say it that way, makes him out to be low down; mean speer-ited. Makes me think he didn't really k'yer 'bout us, but only his boy's money."

"Course he didn't k'yer 'bout us! Would 'a' killed us, soon's the money was got, and he had it in his hands."

"You don't really think so, do you?"

"Dern right I do! I is sick of him. Don't mention him agin. Check on the girl. Make sure she's cain't git away."

"Hey! Look at the li'l girl! She's tryin' to break loose."

Becky, restrained with rope, trembled.

"Won't do y' no good, girlie girl! Them ropes 'll hold!"

"Y' sure they'll hold her?"

"Course."

As Becky shook from her mysterious illness, she repeated over and over, "Won't go insane. Won't go insane." When the tremors ended she leaned against a large rock, still repeating, softly, "Won't go insane. Won't go insane. Won't go insane."

CHAPTER 19

Tom, paddling to town with all his might, did not turn around. He didn't know who shot at him, and he didn't care. Twenty yards to shore, the stick he used to paddle splintered in half, and he fell overboard; but, keeping one hand on the raft, pulled himself back on. Then, tragedy.

"The rifle! Where could it be?" Tom now looked towards the island. "Must-a fallen off, in my rush to flee."

Crestfallen, Tom swam the rest of the way to town, where he brought himself out, and up onto the sand. I'll have to go back there, when it's safe," he resolved. "Drat!"

Time passed. The warmth of the sun, and Tom's own body heat, dried his clothes. He fell asleep for part of the time. The sun's soothing, relaxing beams soaked through the pores of his skin in such a way as to "put him under". Becky's fair image faded into Tom's mind. She seemed to be pleading with him to hurry to her rescue, and wondering why it took so long.

A noise brought him back to reality. A familiar, most satisfying, ear-pleasing, non-human clamor as he had heard in a long time. His favorite sound of all—the whistle from a river-boat.

Tom eyed it with great interest, admiration, and pure gratification. Of all the inventions, Tom believed the river-boat the noblest. River-boats took people places; far away places, filled with wonderment, excitement, adventure; abounding with riches, and rich history, where

famous people lived and dwelled, and called home; where important
dignitaries vacationed, and made a historic mark upon every inch of
ground they trudged over.

Tom thought St. Petersburg a far cry from such monumental places.
Like most villagers, he spend the majority of his life in town, and had no
real idea what lay beyond it, but what he read in books. He envied
Becky, for she hailed from Constantinople, and "had seen the world".
Though only twelve miles away, to a young boy, to anyone, who has
spent their entire life living in a very small town, a distance of twelve
miles seems to be "going places".

As the people left the boat, Tom noted some would stay, while blessed
others wouldn't. But everyone would rest before the journey began
anew, and soak up what little ambiance this little town had to offer, and
then forget it wholly, after they had put distance behind it. Tom revered
each and every single person he saw walk off the boat, though their
moods did not become them. They looked displeased, and Tom felt
their displeasure derived from having to stop here. Still, he revered
them. *They* would not be in town long.

Tom always dreamt of riding on a river-boat. Not to a cave, or to
bring up the body of a dead comrade. Rather, to whisk him far away,
where he might see for himself the world in all its splendor. Books were
the closest thing he had, and Tom relished and marveled in them all. He
memorizing the text to acquire a "feel" for how the other side lived and
existed so *far* away. While imagining where certain people hailed from,
a man, hastily walking off the boat, caught his eyes. Tom followed him,
at a safe distance behind, to the livery stable. He now saw the man up
close.

"Why, Muff! It *is* you."

"Wh-!" Muff Turned. "Oh. You gave me a fright. Shh! Now don't be
yellin' out m' name, please. You know I don't want the whole town
knowin' I'm here, yet. Well, come ahead on over. I'm right glad to see
you, Tom. Really I am."

"I didn't hardly recognize you, with your face clean shaved. How'd you ever get passage?"

"A lucky break. Happened to know the captain from a long time ago, and he allowed me to ride up here with him. I done him some favors in the past. We bargained this 'd square us. Almost didn't make it. We started out when the storm hadn't quite settled. Matthew, thas his name, he'd go out in any weather. Punctual man. Never missed a schedule. Gave the people an ultimatum. Come now, or wait days b'fore another boat 'd be at the ready."

"I reckon *that* explains all the scowling faces."

"Reckon so. Tom, I found somethin' on Ben."

Tom's eyes lit up. "That what had you lighting out so fast before?"

"Yes. Had to. That town, Mission, got me curious." Leaning against a haystack, he recounted. "Ben didn't lie about the feud. It's a mess down there. Two people got shot dead, day I arrived. A woman who worked 'long side Ben told me what happened. Said Ben had come up years earlier, after another doctor got shot dead."

"I bet he took off with one of the daughter's from a feuding family."

"Tom! He did exactly that!" The boy, having read many books regarding these incidents, did not fall over in amazement. Muff continued. "Well, not too long ago, somethin' happened betwixt Ben and another man."

"Did he steal away one of the man's daughter's too?"

"No. No, 'twas a strange account. I might 'a' said that woman was greening me, but with Ben, I've learned, anything's possible."

"Go on," Tom eagerly pressed.

"Well, one of the feudin' men owned a certain colored man. Big, strong, loyal, trustworthy. The master always took his colored man with him, fer protection. Well, this one day, as they started home, shots rung out. Colored man jumped in front of his master, and was hit. Master brought him to Ben, but warn't anything he could do. He died three days later, and Ben had him buried right away. When the master found out, he was furious, 'cause he wanted his slave buried proper, and on his land. After-all, he did save his master's life. Ben was apologetic. He said he would talk with the undertaker as soon as he could about digging up the coffin, and have it brought back to the master's home for reburial. This seemed to be satisfactory, but for one thing."

"What?" Tom asked.

"When the coffin arrived, two days later, the master ordered his slave's body removed to a more dignified coffin. Thas where the trouble started. 'Cause when he opened up the wooden lid, all he found inside was sacks of dirt, but not his slave. He went into town to confront Ben, but he had left shortly after his talk with the master. Told his nurse he had had enough of the feud, and the killings." Muff rested against the hay. For a time, neither spoke.

Tom broke the silence. "Must be a logical explanation for it all. Maybe, grave robbers? No, I reckon not. What would they want with the body?"

"Mighty suspicious," Muff yawned. "I wish now I had thought enough to tell them people down there where they could find Ben. Had it mind to find that master, but when I got half way to his place, they was shots all around. I didn't feel much fer gettin' shot myself.

Leaving Muff did not appeal to Tom, but the man began to doze off.

With the day winding down, Tom knew he must soon return home for dinner. Absence would spell disaster with a capital "Polly". One last stop remained.

"It's a long shot. And I've been there twice already." Shortly, Tom, with reserve, entered the Stantan Home. He walked near to where he and Becky took their oath. "Well, you ain't here, Becky. I thought perhaps you might. I reckon Jimmy is smarter than I give him credit for. He's got you hid away somewhere only he knows about. Somehow, I got to find out where that is. What's this?" Somehow, without knowing how he arrived there, Tom stood at the secret passage, grieving. "Will we ever know what lays beyond this dirt? Well, I'll not move a single grain 'til

Becky is safe. Then we can both of us excavate it, and find the treasure together, like we planned. It don't seem to mean anything without her here. Please Becky, please be safe, wherever you are."

Tom, intending he should go straight home, even willing, headed in that direction. However, he saw two men slinking into town. Unshaven, unkempt, unsavory, and one of them the spitting image of the sheriff underneath the expanse of dirt and grime covering his face and neck. The other, taller, unrecognizable man, carried two jugs. Tom instantly became curious. He knew Judge Thatcher despised Cal, and hoped to produce evidence of corruption. What if Tom could produce such evidence for him?

"They're headed for the sheriff's office." Tom stalked them all the way, and crouched under the small window, patiently waiting for Cal to open it. He didn't. "How ever shall I listen to them now?" Tom put his ear against the wall. "Confound it!" he muttered in disgust. Unable to hear anything, he left, bitterly, and sadder than ever.

It *is* a pity Tom could not eavesdrop upon them. How satisfied and content the reader may feel, knowing he or she *will* hear their conversation. It is merely an assumption.

They talked, while cleaning and shaving themselves, and downing whiskey in excess; for they had lacked that savory taste a fortnight.

"He's nowhere in Illinois, you understand. Give up that notion."

Images of Cal's father and grandfather hideously swirled around his head. "We got to try looking there, at least. He must have crossed the river. Even *I* thought of that, earlier. Where else could he be?"

Cy, with a menacing ogle, bellowed. "I won't have that talk. I've *hurt* men for less." He relaxed his tone. "Might be drowned in the storm. Well, now that it's over, I want to check that island soon. Blasted storm kept me away from it too long. Couldn't have come at a worse time."

"I ain't been there myself. Them town folks tell me there's a lot of caverns up high. Lot of places to hide."

"I am well aware of that, you understand. I told you, I was here once, years ago. We'll head down south first. If there's no sign of him past Hookerville, then we'll try the island."

"Why don't we try the island first?"

"We will try the island! On my time. On my time, you understand." Cy cringed. Jackson's Island, he knew, rested part way on the Illinois side. Stepping foot on northern soil grossly disturbed him. He never could tolerate anything to do with the north.

"You reckon the nigger had help?"

"Another nigger?"

"No. Abolition."

"It's crossed my mind. Getting too common. Damned Northerners."

"Southerners do it too."

Cy pulled out a large knife. "Don't you say it!"

Quaking, Cal stepped back. "Oh!" Sweat rolled down his face.

"Abolition may occur within the south, but don't you ever tell me southerners partake in it. It's these damned northerners." Cy waved his knife. "*They* come down here. *They* steal the niggers. *They* disrupt our economy, *our* way of life, *our* traditions, *our* heritage." After Cy regained control of himself, and put away his knife, Cal's sweating stopped.

"Well, it's traitorous, whoever does it. Founding fathers fought and died for our freedom, and look what some of us do. How *can* a white man degrade God's inspiration that way?"

"Stop that nonsense. What have I told you I'd do to you—,"

"I can't! Isn't the Constitution sacred and divine? Course. Oh, they debated slavery. But if they'd 'a' wanted an end to it, they'd 'a' ended it. They weren't cowards. As I always say, as my own father used to tell me, if the founding fathers all could come together to whip a tyrant of a king, they sure is hell could whip slavery. Well, slavery was never abolished. They had a chance. But God inspired them in the other direction. Slavery is here forever. America can't go against the founding fathers wishes. They who fought and died for us. Slavery wrong! Who will say slavery is wrong? Who will say the founding fathers were wrong? Because if slavery is wrong, our founding fathers were wrong. And if they were wrong, God was wrong. And where are we as a society, when we start to believe God makes mistakes!"

"Oh! Do shut up with your nonsense. Is it not cruel enough I must return to my wife, Judith, who babbles constantly as well? I don't need to listen to you as well. Damn woman." He shuddered; he always shuddered when he thought about his wife. "Well, you don't go anywhere. I want you here when I return. I won't be made to wait, you understand."

Cy did not always disrespect his wife. They were once a very happily married couple, up until ten years ago. But she had kept from Cy a dark secret, which she chose to disclose with him, never thinking he would react with such condemning hatred. His coldness, and his distance, have turned Judith into a very lonely woman. If it had not been for the hospitality shown by Tom's Aunt Polly, Judith would never have known what to do in this strange new town; for she was indeed a very lonely woman.

She had been pacing the floor for hours, uttering only one single word repeatedly, constantly, irritatingly—"Where! Where! Where!—until she heard a rap at her door. She at first thought the rats were on the warpath again. These creatures had driven Judith nearly insane; always poking out their heads, twitching their noses whenever they smelled food; even the smell of boiling water drove an army of these hideous, revolting animals out of the woodwork. The woman's temper mounting, her frustration causing her no end of anxiety, she must do something! Without thinking, she had taken a loaf of bread and stuffed it into the largest hole. The rats were quiet after that. And yet, even the reigning quiet unsettled her; for now she had only herself to listen to. "Where! Where! Where!"

The rapping on the door turned to violent, furious banging; scathing pounding, and thunderous outbursts of the most vile, coarse, vulgar language to resound from within the small town of St. Petersburg. Still, Judith thought she only heard the rats, at their pranks again.

"Dern those inconsiderate animals. Didn't I just give them bread? Now they cry for more! Oh—Where! Where! Where!"

"Judith!"

The door, having taken all the abuse a door can endure—and should be required to endure by law—rattled, loosened, and "flew off the handle". It came crashing down, nearly flattening Judith. She turned to see her husband standing behind her, atop the door. His appearance and manner were such, the rats would have made better company.

"Where!" she cried out to him. "Where have you been all this time?" She curled her fingers, clawed them in the air, as a cat claws at a ball of string just above its reach.

"Why did you not answer me? I have been standing out there for five minutes. My knuckles are red now. They had better not become swollen and useless, for your sake, you understand?"

"What's taken ye so long? You've never been gone this long."

"Don't take that tone with me." He walked passed her.

"Is it too much to ask your whereabouts?"

"You know I've been out hunting the runaway nigger. And that's all you need to know, you understand. My business, is mine, an—. Stop that woman!"

"I thought perchance your neck was sore, and actin' up agin."

"Never mind it. Why did you not answer me earlier?"

"I didn't hear you."

"How could you not hear? The whole town likely heard."

"I thought it was the rats, wanting more food."

"Don't worry about the rats. The storm brought them up this way. They'll head back down shortly."

"Hope so. I've given them one loaf of bread; I'd hate to use another."

"You did what!"

"I, I stuffed a loaf of bread in the hole over yonder."

"You stupid woman. How could you be so careless? For yourself, I mean. If you hadn't rat problems before, you have them now." He left for a moment. When he returned, he carried with him a crate.

"What's—,"

"I don't know why I bother, but, well, use these on the rats."

"Lead bars? They're heavy. I might miss."

"It doesn't matter. The noise itself will scare them, for a time. And the vibrations will unsettle their spirits. But if you do happen to hit one, and kill it, it is your responsibility, you understand."

"Where are you off to *now*?"

"Mind your business. I've things to attend to. I'll return in due time, for the door."

"You hain't been here but a few—." Cy, grumbling, walked out the door and, again, out of Judith's life. "Wait! I didn't get a chance to tell you." Cy walked on. "Why does he even bother to show his face? He only stays a few moments. What possesses a man who clearly despises his wife to keep returning? I can't get nowhere with that man. Not since I— . Lies have done it. Lies have turned him agin me. I deserve it, I suppose." The rats began moving, apparently awakened by the noise; or perhaps they felt more secure with Cy gone. Judith vaguely perceived them. "Won't be long now, 'til I got to use these bars. Maybe I could wrench my arm. Polly's been so good to me, she could care for me, and nurse me. Oh, what a blessing she is! What a beautiful family she has. Oh what a lucky, lucky woman. Lucky!"

CHAPTER 20

The next day, Tom, after an unsuccessful return to Jackson's Island to look for his rifle, moped aimlessly into the forest. He hadn't spent five minutes looking for it, when a sudden shivering overcame him. He promptly left; and though fear gripped him, he refused to admit it to himself. Back, and seated upon the decaying log of contemplation, he absently bit upon the stem of his pipe.

Tom muttered half heartedly. "If it warn't on the island, it must 'a' fallen in the river. How am I ever to rescue Becky?" He felt the swelling frustration poking against his ribs, jabbing incessantly until it hurt. No, not frustration. Becky's pipe! Swiftly, he swapped his own for hers.

"And will she never again lay her hands upon her pipe? Blame *me*, Becky. Blame me. Oh, how you must loathe me, and rightfully so. I'll get you out, honest. If only I knew where you was."

In deep mental anguish, Tom pressed the pipe bowl against his lips. Now, he had the urge to smoke from her pipe. Instantly he prepared it, and watched the smoke curl up, up, up. After a few minutes, the fire within the bowl extinguished on its own, for there had been no prompting.

"Blasted! Can't I do anything right? If she knew the failure I really was, she'd never speak to me again, if she was released and found out I hadn't done anything to help rescue her. *If*! I say *if*. I might never really see her again. But if I set on my hands, and don't do anything—."

Tom fidgeted with Becky's pipe, twirling it in-between his fingers. Suddenly, he relit it, and furiously puffed *Together Forever*. Becky's fascination in the secret code far exceeded Tom's. With her gone, and her fate unknown, *Together Forever* took on new meaning, special meaning. Tom began to cherish it as he thought he never would; for Becky had created it. Little did he know a man, watching Tom from behind a bush, formulated his own interest in it. Excited, he jumped out.

"Hey! You thar!" Tom too jumped, white as a ghost, not sure whether to run or stay. His feet took control, however, and planted him firmly where he stood. "No. You needn't fear. I ain't gonna hurt you."

"Wh-what do you want?"

"I was away back behind that bush. Now, I warn't meaning to spy. No! Jus' passin' along. But I saw you settin' thar, smokin'. I seen what you done with the pipe, and I says to myself—I wish I could do that with mine. I got s' caught up in it, I jumped right out. I didn't mean to frighten you."

Feeling more secure, Tom sat back down and reflected.

"Well, if that's all."

"Oh, it is!"

"Ain't nothin' I reckon. Why, any *body* can do it that's got a mind to."

The man sat down next to Tom.

"Could—. Do you think *I* could learn to create it?"

"You? Oh, I don't—." Tom looked the man over. Obviously this man would pester him no end, for the rest of his life, until he showed him.

"You…don't think you c'n learn me?" Rejected, his body sagged.

"No. It's not that. Takes an awful lot of time, and practice."

"Looks complicated, anyhow."

"It is, but—." The man looked to Tom. "It ain't impossible. I'll show you how to do it. Then you can practice on your own."

"Would you!."

"Have you a pipe?"

"Right here."

"Fine. Watch me a few times, then you try." Except for Becky, Tom never had such a captive audience. "Now, you give it a go."

The man quivered in delight. His first attempts were dismal failures. Yet, he persevered.

"It ain't workin'."

"Puff harder. Yes, that's better. It takes time. And you must make sure the stem is clear of any debris. The air pushes through easier that way. Anything stuck inside will naturally block the flow of air."

"Oh. Likely that's it then. Don't recollect ever cleanin' out my pipe. Usually throw it away and make a new one. Makes sense. I'll do it too. And I'll practice as long as it takes, 'cause I really wanna learn it. Uh, how *long* will it take, to learn?"

"D'pends on how much time you put into it. Up'ards of two, three weeks maybe, if you only practice occasionally. Three, four days, if you can set aside a few extra hours each day."

"I'll do it! And when I get it down, I'll come find you."

Tom did not think much about his last statement. He hadn't really heard it to begin with. When the man left, Tom thought, "He is a curious sort of lot, but who am I to judge."

Chapter 21

Cy hadn't fixed the door when Aunt Polly came to visit Judith. So when the woman saw the mess, she immediately thought the worst.

"Judith!" Aunt Polly nervously called out. She hesitated to enter, lest she might walk in on a body, or two. Instead, she poked her head in, slightly. To her relief, there were no dead bodies.

"Yooou! Polly!" came a distant cry.

"Judith!"

Judith, fifty yards away, raised her arms in the air. "I'm over here."

"Thank the Lord. I nearly went out of my mind. I thought—. Well it's not important now. Oh, let me look at you. You appear alright. Ere you?"

"Indeed. I am, Polly." She smiled, gaily. "You worry about me too much.":

"Well then, how ever did the door—,"

"Come in. I'll tell you about it. 'Twas the wind that done it. Blows awful strong off the river at times. I was asleep. Husband hadn't come home yet. Out on business, you see. I stayed with some folks down the way. They were nice enough to let me spend the night."

"Oh, well, is that all?" And Polly breathed easier. "My heart most stopped when I saw the door lying there."

A rat scurried out of its hole and darted passed the women. Aunt Polly picked up her feet and yelled. Judith, used to the rats, merely watched as this one darted under the chairs and table.

"It won't hurt you, Polly." Speaking to the rat, she said, "Be glad I got company, and ain't near the lead bars. I'd clobber the likes of you."

"Judith! Land sakes! How ever can you deal with those creatures?"

"Tain't bad. I've dealt with—worse. They came up during the storm, to drier ground, husband says. He says they'll head down soon. He's been so good. I ain't got a bad word agin him. Takes good care of me. I couldn't ask for no better man than husband. Well," she sighed. "Has there been any sign of the nigger? Or that Jimmy Finn?"

"No. Ne'er a one. Most of the town's given up on Jimmy. Judge Thatcher put a two hundred dollar reward on him the day after he escaped. But Jimmy could be anywhere. Most is still looking for Miss Watson's Jim, who's worth a sight more than Jimmy. *Three* hundred dollars. He can't be too far."

"What with the river just out there, I've heard so many stories about the both of them. All that gossip floatin' by, and some of it f"om children. I've never heard children talk so."

"You don't know my Tom well enough. Children do like to imagine."

"You can believe I wouldn't tell any child the truth. I'd lie, and make up a story. I'd tame it down, at least. You know the folks I stayed with? They got young 'ns. Heaps of 'em. Most under twelve. And what do you think? *They* tell such stories, Polly! Each one more horrific than the last. I hope to be struck down dead, if ever I repeat what they said, to any child. Polly, they know husband is a bounty hunter, and looking for the nigger. Now they want to know has he found him, and would he hang him first, then drag the body in to town. Polly! These are children. No. Better to lie to a child, then tell the truth. Better to lie period. Somes just can't handle the truth.

After two hours, Aunt Polly left. With Sid ill, she had to relieve Mary. She missed Cy's return by thirty minutes. Judith was inwardly glad.

As Cy entered the cabin, carrying supplies for the door, Judith said, coldly, "'Bout time you got back."

"What have I told you about your tone with me?"

"Dern the tone. Was never like this years ago."

"What wasn't?" He looked to Judith, puzzled.

"What d' you think! You going off, leaving me alone for long stretches."

"Keep it to yourself!"

"I have been. For years. I won't any longer. I can't hold back. It's because I told you the truth about me. You've been distant ever since. I can say it now, without fearing. Fear! What's to fear?"

Cy said nothing for ten minutes, while he fixed the door. Judith watched, silently gazing at his progress.

"The door's good as new. Better, perhaps."

"Yes, yes, the door is. A door is easy to fix, or replace. Other things are not that—that simple."

"Are you to pester me all the while I'm here?" Cy swung the door back and forth several times, examining his work, well pleased with himself.

"I can't help the truth being what it is."

"Oh, woman! Out of my way." Here only to fix the door, Cy picked up his tools and began to leave. It was a strange and confounding urge that always compelled him back to his wife. He so desperately wanted to leave her for good; yet, he was not strong enough, mentally.

"Wait!" Judith threw herself in front of him. "Don't leave just yet. Not just yet. I have something to tell you."

"What then? And be quick. You see may patience has dwindled."

"It's about the runaway nigger."

"What have you to tell me about it?"

"I think I know where he might be held up."

"So does half the town. But he hasn't been caught yet."

"No. Wait. An island! Jackson's Island. He may be up there."

'Oh, you fool. I already know that. I've known about that island for, well, a good long time. He may be. He may not be."

Judith's spirits sunk. She hoped telling him about the island might help win back his approval.

"You've seen the smoke then?"

Cy turned quickly to Judith. "Smoke! What, smoke?"

A chance! "I, there was smoke last night, and before the storm."

"This I did not know. Judith, for once you've done right." His mood mellowed. His eyes softened. But only for a moment. Now within those eyes a storm brewed. "What is this...*before* the storm?"

"Well, there was smoke on the island the night I arrived."

"And you didn't tell me!"

"Wait! Before you do anything you might regret later on, wouldn't you do well to start out now, lest you have the nigger give you the slip again?"

"I never do anything I later regret, you understand. No, not even *that*. I never once have. I *will* be on that island...tonight. I and another man. I'll have the moon to see by. That's all I need, you understand. The nigger won't see me, but I'll see him."

"No!" Judith cried. "Don't leave!"

Cy did leave, humming a tune to himself to drone out Judith's screams. He headed for Cal's office, where he slept four hours, waking shortly before sunset, well rested, and very alert.

Long after nightfall, Cy and Cal stood on the docks. *Cy* stood. Cal paced unevenly, waving at the empty air where he thought his father and grandfather hovered around him.

Cy smoked three cigars before setting sail; both because it gave him satisfaction, and to help measure the passage of time when clouds ruled the skyway for a long time. He calculated each cigar lasted three quarters of an hour; for, although an impatient man, he savored his cigars, his *pets*. This night no clouds were about, so he smoke merely for the pleasure they bestowed.

Just after eleven they shoved off, paddling softly towards Jackson's Island. Though dark, Cy's photographic memory guided him exactly where he wanted to go. The moon's light also helped pinpoint the shadowy outline of the island as the men neared their destination. Landing before midnight, Cal, grudgingly, and by himself, brought the canoe up on shore, and tipped it over; then covered it with newly fallen leaves and branches.

"Stay close," Cy whispered, though he still bellowed. "Make no sound. Whatever you do don't light anything. I can see well enough in this darkness, you understand. But bring this lantern, in case we tree the nigger."

Cy had the eyes of an owl; the intelligence too. Bristly twigs littered the landscape. Cy distinguished this danger ahead of time, taking necessary precautions to avoid a disastrous outcome. Not so with Cal. His clumsy feet trounced upon ever twig; and with each broken twig Cy's animosity towards Cal grew. Yet, every great hunter needs a lackey. Someone to carry the heavy equipment, prepare the food, ride on ahead to make sure the road traveled is safe; a man who works for nothing, and sustains all the abuse heaped upon him. Cal played this role so deliciously in the past, and now was wondrously adapted and trained—if only he would cease stepping on those infernal twigs!

"Oh!" Cal yelped, bumping into Cy, who stopped without warning.

"Quiet. Look out yonder. There's a fire burning."

"We got him now."

"Walk carefully. If you step on another twig now—."

The men hid behind a group of tall bushes only yards away from the fire.

"We wait here." They did wait, for over an hour. Each passing minute made them more restless. Cy became uncomfortable. "It's wrong."

"What's wrong?"

Cy walked out. "It's bait. And I fell for it," he sternly and bitterly said. "This fire was made in a hurry. Hadn't been going long when we arrived. Damn me! We never made a sound coming up here. No way for him to know our whereabouts, our presence, you understand. Yet, he never returned."

"He must still be here, on the island, hiding."

"We'll comb every last square inch."

Searching low ground first, they circled the island twice. Having no luck, they ascended the hills, up to the caverns. Most were empty. Some contained artifacts of old, worn and rotting, and covered with the dust of a thousand years perhaps. The actual date of an artifact didn't matter, if it turned out not to be exactly what they were looking for. One cavern, however, stood out. When Cy gave the signal to light the lantern, both were astounded at what they saw. Clothes, scattered everywhere; cooking and eating utensils haphazardly circled a fire pit; blankets scrunched up against the walls.

"Everything is set perfectly, as if the occupant left in haste. Shine the lantern down on the pit. You see, it's fresh yet. Put out only hours ago. The smell of burning wood is still strong."

"The nigger's! We'll surprise him when he returns."

"Whoever made this fire will not return. When they left, they did so in a hurry. You see, that camp fire *was* bait. Something of a genius.

"*Who*ever? Didn't the nigger make this and the other fire."

"I don't know. Footprints have been wiped away, with considerable care. Look around. Two people were here. Look!. They didn't wipe *this* clear."

"What is it?"

"An imprint of a man's arm. Stretched out, lying on his side, perhaps just after he ate. Perhaps gazing into the fire, he planned his next move. This fire looks to have been put out just as we struck upon the first."

"Meaning we missed him by minutes?"

"I don't mean anything! We've been made fools. I don't like being played for a sucker, you understand."

"How could he have known we were coming?"

"Don't you see? He *did* have help. Damn! Now we must refocus. Damn! Damn those northerners."

"You don't think it could have been a southerner?"

Grabbing Cal by the throat, Cy threw him against the wall. "I told you I'll not have my south slandered. Southerners don't partake in abolition, you understand." Cy slammed his fist into Cal's face, sending him hurling to his knees. "You find your own way back. I'll take the canoe, myself."

About this time, Tom Sawyer awoke from a restless and tormented sleep. Something nagged at him all during the night. He had no idea what—until now.

"Oh my! It can't be. Oh, how could I be so blind. What a *fool* I am!"

A realization brought Tom out of restless sleep, and into restless wakefulness. A *dreadful* reality! One he would never forgive himself for, if it ever proved fatal.

"The man! The man! In the forest. The one who—. He was one of them. One of the two strangers! One of the kidnappers. Oh! Curse me!" Tom fell back against his pillow, destined to remain awake for the rest of the night.

CHAPTER 22

Tom assumed correctly. *Sim* had been that man; and with the descending sun, he quickly returned to his and Jed's new hideout, to use the remaining light to "create"; and when Jed returned, and saw half his brother's body arched out a second floor window, he shook with anger,

"Sim! You idiot! Git away from there. You want to be seen?"

Sim turned to his brother. "Nobody saw. B'sides, they'd only say it was a speerit."

"*I* saw you. Smokin' that infernal pipe. What I tell you 'bout smokin' pipes?"

"I warn't smokin'. I was creatin'."

"I don't k'yer what you was doin'. Don't do it period. Ain't nobody gonna take you fer speerits."

"How come?"

"Do speerits smoke on corn cob pipes?"

"I reckon they smoke on whatever they're set on smokin', and don't worry 'bout what t'other fella's gonna say about it. Anyhow, I warn't smokin'."

"Git away from the window! You want t' smoke, do it after dark, in the room, but not hanging out no infernal window."

Sim pouted. "But it's dark in here. I can't see the creation."

"What creation?"

"A boy showed it to me."

"Boy! What I tell you? What I tell you? Sim, y' got t' stay away from people. Folks is still talking 'bout Jimmy's escape. We helped in it. Rot him. Well, they might remember our voices."

"I jus' wanted to create." He hung his head, remorsefully.

"Don't git that way. This house is our last resort. If we got t' leave, where do you think we'll go to, totin' 'round a girl 'at ain't even ours? A girl any townsman is bound to recognize."

"Well, I reckon I see yer point."

"Hall-lay-loo-yea! Will ya go check on the girlie girl now? What with you hangin' out that window, you'd never know if she escaped."

"That ain't nice."

"Oh! Go see to the girl. I'll be back soon."

Becky, locked in a closet, much smaller than her pit inside the cabin, comforted herself, knowing this closet hadn't any water to wade through. Joan of Arc, her inspiration at the cabin, remained her sole strength here. The only draw back now? Jed had tied and gagged her, worried she might escape.

"I'd rather have the mud, and water up to my neck again," Becky sighed. "It's so hot, so stuffy. No. Now Becky, don't make it worse for yourself. Be like Joan. Be strong. It ain't easy, but you must."

Sweat profusely matted her hair, and clung to the sides of her cheeks, accumulating, trickling through her thin and holey gag. Becky sucked in it, to replenish what liquids she had lost. "It's my sweat," she told herself. "Even though the gag isn't." Becky hoped this only a temporary way to obtain water. There were other, more drastic, ways. If the time ever came when she must employ those measures, she wondered if she would have courage to go through with it. "Joan would," Becky reassured herself. There were no tears. Perhaps because she had so little moisture left to make them. "But I won't allow myself to fear. I may be hungry, starving really. And extraordinary thirsty. I may need to relief myself. I can't allow any of this to affect my mentality. Don't you ever go insane, Becky. You know what happens to people who go insane. If Joan of Arc could endure it all, then Becky, you can wait a little longer for food and water, and bowel relief. They burnt Joan at the stake, remember. This is not going to happen to you. Rest easy, knowing this. Yes— *rest*! Sleep as much through this as you can."

Becky gently leaned against the closet wall and closed her eyes. "Like being treated as an animal." She thought back to her home in Constantinople, her youth. She had a cat, Mrs. Sherry. This name Becky gave her cat after it jumped upon the kitchen table and began drinking, or "lapping", as cats do, from her father's wine glass, which happened to be filled with sherry.

As Becky's cat, Mrs. Sherry depended on the girl to feed and clean up after her. What an awesome duty to levy upon a person! Becky never gave it consideration then. Now, as she sat bound and gagged, and helpless, Becky arrived at a gripping and scarey fact.

"I'm at their mercy, as Mrs. Sherry was at mine. But Mrs. Sherry could always count on me for food and water." Becky could not yet face facts and admit she saw no indication Jed or Sim could be counted on for anything.

As soon as Jed left, Sim let Becky out, freeing her hands and mouth from insufferable bondage. He handed Becky a canteen of water, which she promptly emptied. So he could smoke his pipe without angering his brother, Sim lit a lantern and began the work of replacing the wooden boards over the window.

"They's ham and bacon on the little crate. It's mine and yers. But I ain't hungry, so you can have it all."

Becky didn't argue. She had consumed both their meals, never once thinking of escaping. Not with Jed lurking close by. And Jimmy! They hadn't told her the awful truth. Instead, they lied. Jimmy, Jed told her, left to deliver the ransom note. "Wouldn't people see him?" Becky had questioned. Jed gagged her then, without answering her. Hours later, all three made a daring escape of their own, when the river rose and swept the cabin away.

Finished eating, Becky stretched her arms and legs, knowing she might not have another opportunity for a long time. She again asked about Jimmy.

"Hasn't Jimmy delivered the note yet?" Sim, absorbed with creating, paid no attention to the question. She asked once more. No response. Sim blew, with earnest passion, on his pipe. Becky watched, curiously, as he labored for five minutes. Sloppy attempts in the beginning. Slowing, taking his time, a partial replica of the secret code emerged from the smoke. Enough, at least, for Becky to speculate. Sim looked up at her and smiled.

"You like it?"

"What is it?"

"Don't rightly know. Jus saw it, and thought it was real good times."

"You saw it? You mean you saw someone doing it? Where?"

"Out in the forest. Came upon a boy—,"

Becky gasped. "A boy! Who?"

"Didn't git his name. Sad case though. I didn't ask him what the matter was. I didn't wanna pry. I jus' wanted to do this."

It couldn't be but Tom!

"Sim!" Jed stood at the doorway. "I leave fer a few minutes, with orders not to smoke that pipe, and you go and disobey me."

"No, Jed. It's alright. I covered up the window. See."

"That ain't the point. Put out the pipe. We's movin' agin. There's a cellar out to the other side of the house. It's perfect." Though Becky knew the way, she allowed Jed to lead. "This is it," he announced. It's big enough for us all. I'll have to tie you back up, girlie girl. But you needn't fuss. I got somethin' that'll let you roam around freely. Pick a spot to call yer own," Becky casually meandered over to the boxes standing guard over the secret passage.

Hours later, Becky awoke. She heard a loud thump, and felt something cold being applied to her ankle. Then she heard a "clasp".

"I wake you?" Jed asked insincerely.

Groggily, Becky sat up. "What are you doing?"

"It's so you ain't got to be tied up no more." Jed tilted the lantern.

"What, I. What's this?" Becky groped the object. It feels like—,"

"That's it. Go on," Jed prompted.

"A ball and chain."

"Try walking around in it." Seeing the difficulty Becky had walking, he grinned slyly. "You ain't going nowhere. Not with that 'round you."

"Oh, Becky, be strong. You have to be. Least you ain't tied. Joan endured a similar treatment once. You can too, Becky. Becky? You *can*."

Cradled, Becky rocked herself to sleep. When she woke, she wondered how long she had slept. A lantern burned upon a small crate.

"Must 'a' slept a long time. They're both gone. But, will they return? Nincompoops! What am I to do? Have I food? Drink? No! Nincompoops! Well, first things first." Becky opened up the passage and entered. "I need a box. *Empty*. Except, a layer of dirt. They'll have me live as an animal. Only, I won't *be* an animal." Becky overturned one box, letting most of the dirt spill freely. Saving a small layer, she placed the box inside the passage. "I can relieve my bowels now. There's plenty of dirt. This'll be my outhouse, for a time. Well, it shouldn't be for too long. Even Joan didn't have as much."

Having relieved herself, Becky dared to ascend the steps leading out of the cellar, out to freedom, her freedom.

"They're probably right about the stairs being to hard to climb. But I have to try. I have to do at least that much. I *have* to."

Chapter 23

"Oh! Drat!" Becky muttered in pain. Trying to lift the ball and chain up one stair, she dropped it, nearly atop her foot. "They were right, those nincompoops." Becky slithered away, dragging the heavy ball behind her. "I couldn't lift this without breaking my back. I could yell. Yes, I *could* do that. From the bottom of these steps, and who would hear me? Not a soul. I'm stuck here. Well, and what am I to do? How do I even know they'll come back? And where is Jimmy, anyway?" Becky stopped. "Look at you, Becky. What would Joan think? You need something to occupy your time. To keep busy. They'll come back. They have to. Oh, drat! I am becoming a babbling idiot." As Becky thought how she might keep busy, Jed and Sim, inside and abandoned mill, debated her fate.

"No! How many times I got to tell you. We can't let her go. We're stuck with her. Once we free her, she'll go straight to her pa, and then we is deed like Jimmy. They'll kill us, Sim. In cold blood! And thas legal in this damned country. Sim! Pay attention! Stop smokin' that pipe." Jed ripped Sim's pipe from between his teeth.

"Hey! I nearly had it too."

"Sim, I'm talkin' 'bout our lives. Don't you understand, with Jimmy deed, we got to think of a way out of this, without ending up *like* Jimmy." Jed did not want his brother to discover the true terror that gripped him. "We should 'a' left her on that island. Somebody would 'a' found her. We'd 'a' had a head start fer Canada, then made it west, to

'Fornia. Out west, thas where people like us b'long. Wish I'd 'a' thought of leaving her on that island. Too late now. Sim, las' night, after that girlie girl fell asleep, I thought about the island. Got mad at myself. I tried to strangle her."

"Jed!"

"Oh, now quiet. I didn't. I couldn't." But they could kill me, and you. Both of us in cold blood. Easy! Don't y' see what a terrible mess we're in? If we let her go, they'll kill us. If we kill her, they'll kill us. And it's this damned country's fault. Until we can figure out a way to stay alive, we got to hold on to her. Damn Jimmy, him deed and no worries. Wish I never got involved with him. Was never like this with Joe."

"You mean, *Injun* Joe?"

"Who else 'd I be talking about? We know any other Joe's? Joe could murder anybody 'thout blinking an eye. He done it enough times. Course, he got himself deed too. Well, like I say, we got to keep her. Not always. Jus' 'til we can think of something that'd save us.

"If we could write an apology note, maybe they'd go easy on us."

"Sim, it don't make any difference. They'd kill us in cold blood even if we got down on our knees and begged for mercy. Well, we can't neither of us write anyhow, so it don't matter."

"Well, I can, some."

"You!"

"Remember, when we was little. Them missionaries tried learnin' us."

"I remember they tried convertin' us. I didn't want no part of that. Tried to turn us into something we never could be. Something society never would let us be. Damn missionaries, they never k'yered 'bout learnin' us. Jus' thought that by tryin' to, they'd git some kind of a reward after they died. That's all they k'yered about. Didn't they come out 'a' the same society that condemns us for what we are? You never heard the awful names those damned missionaries called us. I did. Hypocrites!"

"I can write some. I can write my name, and yours. And—I'm sorry."

"What! Apologize for doing somethin' society made us do, forced us into doing? It's this damned country's fault that girl got kidnapped. I ain't apologizing for that. I don't know what to do."

"Then I will, if you got a pen on you."

"I don't carry round sech truck. We ain't writin' no 'pology. Well, it wouldn't do us no good anyhow. Don't neither of us remember where that judge lives. 'Twas dark, and I weren't lookin'. Were you?"

"No. I don't r'call either. We could ask somebody."

"If you think I'm goin' up to one 'a' these here town folk and ask where the judge lives, knowing once we release the girl, and the whole damnable kidnapping comes out, *and* knowing that resident is gonna remember me, and have my likeness drawed on a poster, and hung all over the western territories, and all over these U-nited States, so I can't never find a place to hide nor sleep nor settle down fer jus' a few minutes—yer a jackass! I ain't gonna do it."

"Jed. What do you think it is that unites these states?"

"What? Sim, don't ask nonsense questions. Listen t' what I say."

"'Twas only a question. Maybe an ignorant one. I reckon they 'd know the answer to that in what they call Washington. They know jus' everything down there. Thas what the missionaries say."

"Oh, damn the missionaries!"

"What about the li'l girl?"

"Damn her too."

"No, I mean—ask her where it is she lives."

"The hell with it! If she finds out we don't know where she lives, it's jus' like her findin' out Jimmy's deed, and that we cain't read nor write, and that there ain't no ransom note. Sim, I don't trust her kind. You know I don't. Damn white-skins. Damn missionaries. Damn Jimmy. Jimmy! Well, it's all Jimmy fault anyhow. And him deed and no worries."

"Well, who killed Jimmy?"

"Never mind. Jimmy killed hisself. It's his own fault. Well, we ain't nowhere. I wanna go down to the ferry landing and see can I get some whiskey. I ain't had a drink in two, three days. You comin' with?"

"No. I wanna go back to the cellar."

"Good. It'll keep you out of trouble."

"Give back my pipe though, so I can practice."

"Practice what?"

"The creation."

"I don't even know what that means, and I don't k'yer. Why you got t' smoke this damnable thing I don't know. As fer me, I *hate* 'em! Well, maybe I'll have an idea once I get some liquor in me. I can't think sober. I'll got to go and steal something to git it. Damn people. Won't jus' give it to me. Well, it's their own damn faults I got to go steal what anybody else 'd git fer free. Any *white*-skin, anyhow."

Back in the cellar, Becky crawled into the secret passage.

"Should I?" Becky pondered. "I must occupy myself, but—. What if I find treasure, and Tom is not here with me?" Becky crawled in and out of the passage several times, unsure whether she should progress. Joan of Arc persuaded her otherwise. *You must remain strong, Becky. Dig out the dirt.* "If I do nothing, I'll surely go insane. I'll, I'll—. Oh, alright Joan, I'll dig." Though the ball and chain tugged at her leg uncomfortably, Becky gritted her teeth, refusing to quit, refusing to succumb to insanity. "It hurts at times. But I must. I must. Oh, I must find a place to put all this dirt. Drat! Hadn't thought of that. What'll I do, Joan? No. No, I mustn't disturb her always. I, well, I could spread it out on the ground. Would they notice? Or care? Will I be here long enough for the dirt to pile high?"

Even before Becky could answer one of the questions, she scooped up a handful of dirt from within the passage and laboriously hauled it over to the farthest corner of the room. Dropping it, she spread it evenly out with her unchained leg. She repeated this numerously, each time moving away from the corner, so that the dirt did not pile up.

While inside the passage, Becky thought she heard the deep groaning of the cellar door swing open. Quickly, the handful of dirt Becky held smacked onto the passage floor. Slowly, Becky maneuvered her chained leg out, paying no attention to the clasp's edging that "bit" against her ankle. It felt like a saw, methodically rubbing into that part of her anatomy, amputating it. No blood drew, however. Becky would live with the pain. "I must," she convinced herself. Stacking the boxes became difficult now. Having used most of her energy already, the six boxes she desperately needed to replace seemed heavier than she recalled.

"There!" Becky, exhausted, slumped down against those six boxes and waited. The footsteps belonged to Sim. "He'll never suspect a thing."

"What you been up to li'l girl? You look 'bout ready for the grave."

"What do you expect? I have to walk around with *this* around my ankle. Ain't easy you know. Did you bring food? Water?"

"No."

Becky did not expect he would. "Don't you reckon I might get hungry? Don't you know I need food and water to survive?"

"Well, I, Jed takes k'yer of it mostly."

"And where is he?"

"Lookin' fer whiskey. He might bring—. Did you light the lantern?"

"I thought we were talking about food."

"I know. But this's important. Did you turn on the lantern?"

"Of course not. What kind of—,"

"No? Oh. It must 'a' been me that left it on." Sim began to worry. "If Jed came down here and saw it on—. You won't tell Jed? Please don't tell him I left it on. 'Twas only a mistake."

"You mean you left it on accidental? You'd 'a' left me in the dark?"

"Well, sure. Jed wants to save matches."

"Don't you know that's dangerous?" Becky angered. "You can't leave me in the pitch of dark. Don't you know what happens to people?"

"No. What?"

"They go blind."

Sim sat down. "Really," he asked, child-like.

"It happens when one is left in the dark too long. There was a girl once, who wanted to explore inside a cave, alone. She refused the lantern and candles they gave her, 'cause she thought she could do without them. She believed she could see better'n anyone in town, which was true, but *oh*—was she high on herself. She thought she could actually see in the dark.'

"Packing food and water for a week, she entered, determined to prove herself. Well, after *two* weeks she hadn't come out, so they sent a scouting party after her. Do you know what they found?"

"Oh, please don't say a ghost. You won't, will you?"

"No. No, not a ghost. They found *her*. Just coming out of the cave, crawling on the ground on all fours, groping the walls. She heard footsteps and exclaimed, 'Oh, if somebody's there, mightn't you help me out of the cave, where the sunlight is? I want so much to see again.'"

"Did they?"

"Well, don't you understand? She was coming out, *into* the sunlight. But she didn't know that. Turns out she'd gone blind. 'Twas later found out, on careful inspection of the cave, she hadn't traveled twenty feet inside, but had turned a bend where there was a large room, and she walked around it in circles. Poor girl, lost sight of where she was from the very start. She took the news hard. Never was the same. So you see how dangerous it is, keeping me here in pitch dark? I don't want what happened to her to happen to me. I'd like to keep my sight a while longer."

Sim scratched his head. "Wanna watch me create?"

"What!" Becky's voice boomed loudly.

"Create. On my pipe. You liked it b'fore."

"Didn't you hear what I said?"

"Yes. Makes sense too." Sim lit his pipe and began "creating". "I'm gonna see can I hunt up that boy tomorra. Hope I can find—. Hey! Did you see that? Pert near got it now."

"Unbelievable. He never hears a word. Nincompoop! That's all—,"

"Don't you wanna watch?" Sim shook Becky's shoulder's, jealous her interests lay in other affairs besides paying attention to him, and concerned her eyes were not as focused upon the "creation" as his.

"What! Oh, you startled me."

"'Twas the only way I could git yer attention."

"Why?"

"Why! Don't you wanna watch anymore? You was awful curious b'fore, the first time you saw it."

"Where's Jimmy? Why hasn't he returned with word from my pa?"

"J-Jimmy? Oh, why he's—. Well, Jed 'd know. You ask him."

'I don't want to ask him. I don't like talking to him. You tell me."

"I, I cain't. Please don't make me." Sim nervously twiddled his pipe, trying to "create". "Now see, I cain't do it no more. What'll I tell him, if I see him? He might be disappointed."

"Him who?" Becky's frustration became evident, but only to her.

"Well only the boy. That showed me the creation."

"Oh. Yeah." Sim returned to "creating". As he did, Becky, her agitation waning, her mind refocusing, finally realized what Sim tried so hard to create. "Of course! Well why couldn't I-? I'm so physically exhausted is why. And hungry. I call him a nincompoop. What does that make me? It's Tom. It can't be any but him. Somehow he met up with Tom. Poor, poor Tom. He didn't even realize who he was talking to. Poor me, as well, I suppose. Wait! If he sees Tom again—. If he sees him, oh, Tom has got to know who he is somehow. I must, oh—." Becky's head spun as she tried thinking up ways to let Tom know about Sim. "A message! N—. Oh, but how? It mightn't *be* Tom after-all." An inspiration formed.

"Hey!" Sim shouted in delight. "I got it that time. Did you see?"

This time, Becky ignored Sim's question. "If you see the boy tomorrow, tell him there's another person who think's it gay."

"He'll like that. Who?"

"Why *me* of course. In fact, I think it's pulchritudinous."

Sim nearly dropped his pipe. "What in tarnation is that!"

"Pulchritudinous? Means beautiful."

"An awful big word. Lot's o' letters."

"A fancy word used by dignitaries and senators and presidents and such. My pa learned me the word. Say, I've an idea. S'pose you find this boy. Well, tell him this creation is pulchritudinous. I bet he'd be taken back. Might even envy you."

"Never had anyone envy me b'fore. Spit on me a few times, but never envy me. That'd be real good times. But wouldn't he be curious to know jus' where a fella like, well, like me, learnt sech a word? He'd never b'lieve I came up with it on my own. *He*'d take me fer a liar, then he'd want nothin' ever to do with me agin. Well, bein' envied was nice while it lasted."

Tell him, tell him you learned it off your sister."

"I hasn't got no sister."

"He doesn't have to know that."

"I dunno. Might see through it. He seems intelligent. He might ask her name. All about her. Then where am I? I'd be there fer days sweatin' to come up with a name."

"Tell him your sister's name is, is *Becky*."

"Where'd you ever come up with a name like that, so fast?"

"It's a name I've always cherished, and been very fond of. You tell him your sister's name is Becky. You can even use me to describe her, if he asks. That way, you won't have to sit all those days, sweatin'."

Hey, thas smart. Down right pulch-right-too-dinnus. Is that it?"

"Close enough. You practice on that word, like you do your pipe, and you'll sound it out right in no time."

"I'll do it!"

With that accomplished, while Sim busied himself, Becky "borrowed one candle and one match. "If I am to see the light again, it must be on my own power." Hunched up against the boxes, her stomach squealed with a familiar hunger. Becky rubbed it, as she had a year ago while trapped inside the cave with Tom. "You never knew the pain I endured Tom, while you stowed away looking, looking, looking. Always looking for a way out. I am almost glad I suffered then. For, now I am experienced. It is almost comforting." Her stomach barked madly. "There. Hold on. Soon. It will be soon. I promise you. We've survived this once. We will again."

For hours Becky lingered in and out of sleep. Each time she woke, the intensity of her hunger dramatically enhanced. Each time, she rubbed her stomach, coddled it, babied it, lied to it. She shook once that night, in her sleep. She never knew she had.

Awake now, knowing she had slept, but not knowing for how long, Becky listened for sounds, anything to indicate Jed and Sim's presence. She heard only those noises created by her own body.

"Hey!" Becky called out. Softly at first, but her successive calls grew in pitch and tone, along with her courage. "They're gone. Of course they are. They would have told me to shut up otherwise." Feeling around for the one candle and one match she hid behind the boxes before falling asleep, her fingers stumbled across the inseparable two. "Do I?" She did not hesitate. Why should she? "I do." Just as Becky thought. "Alone."

Weakened by hunger, Becky dragged herself over to the lantern and lit it. She then extinguished her own candle, saving this precious bit of wax for future use. Something to eat, anything really, at this stage, would have delighted Becky. She looked, but found nothing humanly edible.

"No food. No water." *Be strong, Becky. Make me proud of you.* "Joan! Is that you? Where are you?" *Inside the passage. Behind the dirt. I have food. And water too. A whole stream filled with cool, clear, fresh water. All for you, Becky. All for you.*

Becky entered the passage, clumsily stumbling over her latrine. Debris tumbled all over her legs. Frenziedly, she scooped up what she could, and threw it back into the box.

"Damn them!" Becky swore, without realizing. "No food or water. No place to relieve my bladder and bowels. How did you do it, Joan? What did they give you? Ain't like in the books. People in books never have to relieve themselves. Not even prisoners. Some of *them* spend years chained to the same wall. Look at Princess D'Laney. Wasn't she chained to a wall for years by her evil sister who wanted the throne to herself? Wonder how she made out without ever having to relieve *her* bladder. Or bowels. Well, nobody ever bothered to feed her, so that must be part of the reason. Isn't but one book I can think of. Gulliver's Travels. Yes! When I squat over this box, and relieve my bowels, I will think of that book. My bladder? If only I could relieve my bladder as I used to. Thirst. How thirsty I am. I must work up a sweat. That's all I'll get. Well—."

Becky again thought about taking drastic measures. For now, however, she was not convinced. "Mrs. Sherry never had to. But, I was good to her. Oh, I won't argue. I won't argue. No, I won't do it. What good does it do me? Whatever it takes to survive. Right? Oh, I do hope he finds Tom. Tom, Tom, what are you doing without me? What *is* Tom doing without me?"

If only Tom could have heard her plea. He may know where to look for her. It never occurred to the boy, having already searched the Stantan Home twice, to search it a third time. In fact, he forced himself not to go there again. Painful the first time, and even more painful the second, a third time might kill him, he believed. Combing the town once again, per his daily routine, Tom, horribly sickened, and ashamed at himself for not recognizing the man who begged him to create *Together Forever* sooner, he hungered for a delicious reprisal with him.

Tom, amazed at the amount of men still lining the Mississippi in search of Miss Watson's Jim, from far north and south, and on anything that could float, attempted to listen in on the closest groups as they talked. He took a keen interest in two conversing groups. Not so much for the coarseness of their language, or the indelicacy of their stories, but rather for the rumors they echoed. Rumors Miss Watson's Jim had help. Another slave? Or worse? Tom had not time to absorb who the "worse" person might be. Ideas floated, swifter than any of the unmanned rafts and other debris on the Mississippi. And like this debris, these ideas swirled chaotically.

"Whatcha up to?" Tom whirled. A man, standing two feet away, a pipe nestled in-between his teeth, blew smoke out of the bowl. He and Tom watched it rise and curl in the air. "Some might call that beautiful. Not me. Says I, thas pulch-rit-tudinnus."

Tom's eyes widened. "What did you say?"

Sim lowered his head. "Y' mean, pulch-rit-tudinnus?"

"Where did you hear that word?"

"You kind'r envy me, don't you?"

"I, alright. Yes. Only, tell me where you learned the word."

"My sister."

"Sister?" A hazy dizziness filtered through Tom's head.

"And was she excited. More than me."

"More than you?" Tom felt lightheaded.

"You should 'a' seen her eyes. They was tears in 'em. Thas when she said the creation was pulch-rit-tuddinus. And asked me to tell you so."

"She asked you? She *wanted* me to know?"

"Uh-huh."

An idea formed. Tom removed Becky's pipe from his vest pocket. "Would she maybe like to have this? It belonged to *my* sister, up 'til she died. She made me promise to hold onto it, wait 'til the right person came along who could best take of it. I think my sister would want your sister to have it. You'll take it, won't you?"

Sim stared long at the pipe, daring to touch it. But every time he struck out his hand, he pulled it back into his own body.

"I ca-cain't seem t' tech it. You sure yer sister won't mind?"

"Mind! Course not. It ain't gonna hurt you. Look. It's just a pipe. Same as yours and mine." Tom turned the pipe to one side, then the other, showing Sim it consisted of nothing out of the ordinary. Turning it upside down, Sim noticed writing on the under-side of the bowl.

"Ain't them letters?"

"Letters?" Tom looked too, forgetting he had carved Becky's name there the day he made it. "I, yes," Tom sullenly acknowledged.

"Lemme see." Sim no longer feared the pipe. This time, he reverently placed his hands upon it. "B-Bec-Beck-y-y. Becky!"

"It's my sister's name," Tom blurted out, afraid Sim might become wise, and realize both Tom's "dead sister" and Sim's "sister" were one in the same. "Now you'll give it to your sister? Of course you will. It'd mean an awful lot to mine. And it's sure to bring both our sister's closer together. Maybe even—together forever."

Sim studied hard on something. "Seems your sister, and my sister, has got something in common. But I cain't remember what."

"Well, it'll come to you. You'll give her the pipe?"

"Who?"

"Your *sister*!"

"Oh." Sim's knees quaked. "Oh, sure." He respectfully transferred Becky's pipe from his hands to his vest pocket.

"Good." Sim stood to his knees. "Tell her something for me, about the pipe." Finding no comfort, Sim started walking away. "It's most important!" Tom called after him, following the man. Sim's speed picked up. "Tell her it's hers always. She'll be with my sister—together forever. Together forever!" Tom followed Sim into town, from one building to another, without letting the man see him. Tom waited, as Sim slunk into one building. Tom would not see him exit. His cousin, Mary, who had been all over town looking for Tom, spotted him, and carted him off home, under heavy protest. Had it been Sid, Tom would be there yet. But he could not win with Mary, and Aunt Polly knew that well.

CHAPTER 24

That night, though Becky did not know night had come, she worked furiously within the passage to remove dirt and spread it as evenly and as clandestinely as she could. Jed and Sim stayed out longer than usual; and she, always suspicious as to their return, wondered if maybe this time they had left her there for good.

Fatigue wormed its way into her. Becky, weakened from over exertion, and starving both from lack of food and oxygen, and near the point of becoming disillusioned, had momentary fits of crying.

"What *has* become of you, Tom? You know where I am by now. You know I'm here. You—. Well, he found you, didn't he? He told you. Pulchritudinous. Pulchritudinous! The word. He told you, Tom. It must 'a' sparked your curiosity. You asked him questions. You tricked him somehow, to find out my location. You played him good. Tom! Tom! Where are you! Where, w-where, o-oh, oh, no, no, n-not again. Why, oh, w-why d-does it happen? Hold o-on Becky. H-hold yourself t-tightly. It'll stop. S-stop. S-stop." Becky collapsed against the pile of dirt. She remained there, lying in a fetal position, talking to herself, to Joan of Arc, to Mrs. Sherry, for a long time.

Jed and Sim, meanwhile, were down near the ferry landing. A parade of rafts skipped calmly over the Mississippi; their lanterns and torches

lighting the night, reflecting the greatness, the awe-inspiring and mysterious beauty of the river under the watchful protection of the moon.

"Sim, it is too him. Look. Look at his face." Jed pointed to a large man
standing upon one of the rafts. "Remember that day we was with Injun
Joe, and robbed that bank. Well, he was there. Maybe you didn't git a
good look that day. Maybe thas why you don't recognize him hardly. But
I did. Them shots, remember 'em? They near hit me. I heard one jus'
above my ear, and thas when I flinched my head back. Thas when I saw
him. I ain't never forgot that face. And I'm tellin' you, Sim, thas him."

"Well, what'll we do then? It's night now. But s'pose when day come,
and we be walkin' down the street, and all a-sudden he pops out b'hind
a corner, like he done two year ago? We ain't got Joe with us this time.
We ain't got but us. You and I. Me and you. Jus' the two—,"

"Alright! I swore two year ago I'd kill 'im if ever I saw his face agin."

"But that warn't said but in anger and haste."

"No. 'Tweren't. Sim, if that shot 'd hit me, and flung me off my horse,
I'd 'a' been hung deed, sure."

"No! No, I'd 'a' pulled you up on my horse, and we three would 'a' got
away. You, me, and Joe."

"Joe! You think Joe would wait? If you had stopped to pull me up,
you'd 'a' been caught too. And hung."

"Well I don't k'yer. I wouldn't 'a' left without you. I druther 'd be
hung with you, than live without you. I never been away from you
hardly a moment since, since we ran away from them missionaries
together. We was young, but we had each other. I don't know no other
life."

"Neither do I," Jed whispered.

"What?"

"Nothing. Nothing. Sim, it ain't no use. I'm gonna give it two, maybe
three days more with the girl. Don't anybody know who we are. And
don't nobody know the girl's been kidnapped. Thas the one smart thing
Jimmy did, was tellin' her family to keep mum. And thas all we got goin'

for us. If I cain't think of a way to git shed of her, 'thout gettin' us both shot deed in cold blood, well, we'll leave this town for good."

"Y' mean it! Oh, Jed, say you do. Say it's so."

"It's so. But—,"

"But, what?"

"We'll leave her. Down in the cellar. 'Thout takin' off the ball and chain. Jus' leave her and be done—,"

"Jed, you cain't."

"Now Sim, it's got to be that way."

"No it don't. We'll, she'll—,"

"She'll be fine. And what's more, *we*'ll be free, finally."

"No we won't. Either she'll die, or she'll bust free somehow and git help. Then they'll be after us. They'll be mean. Ornery mean. If we was to *let* her go, and leave her with a 'pology note—,"

"No! I ain't apologizing for what's this country's fault. What's Jimmy's fault. What's them damned missionaries fault. I ain't apologizing. Jimmy couldn't 'a' got hisself killed at a *worse* time."

"Well, how's she s'posed to survive down there? If she cain't git free now, what's to say she can when we're gone?"

"I don't—. It don't matter. If she dies it's her fault."

"*Oh*, Jed."

"You know what she said to me t'other night? Said she couldn't wait to be shed of the likes of me. Likes of me! Thas a slur. That little girl slurred me, Sim. Bad enough older people do it; bad enough them missionaries did it. Bad enough ever'body does it. Likes of me! But, but a little girl, well, well, thas the worst, I think."

"You cried, didn't you?"

"Course not. What kind o' a fool question is that? I don't never cry. Ain't healthy. Them damned missionaries beat me every time I cried. Remember? Remember how they took the stick to me? Oh, they'd 'a' done it anyhow. 'Cause they didn't never k'yer 'bout savin' nobody nohow. Jus' liked the power they had over people. Jus' liked to believe they was doing what they needed to git that damned reward they is alwus saying everyone is entitled to. White folk! Don't nobody but white folk git the reward. We's half white, ain't we? Where's that put us, when we's deed?"

"Jed. How come you didn't never learn to read nor write, but gave it up only after a few weeks?"

"What! What, Sim! Here I am talkin' 'bout the girl slurrin' me, and how we's gonna git out 'a' this thing alive, and what do you ask me? Yer alwus doin' that, Sim. Yer alwus off somewhere y' ain't s'posed to be. I'm talkin' 'bout one thing, and you bring up something entirely different. Why!"

"I, well—. Oh, Jed. I dunno. I wisht I did. But you got to talkin' 'bout the missionaries. I saw 'em in my mind. Plain as if we was there now, in that camp. 'Twas so real, I could 'a' reached out and teched 'em with my hands. You never told me why you gave up readin' and writin'. I was only curious is all. Jus' curious."

"That damned man out there on the raft could spot us any moment, and you wanna know *why* I gave up readin' and writin'. If you don't know b' now, then yer a harder lot than I thought."

"Tell me," Sim pleaded. "I jus' got to know now."

"Oh. Listen, if I tell you, will you stop pesterin' me 'bout it? I mean, never agin ask me? You swear?"

"I *do*, Jed. And you know I alwus keep my promises."

"Ye—. Sim, I didn't never want to tell you. You remember that. You remember it was *you* begged me to tell you. It's yer own fault if you don't like what you hear. Sim, I didn't give it up 'cause I wanted to. Was forced. They stopped me. Them damned missionaries. And they stopped you too. Only I lied to you then, to spare you, you see. They didn't want us gettin' smart. Them missionaries *wanted* to keep us dumb."

"You never told me that."

"I know that. I jus' got through tellin' you th—. Look, 'twas a lot I never told you. 'Twas to spare you, 'cause I knew you was diff'ent. Thas the reason yer the way y' are today I reckon. Be glad you are. Ignorant of the world. Be glad yer not wise to it, like me. The only right thing them damned missionaries taught us was that ignorance is bliss. It ain't no fun livin' in a world, when you know the truth. Why do you think I hate pipes? Everything 'bout 'em."

"You never said. I been askin' fer years, but you alwus tell me to hesh. So, I hesh fer a while, 'til I git curious agin."

"Well, it's b'cause it reminds me too much of what I am, and of what I ain't. Them damned missionaries learnt me *that*, while they beat me."

"But, Jed, that—,"

"Well, looks like them rafts is thinning out."

"But, the pipe."

"I don't wanna talk 'bout it no more. *Please*, Sim. Jus' let it be."

Sim never before heard his brother beg to anyone, let alone him.

"Alright, Jed. I, I didn't mean to make you mad."

"Oh, oh, you didn't, hardly. You didn't know any better. Well, I hear tell the hunt for the nigger is about gived up. Least, in these parts. Maybe that fella 'll leave. Then we'll be safe a while longer. Hope so. Don't know how much longer the girl's parents can hold out, with no ransom note."

"They must be 'bout ready to tell everyone their li'l girl's been taken. We got to be long gone by then."

"Thas what has got me worried. We never had no grudge agin that judge. Jimmy did. He got us into this. And it's him who'll git us killed. C'mon, Sim. Let's go." Jed jumped to his feet. "Y' see? He's pulled away from the other rafts. Comin' back up on shore. I don't wanna bump into him, yet. You go back to the cellar. I, I, well, I got things to do. Look around town, y' know. Make sure things are still safe fer us."

Jed and Sim hurried off before the man they so feared had both his feet on dry land. This man, in an obvious rush, leaped off the raft, which lazily drifted in towards shore, three feet away. Another man, who waited the extra three feet, moved his legged doubly quick to catch up.

"Cy! Cy! Don't walk so fast. You know I can't keep up."

"You have nothing more to say to me. You've made your decision. You know what I do to people, Cal. You know what I do when I am crossed."

"I—. Wait! Perhaps I, I spoke ha-hastily. I'm tired is all. Haven't slept in two days. My head's not clear. I can be reasonable now, now that I've thought the matter over."

Cy halted. "You'll find me one then?"

"Well, I—."

Cy resumed his fast paced walk. "Your hesitation will be your undoing."

"No! Stop. You didn't let me finish."

"Again, Cy stopped. "Pray you are not wasting my time. Pray you don't make me stop once more. I will finish this discussion right here, you understand. Now. Will you bring me what I desire?"

"I—. Y-yes. But give me a few days. You have to give me at least that much time," Cal begged. "I have to pick just the right one. Just the right one, that nobody will care about. That nobody will miss, o-once it's over."

Slowly, Cy's fingers twisted into fists, cracking under immense pressure from his knuckles.

"Nobody will care, regardless of the one you pick, you understand. Two days. No more. bring it to your office. Don't make me come find you. I am not in high spirits now, you understand. You've seen me show my anger. You've seen me take my anger out on people." Cy placed a hand upon Cal's shoulder, and squeezed. The pressure sent a shivering sting all over Cal's body, paralyzing him. "You are in terrible pain, I know. And until I release you from this grip your suffering will only increase. Your reflexes have been rendered useless. Even after I remove my hand, you will be sore for some time. Take heed. Pray you do not disappoint me. For what I will do to you, you will only wish is as equal in pain to this grip. But it won't be a damn sight near it! Now go. Find me what I desire."

Cal placed his own hand on the hurt shoulder, rubbing the area Cy had damaged, as he limped off into the night wondering how he made it out alive, and wondering how he could maintain this state of being.

"Two days!" Cal muttered, breathlessly, all the way back to his office. "I don't see how I can manage it." He heard the incessant voices of his father and grandfather calling him a coward, calling him a traitor, and un-American. "It ain't so!" he howled back.

Cy returned home with a bitter conscience. Standing but a few feet from the door, he prepared himself for who lay on the other side.

"It's always difficult. Damn her for making it so. Why this magnetic compulsion to return I *don't* understand. How often I contemplate, how often I pray she had kept that truth to herself. If she loved me, if she respected me, if she had but an ounce of integrity, she would have committed that lie to herself, and only herself. How it burdens me. How it crushes me. Oh! Blasted!" Cy, shaking his head disgustedly, threw open the door. His eyes immediately met Judith's, who sat, rocking, in her chair.

Judith, startled for the moment, then realizing it was Cy, apathetically rose to her feet. Without the love and compassion that for all this time had burned within her, she coldly, but sadly, moved her eyes abstractedly up and down her husband of more than twenty years. Cy's eyes told her the time they have left together was very short.

"Back?"

Cy walked around the room before answering. His eyes intentionally roamed every square inch of the room, except the space which Judith stood.

"You've had some company, recently? That woman?"

Talking just above a whisper, Judith, faintly hostile, replied, "Polly? No. That is, I've seen her. But I've been to her place."

"Somebody else has been here. I see two chairs pulled out from the table, positioned so that each occupant would face one another. Another man?"

"Oh. Oh, no." Judith moved around in small circles. "Nothing but a boy. Lost. Hungry. He came the night you was out on Jackson's Island. Seems like an eternity ago, now. We talked, then he left. Has an uncle lives up in Goshen. Some drunk told him this was Goshen. I set him straight. I, I wondered when you'd, when you'd next show—,"

"Judith," Cy painfully groaned. "No, no more." He pointed a finger, which shook on its own power. "I don't know why I've let it go on this long. You have no idea how I've suffered these years. You don't know what you have done to me. You had no right to keep me here. To keep me coming back here. You've been so unfair, not allowing me to leave."

"Me!" Her blood, frozen for years, melted, and boiled. "You think I could keep you here? You think I didn't know, all these years, how you felt? The moment after I told you the truth about me, the very moment, and not a second more, I knew. I knew, 'cause I saw it in your eyes. And it's been there ever since."

"You knew who I was before we married. You knew how I felt."

"Yes. I wrongly thought I could change you. I wrongly thought our love was stronger. It took ten years to tell you. Ten years to realize the truth. During those ten years I silently suffered with who I really was, and who you really were. The night I told you, remember it? I had more than one reason to tell you *that* night. Well—." Judith, having taxed herself beyond any limit she had ever gone before, weakly dropped back into her chair. Gravely, she said, "By then, it was too late to do anything about it. Oh, how I loved you. What *I've* done to you, *indeed.* I've lived my life for you, twenty years. Now, now it's time I lived it for myself. My only regret is that I didn't come to my senses years ago. Well, that's past. I've my future to think about. Won't be a lonely one. But—it'll be absent *you*."

Cy, pacing furiously, had long and painstakingly waited for this moment. Shock, instead, overcame him. A drying throat, a tormenting swallow, a sobering hangover—it all crept up on him at once.

"Ju—."

"Well, go long with ye," Judith said softly, staring at the floor. "Ain't nothing holding you here. Don't know whatever held you here in the past, but—. Well, go long."

Cy would not look at his wife. He sincerely wanted to, more so than ever before. But with his eyes pulsating, throbbing, and pasted to the floor, even he could not find the strength to lift them those few inches upwards. Weakened and vulnerable, and despising himself, Cy thumped his way to the door. The last remembrance of Judith would be her heavy breathing.

After slamming the door behind him, Cy kept his hand lodged over the knob, and for ten minutes stood there. It took the power from his other hand to remove all five fingers, which had welded and fused themselves to the knob. A chill fluttered in the night air, and Cy felt it. He walked carelessly to and fro, all over town. When he looked up, he found himself standing one hundred years in front of the Stantan Home. He had no idea how he came to be there, but a slight inclination told him why. No emotion poured from him; no sign of life. Yet, he subconsciously knew the reason he had strolled forth upon the old mansion, and what the meaning of his visit here evoked. He removed a cigar and proceeded to smoke it. Three quarters of an hour later, the cigar, half an inch long, extinguished on its own. Cy flicked it forward, towards the mansion. Whatever demons he struggled with during these forty-five minutes were exorcized. Cy left them to the mansion's supervision.

CHAPTER 25

Of course the Stantan Home contained no demons. Only Becky, who, for hours, lay up against the boxes, too weak to continue in the passage, too weak to care about removing the dirt and finding treasure, too weak to do anything.

"Oh, pa," Becky moaned. "Oh, ma. How I wish I was at home with you both right now. I don't even mind the whippings. I'd rather be home right now getting whipped, than here. Maybe she is glad to be rid of me. Maybe I was too much of a nuisance to her. I don't wonder if maybe she is not remorseful. Oh—it must be something of a relief to have me gone, and out of the way. What they must be doing. What they must be thinking? Ma. Ma—if I ever get out of this alive, I'll make a better effort. I promise I will." Becky quieted. "No. This is not helping me. I'm not remaining strong. I've got to keep a—." Footsteps shuffled down the stairs. She sat up, a little; then, exhausted, leaned back into the boxes. "Why don't they either feed me, or put me out my misery." Becky moved her eyes upward to see which one had come down, albeit even that caused her great difficulty. "Oh, it's you," she said of Sim.

"Tired? You look it." Sim removed the water canteen from around his shoulder and proceeded to unknowingly taunt Becky with it. "Ah," he sighed, after he had his fill. "Don't take much, but I warn't very thirsty anyhow."

Becky stiffly lifted her arm. "Please. You might give *me* some water."

"You want some? Well, I don't see the harm." Sim placed the canteen in Becky's hands. She drank down the remaining water before Sim could protest.

"More. Please, more water."

"What? You drank it all? 'Twas near full."

"What do you expect? Leave me down here, without anything to drink. Do you have any idea how hungry I am? I'm starving. When did you think you'd get around to feeding me again? I ain't ate in, well, how am I to know, when I don't even have a window to look out of. Can't you see your way to finding me something, anything, to eat? I'd eat that fish again, I'm so hungry."

"I didn't think—,"

"Darn right you didn't. Where's your brother? *He* out getting food?"

"Jed? Oh, he, well, he had things to do, he said. But I know him better. He don't like comin' around here much, anymore. He's afraid."

"Afraid? Of what? Ghosts?"

"Y-yes. Well, no. Well, he has got his own ghosts hauntin' him. He don't show it much, but he's feelin' mighty guilty these days, I know it."

"He *ought* to be feeling guilty, keeping me here, chained like this, starving, dying of thirst, just plain *dying*. He's a bad one, your brother."

"No! No, it ain't that way. Please don't you say nothing agin him. Please say you won't. He's guilty enough. Course, he don't never tell me—."

"Do you think you could see your way clear to getting me something to eat? If I die—,"

"Die!" Sim's voice echoed. "Oh, you ain't gonna *d-die*? Are you?" It never occurred to Sim she might die. And Jimmy's death haunted him still.

"Don't you think I *might*, if I don't eat? Can't you see how weak I am?"

"Weak? Oh, I, I only thought you was tired."

"Well I am, tired. Starvation does that, or don't you know?"

"Y—. Well, I reckon when me and Jed was with the missionaries they ate high on the hog, 'thout giving us much. Not even the bone, at times. You're really starving?" Sim tried to approach her, but couldn't.

"Yes!" Becky nearly cried.

"Oh." Sim quivered. In his mind it was not so much his fear of Becky dying of starvation that bothered him; but rather that if she did die, he would realize it to be his fault, and fear she might haunt him for the rest of his life. That fear, above all else, prompted him to dash out of the cellar and find food before it was too late.

As Sim was leaving—scurrying frantically as it were, and bumping into the walls, Becky shouted, "Water! Don't forget water!" She heard the thumps as his feet pounded against the stairs, then the hideous squeal from the door. "Don't, don't for-forget the w-water."

A long time passed. It *seemed* to be a long time. When there is no way to know how much time has elapsed, one always imagines the disappearance of a great and vast length of time. The canteen of water Becky drank in one sitting worked its way through her.

"Oh," Becky moaned. "Almost wish I hadn't drank it. No. No, don't say that. No matter your weakness now, Becky, the water has given you some of your strength back. As she entered the passage, she heard Joan of Arc talked to her.

Becky. Becky, I know you can hear me. Becky? Listen to me. You're not so bad off. I suffered worse, you recall. You must remain strong. I know it is hard for you. I know what you are enduring. Everything you are going through now, I have gone through. I remained strong 'til the end. It wasn't easy. And at times I even broke down. But I conquered. I overcame. Even when the flames were upon me; even when I felt my skin dripping off my body, I knew, I knew victory was mine. Persevere! Becky, persevere. It's never easy. It's never like in a book. It takes courage. Real courage. You have it within you. I know you do. I know you do.

With her bladder relieved, Becky stood, staring into the immense pile of dirt. The lantern gently swung overhead. A strange feeling seized her;

a warm numbing, all over her body. She forgot her way out of the passage. Fear, too, whispered close by. A sudden, and urgent, need to vacate now escalated into a full scale emergency, as she could feel the dirt walls pressing up against her on either side. But her senses were backwards. Becky believed the only way out to be through the dirt. She even turned around. But with the lantern shining towards the dirt, Becky saw only the fierce, pitch darkness. In her mixed up, skewed, evaporating mind, the way out must be through the dirt. One horrifying option presented itself.

The event which occurred next struck Becky with lightning speed. Setting the lantern down, the girl stepped towards the pile of dirt as one would, without the least bit of fright, step up upon the gallows. Minutes, tens of minutes, *hours*—what did time matter to her now! Unbeknown to her, dirt began flying in every direction, raging wildly passed her body, some just behind her feet, a great quantity more outside the passage, as her anger worked itself into a frenzy. Becky bent her body into the dirt, and like a dog, shoveled it in-between her legs. The harder she worked herself, and the faster her movements, the more hostile were her fits of unconscious outrage.

"I love you Mrs Sherry!" Becky shouted several times. This once best and only friend of Becky's, in her earlier youth, provided the only comfort, the only joy, the only happiness she had then known.

Minutes, tens of minutes, *hours*—Becky took a comatose view of time. The oxygen levels withered, while the lantern silently laughed. Difficulties in breathing arose. So too did Becky's temper, now desperate and hysterical and distraught, and wanting with incredible favor to explode.

"I took good care of you, didn't I, Mrs Sherry! I fed you! Every day! I gave you water! I cleaned all your messes in the house! Mama never found out about them! I never complained! I loved you! Didn't you love me too! Wouldn't you have fed me! Given me water to drink! Cleaned up my messes!"

Becky wailed; she howled; she lashed out, as would any victim. No longer did she throw the dirt, but pounded her fists into the pile; for she fully believed it was attacking her, and she defended herself against this immobile, inanimate aggressor as gallantly as any unstable human being would.

This continued a good, long while. The screams, mixed with heavy panting, dried her mouth severely. Becky now suffered from a thirst greater, and more intense, then when trapped in the cave. She never told Tom of her wandering thoughts then. Thoughts of death, of wanting to die, of thinking she had died, for a while. Then Tom returned and told her he found a way out. Through all of that water had existed for her in the cave. She never had to worry about drastic measures then. *That* never crossed her mind, until now.

"Oh. So thirsty. Joan, Joan, what shall I do? Joan? Please, Joan, tell me what to do. I need water, Joan. Guide me to the water, won't you? Joan! What do you want to be so mean for? You *know* I am ever so thirsty, and yet you deny me water. Joan. Joan? Joan!"

Becky. I'm with you, Becky. I know where there is water. I know where you can find water to drink. You follow me. For me now. That's it.

Becky, on all fours, walked in circles around the passage, a hand out-stretched, clutching the air, though Becky clearly saw the hand of Joan sweetly caressing hers. She followed Joan into a dark forest, deep, deep inside, stopping when the sun poked itself out. Becky really only stared into the lantern.

There, Becky. Don't you see the stream? Over there. Dip your hand into it. Feel it. feel how cool it is.

"It's not cool at all. It's warm, Joan. Oh, but I don't care."

Drink, Becky. Quickly. Quickly now. It's a magical stream, and won't last much longer. It will be dry soon. Drink your fill. That's it. That's it. Hurry now. Don't you see? It's drying up.

No! No, not yet. Please, Joan. I'm still thirsty. You must not let the stream disappear, ever. Please, Joan." But after a few minutes the stream vanished. "Thank you, Joan. I'm still awful thirsty. But I think I can manage now, for a little while. You're always so very, very helpful. I don't know what I'd do without you."

With what strength remained in Becky, she pulled herself out of the passage, and, intuitively, sealed it. She lie awake, swallowing the liquid that trickled out the pores of her cheeks, and from under her tongue, and that accumulated in the back of her mouth.

"Sleep. Where are you sleep? Where are you when I need you? Don't make me lie awake. Don't make me know how hungry I am."

Courage, Becky. Perseverence. Remain strong.

"I can't. I can't, Joan. Not any longer. Not without food. I—,"

Do you think they fed me? Hardly! What food they threw at me—threw at me—was slop. Slop, Becky! Slop! Molded bread and stew that turned even the maggots stomachs. Water! Diseased water that upset my bowels so, I most wished for death sooner than it was given me. I had no other place to evacuate my bladder, no other place to evacuate my bowels, than in a corner where lay a small bed of rotting hay that had been there even before I arrived, and never was replaced while I remained. I had no dirt to cover up the stench with. And, Becky, I was not a character in a book. I lived. Becky. I was real. I was real. I was real.

Joan's words worked as a lullaby, soothing Becky, singing to her. She drifted into sleep; thought, had she known her impending dream, as torturous and hideous as this wakeful nightmare seemed to her now, she gladly would have succumbed to it, rather than suffer through the vivid nightmare brought about by sleep. In it, she and her cat, Mrs. Sherry, reversed roles. Becky became the animal, and Mrs. Sherry, the caretaker. Their sizes reversed as well; and Becky's beloved pet locked her inside a very small cage, denying her food and water that lay outside just out of reach, beyond the bars, inches from her grasping, clawing fingers. Even in her sleep, Becky experienced the pangs of starvation. When she awoke, her body dripped with perspiration and tears.

"I, goodness. I've been crying in my sleep," Becky sobbed. "Oh, that *dream*! I loathe dreams as those. I loathe remembering them. Poor Mrs. Sherry, dead almost four years now. She never would lock me in a cage, and deny me food and water. I never did that to her. Why would I dream such a sad dream? It isn't fair. That's not reality. It can't be. Oh. I suppose I know why I dreamed it. I know. I—. What's that smell?" Becky sniffed. "It, it smells like—. Oh, but it can't be. But it does smell—." Becky sniffed again, deeply. "*Watermelon*! Big and ripe and juicy. I must still be dreaming. Cursed, cursed nightmare."

The aroma's intensity grew stronger, rising, rising, rising; passing through her nasal cavities, soaking them with their essence. Becky's eyes were long in adjusting to the lantern's light. When they did, her vision played the cruelest prank upon her yet. She not only smelled the watermelon, but she saw it, right under her nose, at her side, already cut in half, just waiting for her to plunge two or three fingers inside the soft pulp and pull out the sweat treat.

"Oh, goodness! No!" Becky cried out as her hand struck against the shell. "I touched it! I, I actually touched this, this mirage. It *is* a mirage?" Her fears worsened. "Better my hand pass through the watermelon; for then this dastardly apparition would disappear and taunt me no longer."

The watermelon did not disappear. Her fantasy must be satisfied. Becky scooped a portion of the delicacy from within its casing, bringing it to her lips, caressing it, for a moment. She gave it entry inside her mouth, sucking on it, allowing the tender juices to melt, and to traverse slowly down, down, down, inside of her, to wage war against the enemies that dare to cause her needle points of hunger, and hot iron pangs of starvation.

Nothing in all Becky's life equaled the delicate smoothness, the rich texture, the savory after-taste, as had this watermelon. She devoured half of it in one sitting, thus over-eating. But, leaning back against the boxes ever guarding the passage, and sighing as tenderly or felicitously as she had in so long, Becky didn't care. Her hands rested comfortably, upon her aching stomach. *Aching* stomach!

"The pain is so good, so refreshing. I'd rather feel bloated and heavy, than starving and weak. Not the first time I've over-eaten. It'll pass. It always does." Within an hour and a half it did; and Becky, crawling outside the passage, stood and stretched, in almost as gay a mood since the night of her kidnapping. "I never thought moving my bowels would be so enjoyable, but I'll always relish it from now on. Funny, what starvation does. I never before liked the after-affects of overeating. Now— now, I wouldn't trade that feeling for anything. Well, accept to be free. But—I must still be starving. This has all been a fantasy, hasn't it? This watermelon didn't find its way in here, cut itself in half, and sacrifice itself for me. Strange I should carry the fantasy, splendid as it is, this far. I *feel* awake. I feel partly refreshed. I don't feel the pangs of starvation any longer. How can it be? Why, this watermelon *is* here! Somebody brought it, cut it open, and placed it in such a provocative position that I *might* smell it, and taste it, when I woke. Strange, I seem to remember smelling it in my sleep too. I, I think that is what I was grabbing for when, when—oh! I don't wish to think about it. *He* must 'a' came while I slept, the nincompoop that he is. Well, I'm still partially weak. Too weak to continue digging right now." Becky paced sluggishly around the room, though not so much for the burdensome ball and chain around he ankle. Her strength had been deteriorating. Every time she needed to enter the passage, it became more difficult. Finally, disgusted, she said, "If I continue to grow weaker, I'll have to relieve myself out here, somewhere."

Be strong, Becky. Always, be strong.

"Joan? Is that you again? Oh. Oh, I'm sorry. I, I'm awful sorry."

Don't be sorry. Be brave. It isn't easy. But you must. You are stronger than you know, Becky. Much stronger.

Yes, perhaps. It's Tom's doing. Tom! Tom, Tom, Tom. You've done so much for me. I'd hate to think what my outcome would be if we never met. I'd be dead sure. There is no doubt. If I could only reach you somehow. I tried with *him*. But I don't know as yet if he has found you. All I can do is wait for him to return."

"Wait for who to return?"

Becky whirled, nearly tripping over the ball and chain.

"You! I—. I was—. Did you leave the watermelon?"

"Why, yes. Did you eat it?"

"Well, yes. some of it. Why? I mean, why did you leave it?"

"'Cause you told me you might die. I didn't ever think you might. I ain't never kidnapped no-one b'fore. Neither has Jed. Now, who was you waitin' for to return?"

What? Oh. Well, you, of course. I wanted to ask you if you found the boy you were looking for. And if you had a chance to use the word."

"Oh, sure, sure. But that was long ago. Near two day now, I think."

"*Two* days!"

"Haven't seen hide nor tail of 'im since. Been lookin' too. Shame. You know, he *was* right impressed with that word. Oh, that reminds me." Sim rummaged around his vests pockets. "He wanted me to give you something. Said he had a sister, died 'bout a year ago. Name was, was—. Oh, confound it! I forgot. But it's the same as the one you gave me to tell him. I remember that. Ah! Here it is!"

Becky's eyes glowed, as she instantly recognized her pipe. Sim handed it to her, and the girl embraced it as touchingly as Sim had.

"'Twas the boy's hope you'd take it for your very own. Said his dying sister wisht it might belong to someone like you, who could care for it the way she had while she lived." Sim choked back a few tears, watching Becky caress the pipe. "He wanted me to tell you somethin' else too."

"Wh-what?" Becky whispered hoarsely.

"He said, said—. Dern it! What *did* he say! Was important too, I know. 'Cause I'm alwus forgettin' the important things. Oh! Said if you liked the pipe you can keep it. And, uh, uh—oh *dern* it! Oh! That you and the pipe can be, be—together forever. Thas exactly what he said." A relief filled Sim, from the tips of his toes, to the top of his head. "How you like that! I finally remembered somethin'. First time in my life, I think."

Becky's eyes bulged. "Did he say *that*? Together forever?"

"He did too." Sim's excitement abounded. He jittered and shook. "I ain't seen you smile, long's you been here."

"I, I never had reason to smile."

Sim jumped to his feet. "I bet he'd be pleased as pie to know it. I—. You know, I'll tell him. Right now. I-if I can find him." Sim moved like a tornado out of the cellar.

"Wait!" Becky called out. "Why is he always doing that? Well, at least I know Tom knows about me, and who the kidnappers are. But he doesn't know where I am. Else, he'd find a way here. Tom's no, no *coward*! Nonsense! I won't believe it. Don't you tell me such things. Tom, a coward? He just doesn't know I'm here, is all. That's *all*. You here! Now, you just stop that talk. Soon as Tom realizes I am here, he'll come. Course, how *soon* is soon? Can't chance *he*'ll slip up somehow, and tell Tom. And pa! What he and ma must be going through. Close to what I am, I s'pose. Whatever is holding up the ransom? Oh, oh my head! My head. All these thoughts, these terrible thoughts that enter my head when I can think straight. I wonder if insanity might be better for me. No! No! I didn't mean that, Joan. You needn't scold me. You needn't. I'm just thinking. Just trying to make sense of everything. Don't scold me, Joan. Joan? Are you there?" Becky tilted her head in every direction, but heard not a sound out of Joan.

"Well, then. I've got to send another message to Tom, telling him where I am. Isn't that so, Joan? Isn't that the best way? Well, *I* think it is. No secret codes this time, but right to the point. And how to deliver it without him becoming wise. Can't just hand him a note and ask he not read it. I've got to conceal it in something. I've, I—. Hmmm." Becky held her pipe up close to her eyes. "I does seem inane. But, it *might* work, if I can roll the note up tight enough. Yes! It must. Well, now that

I have *that*, I need something to write on, and with. Neither of which I have." Becky bit her lip in frustration. "Oh, what shall I do *now*? Wait. What do they do in the books? They improvise. Well, so will I." As Becky planned, she absently inserted the pipe's stem in her mouth. Tobacco-less, Becky smoked the pipe all the same, as though the sweet tasting tobacco was engulfing her mouth.

"That's it!" Becky exclaimed. "If I can rip a piece of my undergar-ment, where it's not dirty, I—. Drat! Come on, *tear*. Tear, why don't you—Oh! it's no use," she panted. "I need something sharp. My arrow-head! That'll answer." She removed the precious trinket from it's place of hiding with immeasurable joy and fervency. However, upon close examination, she found the tip dull and pointless. "Must have happened when I scraped all those holes in the wall of that cabin, to remove the water."

Becky, not quite ready to give up, entered the passage. Near the entrance, in a random pile, were rocks she had dug out from the dirt. She had no other place to put them, and always thought them to be a nuisance, until now. Some were of a harsh and bristly and gritty nature, and could easily peel away layers of skin. Perhaps one of them might be employed to sharpen the arrowhead. Rummaging through the heap, Becky found one with a wide enough surface, with many ridges, and gritty areas and crevices.

Becky lightly scraped the palm of her hand across the rock's surface. "Nothing smooth about this rock! Will it work on—yes! It's sharpening the arrowhead. Yes; yes; O.K., that's plenty sharp. Oh, yes, the dress tears easily. Not too big a piece; not too big. Good. Now." Becky breathed in deeply, preparing herself mentally for what she believed might be the hardest decision of her kidnapping to make. "Do I dare? I don't know that this hasn't been laced with some type of poison. Perhaps I've whit-tled the most of it away. Seems I read somewhere poisons are rendered ineffective if heat is applied. Did I read that, or am I only fooling myself?" Before Becky answered herself, she placed the arrowhead over the flame of the lantern. For a short period she held it there. "O.K.. Good. It's do or d——. No, I won't act so. Everything is in place." She counted. "One. Two. Th——. Oooh!" Becky cringed. "Ooh-right, no time to waste." The blood slowly dribbling out, she laid the piece of under-garment flat across her lap and wrote a brief message to Tom, blew on it to speed up the drying, then rolled it up tightly.

"Come on! Come, fit inside. Why do you want to be so difficult? Why don't—there! Don't ever scare me like that again. Let's see you try and escape now. *You're* in tight enough."

Tiredness overcame Becky. She slumped against the boxes, wonder-ing if the arrowhead *had* been poisoned. "Well, I have been yawning for some time; and well before I pricked myself. I'll rest for a few minutes. *Only* a few minutes." Becky closed her eyes, and did not open them for hours. When she did, she saw Sim standing over. Startled, she curled herself into a ball and exclaimed, "What! What do you mean, looking at me, while I'm asleep?"

Now Sim became startled. "I, oh, well——. Well I didn't mean no harm. Y' see, I went out lookin' fer *him*, but that was earlier. Likely he was still asleep, and thas why I never came acrost him. Then I went and found Jed and kept him company. He's so lonely these days.. But he don't like me hangin' 'round him so often, when he's sad. So he told me to come check on you, which is his way of tellin' me he wants to be alone, with-out bein' mean to me. So I came back here, and saw you was sleepin'; and I didn't wanna wake you, so I jus' watched; jus' watched. I didn't mean no harm, honest. I lost track of time, I reckon. Well, it's later in the day now, I s'pose. I'll go back out and look fer him."

Becky relaxed, somewhat. She eased her legs back into a straight position on the dirt floor. "Well. Well, I reckon I might have overre-acted. Anyway, if you find him, you got to give back his pipe. You'll do that for me, won't you?"

"*Give* it back!" Sim sank to his feet, and nearly fainted. "You can't mean that!"

"But I do. I'm, well I'm uncomfortable with it. I fear his sister's spirit might be trapped inside."

"Speerit?"

"I've been haunted with vision's of his sister's spirit, well, for a good long while. Long enough to make me think you ought to return the pipe to him, and have *him* release the spirit, if she is in there. I wouldn't want to take any chances, you see, of lighting the pipe, and then have her spirit fly out at me. Why, I might have lit the pipe—." Here, Becky paused for a calculated moment. Then, staring at Sim, said, "while *you* were here."

As expected, Sim shuddered. "No. No, I wouldn't want that. No. Not at all."

"Of course not. Nobody would. So, will you return the pipe?"

"I s'pose there ain't no other way around it."

"Good. You tell him, when, or *if*, you find him, to *release the spirit that dwells within the pipe*. Be sure to tell him exactly that." Sim took the pipe from Becky, with as much care as one transfers a baby from one embrace to another, and rose to leave. "Remember what to tell him. *Release the spirit that dwells within the pipe.*"

"Release the speerit that dwells within the pipe."

"Yes. Oh, tell him one more thing. Tell him, tell him that once he releases the spirit—tell him *then* that we can be together forever." Before tearing out of the cellar, Sim agreed to Becky's request. "Oh, I truly hope this works," Becky sighed.

CHAPTER 26

For Becky's plan to work, Sim must find Tom. He hadn't seen the boy in two days, strangely. Tom, having committed an offense worthy of punishment, Aunt Polly kept him indoors two days. The only comfort came when he learned Widow Douglas, now fully recovered and in perfect health, would shortly hold a celebration party at her mansion.

Fleeing the harassing eye of his aunt, Tom dashed out the door nearly at the speed of light. Rampant thoughts whizzed and whirled. The two days he spent in confinement were brutal; for he assumed the worst—that Becky was no more; that she had died loathing him with all her heart, for not rescuing her. Now out of the house, Tom's mind began to clear in the fresh, open air. Still, he could not help fear that even if and when he did find and rescue Becky, she would loathe him for all eternity for his slowness. Near the forest's entrance Tom impatiently wondered where he should start his search for Sim first, when…

"Hi-hi!" came the booming cry from behind. Tom turned around.

"*You*! But I—. Where did-?" Tom could not fathon the quickness in which he encountered Sim. It seemed to him all to unbelievable. However, at this point he did not care, nor did he question it. Before he could utter another word, Sim spoke up."

"Oh, I'm awful glad I finally found you. Been looking fer you long and hard fer days. Well, here you is. And here is yer pipe back." Tom, in a state of confusion, held out his hands to receive the pipe.

"I, well what's wrong with it?" An instant, horrifying picture flashed in front of Tom. He saw Becky, in disgust, throw down the pipe, and demand it be returned. She had waited impatiently for his expected rescue, but Tom had been too long in coming. So, now, Becky loathed him, everything about him, and would never again have anything to do with him. "She, she didn't like it then?" Tom spoke meekly, choking on his words.

"No! She was afraid they might be a speerit in there."

"S-spirit?" Tom looked up, bewildered.

"Of yer sister. She don't want to light the pipe, and then have yer sister float out with the smoke. Neither do I. She wants you to, to let out the speerit that dwells within the pipe."

"Let out the spirit that dwells within the pipe?"

"Yep."

"She wants, she wants the pipe back, though?"

"Oh, oh deed she does. She's took with it. Why, you should 'a' seen her sleepin', with her hands cradled around it. Why, I mean, well, can you take the spirit out 'a' the pipe?"

"Well, well sure, sure. I, she really likes it then? She didn't throw it down in disgust?"

"No! Handled it like it was a baby. Will you do it now? Release the spirit, so's I can give the pipe back to her?"

"What? Oh. No. No, a thing like this has got to be done at midnight, you know. Certainly, not in daylight."

"Oh. I reckon there's sense to that. Well, she'll be sad, but I know she'll be more 'n happy to wait."

"You come back here tomorrow then, same time."

"I will." As Sim turned to leave, he stopped. "Oh, I almost forgot. She wanted me to tell you something."

"Tell *me*?"

"Uh-huh. She wants to be together forever. I reckon she meant the pipe, but I forgot to ask."

When Sim left, Tom contemplated Becky's reason for giving back the pipe. His first assumption, thankfully, being wrong, he knew Becky did not really believe a spirit haunted the pipe; not of a nonexistent sister.

"Let out the spirit that dwells within," Tom repeated over and over. "Got to be a clue. She means to tell me something." He laid under a tree and mulled over any possibilities. "Well, it's baffling. But she figures I can solve it. And so, I must. Let out the spirit that dwells within. Let out—. Perhaps she means I should take out something from the pipe. Don't look any different though, then when I first made it. The only logical place a body could conceal something is—." Tom lifted the pipe to his mouth, as if to smoke it. "Why, it's blocked. Can't get any air through it. Warn't that way when I,.when I gave it to him." He removed a pin from his vest and poked it inside the stem. Something emerged. His body tensed. Carefully, Tom removed the unknown object. "Looks like a parchment, centuries old. But it can't be." Tom unrolled it. What a sight to behold! "This is what she meant!" Tom marveled. The blood had smeared somewhat, obscuring the words, tinting it, but Tom easily deciphered it. The note read—*Stantan Home cellar BT*

"But I—. She can't be. I checked!" Tom's mind swirled. "What insensitive impudence has prevented me from ever returning? Oh, I haven't a minute to spare!"

Tom gathered his feet and ordered them away to the Stantan Home. As he picked up speed, the wind whipped through his eyes, blurring them, sending streams of water pouring out. Visibility decreased. A carriage popped into existence, from virtually out of nowhere, and Tom nearly did not make it to his destination that day. Lucky his spry and agile feet held him in check, sparing him, for now. The horses were shaken; the passengers were startled as well; they being doctor Towers at the helm, Widow Douglas at his side, and Miss Watson in the rear.

"Whoa!" doctor Towers cried. He held a hand on the ropes; another on Widow Douglas, to keep her from falling off. Miss Watson, who had no-one to hold on to her, bounced back, giving a "yelp".

"Thomas Sawyer!" exclaimed Widow Douglas. The boy abruptly stopped before any harm came to him. Once order returned, three faces stared blankly, but sternly, at Tom.

"Are you alright, Tom?" Widow Douglas spoke with concern. "You really ought to be careful, and watch where it is you are going."

"I know it now. I'm awful sorry."

"Well," doctor Towers sighed, "no harm done. But you be careful in the future. I've doctored many an adult stomped on by horses. Never a child. I'd hate to ever have a first."

"The boy ought to be arrested," rung the familiar voice of Miss Watson. "He might have gotten us all killed, the rapscallion."

"Now, Miss Watson. You gave your word you'd be on your best behavior."

"I said I would act accordingly. I have always done so. Is it not enough we are almost smitten down by this vagabond, I must be the one not saying anything about it?"

"What's done is done. Let the boy pass. You may go now, Tom. But I beg of you, as we all do, in future times *do* keep a sharp eye out."

"I regret it wholly, Doctor Towers."

"Mmmmph!" Miss Watson emphasized under her breath.

Tom, allowed to leave, hurried down the road, but at a slower, more cautious and time consuming pace. All three in the carriage watched after him as he disappeared down the street.

"I wonder what has got him in such a rush?" Widow Douglas questioned.

"It's the devil sure, if you ask me."

"Nobody did. Hey-ya!" Ben called out to the horses. The animals obeyed straight away.

"It's good to be out in the fresh air again. I feel so young. Younger than I have felt in so many years."

"You look it. Isn't that right, Miss Watson?"

"I—. Don't talk to me until you apologize. I'm entitled to it."

"Sis, be grateful to Ben. Wasn't it he who found your necklace?"

"Strange he found it in exactly the place he said it would be."

"There. It proves he knows what he is talking about."

"He may have you fooled, but not me."

"Must we constantly fight and bicker? My voice is finally healed, thanks in large part to Ben. I don't want to have to chose between the two of you. It's unfair you make me do it."

"I'm only looking out for your best interests."

"I know what it is your doing."

"Anyway, you should have heard the horrible thing he said about me. He said I am the way I am because I was never married."

"You said that, Ben?"

"Well, I—. It might have slipped out, in the heat of the moment. It was wrong to say, I know. And seeing that it brought tears to your eyes, I promptly apologized for having said."

"Nonsense!"

"Did you cry, sis? Be honest. It's alright, you know. The last time I remember you to have cried was when Mr. Johansson left for Mexico."

"Enough! How many times must I remind you not to repeat that name. My private life is my own. I wish you would respect that. Do I go around town telling your private life?"

"I didn't say you did. I only thought that if Ben knew, I thought he would understand you better. Oh, sis—you cried, didn't you?"

"I don't see what any interest there can be in whether I did cry or not. Why, in Heaven's name, did you bring me out here?"

"It's a beautiful day. We thought you could use the fresh air. You are in desperate need of it. Ben told me about the spells you've been having."

"He had no right. I ordered him not to."

"You're my sister. I have a right to know."

"He had no business. Well, your health has returned. It is unnecessary for him to remain at the mansion."

"It *is* very necessary. Sis. Well, I didn't want to bring it up until later, but—. Sis. We are to be married."

"What!" Miss Watson rose, then collapsed back into her seat.

"Not right away of course. But in time, after a proper courtship."

"You *can't* be serious." Miss Watson, in disbelief, fanned herself; more for show and sympathy than for any other reason.

"It's true, Miss Watson. I, I hope you can be, well, *happy*, for us."

"Happy! Happy! Oh! What a horrible, cruel thing to do, to bring me out here under false pretenses, and announce such a catastrophe upon me. Could you not have shot me instead?"

"Don't say that sis. It pains me to hear you talk so. It wasn't under false pretenses. We had no intention of even telling you until later. But now its out. And please, sis—*do* be happy for Ben and I."

A group of people, growing larger by the minute, were assembling outside the sheriff's office, a good distance up the street. However, neither doctor Towers, Widow Douglas, or Miss Watson, heard the rising shouts.

"Anyhow, a woman at your age—,"

"I'm not yet forty-two. I'm still young. Young enough to want to enjoy the rest of my life; and young enough to want to share it with someone else."

"Well aren't you the lucky one. Having the advantage of *two* husbands, when I have not had the pleasure of one."

"It's time you put away those old grudges."

"Oh, so they are old grudges?

"Brittany's right," Doctor Towers said, awkwardly, turning to face Miss Watson, determined to speak his mind. "Where I came from there's a thirty year old feud going on between two families. Nobody remembers how it began. Not even those doing the killing. Yet, they continue to slaughter one another." While talking, he started the horses back towards town, at a slow, leisurely trot. "I'd hate for you two to end up that way, at odds with one another. I'd hate to be that reason, and know I was."

A man, spying Widow Douglas, split from the main group of people assembled outside the sheriff's office, and ran towards the carriage as fast as his rotund body could sustain him, waving one arm high above him, while he pinned the other arm to the hat upon his head, to keep it from flying off. The ash from his cigar he clenched tightly in his mouth burned and glowed furiously, the faster he ran. He, like Tom, nearly collided with the horses.

"Stop, stop the carr'ge!" This man, on pins and needles, hopped about, wringing his hands and wiping the sweat off his brow. "Widow, doct'r—whoa!" He grabbed hold of the lead horse. "Hold them horses! Whoa!"

"What's this all about?" asked doctor Towers, angrily.

"Whoa! There now, that's better. What's it all about? Well sir, I'll tell ya. We got 'im. We got the son of the devil. Oh, pardon Miss Douglas."

"You have got who?" replied Miss Watson. She had fallen to the floor of the carriage, and stumbled trying to regain her composure.

"Oh, why Miss Watson, I didn't see ya. What're ya doing down there?"

"Never mind you idiot. You caused us great trouble. Now, you better have an answer."

"Oh, yes. Why, I mean, that is, *yes* I do. Oh, by golly."

"Well come on, out with it. I haven't all day."

"You mentioned you had someone. Who do you have?"

"Well, I'm a bit nervous to say it, but we got the one that helped Miss Watson's nigger escape. He's down to the jail. Well, right this very instance he's being interrogated—,."

"Am I to understand correctly? A man has been captured—,"

"Oh, no, Miss Watson. Not a man. Another nigger."

"What!" all three cried out.

"That's why ever'body is racing all around. News is too unbelievable to keep under hat."

"Another nigger stole my property?"

"Miss Watson, it's true. He's confessed it all. Oh, lordy, lordy, lordy. Look at me. I'm all goose bumps. Got to go, to tell others. But it was a privilege telling *you*, Miss Watson. He'll hang sure!"

"*Hang*, did you say!"

The man, already down the road, stopped, twirled, and, with a hand upon his hat shouted, "Yes, doctor Towers! This day!"

Doctor Towers, keeping the horses motionless, looked uncomfortably out into the distance. Miss Watson impatiently snapped at him.

"Hurry! We haven't much time. I want to see that nigger."

"I don't know sis." Widow Douglas said, uneasily.

"What's to know? If he had stolen *your* nigger, *your* property, worth a great sum of money, *you* would want to see him. Move on!"

CHAPTER 27

Cy, from within the darkened sheriff's office, silently, stiffly, eyed the mounting mass of people huddling together in the middle of the street, awaiting the emergence of the condemned. He flirted with an imperceptible smirk, the kind which only slightly stretches the lips, but never shows any teeth. His massive body permitted little sunlight in the office. Those minuscule rays of light that did enter offered no comfort for Cal, who paced nervously alongside the ghosts of his father and grandfather. The condemned, seated in the middle of the room, had no thoughts of escape. He tried once, but Cy removed any lingering dreams of a second time.

"M-must be the whole town out there," Cal muttered nervously, and white as the ghosts of his father and grandfather.

The only movement from Cy came from the deep squinting of his eyes. "You're not *turning*, on me, are you? You know how I get when I am betrayed. You do as I say, you understand. We agreed this would be for the best."

"*You* agreed. But, but if someone were to find out—,"

"I would take care of him. This will buy us time. I know the nigger is heading downstream. I know he will make his way to Cairo, as many of them do. That is all the information I need. I'll have no trouble finding him."

"What if you do? When you bring him back, he'll deny this nigger helped him in any way to escape."

"What of it? Nobody takes the word of a nigger, over a white man's. Besides, I may not bring him back at all."

"Not bring him back! Well what in tarnation would you do with him?"

"It's so easy to forge documents these days. I could make double, *triple*, what the reward is. I know many people, and have even more connections. It wouldn't be the first time."

This time Cy flinched his head towards Cal, ever so slightly. Something about his ice cold stare, blank to all the world, reminded the sheriff of the bounty hunter's true nature. He flashed back to a time, years earlier, when the two were together. Cal had erred against Cy. Words were spoken. "I've broken many an arm and leg for less than what you've called me, From you, I take but one finger."

"Oh," Cal cringed, remembering the incident, and feeling the pain creep back into his finger, years afterwards. He wiggled it, as he had done then.

Cy returned his stare outside. He pinched his lips. "It's time you go out and prepare the people. Do not involve me," Cy warned. "Do not mention my name. Do not include my presence in the apprehension. I have my reasons, you understand. And," Cy doubly warned, "do not make me come outside."

Cal did not have to be told twice. With Cy watching every move, Cal pushed the barrel of his rifle in the back of the condemned, ordering him outside.

Most of the townspeople had gathered together by now. Men, women, and children alike. Many of the men just arriving were from neighboring towns. In disbelief, and heartbreak, they these men bowed their heads in remorse and pity, as if they were attending a funeral; for their search was now over, and for all the days of sweat and toil, the sleepless nights—all that time, was considered wasted, lost, forever taken from their lives. And worst of all was the fact they would not see any money for their troubles. They sorrowed not for the condemned, but for themselves, their financial loss.

Aunt Polly and Judith Loftus, who had taken the occasion of this warm, beautiful day to stroll through town, quickly found themselves immersed in something they, like everyone else, could not turn away from. This burdened Aunt Polly. She was witness to Judith's internal suffering, her deep, ailing depression. She cursed herself for ever punishing Tom, for she had also punished Judith, without realizing it.

Doctor Towers pulled the carriage up. Though Miss Watson attempted to act serious and dignified, her nerves showed through. She watched Cal swagger, as Judge Thatcher had at Jimmy's preliminary hearing. He swung the "hanging" rope as innocently and as casually as one would swing a jumping rope, or, perhaps, a cat. Miss Watson folded her arms into her body, tightly, and hid her hands underneath; for they shook noticeably. The noose bobbed up and down, up and down, up and down...

A tall oak tree stood boldly upright near the side of the sheriff's office. This tree had been planted long ago to provide a comfortable shade, and to cool the office from the sun's rays that beat against the window. Now, it would serve another purpose, a less thoughtful, less sincere purpose than originally planned for.

The people lowered their voices as Cal walked the condemned over to the oak tree. Though most of the townspeople hadn't any aversions towards hanging, there had not been one in St. Petersburg for years. Some, who had never witnessed a hanging before, rationalized their fears by shrugging their shoulders and saying, "Well, it's only a nigger, anyway."

Cal faced the crowd. The sun beat down, baking him. He had a mind to remove his black vest, but resolved against the idea. The way in which his heart thumped, Cal deemed it best to leave the vest attached to his body. After wiping his forehead, Cal raised an unsteady hand in the air. His other hand remained firmly attached to the rifle.

"People!" Cal hailed. "P-people of St. Petersburg! By now you have heard, you know what has happened. This, this nigger here, by my side, this nigger helped in the escape of another nigger. *Miss Watson's* nigger. He has confessed to the high crime. And will hang for it!"

The condemned turned and bowed his head away from everyone, silently weeping to himself. Loud, viscous murmuring occurred. Everyone had his own opinion. The condemned's master was in attendance, and silently uttered his own remarks. He had paid over two hundred dollars for the condemned, and would not be compensated at all for his lose

Spouted one man—"What's the use 'n hanging him? Sell 'im down river! A *live* nigger is a *useful* nigger, I always say."

"Let's all take turns whippin' him."

"Hang 'im half way. Let 'im know how close to hell's brimstone and fire he came." As an afterthought, this man said, "Then you can go ahead and whip 'im some."

"No!" The condemned twisted his body grimly towards the crowd of people, facing them eye to eye. "It ain' true. I, I din' ha' nuffin' t' do wid it. Please! Please, b'lieve me." Tears streamed down his cheeks.

"Quiet" Cal stammered, gritting his teeth.

The condemned, flustered, looked nervously out into the crowd, seeking something, anything that might yield a positive response in his favor. So it came as a shock when Doctor Towers stood up on the carriage and, with a tongue less tart than the others, hailed the townspeople's attention.

"*Good* people of St. Petersburg." Doctor Towers waited until he had control of the audience's attention. "I am relatively new to your town, so you may be skeptical of my voice; the power of my speech may dissatisfy you; you may find cause to turn your ears away—please! Don't. I appeal to you all, as a gentleman, a doctor, and as a human being when I say—there is no warrant for hanging this slave."

An unexpected hush fell over the crowd, making it harder to determine who was more uncomfortable. Doctor Towers, or Cal. The sheriff peered through his office window, then quickly diverted his head away. Cy's haunting glare unnerved him. The glowing red he saw in the bounty hunter's eyes proved too unbearable. He must speak up, and protest.

"Now hear!" Cal objected. "He, he hangs. He hangs."

"But you've just heard him say he didn't have anything to do with it."

"It don't matter what he says *now*. The fact of the matter is, what he said before. He confessed. He hangs."

The condemned, regaining a small portion of his courage, spoke out once more. "De she'ff is lyin'. I din do no sech a thing. Y' all may hang me t' day. Y 'all may take de life f'om me. But ain' nobody gonna take de *spirit* f'om me. An' wheen y' all fin' out de tooth, dat de she'ff is lyin', den I be more a man den any o' you. 'Cause I'll *has* my spirit."

"I said quiet." Cal pushed the condemned against the wall. "People. I didn't intend this to go on so long. I apologize. He should've hanged by now. But he will hang—,"

"Wait!" doctor Towers pleaded. "I still have a few words to say."

"I told you, you ain't got anything else to say. We're not here to debate the hanging of this nigger. We're here to *watch* it; to make an example of him to other niggers who might harbor ideas of helping them to escape. He has got to be punished for this crime."

Doctor Towers turned to the people. "In this great country of ours, in this great country, where we have proven that men—good, hard working, honest men—*can* govern themselves, and set rules and laws, and *abide* by them; in such a country as this, must we kill a person without a trial? A trial that clearly and legally defines the facts? Was this not the hope of all those who fought and died, and eventually won freedom for us all, and of the founding fathers who framed the Constitution, and guaranteed that freedom, that not one of us might ever be abused by those in authority again? My own father fought in the war, and lived to tell me about it. Tell me how important a war it was, and will always be, so long as America exists. And what about our founding fathers? I ask each and every one of you—what would our founding fathers say about the proceedings unfolding here today?"

Cal slapped his side, in utter disgust and contempt. "They weren't talking about niggers." "Whites! *Only* whites. Our founding fathers knew the importance of slavery, and what a precious commodity and benefit they were then, would be today, and always will be. Listen to the voice of reason. Just, listen If they had wanted an end to slavery, they'd 'a' ended it. Were our founding fathers *cowards*?"

"No's," murmured through the wall of people.

"No." Cal shook his head. "If they could come together to whip a tyrant king, they could have come together to whip slavery. It wasn't in their best interest. So slavery stayed. And long live it!" His voice rose in pitch. "What's good enough for our founding fathers must be good enough for us, for all times."

"Yeas" emanated from certain section of the gallery, from men, woman, and even children, no doubt echoing their own parents beliefs. Others, looking desperately from face to face, held their tongues.

"Let me tell you this. My grandfather, my own grandfather, fought in the revolution. Yes, that's right. I'm sure many of you out their have relatives who have fought in the war also. You doctor, you said your father fought. Let me tell you, let me tell you all, my grandfather fought for my freedom, for your freedom, for all our freedom. He fought, and he *died*. He died. But not in vain. He died so we might know the savory taste of freedom; freedom from tyrants. Our founding fathers, our forefathers, won that war. They had framed a Constitution, so they might live according to their own laws and rules. Well, slavery being a vital part of our economy, and heritage before the revolution, our founding fathers thought nothing for ending it afterwards. They made no attempts to end it! Slavery has been legal in these United States ever since."

"That's not altogether true," doctor Towers interrupted.

"Don't you tell me what's true. Our founding fathers could have abolished slavery. It is for the very fact they did not, we law abiding Americans must accept slavery now and forever. Y' see—it's all about ideology." For the moment Cal forgot all about the condemned. Even Cy escaped his mind; for whenever he talked about the founding fathers, nothing else could interrupt his train of thought until he had spoken every last word he had to say. "Founding fathers lived by slavery. They wanted it; they wanted it to continue. They owned slaves, didn't they? Course. They didn't have no ill will against slavery. Are we to snub our noses at our founding fathers? No! We must always abide by their wishes. They had a marvelous vison for this country—slavery included. You either believe they wanted slavery, or that they were cowards. Ain't no other choice. For the sake of our founding fathers, to abide by their wishes, divinely inspired as they were, slavery must always be. Oh, there might be those wishing to stop it. Traitors! We must always live for what the founding fathers wanted. Any other way of life is sacrilegious."

Doctor Towers again interrupted Cal. "Not all of our founding fathers believed in slavery. In fact, a number of them wanted it abolished with the signing of the Constitution."

This statement only provoked Cal further. "You *dare* to split our founding fathers apart? Might as well split the country apart! They were all united in their decision to let slavery stand. That's what made them strong, and why we will always regard them with a reserved specialness. No American can ever say anything bad about a founding father without forever more being stamped—*traitor*. The founding fathers were perfect. Perfect because they had divine inspiration. How do you think the Constitution came into being? God! God inspired the Constitution. A most perfect and errorless God, who loves the American people. God breathed every word of the Constitution into the minds and hearts of the founding fathers. We all know that to be fact. If God had not wanted slavery, he would have willed the founding fathers to abolish it. He didn't. And they didn't. Therefore, God believes slavery is good. To suggest the founding fathers were wrong not to abolish slavery, is to suggest God erred. To believe that, puts American society into a threatening situation.

Doctor Towers replied, "Then the law must be changed, and changed in a hurry, to accommodate the grievous error our founding fathers made. They were obviously wrong."

Wrong! Did Cal hear right. How could any loyal American in their right mind suggest the founding fathers were wrong?

Cy watched on, fuming.

"You traitor! You all heard what he said. How could the founding fathers be wrong? How could they be wrong about anything they did? Didn't they acquired their knowledge, their insight and foresight, from higher powers, too supernatural to err? And too loving and prudent to guide these framers of the Constitution the wrong way?"

The people rustled, uneasily, becoming edgy, uncomfortable. Perhaps it had something to do with what Cal tried to convey. Many of them sided with him. For they too believed in the founding fathers "unfathomable greatness", their "absolute perfection", "acute sense of what is right and what is wrong", and their "time honored bravery to stand up against anything that might impede their way of thinking".

Most would not deny, outwardly, that our founding fathers were divinely perfect, or divinely absolved from erring; that because of their divine inspiration, God's hand went into the making of the Constitution. As a result, and because God had been the true author; because God had not seen fit to abolish slavery; because slaves were not freed then, and allowed to live as men and women; because the hand of God did not intercede within the framing of the Constitution, therefore God, in his absolute and infinite wisdom, showed favor towards slavery. So this must be why, when the founding fathers framed the Constitution, they allowed slavery to stand—legal, moral, and most importantly, divinely proper, and Constitutional. If slavery was good for the inspirer of the Constitution, it must be good for those who wrote it; for they were merely transcribing the breath of God. So many people believe the Constitution and the Declaration of Independence to be almost—*biblical.*

Cy continued to watch this spectacle inside the office. His eyes deepened. He did not want to emerge from the office, from hiding. He did not want his involvement known; for if anything went wrong, Cal would be entirely to blame. However, for the condemned to ever be hung, Cy saw no other alternative. He would make Cal bitterly regret making him show himself.

Cal, trying to regain attention, and order, heard the opening of his office door; the loud, distinct, footsteps behind. Then, he felt the heavy breathing on his neck, and as it descended down his back. He knew he would have welts and blisters on this area come morning.

Cy whispered in Cal's ear. "I'll deal with you later, you understand." Cal gasped. So too did one other, a woman, when she saw Cy emerge. Judith let out a deathly gasp which both scared Aunt Polly, and confused her.

"Judith! Why, what is it?" she asked of her best friend.

"It, it's husband!

"Your husband! I, well I, I never knew it. I, well you never introduced me to him."

"For good reason, Polly."

"He was always away."

"That ain't it."

"That was the man I told you about the other day. The one that scowled at me. And told me to move out of his way. Why, Judith, I said such horrible, sinful things agin him. I'm sorry now."

"No! No, don't be. Don't ever be. Tis me ought to be sorry. The Devil himself would be afraid to pass by him at night. Oh, Polly. I hadn't any idea he was involved in this, this—. Why, I knew he was huntin' the nigger, but—. Polly, there's much I need to tell you." Judith broke down, quietly sobbing. Aunt Polly took the woman in her bosom and held her.

"There now. I'm with ye." She sensed Judith had been wronged by her husband, though at that time not fully understanding exactly how.

"You wanted to know what was bothering me all along? Well, it's him. Oh, Polly, I have to tell you everything, everything, everything. Take me home, Polly. I feel faint. I'll tell you everything there. If only, if *only* I can find courage. Oh, what it will do to us, to our friendship. But I've suffered, suffered for it rightly, I suppose, over the course of my life"

"Be still, Judith." Aunt Polly, consoling Judith, lead her slowly away. Their eyes watered so, making it difficult to see in front of them. "It'll all turn out for the better. Nothing could interfere with our friendship."

"You say that now, not knowing. I pray ye be right. But—," Cy addressed the people, forcing Judith to cringe, and halt her step for a moment.

"People. People," Cy thunderously bellowed. "There will be enough of this talk. This is a nigger, and only a nigger. Remember that. We ought not be having such a debate. He hasn't any rights, you understand. He has confessed to the crime of aiding and abetting in the escape of another nigger. That nigger has escaped over into the Illinois side, and is making his way to Ohio. He will be apprehended soon, now that we know where he is going. What this nigger did is against the law, punishable by any means seen fit by whatever law he is under the jurisdiction of. Under the jurisdiction of *this* law, he hangs."

"Who are you to be saying that?" a man spoke out.

Cy would deal with that man later, as he would Cal. "Who am I? I am the sheriff's deputy. And I was there when this nigger confessed. I will testify to that in a court of law, under oath, if it ever becomes necessary, which I highly doubt it ever will, you understand." Cy pointed to Cal. "Ready the rope, Be quick."

Cal obeyed, leading the condemned to the oak tree, under a thick, portly branch. He hoisted the rope up, up, up. Not one eye blinked as it ascended, gliding freely, in the air; or while it fell, bowing to the laws of gravity. The noose stopped, in front of the condemned, and bobbed up and down for a time. Then, came to a deadly halt. He turned once again to the people.

"I din' do it. I won' run away, 'cause I know dat means y' all think I did. I don' wanna die. But I ain' gonna run. No su'. I din'—," Cal applied the noose around the condemned's neck, squeezing tightly, thereby preventing him from talking any further. In fact, if cal had squeezed any hardly, there might not have been any need to hoist his body.

Widow Douglas put a hand on doctor Towers shoulder. "Ben, I've a feeling he is telling the truth."

Doctor Towers, also finding great cause to believe the condemned, tapped Widow Douglas' hand. "I tend to agree with you." To Cy he said, "I still believe he ought to have a trial."

"Don't interfere! He's only a nigger. Don't any of you interfere. Hasn't the sheriff told you he confessed? Haven't I told you he confessed? That ought to be good enough for the whole of you. This is the south. Don't forget that. You all take a good look around. Many of you hail from out of town. But those of you that live here, if this nigger is given the least bit of credibility over a white man, how does that look to your state, to the rest of the south? You want to be ridiculed? Why, just you all think. If that nigger don't hang, then you all will have hanged yourselves in his place."

That statement resonated throughout the crowd of people.

"Ah, he's only a nigger," a man said. "Let him hang. What's one nigger?"

"Yeah. Ain't that big a deal," another said.

"There's more where he came from."

"Hang him!"

"Hang him!"

"Hang him!"

Except for doctor Towers, and Widow Douglas, and a few others, the people were swayed. Miss Watson, having been quiet all this time, remained silent. She did not dare open her mouth. Ever since the noose had been wrapped around the condemned's neck, a queasy feeling developed within her. She feared what might result if she tried to speak.

Doctor Towers tried again to stop the hanging. "If you would only listen. All of you, please. Does he look guilty? Does he act guilty?"

"I said don't interfere. I am getting mighty upset with you." Cy shook his fist at doctor Towers. "It's not any of your concern, you understand."

"No, I don't understand. I disagree. Something is amiss."

Cy doubled over in seething anger. "He has committed a crime, and that is a fact."

"Ben," Widow Douglas whispered, "this wouldn't be happening if Judge Thatcher was here. Where could he be?"

"Somebody said he went to Constantinople. But that was many days ago."

"Con—. He has relatives there. He must still—. He picked a fine time to take a vacation."

"Now, Brittany, he couldn't have known."

"No, I suppose—,"

"Enough!" Cy, with one booming moan, silenced the entire town. "The law is on our side. Let us end this farce *now*. There is much at stake if this nigger does not hang today—*now!*" What was really at stake, so far as Cy was concerned, was his profit from selling Jim down river himself, when he caught him. He knew he could easily make a thousand dollars.

Cy moved over to the condemned, taking the rope in his hands, feeling it, tugging on it. With a "heave ho", and before doctor Towers could utter one more protest, the bounty hunter lifted the rope, high, high, high in the air, with all his strength. The townspeople were caught off guard. Not even the condemned knew the rope had been pulled, until he looked down and saw how dreadfully high up he was. The noose had been purposely placed where the condemned's neck was sure not to snap instantly. Yet, breathing became more difficult for some of the townspeople, than it did for the condemned. Two of these townspeople—Aunt Polly and Judith Loftus—were witness to the hanging, though they did not want to be. They had not been moving fast enough. When they heard a terrifying "H-yaa!" from Cy's lips, as he hoisted the condemned in the air, they both automatically turned; and regretted the action.

The condemned had been left to dangle, as it were, exposed to the onlookers. Without his hands or feet bound together, without his face hidden, this posed an uncomfortable dilemma, for most of the gapers, anyhow.

It took all of a few moments; and, perhaps more to the town's relief, the condemned lay upright, in the air, at peace with the world. How many in that crowd could feel that same way; how many witnesses would go home that night and sleep as easily and as soundly as the condemned would be for all eternity! One person would be destined to suffer the most. She was rushed home without delay on her firm assistance.

The others were not so lucky. One final humiliation befell the condemned. As the dispersing commenced, somberly and sullenly, by the majority—for there will always be those who enjoy any hanging—a strange, eerie noise loomed overhead. Heads turned to watch as the branch holding the condemned's lifeless body split from the great oak, and tumbled to the ground, toppling onto the condemned, crushing him, insulting him one last time.

Said Cy, "It isn't worth flinching over." Many, however, did.

Only a few people slept soundly that night; only the strong and apathetic at heart. As for the others—well after darkness had settled in, when the stroke of midnight was but a few ticks away, and owls hooted sadistically, and dogs barked hideously, and a myriad of little, insignificant noises spoke up, and seemed as though they would progress throughout the remainder of the night, did these individuals find blessed relief in sleep.

Cy made good on his threat to Cal, beating him severely that night, and leaving inside his office, alone, desperately needing medical attention, but unable to move any part of his body.

"Here," Cy said, wickedly smiling. He placed a gun next to the hand he did not break. "It contains one shot. Do yourself a favor, and use that one remaining shot to end all your misery." At the door, Cy whispered, "This partnership is over, you understand."

Though Cal suffered immensely, nobody suffered equally, or more cruelly, than did one person. She demanded she be returned home promptly, and did not hesitate to jump out of the carriage even before doctor Towers brought it to a complete halt. She sped inside, knocking over anything, or anyone, that had not sense enough to get out of her way. Making it to her room, she locked herself in. There, she became gravely ill, and stayed that way for a week. During this period she refused to come out. Meals sent up to her barely were touched the first few days. After that, they were left outside her door, rejected altogether.

Doctor Towers and Widow Douglas sincerely worried over her condition during that week. Yet, neither attempted a forced entry; each for their own reasons. Miss Watson closed and shuddered all her windows, shutting herself up inside, and closing herself off from the outside. It did not take long for the air to turn musty and stale; sticky and humid. The dust Miss Watson lividly detested in the past, often screaming in horror if one particle was left to graze upon her furniture, now not only grazed, but took up living quarters. Soon, whole families of dust particles arrived, and multiplied like rabbits, mounting and layering upon every stick of furniture, clothing, antiquities, carpets—*everything*. Whatever Miss Watson did in her room, isolated and alone, her sister could only ponder, and dread.

"I distinctly hear her crying in there," Widow Douglas told doctor Towers the night of the hanging, "It frightens me. I hate thinking that to some degree sis is suffering in there. And yet, I know she is. And, and I know I can do nothing about it."

"Perhaps it is good then. The crying I mean. She's letting everything out from within her system. Everything that's been bothering her. A good cry never hurt anybody. Let her be. Perhaps she'll feel better in the morning."

When Widow Douglas retired for bed, earlier than usual, the soft cries she swore she heard coming from the other side of the hall kept her awake; those soft cries would keep her awake long hours for the remainder of the week.

The night had been cruel to just about everyone that saw the hanging.. Aunt Polly included. Sickening thoughts evolved inside her head as the hours crept towards midnight. When ten o'clock arrived, a new thought emerged. *Where was Tom?* Poor woman. She had forgotten about him, in all the mess of the afternoon. Now she became frightened for him, for his safety. In her weakened state, she could hardly find the strength to rise up out of her chair and go look for him.

"And Mary's off on her vacation to St. Louis," Aunt Polly sighed out loud. "Sid's too small, among other things. Well, it ain't his first late night escapade. He's resourceful. He'll be back. Alwus is." The events of the afternoon clung deeply to her. Soon, the unthinkable happened. Tom slipped from her mind altogether. Shortly, so too did Sid and Mary.

CHAPTER 28

Tom did not see the hanging, nor did he know anything about it, nor would he have cared. Not when Becky needed him, and he now knew where to find her. After his near brush with death, Tom, once out of Widow Douglas' eyesight, picked up his pace and flew to the Stantan Home, hoping he would make it there in time, before—. Well, hoping he would make it there in time. The girl in question, inside the passage, wearily sank to her knees, exhausted. Physically, mentally, and emotionally worn out, she sighed, sadly.

"I don't know why I keep digging out this dirt. It's all a waste of time anyhow. There don't seem an end to it. And it looks as though I may never find an end to it. I've dug as far as I can go. "I'm pooped!" Becky crawled out and sealed the passage, for the last time she believed. "Now I've nothing to do; nothing to pass the time. Tom ought to have the pipe by now, ought to know what to do with it, ought to be on his way right now. Well, he *ought* to be is all! Oh, Becky, Becky. Oh, Becky."

Be strong, Becky.

"Joan?"

Tom will come. You must believe he will. You must believe in him.

"Oh, I *do*, Joan. Truly I do. But when? When will he come?"

Just believe he will come.

Becky did believe Tom would come. And soon. During the wait she swore she heard the door creak open many times, and footsteps descending the stairs. "Oh, Becky. Poor Becky. Was only a matter of time before you went insane. At least it's not as painful as I thought it would be. I wish Joan would talk to me, and comfort me. I do so enjoy the sound of her voice. Wait!" She lifted her head. "I do hear a voice. Joan? Is that you? Joan? What are you saying, Joan? I can't hardly hear you. Joan? No, it's not Joan. Sounds like, like, Tom." Becky lowered her head, tucking it into her bosom. "Well, you tried Becky. Nobody can say otherwise. Poor child. Joan of Arc was one of a kind, I suppose. Wish I could 'a' been more like her."

Tears moistened her eyes. Becky, still determined to remain strong, quickly brushed them away, hoping Joan hadn't taken notice. Feeling sorry for herself, Becky sat with her head facing the dirt floor, methodically shaking it back and forth. How long she sat in this position she was unsure. But she knew, or at least thought she knew, insanity breathed right around the corner.

"Oh, insanity. I feel your cold, cold chill, breathing down my back. Or, or maybe it's d-death. That makes sense. I've died of fright. Well—,"

Becky felt pressure being applied to her shoulder; the type of pressure only a hand could make. She tensed. Then tingled. Encouraged Death really had visited her, Becky prepared herself, as best she could. First, fear struck her. Relief followed, as she willingly succumbed. But when nothing happened, and the hand still lay lightly upon her shoulder, the girl began to puzzle why. Slowly she composed herself, daring to turn her head and see by her own eyes whose hand lay upon her shoulder.

"Well if Death it is, I want to see him, for what he really is." Before turning, a familiar voice whispered to her.

"Becky?"

Becky instantly pushed her eyes upwards, though her head remained tucked in her bosom. She hadn't the heart, or courage, to tilt her head, yet.

"Could be a trap, to draw me off guard. Well, but I can't take the suspense." Cautiously, Becky turned her head, just enough to focus upon the face, much shadowed by the dim light.

"W-who, who is it?" Becky asked, shyly, mustering whatever courage she had left inside of her. "Is it Death, come to saddle me upon his horse and ride me off into another world?" She gulped, half believing the answer would come back "yes".

"No," came the gentle reply. "It, it's me, Becky. Tom Sawyer, Avenger. Come to res-rescue you."

Becky could scarcely believe her ears.

"Say, say it again. Say your n-name."

"Tom Sawyer."

"Is it really you? Not some imagination of mine?" Tom threw his arms around Becky, letting her feel him, so her thoughts may finally be at ease. "You found the note then? Inside the pipe? Of course you did. Silly of me to even ask. Oh, how I mumble."

"Becky—,"

"They put a ball and chain around my ankle. See. That's why I couldn't escape. I tried. Oh, Tom, I tried. But I couldn't make it up the stairs."

"Becky. We have to—,"

"They said it would be impossible. Drat them for being right. Well, when I found out you had made contact with one of the kidnappers, I knew I must send you a message, to let you know where I was."

"I know, Becky. But—,"

"If you hadn't given him the pipe, Tom, I don't know *how* I would have reached you with a message. Oh, Tom, there's just so much I want to tell you. I can't hardly spit it all out."

"I know, Becky. It's the same with me," Tom cried. "But Becky, let's get you out of here first. Please! Before they return."

"Is it day or night?"

"Late day, but—,"

"Well then, we haven't much time. Only one of them returns, once in a while. The other one comes down less frequently."

"All the more reason to leave now."

"But Tom, like I said, the ball and chain—,"

"I'll carry you. Come on."

"You can't—. Tom! Wait, don't. I, Tom—." Tom tried lifting Becky. He failed. "I told you."

"Becky. I need the key."

"That's *too* dangerous."

"Maybe. But it's the only way."

"Could you go find help?"

"Nobody knows you've been kidnapped. Jimmy told your pa not to tell anyone, or he'd, he'd do you harm."

"You mean, *kill* me?"

"The key is the only way out. I know it'll be hard, stealing it away from Jimmy, but—,"

"Jimmy! He ain't got it. I haven't seen him in a long time."

"No? Well that's strange."

"First they told me he was out delivering the ransom note. Later on they told me he was in hiding, somewhere. That it warn't safe for him to be here, in town."

"I don't know what to say. Well, we can't worry about that now. I need that key, whoever has it."

"But, that means you'd have to stay here. You would be endangering yourself. I can't let you—,"

"*Let* nothing. Becky, don't you think I'd do anything for you?"

"I, well. You'd really stay? You'd do that for me?"

"Course. I'd do anything for you, to make sure you was safe. And not because it says so in a book. I *know* it's the right thing."

Becky squeezed Tom tightly. "You *are* noble. You'll have to hide in the passage, you know. It might be for a long time, but, but I've cleared out more of the dirt.. It was the only way to kept me from going insane. It gave me something to do, to keep busy while I was down here. I—. Why, Tom, what ever is the matter?"

"N-nothing. I, well, I'll tell you, later. Can I look inside?"

"Well of course, Tom, but, you seem to be holding something back. You're not, are you? Tom, now, Tom. I know that look. You're keeping something from me, aren't you. Please, don't."

As Tom separated the boxes he said, "Alright. I'll tell you. First, let me take a look inside."

Becky handed him the lantern. Before letting go, she paused, slightly, perplexed. For the moment, Tom felt more comfortable inside the passage. How he would explain to Becky what had happened to her parents greatly afflicted his conscience. Crawling inside, and passing Becky's makeshift latrine, Tom wondered whether telling the truth might be more of a sin than lying. He knew she would eventually find out. Would it be better coming from his lips?

"Are you ever going to come back out Tom?" Becky asked, after a long wait. "You must not keep me in suspense forever."

"I know," Tom's voice drearily echoed. Presently, he poked his head out. "You've made real progress Becky. Why, when all this is over, and the kidnappers caught and jailed, you and I will come back here and finish clearing away the dirt. Can't be much left, now."

"Tom, I know you're stalling. Don't. I want to know what's been going on all this time. I have a right, if not a *need*, to know. I don't even know how long I've been away. Please, won't you tell me about ma and pa?"

Tom exited. For the next fifteen minutes he paced anxiously in front of Becky, divulging everything to her. He stopped only when the girl gasped, or sighed, or let out any such noise his ears picked up.

"Poor ma," Becky wept. "Pa, too. He used to stutter when he was a child. He told me about it once. He said it took many years to cure his speech problem. He began talking in front of large crowds of people, about things around town he didn't care for, or that were not right.

Taxes and such, and unfair treatment of people. When his speech improved he decided to go into law. You know the rest. Nobody's seen him since he left your home?"

"No. You see now, why I didn't want to tell you?"

"Tom! I have a perfect right to know. You did right, telling me. I'm glad I found out from you, though. The way you explained it, it was much more sincere and heartfelt. Thank you for that. Poor, poor ma. I so desperately want to see her, to hug her. Both of them. Strange, before this all happened, I might have been glad to be away from ma. Now, now—. Oh, Tom, I fear for her. She may never recover."

"I wish none of it had happened at all. Becky, you ain't gonna faint are you?"

"N-no. No. I don't think I have the strength to faint. I—. Tom, I heard something. There. It's him." Tom knew what he had to do. "Will you be alright in there? No telling how long you'll, well—."

"Don't worry, Becky. I'll be fine. Quickly! Seal it."

Becky gazed into Tom's eyes. "Oh, Tom. If worst comes to worst, if you can't find the key, don't endanger yourself for me."

"Becky—,"

"Shh! He might here you. Before sealing the passage completely Becky leaned forward and whispered, "Together forever."

"Always." Tom replied. "But—,"

Becky didn't wait. She cut Tom off, hoping he could forgive her later on. "I, I know he will."

The clinking of what sounded to Becky like glass, buzzed in her ears.

"Hey! Be careful with them jugs, Sim. You wan' 'em to break?"

"No, Jed. They's got liquor in 'em."

"I know *that*."

"And warn't you right glad we came 'pon them fishermen when they was sleepin'? Course, if you hadn't made all that noise—,"

"I wouldn't 'a' had to shout if you'd learn not to turn deef on me all the time. Yer alwus doin' that. 'Mong other things. They stirred, them fishermen. Might 'a' woke. Don't know. Don't wanna know. Now I got to drink down here. I don't like that. I don't like being down here, with, with—. What're you lookin' at, girlie girl? Stop starin' at me like that."

Becky looked away. The last thing on her mind would be to cause an argument.

"Be easy on her. It ain't any of her doing."

"It's *all* of her doing. Her kinds anyway. Every last scrape we been in. It's all her fault, I tell you Sim. Gimme one o' them jugs." Jed picked an area far enough away from Becky to please his conscience. "Thas the stuff, Sim. Come on over. Bring the other jugs with ya."

If Becky thought she had waited a long time for Jed and Sim to pass out cold, Tom would have gladly challenged her assumption.

Becky thankfully welcomed the silence from the men, as they concentrated solely on their drinking. But this silence came at a price. Becky soon found herself falling asleep, and try as she might, she could not fight it for very long. A fallen jug awakened her, as it smashed into another jug underneath.

"They're out cold. Good."

After Becky let Tom out, he asked, "Did you see where they put the key?"

"Tom, I never saw where he hid it, and I never saw it taken out. All I do know is that the bigger one has it. Jed." Becky pointed to the man.

"Well, I'll check his pockets first. Likely it ain't there. Only an idiot would hide it in their pocket."

"Who do you think you're dealing with? Nincompoops! *Do* be careful."

Tom, staying low to the ground, crawling on his hands and knees. At Jed's feet, Tom wiggled his fingers, loosened them, prepared them. He checked the front pants pockets first, then the back. Nothing. Next he tried Jed's jacket. No key. By Jed's side, Tom contemplated. He knew the key wouldn't be in any of the pockets.

"It ain't in any of his pockets," Tom said, creeping back to Becky.

"Are you giving up?"

"Course not."

"What about 'round his neck. That's where I keep the arrow-head."

"I'll try it." But he found no key there either. Now, Tom eyed Jed's boots. "It's the last place it could be," Tom sulked; for he knew what great difficulty removing the boots would be, as each were bound and secured tightly over his feet. Loosening them meant twisting and pulling and scraping against Jed's skin. That might not go unfelt by the man, even in his stupor. "It'll take time. But I got to try."

The first boot took thirty sweat filled minutes to remove; for every time Jed twitched, Tom had to take time out and wait a few minutes before he could find strength to resume.

The drama unbearable, Becky whispered louder than she wanted. "Well?"

"Nothing, yet. Must be the other one," Tom replied.

It took slightly longer to get the other boot off. Before flipping it over Tom hesitated, perhaps to reflect, or prepare himself for the worst. He placed his hand over the boot's opening, covering every last bit of it, lest the key *be* there, it would fall in-between a carelessly left open crack, and fall to the dirt, and be lost forever.

Tom appeared to be grasping something in his hands. Becky's eyes widened as he Crawled back. She saw the gleam in his face, and knew instantly he had succeeded.

"He's found it!"

"I got it Becky. I got it. Just look."

"O.K. I see it. Now unlock this thing from my ankle and let's get out of here. I'm happy too, but now is not the time to show it." Tom understood Becky's torment, and at once unlocked Becky from her bondage. "Ooooh," Becky sighed. The clasp had chaffed and grinded and bit against Becky's skin. The soothing, relaxing relief made her dizzy. Standing, she stretched her leg to regain some of the lost feeling, and discovered she could not stand on her own power, but would need to lean against Tom for support.

"It'll be slow moving, dragging me along."

"We'll make it. But——."

"Tom!" Tom set Becky down. "What are you doing?"

"I need something to slow them down. This ought to answer nicely."

Tom's motives remained unclear, until Becky saw him place the ball and chain next to Jed, then clasp it to his leg, locking it. Pocketing the key, he scrounged up all the candles and matches he could find.

"This way," Tom explained to Becky, "They won't know you're gone right away. It'll give us more time. But when they do realize it, the ball and chain will slow them down."

"Can you hold the lantern, *and* me? If you can't, I'll und——,"

"Why, Becky! You bet I can. Come on."

Walking to the stairs took little effort. The ascent proved to be more challenging.

"Don't feel you have to do too much, Tom."

Tom understood, but deep down inside the "gaudy heroic pirate" in him took charge.

"Becky, you're as light as a feather," the boy fibbed.

Reaching top, Becky whispered, "Now comes the *real* hard part, Tom."

Tom panted. "What could be harder?"

"The door, of course. Long's I've been here, it's been my friend. It creaks when opened. I always heard it. Now, it may be our undoing."

"I'll turn it fast, to get it over with." Even a fast turn created such a haunting, ghostly racket, both Tom and Becky turned pale and quaked. But it opened, and freedom shined only inches away.

"Oh!" Becky joyously cried, breathing in the outside air. Rain softly fell, moving her to tears. She hobbled out into it, squirming unconsciously from Tom's grip, and falling to her knees, contentedly laughing. "It's finally over." Tom helped her stand. "It's really all over." Yes, finally closed was the kidnapping of Becky Thatcher, and may it be for all eternity!

Becky inhaled her new-found freedom. Before exhaling, she, and Tom, heard another hideous creak. No, not a creak. A shriek. A *human* shriek!"

"Sim! Wake up you idiot. I, I can't move my leg. Oh! Thunder and damnation, my head."

"Tis it yer head, or yer leg?" Sim asked groggily.

Tom and Becky heard the loud shriek.

"Damn, Sim! I think, I think it's on me. Damn! It is!"

"Don't cuss in front of the li'l girl."

"Girl nothing. If the ball and chain is around me, it's off her. She's gone, Sim. Do you know what that means?"

"Yes," Sim replied, half asleep. "And I apologize. You go 'head an cuss and swear all you want."

"Swear! Swear! I'm gonna do more than swear. Where 'd she go first? The law, thas where. We got to git her before she gets too far."

"Maybe it's all a dream."

"Dream! I'll show you how much a dream it is. This feel like a dream?"

Jed must have hit Sim, because he yelled out as if in great pain. It woke him up, at any rate.

"Jed, it *is* around you. I can feel it. Hey li'l girl! Li'l girl? Jed, what'd you do with the candles?"

"I didn't—. Oh, she must 'a' took 'em. Damn her! Damn her kind! Waited 'til we was drunk.""

"Wait, she's here. Yes, I feel her."

"Thas me you idiot. Don't waste time on me now, go find her, before she gets too far. Damn her. She'll be the death of us."

Outside, Becky looked to Tom, trying to speak. "I—."

"I know, Becky. Run. Run with me. We can do it. It's just like the three legged race we were in."

"Yes, but we didn't win. We came in second."

"We'll have to come in first this time. See those bushes out yonder? We can hide in them. But we have to hurry."

"I hear him, Tom," Becky panted between breaths. "He's pounding his way up the stairs."

"We're almost there. Weave around those trees, for cover. There, up ahead. See 'em? See the bushes?"

"Oh, my leg, my leg. Yes, yes, I see them."

"Won't be long."

"It hurts."

"I know. I know. Just a few more yards."

Coming out of the cellar, Sim shouted, "Li'l girl!"

"Hesh!" came the cry from his brother. "You'll wake the whole town."

"Here we are. I told, I told you we'd make it. Can you squeeze in?"

Becky pulled herself inside the bushes; Tom followed her.

"We must control our breathing, else he'll hear us sure."

"I know, Tom."

Sim sped by shortly, then doubled back, stopping near the bushes. Out of breath, wet, tired, and scared for his brother, Sim didn't care about finding Becky. He welcomed her departure, for all the trouble she had caused Jed, and quickly returned to him.

Ten minutes later, Tom said, "He's gone now, Becky. We're safe."

"Safe! How wonderful that sounds."

The rain poured harder.

"We'd better get indoors, before we get soaked."

"Too late for that, Tom" Becky coughed. "Besides, if you only knew half of what I went through, you'd know how good this rain feels to me right now."

Becky shut her eyes, and let the rain pour down upon her. She combed through her fingers through her wet hair, washing out the dirt and grime that had built up over three weeks. *Three weeks!* The amount of time amazed Becky.

"We can't waste too much time you know. He might return at any moment."

"I know. I just want to savor my freedom a little longer. You understand, don't you?"

"Sure. Sure I do."

"Good. We'll leave after a few more minutes; just a few blessed more minutes is all."

CHAPTER 29

Aunt Polly, sitting at the kitchen table, stirred absent mindedly in a sugar bowl; a dimly lit lantern, placed in the center of the table, presented an eerie, ghostly aura. She wanted to sleep, but every time she closed her eyes she saw, in vivid detail, the condemned, suspended between Heaven and Earth, gasping for the breath he knew, and *she* knew, would never be.

Every stick of furniture took on the shape of the great oak tree; the flowers on the window sill that drooped and sagged posed the worst nightmare; for when a gust of wind blew forth through an open window, swaying and bending them, lower, lower, lower, the memory of the branch, stripping from the oak, toppling to the ground, mangling the condemned, shook the woman horribly.

A *click* of the kitchen door roused Aunt Polly. She glanced upwards. For a moment she thought the condemned had come "a-haunting" at her door. But the figure was much too small to be the condemned. Focusing her spectacles on the shadowy figure, Aunt Polly saw Tom. His clothes and hair were drenched. Beads of water dripped from his face. The abrupt ending to the rain had been good enough an excuse for Becky to say, "Let's for home."

Aunt Polly, shining the lantern on him, gasped, amazed the boy had put himself within her reach. "Tom! Well you're a sight. Look at you! Don't you come in here all wet. Shake it off. What is your excuse this time, and never mind 'cause you ain't getting out of this—*My!*" Another shadowy figure sheepishly stepped out from behind Tom. The woman, thinking she looked upon a ghost, nearly dropped the lantern. Her hands trembled as she brought them to her mouth. She stared, shocked, bewildered, and in awe.

"You see, Aunt Polly," Tom spoke, guiding Becky inside. "I warn't out causing mischief."

"Land sakes! I don't understand any of it. Becky! You're here." Aunt Polly cried tears of joy.

Tom furnished a quick explanation. Mostly, he "stretched" the truth. "So, Aunt Polly," Tom wrapped up his lie, "After the two men I spotted at the Stantan Home left, I investigated. Turns out they were the kidnappers, and had been keeping Becky in the cellar. Neither of us knows what happened to Jimmy."

Becky, with chattering lips and teeth, agreed. "I-it's t-true."

"Well, there's *more* to this story. But I won't have you die 'fore its told. Of course you'll stay. Your pa, well—."

"I know about pa, and ma too. Tom told me."

"Tom! You oughtn't to have done it."

"Don't blame Tom. I made him tell me. I had to know. Well, their my folks. It was the first thing I wanted to know."

Aunt Polly tapped her hand against Becky's cheek. "Well, perhaps there's sagacity in that. Certainly! You *would* want to know about your family. A pity, oh, what a pity to have to find out that, that—,"

"It's alright. I, ma 'll be fine. At least she's with relatives."

"Yes. You'd do best to get out of those clothes. I'm sure Mary has some things that'll fit you. She's off to St. Louis, so you take her room."

Morning dawned. Becky woke with a slight cough. Aunt Polly, always nimble when such emergencies arose, heard her and ran up as fast as she could with a medicine box under her arm. Hot and cold liquids, the kind that would roast her bowels, were poured down Becky's throat before she had time to protest. However, her own mother being of the same philosophy as Aunt Polly made it easier to absorb the liquids, rather than expel them.

"There now," Aunt Polly said. "That'll help ye some."

"Yes, I'm sure." Becky saw strain in Aunt Polly's demeanor. The woman's stomach clearly turned more than Becky's, who, having seen the same signs in her own mother, became suspicious. "I'll be fine now. You needn't worry about me. I don't want you neglecting your duties on account of me."

"What? No, child, I—,"

"It's alright. See, those liquids me has stopped my coughing." Becky coughed, involuntary, though she tried to hold it back. This reaction is only natural, and to be expected; for when one does not wish to cough, they most often times do.

"Nonsense child. If you're sick, you ought to cough. It's the coughing that helps heal ye. Just you sit up. Here, use these pillows. The medicine will take hold soon. Alwus does for Tom, and so too for ye as well."

Still, the woman showed signs of nervousness. Becky placed a hand atop Aunt Polly's. It shook, slightly.

"You're worried about something. Or, someone."

"I, no. It's, well, yes. But *you* needn't worry."

"I must. I'm holding you back. And it saddens me. Tell me, won't you? If you don't, I know I'll feel awful guilty."

Aunt Polly looked into Becky's eyes and saw both sorrow and anxiety in them.

"Well, I don't want you feeling guilty. Yes, there is another who needs me too. But she'll understand."

"You've been ever so kind to me, letting me stay here. But you go and do what you need to. I insist. I'll be fine."

"You need someone to look after you. Oh, if only Mary were here."

"What about Tom?"

"Tom? Well."

"I've only a cough, from the rain. He'll manage. I know he will."

"Oh, Becky. With your confidence I reckon you could heal on your own. And fast. But I—."

"No. You go to her. I can see she needs you. And I can see you want so much to go to her."

"I, I'll leave the medicines here, on Mary's table. You don't let Tom give you any. I'll have him bring you your meals. Maybe prop up your pillows. If Mary were here, I'd have her do other things for you."

"Oh, I can handle all the rest. Even if Mary was here."

"You're strong willed. And determined."

"Because I am concerned for you. And I don't want to be a burden while I am here." The sweetness of Becky's voice moved Aunt Polly.

"You're not. I'll go tell Tom." Aunt Polly, standing over Becky, pondered the decision. Walking out she sighed, "Least she ain't any worse."

While Becky waited for Tom she gazed through the window, watching the ascending sun usher in the light, the warmth.

"Mmm, that feels so good. I ain't seen the sun in years. it 'pears." The sun vanished behind a cloud, darkening the room. At that moment, Becky began to shake violently. She clutched onto the bed and held on; her feet flipped in the air, and thumped back down upon the mattress, again, and again; the back of her head repeatedly hit the soft pillow. Tom, coming in, rushed to her side, and as he had before, he held on until her body stilled.

"You're alright, now?" Tom asked.

"I am. I, I wish I knew why it happened. It happened while I was in the cellar. I had only myself then, to hold on to. Oh, Tom! Sometimes it frightens me. I'm so afraid that one of these times, when it happens, it never will stop."

"Can I get you anything? Aunt Polly told me I should look after you while she's away seeing Mrs. Loftus."

"No. Just stay. Keep me company. I'm in sore need of it." The sun gushed forth with unexpected brightness, lighting the entire room, entrancing Becky. "Mmmm, that feels wonderful. Last time a saw the sun was after the storm, when those nincompoops dragged me up to Jackson's Island." Becky rose, with an urge to look out the window. She clasped her hands together, rested her head on them, and simply marveled. "It's *really* wonderful, Tom. I've taken the sun for granted before. A great many other things too. But never again. Never ever again."

Tom did not hear her remarks, however. When Becky mentioned being on the island, his mind became a blank.

"You were on Jackson's Island, just after the storm?"

"Around then, yes."

"I was there too, after the storm. I hadn't stepped one foot on sand but I was shot at. Nearly got hit. The raft did, and I rushed back to town, fearing it would break apart."

"Tom! Could it be? But those nincompoops were shooting at somebody. They were afraid it was the law. Was it *you*, Tom?"

I, I reckon it was," Tom said sullenly, bitterly, shamefully. "Oh, if I knew you were up there, I would have done differently. Honest!"

"You couldn't possibly have known."

"It don't matter. I ran. Like a coward, Not like a hero in a book. I ran because I was only thinking of myself, because I didn't want to get shot. Plain old, well, selfishness. I wouldn't blame you if you never spoke to me again. You must hate me so."

Becky, turning to him slowly, weighed the question in her mind for no more than a second. Even that short amount of time bothered Tom. Certainly she would speak up sooner if she thought differently.

"Tom I—. What *would* give you such an idea?"

"It's—. I understand if you do think me a coward."

"But I—,"

"Well, maybe I am. Maybe after all the books I've read, and all the play actin' I've done, and all the play battles I've fought in, preparing for the day I would need those skills, maybe it was all for nothing."

"Tom—,"

"I reckon I *can't* be the gaudy heroic pirate; or the knight that saves the damsel. I s'pose I learnt my lesson. Rot those books. They put the nonsense in my head. It *is* all nonsense, compared to the real thing."

"No, I—,"

"If I'd been cleverer, I'd 'a' got you out sooner, so you wouldn't 'a' had to go through all them hardships. I apologize for my lack of bravery."

"Tom! Will you let *me* say a word in edgewise?" She went to him, shook him by his shoulders, rubbed his cheeks, in a manner of comforting and consoling. "Listen to yourself. Oh, Tom, *Tom!* You're not a coward. On the contrary, I think very highly of you. You're just as noble now, as when you stood up and took *my* whipping before the whole class, sparing me humiliation."

"But up there on Jack—,"

"Blast the island! Oh, to think rescuing somebody would be that easy. But you did it, Tom. You rescued me. It's the second time too. The first was in the cave. I'll never forget that. And now this time. You came for me, and stayed with me when you didn't have to, when it was so easy to just walk away. You risked being caught in order to get the key. Those nincompoops could have woken up, but you persevered. What *coward* would do all that?"

"But the books! All the books, Becky, with child heroes, that fight villains; don't matter how young they are, or what they use. Sticks, stones—well they and other children lam the villains, usually 'thout any harm to them. And they do it with such class and style as never I could do."

"Those books are wicked fantasies, formulated out of the heads of nincompoops who haven't a clue to the reality of life, nor do they care. To think a child could ever rescue somebody from the clutches of an adult, and with *sticks* and *stones*! Against guns and knives! Utterly ridiculous. Children kidnapped by adults in real life generally are tortured and killed in hideous ways. I know. I've overheard pa going over such cases in his study late at night, when he thought I was asleep. I've blocked the most of what I heard out, it's so gruesome. But let me tell you, most of those children kidnapped by adults never live to tell about it, let alone escape.'

"And what about you and Injun Joe? Didn't you confide in me how terrified you were seeing him in the graveyard; that you dreamt of him, staring at you coldly, with murder in his eyes, 'cause you testified against him? That was reality. You didn't for a moment feel safe 'til he was discovered dead at the mouth of the cave. In a book somebody would have you *fight* Injun Joe, and kill him with your bare hands, just to add a bit of excitement. Or perhaps he'd chase you up a cliff, and at the very moment his hand would reach out to pull you in his grasp to kill you— at that moment, with his fingers not an inch away, what do you think but a boulder would give way and come crashing down upon him just in the nick of time. *In a book*! Did it happen that way? No! He never saw you when you called out; never even recognized your voice. He ran at the sound; it must 'a' been an eerie echo for him, on the run and all. Days later, you found him sprawled out on the cavern floor, dead from starvation. But there's nothing sensational about that, not in any of those romance-adventure novels you read.'

"But we were lucky Tom. You know the only reason they kept me was that they were afraid of what would happen to them if they let me go? They feared being hunted down and killed in cold blood." Becky took a breath "Oh, Tom, please, please, please don't think yourself a coward. In my eyes you're not, and never will be." Becky cried somewhat, as she tried to reach Tom. "We can still read the books, and enjoy them; but one thing I've learned is we ought not take them seriously. Most are joyful. And the play-acting we do, well, I hope we can continue it for a long time. Knights and damsels, and kings and chivalry and all the like. I *hope* we can. But don't take them seriously."

Becky's remarks trickled through Tom's mind; and while he knew she spoke honest wisdom, to break away from books—oh, to break away from books! He did not know if he had it in him. They were his only escape from ordinary life in St. Petersburg. Yet, for Becky's sake, he would try.

"Tom, it don't make any difference *how* I was rescued, so long as I *was*. And for all the books written about people in prisons or dungeons, I've yet to read one that is realistic; that deals with the reality, the true experiences prisoners suffer. I don't reckon there ever will be one. Nobody 'd publish it; it'd be too horrid. For *me*, it was horrid, but not as horrid as others. I'll tell you, every last detail. Right now, I only want to talk about us. But you mustn't think yourself a coward. I'll have none of that."

"Well, no, no, I guess not."

"Tom Sawyer!" The boy stood at attention. "Are you a coward?"

"No"No!" he said with conviction.

"That's more like it. You just don't realize all the help you've——. Why look, look at this." Becky removed the arrow-head from her around her neck. "This saved my life, twice."

"The arrow-head?"

"Yes, the arrow-head. I'll tell you all about it too, later. Tom, I, I know you let me borrow it——. I wonder, I wonder——. I'd like to keep it, always, if you haven't any objections. Oh, It's asking a lot, I know, but——,"

"Becky, I wouldn't have it any other way."

"Y-You mean it! Thank you. Oh, *thank* you." She embraced Tom. "I'll keep it hid 'round my neck, under my dress. I'll never remove it so long as I live. It'll be *our* secret."

As the talk continued, Becky carefully, and slowly, unfolded to Tom everything she remembered having had happened to her. His reaction would be, "My god," after every revelation Becky made; and he quickly realized that what Becky had gone through would never find its way into any book, ever.

After three days Becky's cough ceased, but she kept it up, giving Tom an excuse to stay with her. Aunt Polly insisted Becky remain in bed a week; the usual length of time for a non-serious sickness. Aside from her slight cough, Becky suffered no side effects from being kidnapped. Perhaps she had strength enough to overcome them; perhaps she had repressed some, or all, of them. At any rate, outwardly her appearance stayed tranquil and content. One which may, later on in her life, do serious harm.

With Tom to look after Becky, the wrinkles on Aunt Polly's face relaxed. Now her attention could be focused on Judith, who had become a nervous wreck. In their conversations, which ignited many unkind and unpleasant words about Cy, Judith revealed everything she had gone through in her marriage. They were biting remarks, but Judith said them gladly. Aunt Polly, always the attentive listener, sat with her, held her, cried with her. Then, after Judith told her everything, Aunt Polly wanted to know why he had been so cruel. Judith feared her reaction, for it would most certainly spell a nasty end to their friendship. It would also spell a new life for Judith; one she knew she would never survive. As both women clung tightly to one another, Judith explained the truth about herself.

"So now you know the whole story, the absolute truth, Polly." Judith cried in her friends arms, noticing Aunt Polly's grip did not loosen. In fact, it tightened. "You can loathe me as husband does. I deceived you just as much as I did him. I deceived everyone. I had to."

"I'm not mad at ye, Judith. I love you too much to feel animosity towards you. What you did, you had to."

"Thank you," she sobbed. "Thank you. I don't understand your approval. It might become dangerous for you, if anyone else found out; if husband were to tell anyone. I thought he might understand, as you do, when I told him. But laws alive, Polly! He only looked at me with an icy, cold stare, then walked out of the house. He didn't return for two weeks. He never touched me again, or slept in the same room with me he was so ashamed.'

"The day after he returned he took our son to a nearby pond, to learn him to swim. He'd alwus wanted a son, and was so proud of ours." She cried harder. "An hour later husband returned, without our son. He sat down in his chair and slept. I couldn't understand. Where was our son? I couldn't wake husband. Laws, nobody could wake husband when he slept. Two hours I paced the floor, with him sleepin'. Finally he woke, and soon as he did I demanded to know where our son was.'

"Polly! Without any concern whatsoever husband said, 'He's drowned'. I nearly died. Our boy was dead, and husband knew it for over two hours before he told me. I wanted to know how. He said it was an accident. He left after that, on one of his hunts. The next day I found myself outside, in the back, standing over a newly dug grave. I say *found*, because I wasn't sure how I got there. I had no memory of it. Forgive me, Polly, if I'm wrong. I think husband murdered him. Won't ever be proved, but—. Husband hated the reality you see. Our boy was more *me*, than him. Oh, Polly, you just can't imagine all I've had to endure with husband. Well, I've lived a very sheltered life since I told Cy. I haven't been out much. My mind has softened."

"Oh, you poor, poor—. You come here." Aunt Polly held her friend tight; her own blood boiled and seethed. "Judith, the way that man has treated you all these years; not even the Devil is that wicked."

"I know that now. I alwus hoped he'd change. If only I hadn't told him the truth about me. I know in my heart he'd still love me; I know our son would be alive this day."

"What happened warn't your fault."

"He's gone for good. It's for the best, perhaps. I ought to be glad he's gone. I ain't got to fret nor worry whether he'll ever return. I can sleep decently now. I'm so alone, Polly, now that I have no-one."

"You have some-one. You have me. You'll not live your life alone any longer Judith Loftus."

"Please, don't use that name. I can't bear it."

"Of course. Your husband has treated you revoltingly. Don't you be ashamed of *your*self, not one bit. You were loyal, and all he did was degrade you, time and time again. Don't you worry over him. His day is coming, the scoundrel. He'll *pay* for his actions."

"I know it, Polly. But still, it don't ease the pain much, nor the anguish. He'll live for decades more, I'm sure. And I want him to get his just reward now. Is that too cruel, to say, to *want*, such a thing?"

"I dare say not, after all he's done to you. Why, if ever I come across him—." Aunt Polly curbed her tongue; she came near to cursing, and she had no mind to say anything in front of Judith. "I've noticed your anger and hostility and bitter resentment towards him from the time you arrived. I didn't think much of it; you always praised him so touchingly. But Judith, something constantly nagged at me, and I wanted to ask you about him. The way you speak of him, I knew you wasn't being honest, somehow. I understand now, why you did it. I understand everything. I see the remoteness of your relationship. You never called him by his name, but always—*husband*. Just, husband. He was that distant."

"Oh, no, Polly. You have it all wrong. It isn't that I don't *want* to say his name. It's just, after all these years, I've, well—I've *forgotten it.*"

CHAPTER 30

Widow Douglas dreamt of the hanging five times during the night. After the fifth, though not nearly seven a.m., she vehemently opposed a sixth dream. Rising hastily she threw off her blankets in disgust. Now standing, nothing could induce her from falling back asleep to dream such monstrous dreams. She opened her shades. The room did not illuminate very brightly. It wouldn't until after 7:30, when the sun ascended high enough over her willow trees.

Breathing in the morning air, she watched her favorite trees sway in the wind. Vulgar noises interrupted her thoughts. Looking down, she saw doctor Towers standing near the slave quarters with another, strange, man. They shouted at one another. Though unsure, she thought she heard the man demand something. The object of his desire sounded like a necklace, but he swore so violently, Widow Douglas did not hear anything else. She instantly, and instinctively, closed her window, refusing to hear such talk. However, she watched the strange man shake his fist violently at doctor Towers, then turn and walk away, stomping his feet, presumably in disgust.

This man looked familiar to Widow Douglas, but try as she might, she could not place him. His long drooping mustache, hanging below his chin, made her feel uneasy. She gave up, presently, to check on her sister.

"Go away this instant!" shouted Miss Watson. I'm not having company."

"I'm not company. I'm your sister." Widow Douglas stood at the door, her mouth pressing against it. Had the door been a window, it would have fogged up densely with thick layers of breath. Widow Douglas wished she might see through the door, as the desperate need to know the condition of her sister grew. She had reasons for not opening it.

"I have no wish to see anyone, thank you."

"You've been crying. I can tell it by—,"

"Nonsense! I haven't."

"Have you eaten?"

"No."

"I'll have Ruth bring—,"

"No you won't either. I couldn't hold anything down."

"You *must* eat."

"Must I?"

"Is it the hanging that has you acting this way? Believe me sis, I know how you feel. I saw it too, remember. Cruel and barbaric. Something ought to be done about *it* and the sheriff. Something *will* be done. Ben sent a letter to Senator, to Jonathon for me, after we returned home. You remember him?"

"It's not the hanging; not *just* the hanging," Miss Watson opened up. "It *was* horrible, I admit. How could—. Oh sis, why do you torment me so? Can't you see I want to be alone!"

If only she *could* see. "I know something's troubling you. Please, I do wish you'd tell me. When we were little we told each other everything. It was so much easier then. I told you things, private things, I wouldn't tell anyone. My secrets were secure in your possession, as yours were in mine. Let's put an end to the secrecy. Tell me, what is bothering you?" Widow Douglas paused for a response. None came. "Is it my marrying Ben? We caught you off guard? It was sudden of us too."

"I said I wanted to be alone. Stop bringing up the past." Talking into the mirror she said, "Always alone. All my life I've been alone, isolated from the world. It didn't matter I mingled around people, I was still alone. They could see me, but I was a serpent to them, and they cast me out. Oh, to think how alone I am because that is what society wanted." She shouted at the door. "I want to be alone! Can't you have respect for your elder sister?"

"I have always respected you." Widow Douglas touched the door gently, rubbing it with her fingertips. "This is her door. It's almost like I am touching her. It's as close to her as I can get." The impulse to open the door, to know how her sister occupied her time, expanded by leaps and bounds. Her hand inched towards the knob; a light touch sent a bolt of electricity throughout her body. She ran away, down the hall, down the stairs.

Miss Watson, sensing her sister had left, resumed crying, letting the tears fall without caring where they landed. Her long-length mirror rested against the back wall, and for hours she examined herself, dressed, semi-dressed, in the nude, in different clothing, from head to foot, to find out just what the world found so repulsive about her. Had she known it came from within, she might not have stared at herself for so long.

"All the years I've wasted and toiled away, waiting. For what! Sis thinks I don't cry. I have, every day for nearly ten years. You cursed devil! Why did you do it? How happy I, *we*, would have been. Instead, I'm bitter and resentful. Look at me! Old and grey and wrinkled, and so bitter. How many slaves I thrashed because of you, to take out my revenge, to appease my anger. It was *you*, after-all, in their faces. You made my blood seethe, my body turn crimson with anger, my insides tense and become rigid and unfeeling. Brit was right. I haven't stopped thinking about you all these many sad and lonely years. I've not let go. You were all I had in this barren, depraved world. You were the first; you were the last. You were my only love, and the only one that loved me. Shameful. *Shameful*, you left. I begged you to take me with; I was down on my knees. I knew once you left, you'd never return.'

"To think it took the hanging of a nig—, a nig—. Why, look at me. I can't bring myself to use that word any longer. All my life I have used it fluently. Now, somehow, I can't. But when I saw how terribly frightened he was, why—something about him was so pitiful, so undeniably remorseful, so *human*. And I only thought of myself, my eagerness to make money on Jim. I should never have done it. I killed that slave, sure as if I had pulled the rope. I condemned him by my outrageous actions. I wish I may never have offered a reward. Bless the one that helped him escape. My god!" she gasped. "Did I say that? Oh, why didn't I stop it? I could have, I think. I've influence in this town. Oh, why didn't I? Why do I never do anything right? Well, I mean to do something about it now. I can't save *him*, but—."

A box that had rested comfortably on her dresser, never having done anybody the least bit of harm, flew violently in the air, somersaulting with such grace, Barnum and Bailey would have signed it to a long contract. As Miss Watson rubbed her swollen knuckles, the lid opened. Paper inside floated to the ground, scattering all around. The box finally landed on a chair, displacing a society of dust, throwing it into an apocalyptic nightmare all over Miss Watson's bed clothes. Other contents also blanketed the surrounding area. None were ever picked up.

Running down the flight of stairs, Widow Douglas nearly met doctor Towers head on.

"Oh!" Widow Douglas composed herself. "I didn't see—. I'm Sorry. I, I was with sis. That is, by her door."

"Oh? How is she doing?"

"She won't come out; she won't eat. I'm so afraid for her."

"Perhaps she needs some time. It's the hanging that has made her ill."

"No. It's not. It's not just the hanging. I'm sure it stems back to Mr. Johansson. She was so happy and alive then. After he went to Texas, she curled up in a ball and stuck herself in a closet. Well, such is life, I suppose." In the sitting room, Widow Douglas asked about the stranger.

"Man?" doctor Towers asked innocently. "What man might that be?"

"The man you were with out back. The one who was shouting at you."

"Oh. Yes. Ah, well—. Did you hear anything?"

"I heard vulgar cursing, and that was enough for me. I shut my window promptly."

"Good. Good." A sense of relief came over doctor Towers. "He was a slave trader, he said."

"Slave trader! What on earth would he-! You don't suppose sis has gone and sold another slave?"

"Well," Ben scratched his head. "I believe he did mention buying Ruth. Never mentioned Miss Watson. A scavenger, likely. One of those uncouth sorts who rides into a small town, hoping to buy one or two slaves at low cost, then either sell them at auctions, or down river; always for a higher profit. I've seen their kind in operation down in Mission. Vulgar, filth of a man. He wouldn't take no for an answer."

"What is it with people, that they think they can come upon my property and demand anything they want?"

The following days for Widow Douglas were torturous and endless ones, tending to her sister, standing outside her door, sitting up against it when she tired; often she fell asleep. Many times she wanted to force open the door and drag her sister out. She resisted, having her own, personal reasons.

One occasion, while downstairs shooing away another nosy reporter who wanted to know about her next party, a loud crash echoed from upstairs; undoubtedly, her sister's room. Slamming the door on the reporter, Widow Douglas flew upstairs.

"Sis! What happened!" Widow Douglas banged away on the door; her voice trembled and shook; her face paled, fearing something awful had happened.

"It's nothing you ought to worry over. I assure you I'm fine."

"Fine! I heard a crash. A very loud crash."

"Well, I, I moved the dresser; the mirror toppled over."

"Gracious! What would make you do such a thing?"

"I wanted to see something. Please, go. Leave me be." Though her voice sounded weaker, Widow Douglas did not dare open the door.

On another occasion, late at night, Widow Douglas awoke to a strange squeaking noise. She followed it to her sister's room and listened. Pressing her ear to the door she heard footsteps pacing back and forth; and mumbling; garbled, incoherent jargon from her sister's lips. The only words she deciphered were "Mr. Johansson", and "not fair".

The urge to open the door grew its strongest now. Again, her arm shook tremendously the more she turned the knob; and the electrical shocks she received, pulsating first through her hand, then her arm, then her entire body, were so painful she had no choice but to release her grip from the knob. Once her hands were at her side she calmed. In bed, Widow Douglas lay awake, unable to sleep for hours. She swore she could here her sister pacing in all that time.

Before heading down to breakfast, Widow Douglas stopped at her sister's door. Haunting silence was all she heard. Still, she dared not enter. Not alone. Seeking Doctor Towers, she learned from Ginny he had gone out earlier. An unsettled stomach prevented her from eating until he returned.

Hours passed. A door opened. "Ben! Where were you?"

"Ho, there now," doctor Towers said, caught off guard. "I had something to attend to. Errands, and such. That is what kept me." He would not tell her he had run into Cy, and that the bounty hunter threatened their lives; all because they had interfered at the hanging.

"Ben, she's up there, pacing and talking to herself. I can't stand it any more. And I can't go in alone."

"Well, you want me to look in on her now?"

"I, I, oh! I know it's the right thing to do, and I know we should have earlier, but, but—. Do it! Do it! I can't bear it any longer. It's been four days since the hanging, and she hasn't eaten anything, and I just want to know how she is. I was wrong to wait."

"I was wrong too. I kept saying, 'she's your sister, you know best'. I should have listened to my own medical instincts."

They both walked with heavy feet upstairs.

"She won't like it. But, it's for the best." Reaching the top landing Widow Douglas nearly froze. A voice from the past whispered in her ear. "*You never, ever disturb a person in their own room.*" The scorning voice came from her dead mother. As a little girl Widow Douglas had opened up her mother's bedroom door, without first announcing herself. She only wanted to wish her mother a happy birthday, but instead walked in on her completely undressed, and in the arms of a man other than her father. Widow Douglas left the room, having been severely whipped. Afterwards her mother became distant and cold. The event haunted Widow Douglas, and from that point on she feared closed doors; she feared what lurked behind them.

Doctor Towers placed a hand upon the knob. Widow Douglas involuntarily laid her hand over his, almost preventing the door from being opened. However, Doctor Towers strength prevailed, and as the door swung open, the first time in nearly a week, Widow Douglas' fears returned. Her naked mother, and *that man*, flashed in front of her.

Papers lay, all over the floor; glass from a broken mirror lay in sharp, jagged pieces; clothes, some quite expensive, were scattered everywhere. Dust, unexpectedly, covered the entire room, from one corner to another, suffocating the beauty of everything in the room. In the past, Miss Watson had been particular about dust in her room; she could not tolerate one single speck within eyesight; and would take switch in hand and inflict harm on the one who left it there.

The bed cover Miss Watson picked out at a store in St. Louis half a year earlier, one she had revered and declared the most magnificent and quality hand made spread created on earth, now lay mostly in a heap on the floor near the end of her bed. The rest cascaded over the edge.

"Oh my!" Widow Douglas gasped weakly. Clutching the door frame, she saw

her sister laying in her bed, wearing the same dress she wore the day of the hanging. "She, she tore it. Tore it to shreds, nearly."

"Wait there, Brittany. I'll have a look-see." Meekly, she obeyed. Doctor Towers sat down upon her bed and looked her over.

"Is, is she—,"

"No." He sensed her thoughts. "But very weak. Her heartbeat is abnormal. She's awful warm. But, it's awful warm in this room, with the air sealed off. Her pillow, where she laid her head is soaked."

"Will she be, alright?"

"Can't say. I better open this window. Get in some fresh air, and sunlight."

Miss Watson stirred slightly; her eyes opened and bobbed lazily around the room, falling on her sister. She rigidly lifted her arm and pointed to her dresser, near the door. Widow Douglas believed herself the target.

"I know sis. I know it was wrong of me!" she screamed and cried. "Please forgive me. I know it was wrong to come in here. I know mother always forbade it. You know what she did to me. Please, don't be mad. I love you so. That's why I came."

"Brittany, get hold of yourself. There now, Miss Watson." He put his hand around the woman's shoulder for support. "You just take 'er easy."

The sick woman tried to pull away. She said, "Ungdruther," while continuing to point towards the dresser with her remaining strength.

"My god! Ben, what did she say?"

"Ungdruther," she gurgled again.

"I didn't know it before. But I think it's much worse than I—. Miss Watson, please, say something else. Tell me, how well is your speech?"

The answer came in the form of babbled words neither Widow Douglas nor Ben could understand. Still, Miss Watson pointed forcibly at the dresser and repeated, "Ungdruther," over and over.

"Brittany. Look on the dresser, please. There, it 'pears to be a piece of paper. I think she wants us to look at it." Widow Douglas hesitated, but as soon as she found strength to pick it up, Miss Watson sank back down in her bed. "Brittany, I don't know how to tell you, but,"

"Oh, no! No! No!"

"What is it?

"Come here, now. Look at it. Do you know what it is?

Ben perused it. "It's a letter."

"It's, it's a *will*. She wrote a will. Ben, she, why would she?"

"Brittany," Ben quietly spoke. "Your sister's had a stroke."

"What?"

"She's, dying."

"No!"

"I know it's hard, and I detest telling you in this manner, but you must be strong. I don't know how long she has. She's in pain right now. I've some medicine in another bag. I'm going to get it. I need you to sit by her side; be everything for her, and do everything for her. She needs you know."

"Ben." Widow Douglas cried in his arms.

"I know. We must do everything to make her feel comfortable. I'll be back with the medicine."

Widow Douglas crept towards her sister, sitting upon the bed. "It's as close as I've been to you in many years. I, I don't—." She gripped her sister tenderly in her arms, and broke down.

"Oh, sis. Why, why, why? Why did I wait? My god, but you are in such pain. I can see how much pain you're in. Oh, sis. What am I to do? I, I— oh, sis. I wish Ben would hurry. Does it hurt when I hold you? Oh, you can't answer me. Can you shake your head? No, not hardly. Oh, dear god, sis. Why did I wait? It's my fault. If I'd been more quick—if only I'd overcome my fear and entered sooner."

Five minutes later, doctor Towers reentered.

"Brittany!" he exclaimed in alarm. "You mustn't hold her like that. It's too painful for her. Let her lay back."

"No," Widow Douglas cried. "She has no more pain."

"No more pain? I don't understand. I——. You mean——."

"Yes, Ben. She's, she's gone."

"She can't be. Not this soon." He would not believe it until he felt her pulse. But afterwards he finally conceded Miss Watson had really died. "I don't quite understand. She was very weak, but she would have lived the rest of the week, I believed. Well," he sighed, "Everyone has their own time and place. I reckon this was Miss Watson's."

Widow Douglas gently laid her sister's head upon the pillow. "She's at peace now, Ben. She at peace. She's—oh, god, Ben, she's gone." Falling atop her sister she smothered her lifeless body, crying, crying, crying.

Doctor Towers, uncomfortable around death, became more so with Miss Watson's. Not since Clara's death had he ever shivered. As the woman lay resting upon the bed, peacefully, solemnly, he recalled Clara looking much the same after she died.

So, Miss Watson slept, forever. Widow Douglas laid the lifeless hands upon one another, upon her stomach. She and doctor Towers stood over her, holding a moment of silence. Strangely, they discovered in her something different, striking, and altogether incongruous to her nature. It wasn't that her wrinkles, once imposing and threatening when she stretched them, seemed more relaxed, more tender, now that they were no longer useful. Nor her "Medusa" eyes, which in life beamed and brimmed with hellfire and brimstone, and petrified everyone. Those same eyes now beamed soulfully, heavenly, peaceful, and completely at ease. What on earth transformed Miss Watson into a creature as angelic and sweet natured in death, as beastly in life? And her face glowed! Why, yes! A smile! Of all things, a smile. She never smiled in life; not in public, and not in all the years after Mr. Johansson left her. Every other facial expression had been diligently formed with absolute conviction on those once bitter lips. But alas—a smile! A smile that had never been crafted until this ghastly, horrible hour. A sweet smile; a tranquil smile; not a particularly large smile, but a beautiful smile none-the-less, as far as Widow Douglas was concerned; for it brought the *life* back in Miss Watson.

CHAPTER 31

After seven full days, Aunt Polly allowed Becky to escape the tangled sheets of bed confinement, which the girl did happily, strolling down to the breakfast table with Tom. The two met Sid, who busily ate his breakfast. He watched Becky, particularly, out the corner of his eye, with that ever suspicious, ever sinister, smile flirting about his mouth, waiting for the right opportunity to strike. When that opportunity arose, he said—

"What was it like?"

Tom and Becky stopped their speech, and looked up at him.

"What was what like?" Tom asked.

"I wanted to know what Becky's kidnapping was like; how scared and frightened she was. After-all, being kidnapped is a horrible experience unto itself, but if you're a girl and you're kidnapped, well it's most scarier."

"How do you know that?" Becky asked, whimsically; for she understood Sid's nonsensical nature.

"It only stands to reason. Girl's have no back bone, not being created with one; they're yella, with the stripe right down the middle of their back; and they're afraid of just everything that crosses their path."

"You think so, do you?" she remarked, humorously.

"Why—I *know* so. It's in your nature, your sex, to be scared. It's nothing for you to be ashamed of. I bet they threw you in a room with hoards of rats, and you all the time shrieking and yelling and clawing at the walls. It'd be most horrible for a girl; especially the rats that gnaw at you and nip at your toes and fingers. Oh, and of course the *darkness*— why, I can imagine your terror, being in a room with rats and spiders and all sorts of those creepy crawly creatures, in the dark. They all the time crawling over you, getting in your clothes, and in your hair—your hair especially. It's all right for you to cry now, and let it all out, as you must have cried then you poor, poor child. To think of the many tears you shed because you hadn't a man at your side to protect you and care for you; to capture you before you hit the cold, hard ground all the times you fainted in your girlish weakness; to hold your hand throughout and whisper to you sweet, poetic lies in your ears; sweet, white lies how everything would be all right, and how no harm would come to you so long as *he* was by your side. But alas, poor child, there you were, without that man. Poor, poor little thing, you." Sid bowed his head and sighed in phony despair for Becky.

Becky allowed the boy to finish his pathetic, mocking speech uninterrupted; for, as a guest, she knew her manners. Now, she had to let Sid know her true feelings, guest or no guest. Her face reddened a few moments, while she gathered herself. Her cheeks expanded like balloons. Before Sid, or Tom for that matter, could decipher the girl's response, she made it crystal clear. She laughed. She laughed at such a magnitude it shook the entire house; she fell from the table and onto the floor, pounding it with her fists. Her face turned a delightful, unabashed crimson as she rolled over on her back, clutching her stomach, her head, her mouth, in this uncontrollable fit of laughter. She did cry; but they were tears of delicious felicity.

Sid did not catch on, and so exclaimed, "She's gone mad! I've read about it, so know all the symptoms. Oh, I've recalled the painful, haunting memories too sudden, too soon for this poor, lost child. She couldn't handle it. Ah, such is girls; such is girls." Sid clasped his hands piously.

Hearing *this*, Becky roared harder. Regaining her composure she returned to the table; her mouth still twitching widely.

Tom, feeling he had to say something, attempted to intervene; but Becky stopped him. "No," she said. "I know what I'm doing."

Sid, still unwise, foolishly replied, "I *am* sorry for dredging up those painful memories; those memories you will carry with you for the rest of your life. It may be smart of you to kill yourself, on Lover's Leap. Nobody would blame you. Likely your mind will become such, that you will find it necessary to retreat to a convent and live with the nuns, and pray they whip you, and beat you every day, when you have such outbursts."

"I hope not Sid. I never cared for such places. I'd *really* go insane if I were to live amongst them for any length of time. But never you fear, all that you conjured up is untrue, so rest your over stimulated, weary mind. My kidnapping wasn't a tenth what you made it out to be. It wasn't blessed, but I never once thought of killing myself. No, I never waited for anyone to come rescue me, but took action to rescue myself. But I would have welcomed anyone, even you, Sid, to come rescue me. I never fainted at the sight of rats, spiders, or any creature; why, I made friends with them, and I let them crawl freely over my legs and on my shoulders, and made pets of some of them. None ever nipped or gnawed at my fingers or toes. Such silly nonsense you create out of that fragmented mind of yours. Where ever do you get it all?"

Before Sid could respond, Aunt Polly walked in, sullenly, holding a newspaper at her side; her eyes puffed noticeably.

"Why what's the matter, Auntie?" Tom asked.

"Some terrible news," she spoke softly and withdrawn. "Miss Watson has died." Though she hadn't known Miss Watson well, a death always grieved her. She once cried tears over Injun Joe! Aunt Polly held the newspaper up, to reveal the front page story, and an etchinge of Miss Watson, taken from a painting done years earlier. "She died two days ago, peacefully, thank the Lord, in her sleep. There was a private funeral. In attendance were her sister; her doctor, Ben Towers; and two of Miss Watson's slaves. She was buried behind the house, underneath Widow

Douglas' favorite willow trees. By the way, I heard laughing a few minutes ago. What was it all about?"

Becky hung her head, shamefully. "I'm awful sorry. That was me. I had no idea about Miss Watson. I shouldn't have laughed anyway."

"It's all right, honey. It's good to see you in high spirits again. You been through so much, you need to laugh." Aunt Polly glanced back towards the newspaper. "At least she died peacefully, in her sleep."

Breakfast through, Tom and Becky excused themselves. They had planned a return to the Stantan Home this day, before knowing the fate of Miss Watson. Now the two laboriously debated the properness of going, or waiting an extra day. Both eventually decided to go, and not dwell on Miss Watson's death. Whether proper or not, they weren't ever sure.

So, Tom and Becky bravely forged ahead towards the Stantan Home where, only one week earlier, they fled for their very lives. They carried an abundance of candles, and a lantern Tom managed to hide away; two canteens of water apiece, so that no "drastic measures" need be taken; and two shovels.

Their talk was spry and vibrant; they were gay in the determination that scourge of dirt would finally be removed. Reaching the hilltop this gaiety subsided. The Stantan Home lay a mere one hundred fifty feet away, but a new, unsettling thought seemed to bring it closer.

"Tom, you reckon they *are* gone? I heard one of 'em talking in their sleep 'bout somebody they wanted to get even with right here in town."

"I s'pose they gave up on that once you escaped. They've fled sure."

"Not Jed. Not with that ball and chain 'round his leg."

"Becky! I forgot that. I most wish I hadn't put it on him now. Why, they might be down there yet. *Dead*."

"Tom!"

"Do we dare?"

"I, I'm willing. If you are. And I do want to find the treasure. We worked so hard already. Why should we give up on it because we only *think* they're still down there?"

Tom agreed. How could he say no? He held a stone in his hand, and when he and Becky reached the cellar door, Tom threw it down, listening, waiting, preparing to scurry away if the need arose.

"Nobody's down there, Tom. Else they'd investigate the noise."

"Maybe. Might be a trap. We'll go down, but don't light a candle."

Slowly they descended, clinging to one another for support.

"This is the spot, Becky. I'll light a candle now. If we see a dead body we can run."

And what an awesome sight they did behold, laying only feet in front of them. Not a dead body, but the ball and chain.

"Looks like it's been shot off, Tom."

"It's good they ain't *that* dumb. 'Pears to have taken three or four shots before they finally blew it off. Here's a couple of the ball bearings. Becky, let's keep 'em, one apiece. We can show these off sometime."

"They won't amount to shucks, when we find that treasure."

"That's so. Maybe I'll keep mine for trading, then."

"Well, yes, I didn't think of that." Becky pocketed a ball bearing, then anxiously opened up the passage. "Tom, I know what the books say about treasure hunting, but we can stray, a little. Don't you reckon?"

"I, well, we've lived up to the books; maybe if we *ate* some of the dirt, that would settle it."

"I've already done that. I was so hungry, well I thought maybe a little taste wouldn't hurt. It was terrible; awful gritty and bitter."

"That's to be expected. If dirt tasted good, people wouldn't ever go hungry, 'cause it's lying around just everywhere."

As Becky entered, a blazing lantern held out in front, Tom followed behind with both shovels. Work progressed speedily; and because shovels were used, instead of small hands, it did not take long before the tunnel widened, exciting and encouraging the children. Each curiously noted the passage seemed to dip downwards. When both were able to stand up, side by side, with room to spare, they motioned for a break.

"D'you see how the tunnel is sloping downwards at a greater level, Becky? Well, we're going down. Don't know how far, but you know the Stantan Home sets atop the highest hill. We must be nearing river level."

"I can't stop thinking about all those rumors I've heard growing up; all that money is said to have disappeared. If it's true, then, well it must be down here, at the end of the tunnel."

"Naturally. Well, not too many people in this town care for investing their time in what's only based on rumors. That's what separates me, from them. There's more fact in rumors than people know."

"I believe you're right, Tom. I wouldn't be down here if I thought otherwise." Becky laughed, slightly, as a long forgotten stitch of mental history from her childhood re-emerged after so long an absence. "I went to a party once, with pa, when I was younger; for dignitaries and politicians and such. Well, I remember desperately trying to get pa's attention. I was thirsty, you see. He never noticed, so finally I went in search of the punch bowl on my own. I came across a couple of people talking about the Stantan Home and—Tom, I'd forgotten all this, and might not ever remembered it but for you wanting to find the treasure here. Isn't that strange? Well, one of these fellows was our senator, and he talked grandly and affectionately of the Stantans. Oh, but it's all coming back now. He called them true Americans; but now that they were dead, things would be different. Or did he say things would change?" Becky tried to recall. "I guess I can't remember it all. It was the way he talked about them, that stuck in my mind. I've heard pa talk about them from time to time, but not as that senator did; not with the love and respect he labored to put into every word. I wisht I could've met the Stantans, I said then." After a slight pause, Becky sighed, "Well, it's all I can recall right now." She stood, and brushed the bits of dirt off herself. "Ready to go back in?"

Tom hopped to his feet and followed Becky. In another fifteen minutes their hopes soared, as the dirt, for the first time, began petering out.

"Won't be long now," Tom said, between breaths.

"Can't you feel it?"

"I sure can."

Whatever "it" was, neither exactly knew; but that didn't matter. Their aspirations were soon to be realized. Ten minutes later they threw down their shovels and jumped up and down, relieved and excited.

"We've done it, Becky! You and I."

"I know it. Oh, how I know it."

Gathering their gear, for nothing must be left behind, Tom and Becky crept slowly down the exposed tunnel.

"It's hard to see how much deeper it goes. Maybe you should have brought another lantern."

"Becky, I had a hard enough time getting this one. No matter. We'd been descending and winding for so long, now it 'pears we're leveling off."

They moved along cautiously down the tunnel, until the lantern hit upon something up ahead—something which made them both stop dead in their tracks. Their hearts increased in beats. All their hard work had finally paid off. Tom and Becky glowed with delightful, delicious repose. Ah—but they tingled!

They walked slower, but steadfast. Not a whisper stirred in the air. Closer, closer, closer still! Their bodies stiffened the nearer to the object they came. Closer, closer, closer until!...

"Oh! Tom!" Becky cried out. Tom shined the lantern directly on the object that lay only inches apart from them.

"Becky, I—. I don't know—I don't know what to say."

"Who would? I never—. I, in all my days, I never saw—."

"Neither have I. Stay calm though. Let's not overreact."

"Leaves a person gasping for speech." Both were bedazzled. "Tom, I, I never expected *this*. What can it mean?"

"I dunno. I'm as dumbfounded as you. Must be a, a logical reason."

Becky pointed. "*There are two skeletons down here!* A man's and a woman's, as the clothing would indicate. There'd *better* be a reason."

"Well, pirates always throw a man in with the treasure, and by and by he dies, and all that remains is his skeleton, to warn others who find the treasure to leave it be."

"But there's no treasure."

"Well, no. But the passage goes on a ways more. Maybe these two tried hunting for the treasure, but ran out of food, or oxygen, or—oh, I dunno. Maybe this is only to frighten away treasure hunters. Well, I ain't afeared."

"I wonder who they a—. Who they *were*."

"Dunno. Traitors, perhaps."

"Oh, Tom. I just had a thought. What if, if those skeletons are—. Oh."

"Are what?"

"Are, the Stantans."

"They can't be. You know, as I do, Murrell's Gang murdered them, and threw their bodies in the river."

"Nobody knows for fact it was Murrell's Gang."

"What're you getting at?"

"Their bodies were never recovered. They were only thought to have been thrown in the river. It *must* be them." Becky looked long and hard the two skeletons. "It *is* them! Look!" Becky pointed a shaky finger, pushing it nearer to one of the skeleton's. "Look at that one's finger. What do you think that is?"

"Why, yes. I hadn't noticed before. I was too afr—. Too busy thinking who they was. It's so large."

"Largest diamond ring ever *I* saw."

"Only Mrs. Stantan would wear such a ring."

"That means the reports of them being thrown in the river *were* false. There was an eyewitness, said he saw Murrell's Gang; said he heard them bragging they had just murdered the Stantans. Who? Who was it?"

"I dunno. I—. By jings! Muff! Muff Potter was the eyewitness."

"No! Is it so?"

"Yes! And he was drunk, which is why many people threw up their noses at him and his story. Maybe some was fact; maybe some wasn't.'

"Do you reckon he lied?"

"Muff? Not likely. He was drunk; probably hallucinating. Well, he don't know the first thing about lying. I saw him break down and confess to a murder he never committed."

"I was there too. Do we tell anyone about this?"

"I don't—. Not right now. This may be bigger than we both realized."

"Tom, you're thinking."

"No, I ain't."

"Yes you are. I've hung around you long enough to know when you're thinking about something. Tell me."

"Well, maybe the answer lies at the end of the tunnel. If not, we got to go hunt up Muff; and see can we pump him for anything that might help explain what happened that night."

The shovels were thrown clear across, into the darkness. The lantern had to be held. Cautiously Tom and Becky tiptoed over the skeletons, refusing to breathe, fearing so slight a breath might injure their concentration. Having made it over unharmed, they were relieved, as well as curious.

"That was too easy, Becky."

"Well, I don't care. I wouldn't want to fall on them. Would you?"

"No, course not. Well, let's not tempt our luck any further."

Retrieving the shovels they focused their attention directly ahead. Soon, the tunnel began to veer and wind again, for some time. Then, it straightened, and quickly lessened in height and width, so that Tom and

Becky had to crouch and squat; and before long they were on their hands in knees.

"I hope we don't get stuck, Tom, inches away from the treasure."

"It happens in the books. But," Tom noted, "usually to the villain."

Finding they could not travel side by side any more, Becky scurried out ahead. Even she had dreams of being the first to discover treasure.

"I see light, up ahead, I think. Looks like light."

"Keep going, then. We'll know for certain soon."

Becky's pace quickened. "It is light," she gasped.

"Poke your head out. See where we are. But be careful. Might be the center of the earth."

"No. That is, I don't know. It's all trees and bushes and weeds."

"Can you make it out?"

"I, yes."

Outside, the two looked inquisitively in every direction.

"Where do you think we are?"

"I don't think it's the center of the earth. I can see the clouds."

"And—listen. Don't that sound like a river? Like the Mississippi? Smells like the Mississippi too. And I ought to know."

"How do we get there? It's like an enchanted forest here. Wait. Over there. Is that a trail?"

"Looks to be. Looks old. Mostly covered up, but I think I can follow it." Tom and Becky plowed their way threw dense weeds, and around adolescent trees.

"I hear the river now, too. It's getting stronger. Up ahead, is that it? Out beyond those trees?" Tom did not have to answer Becky. The answer lay in plain view.

"Now I'm really confused," Tom admitted.

"All I know is that there is no treasure. Just two skeletons. And none of it makes any sense. Can you figure it out?"

"I was sure I could, once we got to the end of the tunnel. But I never thought it would lead outside. It don't make any sense. This whole thing don't make any sense at all. And I don't reckon it ever will. Not to me, nor to anybody else, ever. Let's go find Muff, and see if he can shed any light."

Fifteen minutes later Tom and Becky crept along the side of the old mill Muff had told Tom he could be found.

"Muff!" Tom whispered loudly, poking his head inside. Something rustled in the far back, behind a group of crates. "It's Tom Sawyer."

Muff jumped up quickly. A few pieces of straw clung to his newly formed beard.

"Tom! I, I warn't expectin'—," The man yawned ferociously.

"You look like you been up all night."

"I have, Tom. Tolerable hard to sleep when—," Muff stopped again, but not to yawn. Becky walked in, startling Muff. His blood shot eyes widened.

"It's Okay, Muff. She won't tell anyone you're here."

"Tom told me you were back, and part way explained why. I can be trusted! Please, don't be mad at Tom."

"Oh, well, I ain't 'xactly mad, but—."

"Muff, I wouldn't 'a' brought Becky here if it warn't important."

"Well, jus' don't go 'round telling anyone else. Please! Not yet. Let me do it, on m' own time. Now," Muff again yawned. "What's so important? Can't it wait 'til I get some sleep?"

The children hastened towards Muff, and knelt down behind the crates.

Tom lowered his voice. "Muff, Becky and I want to know, from you, what really happened during the night—the Stantans were murdered."

Muff suddenly, and unexpectedly, turned white. His knees buckled. The shock woke him, directly.

"Laws me! 'Pears I must 'a' had a drink when I wasn't lookin'. I could 'a' swore I heard y' say—. No. No, couldn't 'a' been. Derned if I ain't had a drink."

"You ain't drunk, Muff," Tom said.

"Bless you. But if I am sober, why, did I hear you right? 'Twas the name you mentioned, the Stantans?"

"Deed it was. Becky and I are in a sweat to know what happened the night they was murdered. We remembered you were a witness."

"And we were ever so anxious to ask you about it."

"Now what ever fer? Been more than ten years."

"We know. Muff, we wouldn't ask you, if we didn't think it was important. We know you're tired, but—."

"Tom, I *was* tired."

"We need you to tell us about that night. We'll explain why afterwards."

Little did they know, little did anyone know, Muff frequently revisited that unlucky night, in his mind. The liquor he consumed in great and excessive quantities quelled the horrible images he saw. He looked to both children, internally wondering why they wanted to know. He always dreaded being asked again, but never expected the question to come from children. The seriousness in Tom's speech softened Muff. He wavered, took a deep breath, folded his arms into his stomach, and leaned against the wall of the building. For a few minutes he remained silent. Then, when he had composed himself, he said—

"Well, it's like this, children," Muff explained. "And like I told Sheriff Tilman, and the paper. Y' see, I was out that night, like alwus, like alwus. I told the sheriff, and the paper, I didn't remember climbing that big hill leading up to Robert and Marribelle's home."

"Robert and Marribelle?" Becky questioned.

"The Stantans. Robert and Marribelle Stantan. Hmm," Muff sighed. I ain't said their names since—." Muff paused momentarily, then resumed. "Well, I explained I must-a got hold of some bad liquor, and figured the higher altitude would clear my head, which was thunderin' on the inside. There used to be a great big tree set out some twenty feet from the house. But it's torn down now. I used it then, to rest up against, thinkin' I might sleep off the liquor. I never got to," he reflected. "After settin' there awhile, 'twas a noise 't stirred me, coming from near the home. When I looked, I saw some men enter. I didn't think nothin' about it, and all was quiet for a time, 'til I heard the shots."

"You said it was Murrell's Gang."

"Well, Tom, I said it *looked* to be Murrell's Gang. Had all the earmarks. They all come out, one of 'em, most likely Murrell his self, with a box under his arm. The others was carrying something else. I couldn't make out exactly what, but I figured it to be the Stantans. Next a man shouted, 'Saddle! Saddle!'—meaning to get on their horses. They got away, 'thought ever noticing I was there. They was never caught. I didn't know it then, as I told Sheriff Tilman, but as I learnt later, their bodies were never found. So like as not they carried the Stantans off and threw them in the river. Thas what everyone concluded. Sheriff, he locked me up, after I told him what I saw. Jus' so as to sleep off the liquor. Well, that's it, far 's I can remember."

"But there has to be more," Becky sadly moaned.

"More? Well, I know how you young 'ns like a good mystery, but that's all there is to tell about it. I only wish I didn't have to tell it the first time. Now, didn't you have a reason for asking me?"

"Y-yes," Tom stuttered. "Well, we thought we did. Muff, are you certain they ain't any more to tell? Maybe you missed something."

Muff looked inquisitively at each child. His mind raced. He wondered if these children knew something—something that might prove to be disastrous for him, and many others.

"Now," Muff said, "You two said you was *at* the Stantan Home? 'Though you know—everyone knows a law was passed making it a crime fer anyone to go there."

"We knew," Tom meekly confirmed, afraid Muff might actually turn them both in. "We know it was trespassing."

"And we know we could go to jail for it," Becky added.

"We was looking for the treasure."

"Treasure, Tom?"

"Well, Muff, don't you know they was thousands of dollars discovered unaccounted for by a bunch of lawyers, after the Stantans was murdered?"

"Well, seems as I heard such a rumor. Was never any real proof. Is that why you both went up there?"

"Yes?" they both said.

"We didn't find any treasure," Becky said. This seemed to relax and comfort Muff.

"Are you going to turn us in?" Tom asked.

"Oh, heavens no. Jus' give me your word ain't either of you gonna go back up there."

"Well, we might have to, Muff," Tom explained.

"On account of what we *did* find," Becky added.

"Find? What now what the thunder could you have found?"

"Should we tell him, Tom?"

"Tell me what?" Muff asked.

"I've believed for a long time there must be treasure somewhere in the Stantan Home, and I convinced Becky to help me find it."

Muff sat up sharply. "You mean you both went *in* looking!" he whispered, hoarsely. You jus' didn't dig around the home, on the outside?"

"Course not," said Tom. "Where else would it be? And we looked all around for a secret passageway where it would be hid."

"What makes y' think there'd be a secret passageway."

"'Cause every mansion has got one. That's what the books say."

"And we searched all over."

Muff, becoming excited, knelt close to Tom and Becky. "Only tell me—both of you. Did you find anything? Tell, ol' Muff, now."

Tom and Becky looked to one another.

"Yes," they both said, nodding their heads.

"Wh-where? Tell me." Muff was turning paler by the moment.

"In the cellar," Tom declared.

"Oh, god," Muff moaned, leaning back.

"We found a tunnel," Becky said. "But it was caved in with dirt."

Muff suddenly sat up with vigor. "Did I hear right? 'Twas caved in—with dirt?" His color returned.

"I'll say," said Tom. "Took us both a long time to dig it out too."

Muff again turned white. "Dig it—*out*?"

"Well, at the time, Becky and I thought sure the treasure would be only the other side. But it warn't so. We never did find any treasure. A strange thing about that tunnel though—winds all the way down to the river."

"Now, now children, you haven't told nobody else about this have you?"

"No. Becky and me was afraid they'd turn us into the law for being up there."

"Good. Good. Don't tell nobody. Leave it be. You both had an adventure, and now it's over. You didn't neither of you find anything, so there ain't no reason to tell anyone else about it. And you can count on ol' Muff to keep it secret."

"But we *did* find something," Becky said. "In the tunnel."

This revelation stunned Muff. Perplexed, he almost said something he would have forever regretted; but he caught himself in time. He guarded his next words carefully, asking in all earnest, but with haste, "What ever did you find?"

"Two skeletons," Becky said.

"What!" Muff gasped. He rose to his feet suddenly, towering over the children. "You said you found what?"

"Skeletons," Tom said. "We tried to think whose they might be. Well, when Becky seen one was still wearing a diamond ring, we figured they had to be the Stantans."

"We think Murrell's Gang forced them to reveal where the money was hid."

"And so they led Murrell's Gang down to the cellar. To the passage."

"Where they killed the Stantans after they got the money."

"Then caved in the passage to hide the dastardly deed That's when I remembered you had witnessed it, partly. But you never said you seen anyone go down in the cellar. Not when it happened, nor now."

"And didn't you say you saw Murrell's Gang carry out the Stantan's bodies? That's what confused us, and got us to thinking."

"Oh, those poor, poor people," Muff mourned. "If only I knew. It's the drinkin' sure. Had to be. Curse it."

"Don't look so downcast, Muff. You couldn't have helped the Stantans."

"The Stantans? Oh, yes, Becky. Children, I'm mighty glad, powerful glad, you came to me. You did right. Now I see, now I see. Yes, thank ye, you both, fer tellin' ol' Muff. Fer trusting him enough. Just you both never tell another living soul what you told me. Agreed?"

"Why, we was gonna ask you exactly that. Wasn't we, Becky?"

"It's true. But now I'm wondering if maybe we ought to."

"No!" Muff waved his hands. "Well, it wouldn't do no good anyhow. Only stir up trouble, speculation. That tunnel—well, likely they only used it for storage. Don't neither of you think any more 'bout it. And I won't. B'sides, I got enough to worry about now with Ben and his stealing f'om—." Muff bit his tongue, hard. Even sober, he could not keep a clear mind; not now. "I got to go. I really got to go." Muff rose, clutching his body as though he had been severely injured. "You leave the Stantan Home to me, children. You leave everything to Muff." The man ran from the building in a hurry, before either Tom or Becky could stop him.

"I reckon he's right about the tunnel," Tom said. "And I'd almost forgotten about doctor Towers,"

"What about him? Did Muff say he was going to steal from somebody? Who, Tom? And how do you come to know about it?"

Tom divulged everything he knew to Becky; everything he had learned from Muff about doctor Towers.

"Well, we got to do something, Tom," Becky said afterwards.

"We need a plan to stop him, without it ever incriminating us. Right now I'm drawing a blank."

Becky took his hand. "Never fear," she smiled. "As a team we're invincible; we *will* think of something!"

CHAPTER 32

In Widow Douglas' mansion, dreary thoughts and somber silence wafted invisibly throughout, albeit as they bumped up against any human occupant the ghostly sensation was more than noticeable. Doctor Towers and Widow Douglas sat in the grand living room, unusually adjacent from one another, in front of the fireplace. Widow Douglas stared intensely into the extinct pit, while doctor Towers' gaze fell a few feet short, upon the floor.

Widow Douglas, speaking her first words since breakfast, and all too meekly, said, "How could I have allowed it to happen?"

Doctor Towers, who had been mentally going over future plans, and vaguely detecting human sound, perked up. "Hmmm? Did you say something?"

"I should have gone in her room. I should not have worried over its properness, or a silly fear I had. Sis would be alive today. I *know* it."

"Brittany, we've been through this countless times. It's quite possible she could've died regardless. It 'pears she had a stroke. Many people live through it, others don't."

"Because of my stupidity, we'll never know if she could have, will we?"

"Oh, Brittany. You can't go on blaming yourself. *You* may become ill. I don't want that. You don't want that." He leaned towards her asking, "Have you looked at the letter yet?"

"I haven't touched it since she died. It's on her dresser yet. I find myself at her door, staring at it, many times in a single day. I can't, I, I can't bring myself to look at it."

Rumbling echoed from another room; the familiar pitter-patter of feet scampering across the floor. Then, suddenly;

"Missus! Missus! Oh, dere ya is." Ginny, panting, stopped at the living room entrance. "Dey's a man at de door, an' when I opened it up, an' he see me, do ya know what he done? He bowed! A white man bowed fo' me. I ain' never been bowed to by nobody, 'specially a white man. He was awful kind t' me too; patted my head, an' smiled, an' said, 'Hello, an' how are you?'"

Withdrawn, Widow Douglas asked, "Ginny, who did the man say he is?

"He say he an ol' friend o' yers—de senator."

Instantly the color returned to Widow Douglas.

"Goodness! Can it be? Jonathon? But I'm not prepared. I—."

"Brittany," doctor Towers fretted. "You're shaking. Calm down."

"You don't understand. I haven't seen Jonathon in years. Oh, do I look-? I had no idea he would come. If only he would have sent—."

Widow Douglas leapt to her feet and started walking hastily out of the room. Doctor Towers did not know how to react.

"Brittany! Wait!" Before he could persuade her to remain, she had disappeared. Confused, and standing alone, he scratched his head, cynically saying, "I hope this won't spoil things." After that, he followed her.

A well-groomed, elderly gentleman stood in the doorway. His eyes having fallen upon Widow Douglas as she entered, he quickly sucked in his stomach, and held that position for a time, then released it.

"Dear Brittany!" the man exclaimed, extending his arms towards her. She did not flinch. On the contrary, she accepted his embrace, and even returned the favor by applying a friendly peck on his cheek, for which he pleasurably welcomed. Then, the two marveled at one another.

Widow Douglas smiled exuberantly. "Jonathon! Honestly. Have you no shame? Coming here without first notifying me. I would have planned—."

"Ah, dear Brittany, my sincerest apologies. But when I received your letter I—. Well, there was but not a moment to lose. Oh, let me look at you. You haven't changed at all, not since I last had the privilege to lay eyes upon you. No! Still ravishing as ever."

"Oh, now you hush," Widow Douglas joked. "You're always saying that."

"Because it's so true."

Doctor Towers entered sheepishly, not knowing exactly how to react, and in-between the awkward position of wanting very much to leave, but also to stay. He nearly had his feet turned around when Widow Douglas beckoned him.

"Ben! Come here. Ben, this is Jonathon; senator of this great state."

"*Former* senator. I've been out of office four years now, you know. Still, all my close friends call me Senator, respectfully. All except you, dear Brittany. I have always insisted you call me by my given name, because you always say it with such tenderness and emotion."

"Yes. Of course, Jonathon. And this is Doctor Benjamin Towers. The one I wrote you about. The one who saved my life."

Senator extended his hand. "Ah! An honor, a privilege indeed, to shake the hand of the man who saved the life of my dear, dear Brittany."

Doctor Towers tried to smile, but found it difficult. "I've heard about you, this past week; ever since Brittany wrote you concerning the sheriff. Have you spoken with him yet?"

Senator's smile faded. "No. No, it appears he has left. His office is in a shambles, but he is nowhere to be found. Having spoken with some of the townspeople, they have verified his disappearance, and not one person can claim seeing him the day after the unfortunate hanging."

"I didn't know," doctor Towers admitted. "But then, I've been here the whole time, tending to, to—."

"Ah, yes. I understand. Oh, dear Brittany, I am terribly sorry for you. I read of your sister's death on the way. You *will* be alright?"

"I—. If you say you'll stay here, for a while. I know that will cheer me up. You will, stay, won't you?"

"Oh, Brittany. Dear, dear Brittany, you know I could never refuse you. Of course I will. It is alright, doctor Towers?"

"Huh?"

"My staying here will in no way cause any problems, medically speaking?"

"Oh." He glanced towards Widow Douglas.

"Don't be silly. Ben, tell him it's silly."

"It's silly. I mean, the way in which Brittany speaks so highly of you, you will be an added benefit. She *has* been feeling low of late, what with her sister's—Miss Watson's passing."

"Then—I shall. My manservant will handle the luggage."

Ginny, all the while eyeing Senator from behind a wall, half-screamed, "Oh, please, let me!" She had been taken by his charm from the moment he treated her with decency and respect. "I c'n do it. Won't ya let me?"

Senator looked down upon this innocent child. "Now, you don't want me troubling you, when I—."

"It ain' trouble. Please," she begged.

"Well, how can I refuse a girl who has such a beautiful smile."

"I got a bootiful smile?" Ginny had never received such praise before.

"Indeed."

"Oh, *thank* you." She hugged Senator, without realizing it. He returned the compliment as if she were his own daughter.

"Go then, and bring in my bags." She did so, instantly.

"A remarkable child. Simply, remarkable. I am so happy to see her in high spirits. So many of them, so many are terribly mistreated in this region. Brittany, you are one in a few, a very small handful, who don't inflict cruelties upon them. I have always admired you for that. You know, I stopped by the Stantan Home on my way here."

"They would be happy to know you still care."

"Yes. Doctor! You do know of the Stantans, I hope?"

"Y—, why yes. Brittany has told me about them."

Senator lamented. "A pity you could not have known them as we had. They were extraordinary people, benevolent people, the truest essence of human beings. Did Brittany tell you it was I who enacted the law saving their home from destruction? I lobbied for longer but, well, even as powerful a senator as I am, *was*, even I could not save it longer. Perhaps future generations will take up the cause. I hope so, anyway."

"Brittany did mention you—,"

Ginny rushed in with Senator's luggage.

"Where to Missus?"

"What? Oh. The third room on the left, next to, to sis'. It has a nice outside view, Jonathon." With a *whoosh* Ginny flew upstairs.

"A delightful child. Irresistible. It is a travesty—." There, Senator stopped. He finished the thought privately. *A travesty she will grow up.* "I say, what were we discussing?"

"The Stantans," Widow Douglas answered.

"Of course. Of course. My, how the mind wanders in old age. Well, it's a terrible way they died. Some day their home will be appreciated for what it truly stands for. I am uncertain if one hundred years is sufficient time enough—. Oh, would you look at me, Brittany. Here you let me rant on in your magnificent entrance hall. You must scold me sometimes."

"Jonathon, I could never scold you."

"No. I, I am suddenly tired. Well, dear Brittany, talking of the Stantans always takes up so much of my energy. You know that. I wonder, might I lie down?"

"Certainly. I'll have Ginny show you—,"

"Nonsense. Trouble not that spectacular child. I'll find my way. I'll—. Oh, why doctor, I thought you had left. I apologize."

"No need. I, well, call me Ben, won't you."

"Ben? Of course. Anything for the man who saved dear Brittany. Later on, I would very much enjoy your company, for a chat, if you've the time."

"Of course. Whenever you like."

"Splendid. Well, I'm off." He walked upstairs, gripping the bannister tightly, while talking just above a whisper. "The Stantan Home is empty now, and desolate, and lifeless, and—. Well, perhaps it is not *so* lifeless. In time, it will stand out among the rest in, in, ah, yes, in St. Petersburg. It will stand as a symbol of strength, of fortitude, of everything America can aspire to be. Why, it *is*—America! A pity they can't know them as *I* had. Yes, ah yes. As I had."

Widow Douglas, having broken free from her earlier depression, jumped excitedly. "I'm glad he's here. So, so glad."

"Yeah," doctor Towers responded, unenthusiastically. "Things will be, well, interesting." In contempt, he sighed. "More at, chaotic."

CHAPTER 33

During the middle of the night, at one of those odd hours in the early morning when even "non" respectable citizens know enough to come in out of doors, a group of men entered town. Out on a month long hunting expedition, they looked forward to a quiet, leisurely return to their homes and families. However, about one mile outside town the men passed by a camp, where a fire burned strongly. A thirst for coffee impelled them to investigate. What they found unsettled them. A man lay very near the fire, stretched out, and quite dead. Severely burnt over most of his body, the only part of his anatomy left recognizable was his face. His face! What abysmal terror, frustrated consternation, and horrid uncanniness frozen for all eternity upon his face. Each man who saw it quickly turned his head in another direction, daring, refusing, begging not ever to glare upon it again.

By what name had this former, living being gone by? How did he come to meet such a wicked fate? He appeared to be dead by only hours. The men, desperately tired, speculated no further on the matter, but wrapped the corpse up tightly in a blanket and threw him over the biggest horse, inducing enormous effort due to his unusual size and weight.

It would not be discovered until much later this man had been shot numerous times before being kicked without care into the fire where, still alive, he burned splendidly. Somehow enabling himself to pull free of the flames, he lived a short while in constant agony before dying. These men frantically, and unsuccessfully, canvassed the town for their sheriff until coming to a fearful resolution one unlucky man must stay in Cal's office *with the corpse* and wait for his return. The unlucky man sighed, and with the help of his "friends" carried the body inside. As the men left their bosom comrade, they reassured him that the sheriff, probably out on his rounds, would return soon. Five hours later the unlucky man, down on his knees, prayed he might die than spend another minute with the corpse, and cursed his friends for abandoning him. Sleep! How, with a corpse so close he could feel and sense the dead man's absolute and eternal stillness? Most people pass through life never knowing what it is like to spend the night with a corpse. This unlucky man, having done so, wished he might have carried that bit of curiosity with him into his own afterlife.

Becky rose early that morning. She too had trouble finding sleep, but for a different reason. She feared doctor Towers would not just steal from Widow Douglas, but also kill her, and desperately needed a way to warn her, as Tom suggested, without bringing attention to herself. Finally, when an inspiration came to her, she crept into Tom's room and softly nudged him.

"Tom," Becky whispered into his ear. "Pirates are about, everywhere. The house is surrounded." Instantly Tom sat up. Looking around, and seeing only Becky, he fell back against his pillow.

"Oh, Becky. And I was dreaming so peacefully too."

"I know. But I've the perfect way to warn Widow Douglas, doctor Towers is going to steal her valuables, without it getting us into trouble."

"You *have*?" The boy sat up again.

"Uh-huh."

"Tell me."

"Not yet."

"But Becky," he protested. "Why do you want to keep me in suspense?"

"Oh, Tom, I don't. I'll tell you, shortly. I promise. But Sid might not be asleep, and who knows what other spies are nearby. No, we must go to *my* home now. I've wanted to return for a long while anyway, but up 'til now I've been afraid. I'm not afraid anymore, and everything we need is there."

Dressed, they slowly crept downstairs, having no mind to wake Aunt Polly. However, they might have run screaming through the house without disturbing her, for she was nowhere in the vicinity.

Outside, while Tom tried to keep up with Becky's long strides, he pleading with the unwavering girl to know her idea. "Can you at least give me a hint? It's not right you keeping me in such a sweat. *Please*, Becky."

Becky stopped for a moment, giving Tom a chance to catch up. Turning to him, she exhaled her words in haste. "Well, the week your Aunt Polly made me stay in bed, and refused me to leave for any reason, I asked you for some of your books, to pass the time with. And I read them, sometimes into the late hours." Becky picked up her pace. "They *are* filled with excitement and adventure, and they surely do make it easy for me to imagine myself far away from here, and *want* to be far away from here." Again, she stopped. "It was in one of these books the idea came." She kept quiet for a long time, then resumed her pace. "I know it'll work, and that doctor will—. Oh! There." Becky pointed. There it is. M-my, my home. Oh, Tom."

"Your shaking. Is it—,"

"No. I mean, this time it's nerves. I was afraid to return. 'Cause that's where my—. Where it happened. Come with me, will you, Tom?"

Helping Becky along, the two sped cautiously passed the white picket fence, over the narrow walkway, up the stoop, ever nearing the front door. After a pause, Becky pushed open the door, and the two entered.

"It's not so bad, is it, Becky?"

"Well, no. No, thank goodness. I hate it when I overreact. Oh, but still—having someone come with me helps. Tom, I heard something. A creak. From in the study." Tom loathed to admit it, but he heard the same creak. "Somebody's in there, and they're coming out."

Sure enough, only moments later, a man emerged. He stood, towering over Tom and Becky. His attire reeked, and gave every indication he had been sleeping, possibly living in, or nearby, a slaughter house. Strangely, nobody made a move. Even stranger, both Becky and the man looked at one another with the exact air of bewilderment.

In amazement, Becky exclaimed, "My goodness!" and proceeded to run towards the man and throw her arms around his dirty, greasy clothing.

"Becky!" Tom attempted to grab hold of the girl, and keep her from doing anything rash. He failed.

The man caught Becky, but didn't know exactly what to do with her.

Much to Tom's dismay, and more to the man's, Becky shouted, "Pa! Pa, it is you. Oh, don't you recognize me? You do, don't you? I recognize you, even underneath all the whiskers and uncombed hair, and dirty and ragged clothes. Say you recognize me too. Say you do."

"Mr. Thatcher, is, is it you?" Tom wasn't sure, and the suspense ate away at him. By the way Becky clung to the man, he hoped with all his being her assumption to be true.

"Child," the man uttered weakly. "M-my goodness. How d-did you—."

"Pa, you're stuttering again, like you did when you were a child."

"I, I'm sorry. I didn't expect t-to see you, Becky. I d-don't understand. I, g-give me a moment to catch my b-breath. It's q-quite a shock seeing you. I th-thought you, I thought—,"

"Oh, pa, it don't matter. I'll tell you all about it when you're well. The important thing is that I'm safe, and so are you."

"Y-yes, I suppose. It's all s-so confusing."

"I know. I know it is."

"Tell me, the k-kidnappers, are they in jail?"

"No, pa. I don't know where they are. They fled after Tom rescued me."

"Tom! Rescue! Oh, I d-don't understand any of it. I, I, oh, I don't f-fell so well. Let me sit down. There. Now, when did this all take place?"

"About a week ago. A little more, maybe. I'm staying with Tom, at his home, because—. Oh, pa, you're turning white. Let me get you a wet cloth."

"Child, n-never mind me. I'll be fine. I am f-fine. Now that I've seen you. I'm only d-dazed." He did not want to tell Becky he had lost his memory shortly after he left the Sawyer household. "Your ma will b-be happy to know you're alright. Goodness knows how her health is. I haven't been in—. Well, never mind it. N-never mind my problems. They are all s-second rate, now. You say Jimmy, and the other t-two fled?"

"Well, the other two did. We don't know what happened to Jimmy. I hadn't seen him since he threw me in some kind of a pit."

"He threw you in a p-pit!" He man rose angrily. "I'll hunt down every last one and—,"

"Pa, the other two, the other two, they're likely long gone. Probably half way to Canada by now."

"Canada?"

"That's where they kept saying they'd go."

"My god!"

"Pa! Where are you going?" Judge Thatcher ran hastily into through house, striding clumsily up the stairway. Tom and Becky followed. "He's gone in his room. Oh, Tom. I know he'll go after them. I just know. Every ounce of me says he will. I don't want him to. He won't give up until he's caught them. I know it."

When Judge Thatcher descended the stairs, a bit slower, but more confident, with his hair combed, and wearing clean clothes, *and* tightly gripping his rifle, Becky urged him to reconsider.

"They m-must be brought to justice, Becky. It is my duty to make sure they d-do not get away. Now, you stay with Tom. Polly is a good woman. I know you'll be safe under her roof."

"Pa, you're in no condition—,"

"I am f-fine. I h-have a hunch I know where they m-might be."

"Please, pa."

Judge Thatcher stooped down next to Becky. "Everything will b-be alright." He looked into her eyes and smiled; the first time she had seen him smile in ages. Something about that smile, it's inviting warmth and profound sincerity, comforted Becky immensely. Perhaps it would be years until she understood exactly why, but she too felt a strange warmth, a safe warmth. "I p-promise you Becky," he spoke, "We're still a f-family, always."

With that, Judge Thatcher departed. He regretted leaving Becky, but he could never live with himself if he didn't apprehend her kidnappers. Becky slightly understood. Still, like any daughter would, she worried.

"We can leave," Tom said. "And come back later, if you want."

Becky walked up to a window without saying anything, and remained emotionless for longer than Tom could tolerate. Then, out of the blue, an eerie transformation occurred from within her.

"I feel *funny* Tom."

"You wanna lay down?"

"No. He said we'll be a family again. A family! Don't you understand? We're going to be together again, all of us."

A delicious, involuntary, excitement overcame her. Her eyes gleamed and sparkled, and opened like a garden of tulips at dawn's inception, when the first rays of the new sun hit upon each petal. Her lips flickered and twitched, while dreamily watching her father disappear down the street.

A smile, like none other she had before produced, gripped her. A revealing smile! A wild smile! A smile that in less than an instant changed her strained, unhappy, uncertain posture from sour to blushing resplendence. Such a smile as this could never be considered ordinary. A smile as this, new to the world, craved an appropriate name.

Tom saw it. Nay, he discovered it; for it had never before been seen. He tried desperately to think of words he might dare describe what he saw; poetic, grandiose, majestic words; but none came to mind; no words fitting or deserving enough; certainly not in the English language, or any language, perhaps; quite simply no words had yet been invented, or may ever be invented to eloquently and responsibly describe this smile. Such naturalness, such easiness, the way in which Becky wore her newfound smile, as though she had been destined all along to display this wondrous glory. But what to call it! Not a smile. Anyone can smile. No, more of a, a grin, yet more spectacular. Yes! That's it. A grin. A—*mega*-grin. No other tribute comes close.

Becky turned to Tom suddenly. "We haven't a moment to spare! Doctor Towers is after Widow Douglas' money and jewels. It's up to *us* to put a stop to it. Pa would want us to do what's right."

Stunned, Tom replied, "But just a moment ago. Are you saying—,"

"That we must forge ahead? Yes!"

"If you're up to it."

"Of course I am. Aren't you?"

"Well, naturally. I only thought you—,"

"Oh, *pooh* what I thought! I'm alive as never before. "Now, we need quality stationary. That way, Widow Douglas will not think it a hoax."

"Think what a hoax?"

"Well what do you think? The *nonamous* letter of course!"

"Nonamous letter?"

"Yes. That's my idea, and we haven't a moment to spare. That's why we had to come here. I knew pa had quality paper, and ink, in his study. We'll write a letter outlining the doctor's plans, then pick the right opportunity to deliver it to her."

Becky scrambled into the study, while Tom, entranced, tried to recover. He would not be himself, fully, the rest of the day, However, he regained enough of his faculties to help Becky write a "nonamous letter" that Widow Douglas could not possibly take but seriously.

Meanwhile, a corpse still occupied the sheriff's office; and the man left guarding him, near petrified with terror, used the quickest means to leave before his body solidified completely. He jumped through the window, rolled over the walkway, and tumbled onto the dusty road, paying no heed to his bruises, Quickly, he bounced back up.

"There's, there's a m-man, a dead man, a dead man, in the sheriff's office," Every man, woman, and child in the vicinity stopped their activities. Whatever became of the unlucky guard, nobody knew. He had been last seen running out of town, westward.

An investigation of the office must be made; and many, hoping the corpse would be the sheriff, applied for the job. More than a mob of people entered to take a quick glance. However, the body they saw sprawled out on the floor did not belong to the sheriff. It belonged to Cy!

It did not take long for all of St. Petersburg to learn the grim news, which spread with an eerie echo. "Sheriff's deputy dead! Who shot the deputy, but did not shoot the sheriff?"

In under an hour, doctor Towers stood over the body and officially pronounced Cy dead, and ordered he be taken away for burial. More than half a dozen men were needed to carry the body out.

Senator, insisting he come along, stood alongside Doctor Towers. He did not give a specific reason why he wanted to be there; and to his relief, doctor Towers never asked him for one.

A reason did exist. One which Senator guarded with his life. Though never meeting Cy, he knew well of him. So well in fact, all the way down to the sheriff's office a suspect amount of sweat pored off of him. "I must be sure," the man kept repeating, in-between wiping his brow.

In a hidden pocket within his vest, Senator had once secretly tucked away a leaflet with Cy's picture on it; a crude sketch. Until this day, as he bent over the dead man, that leaflet had not been removed. Now, wrinkled, yellowed with age, somewhat smeared, Senator held it close to Cy's face. He wanted the leaflet to match. It did.

"He wanted somewhere?" doctor Towers asked.

"It doesn't matter, now," Senator responded. He stared at Cy for a long time; the only one to do so, whose constitution remained perfectly sound and healthy. Privately, he praised the unknown assassin.

Aunt Polly, overwrought by a wild and horrific nightmare the night of Cy's murder, one of those "premonition dreams" so real and vivid, she discovered herself knocking on Judith's door when her senses finally returned. The nightmare itself dealt with Judith, and while banging incessantly upon the door, she tried, for her very life, to remember every detail. But by then, the memory had faded away.

"Judith! Judith! Judith! It's me. Polly! Don't be afeared." She jiggled the knob, only to learn the door hadn't been locked. She entered, and made a frantic, but hopeless, search for her dear friend. "She ain't here. She ain't here. Well, where on earth!"

Aunt Polly speculated what had caused Judith to leave the security of her cabin at such a lonely hour. The poor woman's head spun, as her mind grappled for a logical solution. She sat down at the table, merely wanting to relax her overtaxed mind; but fell peacefully asleep instead. An hour later the sound of a closing door awakened her.

"Polly!" Judith approached, in a bit of a haze herself.

"Judith! I—," Aunt Polly weakly stood, then collapsed into her chair.

"I—," A strange and bitter silence bit both women's tongues. Talk seemed impossible; and neither Aunt Polly or Judith wanted to explain their circumstances. Neither woman could. "Well, anyway, I'm glad to see you,"

"And—I, you." Reluctant to approach one another, they stood, looking each other up and down, until Aunt Polly said, ""Sit, sit down. Won't you?"

"I—. I, yes. Maybe I—should."

Seated, and faced eye to eye, they allowed themselves to breakdown and cry in each other's arms. Through the early morning, and well after, the crying continued. They talked some, but neither friend asked the other her prior whereabouts. Only sleep interrupted their conversation; and, holding onto each other comfortably, they peacefully drifted off.

The cry from a townsman, rushing past the cabin, awoke them directly.

"Deputy murdered! Deputy murdered! Sheriff's deputy murdered!"

Judith and Aunt Polly looked at one another, as if Cy's murder had not been a shock to either of them; as if they knew it all along, or expected it, and wondered what had taken so long for the news to be delivered.

"Well," said Judith.

"Oh," said Aunt Polly.

"He's finally—. Can't say as I'm sorry to hear it."

"No. Somehow, neither can I." They shed more tears, but not for Cy. Rather, for the relief his death brought. They two women stayed in each others company for the remainder of the day.

CHAPTER 34

Returning to the mansion with doctor Towers, Senator uncomfortably asked him to diagnose his condition. After excusing his manservant to sit atop the coach with the driver, Senator pleaded with doctor Towers to be honest.

"I must not be lied to, or mislead. I implore you, doc—, er, Ben. Yes, you did insist I call you Ben. Ben, I know I am ill. I've seen other doctors, as I've told you. However, I rarely act upon the advice of a few."

"Alright. Well, it isn't simply age, as has been suggested. That much I do know. How long has your memory been declining?"

"About six months. I didn't think—. Now Brittany is not to know of this. I must have your word. She is a delicate woman. I wouldn't want to upset her, or worry her."

"Of course."

"It's worsened the last two months. In the past these spells have lasted anywhere from a few seconds to a few minutes. They're increasing now. I'm going to tell you something, and I'd appreciate you never repeating it. When I received dear Brittany's letter I, I didn't recognize it at first. The hand writing, her name, they were obscure. Imagine! A woman I've revered since the day I met her, and just like that—I forget her. Of course it suddenly came back to me, and then I remembered everything. Strange, this illness, what it does to the mind. I don't forget everything; not yet. But I fear that will be the end result. Crucial matters I take great pains to remember. Other, lesser matters, I've resigned myself in forgetting." His hands shook slightly. "You've seen this before?"

"In older people, yes. Some type of disease, in the brain."

"Disease! This is new. What, pray tell, happens? Don't hold back."

"It progresses, until the memory is completely destroyed.."

"I see. How long would you say is the life expectancy?"

"It's on an individual basis. Some live years; others only a few. One woman I knew, ninety years old, lost her memory completely some thirty years prior. Was told she never drank, swore, or took snuff in her life; never said a bad word against anybody; always smiled; was as pleasant as could be. For all I know she's still alive today. Seems the more fit and healthy a person is, the better they are able to succumb to the disease. That is, mentally."

"I've constantly maintained a positive mental attitude. I'm a believer in positive thinking. It isn't often I allow myself to become upset. Not too often, anyway." The coach pulled into the mansion. "I must ask you again not to repeat this to anyone; especially Brittany. I've made a special trip to see her one last time, while my memory still—. I wouldn't want it, well, spoiled."

"I've always upheld doctor-patient confidentiality. I won't tell her."

"Ah, look at her! Standing out on the porch, happy as a lark." Doctor Towers wisely said nothing, for he might have inadvertently offended Senator. "M'Lady!" he hailed Widow Douglas, stepping off the coach, "What an honor it is to see your beautiful self out on the porch."

"Oh, Jonathan, *really*." She blushed like a school girl, which angered doctor Towers. "I couldn't wait for you to come inside to tell you."

"Tell me? What has dear Brittany to tell me?"

Doctor Towers stood near the coach. He worried for Widow Douglas, who seemed to have recovered from her sister's death too soon. However, he had plans of his own; and with Senator's arrival, he feared "dear Brittany's" old friend would interfere with those plans.

"I'm going to have the party, now," Widow Douglas announced. "The grandest one I ever put together. I've put it off too long, and I *do* want it as much as the town does. I would have had it earlier, but that poor slave was hung; and then sis died; and after that I didn't much care for anything anymore. You've changed all that Jonathan. Just by being here, I feel complete again." Doctor Towers wanted to contradict her, but wisely held his tongue. "We'll set the date for this Saturday."

"Sure, sure," Senator laughed. "Whatever your heart desires."

"It's only four days away I know, but I think everything will be ready." Forgetting about doctor Towers, Senator escorted Widow Douglas inside.

"This is going to complicate things," Doctor Towers sighed. He had plans for this Saturday as well. How unfortunate his plans and the party must coincide. Or, perhaps not. "May still work out. May still work out."

Somehow, within hours, word of Widow Douglas' party leaked; circulars were hurriedly printed, and spread all over town. Tom and Becky read one, and rejoiced, as a shiver of excitement crawled up and down their spines. By mid-afternoon their nonamous letter had neared completion. Now they began planning how it would be delivered to Widow Douglas inconspicuously; for both children constantly dreaded being caught in the act.

The day before the party Tom and Becky were in the kitchen, rehearsing, when Sid entered.

"Becky! Tom! A letter! From Constantinople."

Becky sprung to her feet. "Constantinople!" Rushing towards Sid she grabbed the letter from his hand.

A horrified look assumed Sid's face. "You, you can't open it. It ain't addressed to you. Says, Aunt Polly—,"

"Hush!" Ignoring Sid, Becky tore through the wax seal. Too much for the disgusted boy to bear, and fearing divine reprisal for the sinful act, Sid slunk out of the kitchen in a hurry, before the imminent lightning strike hit. He caught a quick glimpse of Becky reading the letter with absorbing interest, and resigned himself to go to his room and pray for himself, that he not be injured as well.

Anxiously, Tom asked, "What's it say?"

Becky's lips, though moving rapidly, kept mum, until she had perused the entire letter. Tears developed, "Tom. Tom, it's about my ma."

"Your ma? Is she—." The boy bit his tongue hard, but not hard enough to his liking. He made a point to bite it harder, later.

"She's—. Oh, Tom, she's doing much better, *thankfully.*" Becky pressed the letter against her chest, giving it a hearty squeeze.

"That's awful good to hear."

"It's your Aunt Polly's doing. She sent a letter off to Constantinople, to my relatives, saying I was safe and sound now. This letter says ma would babble nonsense for hours, while holding on to a doll. She called it Becky, and wouldn't let anyone take it away from her. Since receiving the letter from your Aunt Polly, ma's health has improved, and continues to with each passing day. It's wonderful, Tom. But—." Becky cast her eyes downward.

"But what?"

"I have to return to Constantinople, immediately. The relations believe my being there will benefit ma's recovery."

"But, Becky—," Constantinople! Tom's throat thickened. For her to leave now, to leave at all, the idea seemed insane. They were sworn friends; inseparable—*Together Forever!* Constantinople lay so far away. He'd never see her again. Protest occurred to him. But then he realized Becky's mother needed her daughter by her side, more than he. Tom could have no role in tearing apart a family. Knowing it his chivalrous duty to let her go, he reluctantly fought back his protest.

"I know, Tom. Oh, I know."

"Will you, will you come back?"

"I—. I don'—. Oh, Tom—I don't know. Not for certain. I hope so."

"It ain't got to be now, has it? You can attend the party, at least."

"I won't leave without pa. If he comes back tonight, I reckon we'll *have* to leave. But if not, then let's make whatever time we have left as special and as exciting as we can."

Tom and Becky collapsed into each others arms, sinking down, down, down to the floor, where they remained, silent, for a long, long while.

CHAPTER 35

So the night had arrived! By seven that Saturday evening, only one half hour before the guests were due to arrive, the mansion reverberated with servants feet, as they finished setting and arranging every last detail to Widow Douglas' liking, while she and doctor Towers waited in the sitting room. The distance between them had widened since Senator's arrival. At a quarter past the hour, the room shook from the first words spoken by either person.

"Ben, I do wish you would stop that pacing. It's very distracting."

The man stopped, then resumed. "Do you know where Senator went off to?"

"No. Jonathan's manservant left word he had business to attend to."

"When will he return?"

"How should—. Stop pacing! I remember you didn't like sis' pacing."

"Have you looked at her letter yet?"

"Ben! How *could* you be so insensitive? Jonathan would never talk to me that way."

"Yes, yes. I *know*." Weariness hampered him. "Senator can do no wrong; never did do any wrong; never will do any wrong." Doctor Tower's nerves were wearing thin, but the reason had nothing to do with Widow Douglas.

"Please refrain yourself from talking about Jonathan in that manner."

"Oh, Brittany." Kneeling beside her he asked, "What *has* happened to us? Why have we become so distant?"

"It is no fault of mine I assure you." She refused to look down at him.

Rising stiffly he retorted, "Very well. I've things to do. I will stay for the party, then—move back into my office in town."

"Leave!" The response caught Widow Douglas by surprise. Before she could muster another word he had left the room. Sadly, she reflected upon her tone towards him. "Oh, what *has* become of me? It's that letter, isn't it? Oh, sis, *sis*. I must read it, in full. She left it for me to read. Oh, but it's so, so gloomy. But it contains her last words. I must honor them. If only I could find the courage. First! First I must apologize to Ben.

The apology would have to wait. Ginny ran in, announcing the arrival of the first guests. "*This* early? Well, I must see to them."

Her obligation as hostess confined her from slipping upstairs; and as the night progressed, and more guests arrived, she lost track of time altogether. Doctor Towers, on the other hand, sitting in his darkened room, had nothing but time on his mind. He kept a watchful eye on the outside, damning everything he could think of while impatiently waiting for the signal planned well before knowing the date of Widow Douglas' party.

Fireflies danced everywhere. A large cluster zoomed through the wooded area fifty yards out in back of the mansion, sparking on and off. Doctor Towers watched them for a while, to pass the time, until his head began to throb, growing bothersome by the minute. He turned his attention away from the forest, and the incessant twinkling of the fireflies, little knowing that just beyond these mysterious creatures of the night a man, tired, breathless, weary, and very confused, hastily brought to a closure his own suspicious activities.

Leaning on his shovel he whispered solemnly, "It ain't what you deserve, but it's a heap more respectable than the passage. Jus', only don't hold it agin me, fer takin' so long. Lordy, if I'd 'a' known sooner, I'd 'a' acted. All these years I thought—. Well, I *wanted* to make sure you'd gotten out. But that damned sheriff locked me up. I couldn't resk going back. Might 'a' been seen. I wish to thunder I had now. I had convinced m'self years ago you'd made it out safely. Bless those two children. Bless them fer comin' to me, and tellin' me about you both. Ah, but bless their, their ignorance. If ever they were to find out the truth!"

Those children would not find out the truth, however; and by now, their minds were clearly focused on delivering the "nonamous" letter. Playing game upon game with the other children, to blend in, they finally found a break to steal away for a parlay.

"It's about time, Becky."

"I'm glad. I'm pooped from playing all those silly games, when I so wanted to sneak upstairs and plant the letter."

"I know. But it's important we make ourselves seen, so when Widow Douglas wonders who sent the letter, you and I will never cross her mind."

"Have you noticed how sad and downcast she is tonight? I saw her once, and she don't seem to have the same enthusiasm she usually has. It's affected her slaves too, I think. I saw one slave woman dragging away a girl slave by the hand. And I could tell the girl didn't want to go."

"Maybe they're Miss Watson's, and with her dead, they'll gonna be sold. Maybe Widow Douglas has got to sell 'em, but don't want to. I—. Derned if he ain't gonna stare at us all night."

"Who?"

"Sid. He's our only obstacle. See him over there, across the room? He's got his eye on us. Hasn't taken it off all night; and if I know him, he won't take it off us ever. It's one time I wish Aunt Polly was here. Then Sid 'd stay by her side all night. But she spends all her time with Mrs. Loftus now; and Auntie hinted she might be moving in with us shortly."

"It must be tough on her, what with her husband being murdered. Oh, drat it! There's Susy Harper again. She's wavin' for me to come over."

"You best do it. She might wonder otherwise. But don't stay too long."

"I know."

"Try to think of a way for us to get shed of Sid, and I'll do the same. Hang it all, if he ain't gonna keep his eyes on me the whole night. We'd 'a' been up there already, if not for him."

Sid's undaunted stare may have bothered Tom, but it saved him and Becky from a sticky situation. Had the two snuck upstairs now, they might have run into doctor Towers. He, pacing behind a chair, looked nervously out his window, waiting for the signal.

"When the devil!" he muttered. False noises surrounded him, as his conscience slowly eroded away his remaining sanity, frightening him into believing Widow Douglas would find out about his plan before it could be carried out. "It's wrong, I know. But—. But, it has to be. She'll not understand. *I* don't understand, hardly." Thinking he saw a human figure slip behind Ruth's and Ginny's quarter's, he poked his head out for a closer look. Whatever he saw, or thought he saw, did not reappear. "Idiot! Where's the lantern! The signal! Be just like him to forget. Well, perhaps Franklin's out there. I've told him I don't like his going out. I'll have to see."

Sneaking downstairs and ducking through a servant's door without being noticed, Doctor Towers crept silently towards the small shack. He knocked three times before entering, pausing in-between the second and third knock.

Ruth and Ginny huddled together in front a dimly lit lantern. Their clothes were soaked through with tears. Ginny had her head buried in Ruth's chest, and her arms wrapped half way around her slim body. The woman looked up and saw Doctor Towers standing overhead.

"She knows," Ruth softly spoke. "I hated t' be de one t' tell her. Was de hardest thing I ever done." Ginny whined quietly as Ruth rocked her.

Wanting to show compassion, but knowing he had not the time to do so, doctor Towers asked, "Has Franklin been out again?"

"Why, no. He wanted to, but I tol' him he got t' stay put, 'cause dis is de night, an' ain't nuttin' can go wrong. He was sore, 'cause he don' like bein' cramped, he so big. But he know 'nough not to cross me, 'cause I low I'd lam him, and he know 't. Is de man out dere?"

"Shortly. You and Ginny stay here. Don't go out for anything."

"Yes'r."

Outside, doctor Towers became worried. "If it wasn't Franklin I saw——." He grit his teeth. "You idiot. You'll ruin everything. You and that damned necklace. It's all you ever cared about. If you mess things up, I'll kill you." His hands slithered inside his jacket pockets as he turned a corner, and stumbled into another man, who had his ear pressed firmly against the wooden structure, "What's this!" Doctor Towers' heart nearly stopped.

The man, briefly, feared retaliation; then, realizing doctor Towers' strength had left him, summoned up courage to speak.

"Y'——. You don't *know* me?"

"Kn-know you!" He looking everywhere, with urgency. "I don't have time for this. Whoever you are, I'm giving you a chance, you see. Leave now, and I'll forget you were ever here. Look, here's some, some money." Withdrawing his hands from his pockets, doctor Towers produced two folded bills and a fistful of loose change. "It's all I have."

Disregarding the money, the man again asked, "Y' really don't know me?" At first, he showed signs of resentment when doctor Towers hadn't recognized him. Now, after reflection, he felt sadness, more than anything.

"I haven't time for this. You're obviously a drunk. I'm giving you money. Take it. Use it to do what you do best."

"Is that Widow's money yer offerin' me?"

"Certainly not!"

"*Clara's!*" Now, the anger resurfaced.

Doctor Towers jumped, slightly. "You're drunk already. Why don't you take the money and leave? Do you want me to set the law on you?"

"If you do, I'll tell them about you. I know what you're planning. I know all about it."

"You don't know anything."

"I know *you*. And once, you even knew me."

"Tongues! You're talking in tongues. I won't have it! I don't know you. Now are you going to leave, or—,"

"You don't remember you're one time best friend? Sure 'nough you remember stealing away my one true love, and then murdering her."

"I was wrong. You're not drunk. You're insane!"

"When I learned you was here, in St. Petersburg, I had to find out why. I knew you was up to no good, but I had to find out yer motives. You've gotten mighty cozy with Widow Douglas. Almost as cozy as with Clara."

"Who *are* you! And what do you think you know about Clara and I?"

"I told you. I was once yer best friend, twenty years ago. Is it comin' back to you?"

"No, I—,"

"I ain't gonna let you hurt Widow Douglas, like you done Clara. I kept myself sober too, 'cause I didn't want my head to be clouded, like it was with Clara that night I confronted you."

"Night you confronted me? M-my god!" Doctor Towers looked long and hard at the man. "Potter! Muff Potter."

"Now it's coming back. No, I don't blame ye fer not recognizing me right off. I've changed. The liquor done that, mostly."

Doctor Towers stiffened. "Look, Muff Potter or not, this is not the time or place to discuss our past."

"You don't know the half of it. Yer wrong. It is our past which has brought me here. I know all about you, Ben. I know what you are planning. I've just been waiting fer the right opportunity to tell Widow Douglas about you." He peered towards the mansion. "Tonight. She will know about you *tonight*!" Muff, walking briskly, breezed past his one time friend.

"Stop! You don't know what you're doing. You'll jeopardize every-thing. You here! Everything!"

Muff paid no attention. He must warn Widow Douglas. He must expose doctor Towers. He must make amends for Clara's death. He must finally put to rest the haunting nightmares *about* Clara's death.

Doctor Towers followed Muff, trying his level best to catch up. Many lives rested in his hands, and on his actions tonight. He knew if Muff did anything rash, the consequences would be fatal for them all.

Meanwhile, Tom and Becky had bribed a group of playmates to let Sid join them in a toned down version of *Blind Man's Bluff*; nothing more than *Tag*, but with the blind fold. Sid, enchanted with being the center of attention, forgot about Tom and Becky altogether.

"That'll take care of Sid for awhile," Tom assured Becky.

"We better find Widow Douglas in a hurry, though. The other chil-dren gave us ten minutes."

Presently, they found Widow Douglas.

"I hope this works, Becky. If it don't, then we'll have to sneak up to her room. Are you ready with the nonamous letter?"

"Aye-aye," she whispered, pleasantly smiling.

The two separated. While Tom approached from the front, Becky snuck up behind her. However, Widow Douglas' state of mind had clouded. Imbalanced thoughts shifted between Doctor Towers to Miss Watson's letter. The glass of water she held jiggled. Feeling her mouth becoming dry she slowly raised it.

"Widow Douglas!" She hadn't notice Tom's advancement. Now he stood directly in front of her. Becky also had positioned herself, ready to strike. She wore a bracelet on her wrist, and pretended to be straighten-ing it. Really, she had tucked away the "nonamous" letter inside her sleeve. However, Tom's outburst surprised Widow Douglas, causing her to spill the glass of water on her dress. Though *only* water, it may as well have been acid.

"Oh! Oh, no. My dress."

Suddenly, all the momentum and desire to carry out the plan, so potent seconds earlier, dissipated in one quick flash. Awkward and embarrassed, for people had witnessed the scene, Tom sheepishly attempted an apology.

"I, I'm sorry. I didn't mean to—. I—." He could not finish.

"Well," Widow Douglas shrugged. "It was mostly my fault. My mind was elsewhere. It's only water. Please, go on with the party. No need to stop everything on, on account of a little water." She tried to laugh, and did laugh, slightly. Soon, and much to Tom's relief, other's joined in. As Widow Douglas walked away, Tom knew how close he had come to really "catching" it.

CHAPTER 36

A second wind surged through doctor Towers, and he caught up to Muff, who had reached the back door of the kitchen. He did not get much further beyond the door, before Doctor Towers grabbed hold of his shoulder and pushed him up against a wall. Both scuffled, trying to gain the upper hand.

"I should 'a' killed you twenty years ago."

"Twenty years is a long time to hold a grudge."

"Clara 'd still be alive."

"Not likely."

"Not likely! Twas *you* pushed her down the stairs. If I'd 'a' killed you, you never would 'a' had that chance."

"You still believe I pushed her down the stairs?"

"Lordy, I *know* you did."

"You should have stayed around town long enough to find out the truth. She wasn't *pushed* down the stairs. She had—a seizure."

"What's a seizure?"

"A sudden attack of irrational shaking, once believed to be associated with devil possession. Clara couldn't control herself. She shook violently on top of the stairs. Before I could reach—I tried to grab her, but she fell from the railing. Her neck snapped. She died instantly. Don't you see? It wasn't but a tragic accident."

"I don't believe it."

"No. Neither did her parents, after you told them and the town I murdered her. You didn't know it, but I too was banished from that town, not long after Clara's funeral. My hopes for becoming a first rate doctor were dashed. I had to settle for being a country doctor."

"Clara's parents were to take care of that."

"Yes. But you don't think they'd give me the money after you told them I murdered their daughter? They put me on trial. On trial! I was exonerated of any wrong doing. No real proof. Only, only hearsay. Gossip. But that's not the worst. The whole marriage was a sham from the start. Well, I didn't even know about Clara's disease until *after* we were married."

"*Alleged* disease, y' mean."

"Listen! I'm trying to tell you her parents were using me. When I was over at her estate, you don't think we ever spent any time alone. Of course not. Her parents wouldn't allow it. They feared she might have another seizure; and they worried I'd call off the wedding if I found out beforehand. Why do you think Clara's parents wanted *me* to marry her? Why do you think they barred *you* from seeing her any longer?"

"Cause of you."

"No! They knew I was going into medicine. They arranged for me to marry Clara, and then to find out about the seizures afterwards, hoping I would somehow find a cure for her illness, or at least devote my life to trying. *And*, at the same time keep it private. They never went to outside doctors; never wanted the scandal to tarnish their name And they were prepared to finance my whole medical education, whatever the expenses."

"Now yer talkin' crazy. Why would they accuse you of murdering her? If she had these, these seizures, as you call them, and her parents knew full well of them, why wouldn't they think her death only an accident? Why wouldn't they have believed you when you told them she'd fallen after having one of these seizures?"

"Why! Why! Because of you. You, and your lies you spread all over town. They used you too, Muff. You and your lies. They used that to their advantage. After Clara's death, they abandoned me, having no other use for me. I became a financial burden to them. And after you spread it over town I had murdered her, don't you see, don't you see how they used that to their advantage? By having you accuse me of her death, they could cut me off, without anyone ever knowing they had only been using me. You, Muff, made it so much easier for them."

"I——. I, well——. No. It still don't make sense. If her parents didn't tell no-one, how did you find out?"

"She *told* me."

"Who?"

"*Clara.* Two nights after we were married I found Clara in our bedroom, slumped over the bed, shaking. By the time I came to her aide, the convulsions had stopped. She told me she had chills, nothing more. And I, the faithful husband, believed her. It wasn't until two weeks later, when I found her sobbing upon that same bed that she broke down and began confessing. Afterwards she begged me to forgive her parents. She begged me not to lose my temper. I did. I *did*! And I'll never forgive myself for what happened next."

"What?"

"She saw the red in my face, burning fiercely. She stood, perhaps as an involuntary reflex, frightful I might lash out. And as she did, another seizure attacked her, quite violently. She ran from the bedroom, and all I know is that when I came running out after her, all I saw was her body tilting dangerously over the edge of the bannister, and before I could move an inch, she plunged down to the lower floor, and ultimately—to her death. So in a way, I *am* responsible for her death. But I did not push her in the gruesome manner in which you suggested I had. And I have had to live with that more years than I care to recall."

"I——." Muff scratched the hair atop his head. "Well, I don't——. Well, y' seem sincere enough, but, but that don't explain the other things. It don't explain your being here." Muff's temper flared once again. "Oh, you! And we was best friends once. Well, that don't change nothin'. That don't change what yer goin' to do to Widow Douglas."

'I'm not going to do anything to her! I'm not—,"

"What is going on!" Doctor Towers and Muff turned to see Widow Douglas standing before them, gripping the wet area of her dress. Droplets of water dribbled onto the floor's surface.

"Brittany!"

"Widow!"

"For heaven sakes, let go of each other. My goodness! Muff? Muff Potter? Is it you?"

"You, you *know* him!" The revelation astounded Doctor Towers.

"Of course. But, I don't understand. Why are you here? And why on earth are the both of you trying to kill one another?" She looked back and forth into the eyes of the two men. Oddly, Muff, who had waited for such an opportunity in the past, now became tongue tied, and fearful. The water soaked deeper into Widow Douglas' dress; she felt the chill against her skin. "Oh, " she grunted. "I need to—. Don't either of you leave. I'll be back. I'm not through with you both yet."

With Widow Douglas gone, Muff faced his nemeses. "Yer up t' no good, Ben. I went down to Mission. I found out about you."

"Mission? Found, found out? Found what out?"

"About the feud and the missin' gold you was accused of stealin'."

"I! I!" Doctor Towers gasped for breath. " I don't know what you're getting at." .

"Mas'r" A new voice, raspy, terrified, and anxious, echoed not too far away. Mas'r Ben! Oh, Mas'r—*Where is yooou!*" Muff Potter and doctor Towers flinched their furtive and virile glances towards the voice, which emanated from outside. The servants entrance had been left wide open, and footsteps, thumping harshly and rudely upon the sod, proved easy to detect.

Seconds later a negro, flustered, peaked, and dangerously out of breath, ran wildly into the kitchen. "Oh, Mas'r Ben. Here you is. Why don' y' answer me? Why d' you make de living speerit jump out o' me?"

Coldly brushing past Muff, doctor Towers, gravely nervous, took the man to one side.

"Franklin," Doctor Towers whispered with trepidation, "I, I thought I told you to, to stay put. You have j-jeopardized everything now. You've put *me* in jeopardy, as well as yourself."

"I had to, Mas'r."

"*Don't* call me that."

"Yes'r, but—."

"There's no excuse for you leaving, Franklin." Doctor Towers raised his voice, though in his state he did not realize it. Muff listened to, and heard, everything.

"Dere's—,"

"There's no excuse. Ruth should have—,"

"Don' blame her. Don' blame Ruth. She de one dat tol' me t' come git you."

"She-!"

"Mas'r. It's dat man. Dat's why I had t' find you. It's dat man. He here."

"That's still no reason to—,"

"*He diggin' up de grave!* Dat's why I come."

"Digging up the grave? Franklin, what on earth are you talking about."

"De Widow's sister. He diggin' up her grave."

Franklin's timing could not have been worse for doctor Towers. Widow Douglas returned, and although she hadn't heard anything prior, the fact that she heard his last statement caused her to nearly wet herself again, though she hadn't a drink in her hand.

"What! Wh—. Ben, what is this man saying?"

"Brittany. Oh, what next?" Exasperation set in.

"Who's trying to dig up sis' grave? Who!"

Muff, having kept silent, prudently held his tongue even now, though he itched to say something. He stood against the wall, and patiently waited to see what would happen next.

"Y' got t' hurry, Mas'r, 'for he dig it up, and pop open de lid, an'—,"

"Ben, I, I—. Do something. If some lunatic is out there, you've got to do something."

"He after de necklace, Mas'r."

"*Stop* calling me that. Alright, let me think."

'There's no time to think. If somebody's out there—. My goodness, did you say...*necklace*?"

"Yes'm."

"Sis's necklace?"

"All of you, stay here. I'll take care of it. Just, only stay here.." A nervous wreck, doctor Towers sped out of the kitchen, past the inquisitive guests, up the long flight of stairs, and into his room, where he withdrew a lengthy, loaded, rifle from under his bed.

Franklin, now in the presence of strangers, became visibly agitated and fearful. However, to his relief, Widow Douglas paid him no attention.

"Wait here! Well, who does he think I am?" Widow Douglas stood stolid, waiting for a reassuring response; waiting for someone to say they would exit with her, and go see about Miss Watson's grave. However, Franklin would dare not say anything more; and Muff felt out of place as well. Finally, after a few impatient minutes, Widow Douglas took a deep breath and exhaled, "Well!" Then, she walked hastily out. Muff, ashamed at his lack of courage, followed closely after her. Franklin followed after Muff, albeit at a farther distance from either of them.

With his rifle in hand, and no time to waste, doctor Towers opened his window and climbed out. Decorative vines clung to the siding, supported by steal beams. He descended swiftly. Grounded, he ran towards Miss Watson's grave, slowing only when the mysterious man became visible. However, the man, completely absorbed in uprooting the dirt with his hands, would not have noticed if a steamboat snuck up behind him and blew its whistle.

Yards away, doctor Towers could hear the man swearing in broken English. "Halt!" he demanded, pointing the rifle at the man. "Halt this insanity at once."

Had it not been for doctor Towers shadow, the man might never have noticed his presence . He looked up, frightened for a moment; then, realizing the face as a familiar one, pushed his hands further into the dirt..

"'Is necklace est mine, ja. *Mine!*"

"Back away this instance, or I swear I will fire."

"Est mine!" the man screamed. "Go. I come when ready. Maybe I tell Douglas woman about you, ja? Ja," he laughed.

Knowing he had but one alternative, doctor Towers readied himself. Widow Douglas, twenty yards away, stopped coldly when she heard the shot.

"Ben!"

The shot, a clean one, entered the man's left breast. He fell atop the grave; dirt still sullied his palms.

"Est mine!" he gasped. Doctor Towers, showing no emotion, pushed him off onto the grass with his foot; for he did not desire any further desecration of Miss Watson's grave. Standing as a statue, he watched over the dead man. Soon, three others joined him.

"Ben! Are you alright? I—. Well, what happened?"

"I had to shoot him. He was insane. He, well you can see what he was doing."

"Oh, Ben. At least, at least he didn't—*dig any deeper.*"

Muff knelt over the man, consternated for a moment. Then;

"I know that man from somewhere, but I, I can't seem to—. It's his drooping mustache."

"Oh dear lord!" Widow Douglas swooned to the ground.

Doctor Towers threw down the rifle. "Brittany!" He shook her until she came around. "Why did you faint? Oh, silly me. Of course you would faint. Of course you would—,"

"Ben. Ben. That man. I saw him." Widow Douglas stood. "That's the man I saw talking with you. The one you said was a slave trader. I thought he looked familiar, but when you said he *was* a slave trader I, I brushed him off. Ben! Oh dear. I don't know how. I don't, I don't—. It's his mustache. That's what I remembered. His drooping mustache. Oh, I can't believe—. Oh!. That man lying dead right there, I know—. I *knew* him. It's *Mr. Johansson.*"

CHAPTER 37

Within moments of the gunshot all of Widow Douglas' guests quickly exited the mansion and hurried out onto the front lawn. Speculation had, beforehand, circulated as to their host's whereabouts; for she had not been seen since making a hasty exit of her own, after spilling water upon her dress. Even Tom and Becky wondered; and feared she might not return again that night, and blame them as the reason she would not reappear.

"She must be quite upset with us, Tom." Becky, near tears, almost induced another bout of shaking. "Oh, what will the people think of us, when they find out *we're* the reason she has not returned? What ever will they think of us?"

"Not everyone saw. I—. Well, look. There's doctor Towers. Let's ask him if he knows."

But the man sped by so quickly, Tom had not time to inhale his question; and by the time he exhaled it, doctor Towers had ascended more than half way up the stairs.

"Well what do you think, Tom? Is something up?"

"I've never seen anyone in such a hurry, unless there was trouble. I caught a glimpse of his face, and there warn't much color in it, 'cept white."

"I'm afraid to question what might be wrong. What if it has something to do with us? What if, after Widow Douglas spilled the water, it dribbled down to her shoes, and she slipped and broke her leg, or, or—. *Oh!* I don't like to think about it."

Talking about Widow Douglas' disappearance did not help; nor did the silence ease their tensions. Not long afterwards a loud ring traversed throughout the mansion, halting all manner of activity. Every man, woman and child were as stone. One man, however, broke free and shouted, "Gun fire!" As if by magic, the petrification melted away, and thus began the exodus from Widow Douglas' mansion.

Barely noticeable at first, as they clumped together in an ever increasing mob, their horrible screeching brought forth the attention of Widow Douglas.

"Ben. They've heard the shot. They'll want answers. *I* want answers. Quickly, so I can explain things. How did you come to know Mr. Johansson, and what connection is he to you, and to, to—. Where did he go? Where did the colored man go?"

Doctor Towers felt the impending pressure, as that of a boil on the back of his neck. He knew he had to come clean. Nay, he *wanted* to come clean. For many weeks now he had lived in fear the secret would be divulged. For many weeks he desperately tried to think of a rational lie, in place of the irrational truth.

"Oh, blasted! I—. I try to, try to do something of value, and what becomes of it? I suppose there really is a supernatural, and that it is completely against me. Well, well—. First of all, Brittany, please, please *do* call him Franklin. That's his name."

"Alright. He did come warn us, after-all. Who is he? He isn't one of *my* slaves. Is he one of yours?"

"I, well, well in a manner of speaking—. Well, it's more complicated."

Muff, without careful consideration, or any particular delicateness, exclaimed, "You *stole* him. Didn't you?"

"Stole?" Widow Douglas stared, perplexed, as a child who has been given instructions she can't quite understand. "Ben? Muff! Do you know what you're saying, what you're accusing Ben of? There's another reason. Of course there is. Ben?"

"And I thought you was only after her jewelry; and maybe , maybe y' still are."

"I am not after Brittany's jewels. That is an outrageous lie."

"Well, maybe, maybe not. What about it, Ben? You steal this colored man from somewhere? Hoping to resell him someplace else? That yer game? I know'd people to 'a' done that. I know'd people to 'a' been hung fer it too."

"I didn't steal him so I could resell—. Confounded! If you must know, I, I *was* stealing from you. I *was* after your money and jewels, just as Muff says. I confess it. I confess it all. Well, I didn't go through with it, so you can't prove anything. And after tonight, you won't have to worry. I'll be gone." Apparently, the irrational lie would suffice, at least, for the time being.

Widow Douglas sobbed. "Ben. Why? Why would you steal from me? I trusted you. I, oh, I—it was than trust. I loved you!"

Doctor Towers breathed silently, staring down at Mr. Johansson's body. He spoke nothing. Subsequently, the soft sobs emitted from Widow Douglas squeezed against his mid-section until he no longer could breath silently, but instead must gasp for precious air. He could have remedied that; but the cure, he knew, would cause him even greater pain.

Muff gazed oddly at doctor Towers. "What was you gonna say, Ben? If you was up to more, best to get it out now."

"I told you what you wanted to hear, is that not enough?"

"Not if it's more lies. Maybe you don't owe me the truth, maybe you don't owe me anything. But you owe Widow Douglas the truth?"

"The truth! She can't handle a *lie*, what do you want me—. Never mind. I've said too much. I've said too much."

Widow Douglas sobbed on. By now the only voices she heard were her own internal ones, whispering wickedly inside of her.

"Why, you wasn't planning to sell that colored man was you?"

"I told you I wasn't."

"But he calls you master, like you own him. A slave gen'lly don't call nobody master, 'less that person *is* his master. Well, there are other times too, I reckon."

"Will you not let things stand the way they are?"

"No. No, I won't. If you ain't gonna resell the colored man, he must already be free, which case he'd have papers to show it. If he ain't got the papers, or if you ain't holdin' on to 'em, they ain't but one other alternative."

The guests were still assembling outside the front lawn when someone shouted from twenty yards away he had people out back of the mansion. Now an investigation must be made.

Doctor Towers sneered. "Save your opinions—,"

"Are they opinions? They's a colored man on Widow Douglas' property. She don't know who he is, and you seem t' be the only one who does. He knows *you*, real well. Why, who did he come lookin' fer when that man Johansson was digging up Miss Watson's grave? Not Widow Douglas. He even seems to know the terrain, inside and out, real well. That means he's been here long enough to learn it. But Widow Douglas ain't ever seen him. She ain't ever seen him 'cause you've kept him hid. Why would you keep him hid?"

"You're barking up the wrong end of the tree."

"No, I don't think I am. I think I finally have it straight. I think you—."

"Ho. There she is! Widow Douglas! Widow Douglas!" Once spotted, it did not take long for the guests to form in a horseshoe around Miss Watson's grave.

Ben, a thief? Stealing from me? Stealing! Those little voices whispering inside her head blocked everything out for a time, until even louder voices surrounded her. Then, she looked up, dazed and bewildered to see so many people standing in front of her. It took her a few moments to remember what had happened.

"Oh. I, I suppose you all heard the gun shot.".

Said one guest. "We, well, we wondered what had happened, and where you went to."

"Thank goodness you are unharmed," said another guest, looking down at the dead body. Little did any of them know the true harm that had befallen Widow Douglas.

"How'd it happen?"

"Who did it?"

"He tried to dig up my sister's grave," Widow Douglas murmured. "Ben, doctor Towers, shot him. He had to." She hadn't much spirit in her voice. "The man wouldn't stop, even after he was warned. I'll, I'll be glad to testify to that."

It did not take much more explaining. "No need," the guests emphasized. Widow Douglas' word stood on its own merit with the townspeople. More than enough men were quick to volunteer their services to remove the body. Widow Douglas thanked them, and then apologized for having the evening end on such a sour note. As the women walked past her, each put an understanding hand upon her shoulder.

Muff, standing the furthest away from the grave, felt a tug on his coat tail.

"Muff!" two strained voices whispered. "It's us."

The man whirled. "Wha-!" He looked down and saw Tom and Becky. "Oh. Oh, it's you, children. I didn't expect t' see you. "

"We didn't expect to see you either," Tom said. "We thought you wanted to lay low, to keep watch over doctor Towers.."

"Well, yes, yes. But's that's over now, I think."

"But wasn't he going to steal from Widow Douglas?"

"Ah, well. Well, no, not no more, Becky. At least, if he was, he ain't goin' to now."

"Ain't he gonna be arrested?"

"They ain't no need for that, I don't 'spect.. He *didn't* do it, so can't be arrested."

"And to think, Tom, all that work we put into the nonamous letter. What's to become of it now, if we can't give it to Widow Douglas?"

"What's this? Give what to Widow Douglas?"

"We was going to warn her about doctor Towers, with a nonamous letter, so as not to get ourselves into trouble."

"I don't hardly understand any of it. Just tell me, this letter, you still got it?"

"Course."

"Good, Tom. Destroy it. Don't never let her see it. It'd only worsen matters."

"Well, if you think so, Muff, but—,"

"Now Tom, don't you argue. It's late. Everybody's leaving. Best you both do the same. Give Widow Douglas some space. There's been a killing on her property, and she'll need time to regain her strength. She's awful weak right now." The guests departed quietly, and respectfully, and above all promptly, leaving the three original occupants to contemplate the night, and what tomorrow would bring. "Well, Ben. It's just us again. You wanna finish tellin' us 'bout the colored man?"

"Franklin! Oh—let it rest, Muff. You've caused enough damage already."

"Muff!" A vigorous spark energized Widow Douglas. "You think Muff caused all this? .Don't lay *all* the blame upon Muff. You're just as much, no, *more* to blame."

"Well, I reckon I know what he's up to. I been goin' over in my mind several things that didn't make sense. The way I add it up now, everything makes sense."

"Nobody wants to hear *your* ideas."

"Well, *I* do. Ben, you've just confessed an awful, awful, well, it's awful what you've confessed. I don't know what I should do. I don't know how I should handle this. Don't you see how it's tearing me apart? I don't know what to do."

"It's tearing me apart too. Oh, I wish, I wish I never set out to do it in the first place."

"If you'd tell her the truth, Ben, you'd save her a life time of grief and guilt, and misunderstanding, and, and a strong hatred towards you. It don't take a doctor to see that."

"Muff, you think you know the truth. You think I have more to hide. Well, if that's true, and if you do know the truth, as you say you do, then you know what harm the truth would bring Brittany. You know what would happen to her if she knew the truth."

"Don't underestimate her. She may surprise you."

"You're both talking in tongues. Why are you trying to say, Muff?"

"It's simple, really," Muff explained. "Isn't it, Ben? Just a matter of—abolition."

"Muff!" Doctor Towers gazed sternly. Widow Douglas held a similar gaze as well.

"My god! Muff! How could you say, you—well, don't say it unless you truly mean it." Widow Douglas stepped away. "Ben? Ben, be honest with me."

Doctor Towers gazed back and forth, from Widow Douglas, to Muff. A look of disgust drenched his face. He went through many unpleasant, emotional phases before he said anything.

"You couldn't leave well enough alone. You had to keep on pressing. I told you she couldn't handle it. Well, well yes, in a manner of speaking. Yes, it's abolition. To think, I try doing something of value, the first time mind you, and what comes of it! It's not so much for myself, but Franklin. Well, now it's out. I don't know whether to be happy, or terrified. Terrified for Franklin, mind you, not me. They'll only *hang* me. Oh, but what they'll do with Franklin. I suppose it futile for us all to make our escape now. You'd only have the law on me.

Poor Franklin. I've failed him, and he doesn't even know it."

"And the other man?" Muff asked. "He in on it too?"

Doctor Towers grumbled. "Him! No, he was never actually in on it. He knew about it. He——. I caught him spying, one night, upon the grounds. I told him I'd have him arrested, upon which he laughed, wildly. Well, he had found out my plans somehow, and threatened to expose me if I didn't get something for him. A necklace. Miss Watson's. He claimed it was his, and he wanted it back. I knew he was insane from the moment I first spotted him. Why I didn't kill——. Well, enough about him."

"He, Mr. Johansson, had given that necklace to sis, a long, long time ago. We all thought he had died at the Alamo. All these years, we thought he was dead. He was so gentle, so kind, so benevolent. What happened to him, I wonder, that made him stark crazy mad?"

"Is that all you was gonna do, Ben? Only steal Franklin out of slavery?"

"Of course. Well——."

"Well what? Was you gonna steal from Widow Douglas too?"

"No! I told you that was an outrageous lie."

"There's more, Ben. You owe it to Widow Douglas."

"Please, Ben. My mind, I'm so confused now. Just a few moments ago I despised you. And now, now——. My mind is dizzy. I don't know what to think of you any longer. You've hurt me. You've hurt in me in ways. I——. I trusted you, Ben. You betrayed that trust."

"I know it. I know it. I never set out to harm you. I never wanted it to come to this. I didn't expect it to come to this. If only he hadn't been married. If only he hadn't a wife."

"Who?"

"Franklin! Ruth, Ruth is his wife "

"Ruth? But she never mentioned having a husband. Well, I never thought to bring it up. I never much discussed anything with her, I guess."

"So that's why you's here. You planned stealin' both Franklin *and* Ruth."

With trepidation, he said, "I admit at first I thought the idea of abolition insane. I suppose I only agreed to it because, well, I thought Franklin would die. Not, not a very pleasant fact, but—. Well not too many survive being shot; nor the amount of blood lost." Doctor Towers shuffled his feet.

"Go on," Widow Douglas urged.

"I, I don't know if, if—. I had to intoxicate him, before removing the bullet. Well I never saw another man go through as much whiskey as Franklin. Halfway into his second bottle he started feeling the effects."

"Takes me 'bout two," Muff absently mumbled.

"On and on he went about himself, his life, and finally the wife he thought he'd never see again. He told me he wanted to die, and wouldn't allow me to remove the bullet unless I promised him I'd take him to his wife if he survived. Well, as serious a condition as he was in, I knew he wouldn't survive while the bullet remained lodged within him. I must admit I had little confidence he would survive with it out. But as a doctor I am sworn to save lives. Suffice it to say, I granted Franklin his desire. I was more surprised than anyone when, after a couple days, his health greatly improved. I had no other alternative but to honor my oath."

"There's more to it than all that," Muff speculated.

"Well what more do you want?" Doctor Towers shot back with frustration and anger.

"I, I know what *I* want," Widow Douglas interjected after some thought and deep reflection. "I want to help."

CHAPTER 38

Not expecting a statement as chillingly treasonous as that from the mouth of Widow Douglas, doctor Towers abruptly took her arm and escorted her back inside the mansion, into the parlor, where he hoped to convince her otherwise. Muff, always the outcast, followed.

Pacing behind the sofa, while constantly mangling his hair with a sweaty, unsteady hand, Doctor Towers pleaded, though not realizing the woman's stubbornness.

"Please, I beg of you, be reasonable. Reconsider. Take back what you've said. It's, it's unbecoming of a woman in your position."

"A what! Ben I—,"

"I never dreamed you should learn about me. I dreaded you ever finding out, because of course I fully assumed you'd turn me in. But, to hear you say, say—. I can't repeat those words, it's far too astonishing." Both had become so overwrought, so enmeshed in their unwavering positions, they forgot about Muff. He stood near the exit, where he felt safer.

"Indeed. It came as a surprise to me too. But I'll not take the words back now. I said I wanted to help, and so I shall. Won't I?"

"Is it not enough you know? You know! You know what I am going to do. If anyone found out you knew, well—. Brittany. Brittany, darling, if I could only make you forget what you know. If I could make you forget, so that if ever—,"

"I don't want to forget."

"But you must. You *must* forget. The alternative is so much more dangerous. Have you any plausible estimation of how many times *I've* nearly been exposed? From the moment I faked Franklin's death, I haven't had but chilling thoughts I would shortly be exposed. Every moment I had Franklin out of my sights I feared doubly more than when my eyes knew his exact location. I had to bring him here, after-all, for fear he had been seen. He had a habit of coming out of the cellar, once in a while, against my strong warnings. It *is* hot in there. One time somebody came to the door while he was out. I don't if he was seen or not; I'll probably never know. Still, I knew I couldn't take another chance. I had to bring him here. I had planned to anyhow, but not that early. Brittany, you just don't know how difficult it has been for me. We, that is, Franklin and I, burrowed underneath the flooring of Ruth's and Ginny's quarter's."

"So that's where he's been all this time."

"And it was no easy task either. Especially with the rains. Oh, the rains. And the ground water kept seeping inside. Franklin spent more time on the floor next to Ruth's bed, than down below. We finished it, the two of us. Unfortunately not before that man came. Johansson. He told me his name was Mr. Farmer, I suppose for obvious reasons. Well then, all my fears came true. Somebody knew, and blackmailed me. No Brittany, it's best you forget. I've slept very little. Too much on my mind. Always too much on my mind. I don't want to see you succumb to my internal sufferings."

"Sufferings! I've suffered greatly already. Don't you see, don't you see how my helping would relieve those sufferings, for the both of us?"

"No. Believe me Brittany, my eternal gratitude goes out to you, for not despising me, for not telling me I am in league with the devil, for not turning your back on me. Why you have taken this position puzzles me, and even worries me. If somebody else, somebody from the out- side, discovered your views, I, well we both know exactly what would happen. I need not say it out loud, I hope. The, the time is growing short. I must take Franklin away shortly, over to the Illinois side, where we'll rendevous with a group of Quakers. Thank goodness for them. They've been doing this for years, they've told me. Franklin and Ruth will be in good hands. But I *won't* leave until I've convinced you to end your aspirations to help me."

"I said I wanted to help. As astonishing as that may sound to you, it comes as an even greater shock to me. Me, who has been raised on a plantation, and has lived all her adult life in a mansion, waited on day and night by slaves. But when you confessed, when you openly admitted your true intentions, I said to myself—*I must aid him. I love him. He means more to me than all my earthly possessions.* That became clear to me after our argument this night, after you left me, here, in the parlor, which you had every right to do. I acted terribly, and deserved your disdain, then. I want to make up for my selfishness. Sis's death has affected me deeply; but it should never have affected our relationship, and for that I apologize. *Let* me help you, Ben. You need all you can get."

Muff spoke up, with trepidation. "She's, (cough), right about that."

Doctor Towers whirled. "What in-! What! Oh. Oh, Muff, you, you—. I hadn't realized. You, well you—." Sucking in his gut, doctor Towers bellowed, "Well, I suppose you'll want to turn me in, won't you? Well you can't prove anything. Anyhow, by the time you come back with the law, I'll be gone. And so will the evidence."

"I don't reckon I had any intentions of turning you in."

"No intentions of—. Oh." The man looked to Widow Douglas, then back at Muff. "So that's your game, eh. You're going to blackmail me too, just like that Far—, er, whatever his name is, *was.* Well, I killed once this night. Maybe—,"

"Ben!"

"Well if he thinks I'm going to let *him* blackmail me; if he thinks I'll let any harm or shame come to you—. Brittany, he heard everything we said."

"Ben, ain't a single body in all of St. Petersburg gonna believe Widow Douglas is an abolitionist, or a party to it. I'd be the one thrown out, not her. B'sides, I ain't got no intentions to blackmail you."

Worried, more for doctor Towers than for herself, Widow Douglas wrung her hands. Stepping towards Muff she said, "Muff, Muff, please, I know it's wrong what Ben is doing, and I know I'm in the wrong for wanting to help him; and I know, I know what I am about to ask you is wrong, dreadfully wrong; but Muff, there now Muff, can't you see the pain you would cause by turning Ben in? I'll give you anything you want. Money? Do you want money? I'll give you money, Muff. Enough to satisfy you for the rest of your life. Your *life.*"

"Brittany, you're over exerting yourself."

"I don't care," Widow Douglas lashed out.

"Miss Douglas, you misunderstand me," Muff explained. "I'm not going to blackmail Ben, nor turn him in. I'm only trying to say i'd like to help him."

Doctor Towers leaned forward. "What!" He nearly collapsed.

"I wanna help."

Doctor Towers threw up his hands. "Oh! I've never lived as trying an evening as this. *You,* help. Leave. Leave and never spill a word what you've heard this night. That's the best help you can offer. And the both of you, just let me take Franklin to the Quakers. Let me get him out of here before anything else goes wrong."

"Wait, Ben." Widow Douglas tugged at his coat-tail. "Muff, I *have* to help Ben, whether he wants to accept it or not. But why should you want to help?"

For a moment Muff stared into the question brought before him. Stared *into* it because he saw the question as clearly, and soberly, as he had seen anything in his life. Every word, every letter, every syllable, breathed its own significant meaning; and Muff, feeling slightly queasy, realized how scandalously important became the question asked.

Widow Douglas, anxious for his answer, prompted him. "Well?"

"W-well," Muff uttered.

"Well?" Widow Douglas again asked.

"Well, maybe, maybe—." Muff looked to Widow Douglas, then doctor Towers. "Maybe I know a thing or two about, well about what Ben's plannin' to do." Muff's hands trembled.

"We all know a thing or two about what Ben wants to do, Muff."

"I mean, I, I—. Oh, it oughtn't t' be this hard. Not now. Not no longer. See, a long while ago, shortly after I stumbled into this town, I got involved, I, well, in the movement. That is, the abolition movement." Muff's eyes dragged back and forth, heavily, nervously, abounding with frightened speculation. Instead, doctor Towers took his own eyes off Muff and slowly paced behind the awed, but bewildered, Widow Douglas. "It seems far-fetched, I know. But y' got to believe me. I don't have any reason fer makin' it up."

"You, an abolitionist, Muff?"

"It's true, Miss Douglas. I didn't rightly think I'd live to say it out loud to anyone. A long, long while ago, over fifteen years ago, and shortly after I stumbled into St. Petersburg, as I said, I got involved, along with, well some other residents."

"Here? In St. Petersburg? Residents in St. Petersburg?" Widow Douglas questioned.

Muff veered his head downward. "Yes."

"But, that can't be. Well the town wasn't much then. It was still forming. I, and my late husband, only moved here twenty years ago, when St. Petersburg was still a fairly young and new town. The founders, God rest their souls, the Stantans, settled here in the mid-teens. I've known everyone who has ever lived here, and not one of them has ever given me the slightest hint they were involved in abolition."

"I didn't know they was abolitionists either, not fer a couple years, 'til I accidently discovered them in the process of moving slaves."

"You seem to stumble into every place you're not supposed to be," an irritated Doctor Towers said.

"Ben, really."

"Well, how do we know he's not making it up?"

"Why would he?"

"I don't, I don't know, Brittany. I don't know anything anymore. I'm too frustrated right now to think clearly. Well, alright, I, I a-apologize."

Satisfied, Widow Douglas took her eyes off doctor Towers, and returned them to Muff, staring at him with eager inquisitiveness.

"Who, Muff? Who were they, the abolitionists?"

"Oh, well, I don't hardly b'lieve I ought to tell. I've already said too much 'bout what I swore an oath to keep mum a lot of years ago. Now, I've let it out and nearly betrayed—.."

"Go on," Widow Douglas said. However, Muff scratched his head, looked around the room with a funny stare, and shrugged his shoulders.

"Oh, I don't reckon they'd mind you knowin'. They always wanted to tell you, but always feared you wouldn't understand, you being brought up with slavery, and havin' nothin' agin it, which is how most folks is. They didn't want no harm to come to you neither. And you always bein' so close, and them all the time fearin' you'd find out anyway, and—,"

"What do you mean me being so close?"

"What? Oh, oh I let my tongue out longer than I should 'a'. Well, at the time, back fifteen years ago, we was a whole underground network. I was an escort. I led the slaves from the house, into the tunnel, and all the way out to the end, where someone else, another escort, would take them to the river. There'd be other escorts to take them across to the Illinois side, and up to a village of Quakers. Same people as Ben spoke of. The Quakers would take them to other underground homes, and eventually into Canada. That Mr. Johansson, the man Ben killed, he was an escort."

"Mr. Johansson?"

"Yes. As I recall he disappeared quite suddenly one day. Put the whole operation in limbo for a week, while two of the leaders tracked him, fearing he had gone to the authorities."

"Leader?" doctor Towers questioned.

"We had three people at the top, or leaders as we called 'em, that took charge of every little detail. They come back 'bout a week afterwards and said things was alright, and not to worry. So I never thought much about Farmer, or Johansson, ever agin, 'til I saw him this night, and recalled the drooping mustache."

"It is not only confusing, but the whole idea of an underground, well it seems so complicated.. I can't think of anyone in St. Petersburg who would have the resources, the means, and the money it must have taken, to carry it out."

"But do you *know* anyone who could have?"

"Know? Well, there have been several affluent families. But the only ones living here fifteen years ago were mine and the, well the Stantans."

"Yes. Yes, I remember those were the only two." Muff quieted.

"So?" Muff said nothing. "Well, if you're implying the *Stantans*, Robert and Marribelle; if you're implying they were connected, I don't, I don't know what to say, except they couldn't have been."

"They were," Muff revealed.

"Oh! It's impossible. Utterly ridiculous. I knew them. My husband and I were very good friends. Why, Robert knew my husband long before I did. They were land speculators, working together, side by side. Even after we married, when he and Robert went off together, I spend my time with Marribelle. Everyday. *Everyday,* do you hear? We threw parties twice a months, either here at my mansion, or at theirs."

"That was how they got the slaves out unseen. Those parties weren't social events. They was the only way to get all the town folk in one location, allowing fer the slaves to be moved out unseen, while everyone was inside. They became more and more necessary the more populated the town became."

"It's preposterous. Well, how could Robert hide such a, a—. Well, wouldn't my husband have found out? For goodness sakes, to think they used my husband and I."

"Brittany, you're over exerting again. Please try to remain calm."

"Remain calm! How? He's telling me mine and my husband's best friends were abolitionists. It has to be a lie."

"There, of course it is. Muff, why you couldn't leave well enough—. Look at Brittany. Look at what you've reduced her to."

"I was afraid this might happen, thas why I resisted telling her fer so long. Thas why I didn't want t' tell her now. But, well, I thought she could handle it. I thought she had a right to know now, now that she hadn't anything agin abolition, and was gonna help you."

"Oh, if it's true, my poor, poor husband. To have been used by his best friend. To have used him, and my, and our home. No! No, I won't believe the Stantans used my husband.

"They—. If it's anything to you, they never *used* your husband."

"Of course they did, if what you are telling me is true."

"No. I mean, all what I told you is the truth, so help me. They thought about telling you, but decided agin it. They didn't know how you'd react. And they didn't want to disgrace you, nor involve you, fearing if they was found out, you would be disgraced, or worse."

"But they used my husband. I don't care that they were abolitionists and stole slaves, but they used my husband to do it. And I just cannot ever believe such a lie as that."

"No. Miss Douglas, your husband *was* an abolitionist. In fact, he was a leader, like Robert and Marribelle."

"You're mistaken. Why are you doing this to me? None of this makes any sense." Widow Douglas slipped from doctor Towers grip, onto the sofa. "You're wrong, Muff. You're so very, very wrong. You must be."

"Ah, but he *isn't*," a booming voice, new, but not unrecognizable, echoed from outside the parlor. "He is quite *right*, dear Brittany."

Widow Douglas whirled. "Jonathan!"

CHAPTER 39

"Pray, forgive me," Senator smiled, entering the parlor without reluctance. "I loathe intruding as I have, but felt it most necessary, most necessary."

Rising lightly, Widow Douglas said, "We missed you at the party."

"Yes. Unfortunate circumstances led to my absence. An, an unclear head. I was resting in my room when I heard a gun shot. When I came down, I heard voices in the parlor. It did not take me long to interpret what was being said, and thus deduce the serious matter in which it was being discussed."

"You heard everything we were discussing?"

"Yes, Benjamin. I could not help but to become intrigued and fascinated."

"Fascinated?" Doctor Towers puzzled the man's meaning.

"Jonathan. Just before you came in, Muff told me my best friends, *your* best friends too, the Stantans, were abolitionists. He told me my husband was an abolitionist also. And then, and then you, you, why, when I told Muff he must be mistaken, why, you came in and said, said—. Oh, I'm so confused."

"Yes, of course, of course you are. It's completely understandable. A great shock." Senator seated himself, not the least bit in a foul mood. "If I were in your place, I wouldn't know what to make of it all either." Becoming serious, he arched his head upwards towards Widow Douglas. "Brittany, oh dear, dear Brittany. I never thought I would be telling you this, not so long as I, I lived. We never dreamed of exposing you, ever. Far too dangerous. I feel it only right you know now. On behalf of the Stantans, Robert and Marribelle; and on behalf of your husband, Peter. Yes, I am confident they would want you to know."

"I'm listening, although I don't understand, really. Not all of it."

Senator motioned his arm out towards Muff. "What this fellow here has said about the Stantans, and your husband, is all true. They all were abolitionists; they all aided in stealing, and then freeing, many, well, hundreds, of slaves, over the years."

"And how do you come to know all of this?" doctor Towers asked.

"Know?" Senator tensed, though he hadn't any objections in divulging his secret. "Well," he laughed, wryly. "There were three leaders in all. Robert and Marribelle, and your husband.. But, but only one man stood above *them*. The one man who orchestrated the entire operation; the one man who recruited the leaders, and for whom they reported to and collaborated with; devised plans, false documents, records, everything; the one man, the *only* man, who had enough power and influence, and knew how to use is prudently; the one man who started it all; the one man who will never forgive himself for allowing the Stantan's deaths, or Peter's, and will carry that regret to his grave."

Widow Douglas sunk down next to him, slowly picking up on Senator's meaning. Her eyes followed the length of his body, up and down, until they rested upon the man's eyes.

"Jonathan," Widow Douglas gasped, hoarsely.

"It's a growing underground movement. I began myself very early on in the century. My own father had been against slavery and, after the revolution, was certain it would be abolished. Our founding fathers never saw fit to do so. Well, slavery was contained mostly within wealthy families anyway, and it looked as though it might not last into this century. And it might not have, if it hadn't been for that da—. Oh, pardon me, dear Brittany. I was about to use a word I ought not to use in front of you. The cotton gin. Well, once that came along, there was no stopping slavery. Don't get me wrong, it's a wonderful invention, and it has been quite an extraordinary benefit to our economy. But it has come at a very high expense."

"And Robert and Marribelle?" Widow Douglas asked. "How did they come to be abolitionists?"

"The same way I did, I suppose. I met them around, oh was it eighteen ten, or eleven. Well, around then. A good man, Robert was. French, on his mother's side. He and Marribelle were living in New Orleans at the time. I convinced them to move up here. The area was opening up, and as people were crossing the Mississippi River, into the new west, they brought along their slaves. A dangerous trend, I believed. It became a perfect locale, for hiding, and moving, slaves."

"All that time," Widow Douglas said, still in disbelief. "And I never knew."

"The Stantans loved you as much as your husband, Brittany. It was out of that deep love and devotion they decided not to tell you. As—. I'm terribly sorry, what name did you go by?"

"Me, sir?" Muff jumped.

"Yes, sir. You, sir."

"M—. Anthony James Potter. Thas my real name, though everyone's been callin' me Muff since I was real young, cause I'm rather awkward and don't do any but fool hardiness.".

"Well, Anthony, when you joined the underground, that wasn't fool hardiness, *I'll* say. Many men, women and children owe you thanks. Even I owe you thanks, for your service."

"I, well, I'm grateful to you. Well, they, the Stantans, yer husband, they talked about you, oh not by name o' course. I alwus wanted to meet you. Never thought I would."

"As I never thought I would meet you, or anyone the leaders employed to help, for obvious reasons of course. Anthony told you correctly, dear Brittany. We made every effort to shield you from knowing about us. In the beginning for fear you'd turn us in. You see, Peter was involved in the movement long before he met you. When he told us you both were to marry, we pleaded with him to reconsider. Selfishness on our behalf, yes. Thank goodness he was always a stubborn one. He convinced us you were worth it; and we had to admit, shortly after the marriage, without the least bit of dissatisfaction, how wrong we were."

"And what would have happened to Brittany had you been exposed," doctor Towers wanted to know.

"Hmm. A terrible scandal. We made every precaution to prevent such an occurrence. And every precaution worked splendidly to our favor. Well, but one, of course."

"The Stantans deaths?"

"Yes, Brittany. That was the one time, the only time, we, *I*, failed. Stealing slaves is no easy task, mind you. There was always the pro-slavery sector to worry about; and they were none too apathetic about our business. We were always careful to watch out for them. This one particular time *especially*, as we were about to embark upon our most extraordinary, and subsequently, most dangerous mission to date. Perchance, Anthony, you recall?"

"'Twas when we was gonna move near thirty slaves over to the Illinois side."

"Hmm," Senator reflected. "Ordinarily we moved between five and ten at a time. Certainly no more than ten. After-all, how would it look to people if they saw a substantially large band of black men, women and children out of doors at night? And with the Nat Turner killings still very fresh and clear on people's minds. No, better safe, than otherwise."

"What changed your minds?" doctor Towers asked, "to make you decide a risky venture with so many slaves?"

"Well, you may call it foolishness, impatience if you prefer. It never seemed as though we were making progress. New laws were always being enacted against slaves; punishments worsened to such an extent—well, we, that is, the leaders and I, agreed an attempt with more slaves might prove worthwhile. But problems arose from the beginning.

Robert and Peter, as they told me later, encountered a storm while shipping the slaves up the Mississippi. It made night passage near impossible. All too often their steamboat hit upon logs, rafts and other debris. They just missed side winding another steamboat; and at that point, both men agreed to put into the next town, and hope the storm would cease by dawn. We were aware of the town's pro-slavery attitude, but had little choice. The storm had overpowered our steamboat, and we couldn't risk the chance of it breaking under the pressure of the current. If only we had known, if only we had some twinkling of knowledge."

"What's that?" doctor Towers questioned.

"The pro-slavers were on to us. Somewhere we erred. The thirty slaves we stole, they were noticeably missed; sooner than we had hoped. Curse *me* for it all, for everything that happened afterwards."

"Now Jonathan, how could you have known?"

"I should have. I should have at least expected *that* many slaves would not go unnoticed. I should have made plans in the advent of retaliation. I had gotten greedy, simply put. That greed led to the worst of all tragedies." Senator's self embitterment heightened. "The time Robert and Peter were laid up was long enough for the pro-slavers, one at least, to catch up. He followed them back to the Stantan Mansion, thus discovering exactly where the slaves were hidden. As if this was not enough, Robert and Peter returned to find out one of their men had vanished, quite suddenly, without leaving an explanation, nor where he could be reached. We never did hear from him again. I, I've always wondered if maybe *he* had something to do with the Stantan murders. Anthony!" Senator turned violently. "Did you earlier say the man Benjamin shot had once been employed with the underground? That he too had vanished mysteriously?"

"He was one in the same."

"Strange, these twists of fate. Well, we couldn't risk the man's disappearance. We moved up the time of the transfer as quickly as we could get word to the Quakers. That became the night of the murders."

Widow Douglas bowed her head, solemnly. "I'll never forget. " Widow Douglas shivered. "Oh, those dreaded men."

"Who?" doctor Towers asked.

"Murrell's Gang. They were the demons who murdered poor Robert and Marribelle."

Doctor Towers squinted his eyes, puzzling over something. "Yes. You had mentioned them to me before. But I, I thought—. What's this about a pro-slaver? Is he at all connected with Murrell's Gang?"

Senator nodded. "Indeed, he was. A very lowly person. An unscrupulous man; a poor excuse for a human being, if you ask me. I took particular delight in glaring over his body the other day, after you pronounced him dead." Senator gestured towards doctor Towers.

"I? The other day? When did you-? Are you referring to the dead man in the sheriff's office? The one you, you said you once knew?"

"Had heard of, yes? His name was Cy Loftus. A bounty hunter by trade, but an avid pro-slaver, and heavily involved in the pro-slavery movement. He had made a name for himself, and we were well aware of his existence."

"That explains his actions before the hanging, why he tried desperately to silence me."

"You see, after he found out where we brought the slaves, Cy went to gather more men—pro-slavers, to help apprehend the slaves. However, Murrell's Gang beat him. I never uncovered exactly everything that transpired, because, of course, I was not there. A small hand full of slaves, that *had* successfully escaped, and found their way to the Quakers, were very instrumental in explaining the chaos that irrupted. I was with them, the Quakers that is, as I always am, when slaves are to be moved. I rushed back as quickly as I could. What ever became of the other slaves that made up the thirty still remains unclear, though it is likely some drowned in the river, while others fled in every direction and were never heard from again. Of these, perhaps, at least I like to think, they somehow found their way to freedom.

"There's nothing to suggest some of them didn't find their way to freedom."

"Yes, Brittany. One likes to assume for the best, as it lifts a heavy load off the mind."

"What did they, er, that is, the slaves, say happened?" Muff asked, stumbling through the words. "I had only left the Stantans minutes before Murrell's Gang arrived. I rushed back toward the mansion after I heard gun shots. I hid myself behind that great tree that used to over-look the mansion."

"Don't blame yourself, Anthony. You, you had no idea. You might have been killed yourself, had you stayed longer. The slaves I spoke to told me that after hearing the shots there was an immediate panic. One of them, in this frenzy, accidentally knocked over the only lantern. Now, in total darkness, they trampled over one another down the winding tunnel in a desperate search to find the way out. In the process, many suffered broken arms and legs, which led me to believe some among the thirty had inevitably drown in the Mississippi."

Muff nearly sobbed. "I never knew it."

"And now, Benjamin, that you know of my involvement in abolition, and the underground, I again offer my services. I know you must be scared to death, both for yourself, and for, for—,"

"Franklin."

"Yes. Franklin. I know these Quakers you have talked about, inti-mately. Franklin will be in good hands."

"Ben. Ben, *let* Jonathan help. You know you need all you can get. Also, I want you to take Ruth. And Ginny. They both belonged to sis, but I'm sure Ruth *should* be with Franklin. I know sis would agree. And Ginny, she's so attached to Ruth, I'd hate to split them apart. As I think on it, I'm positive I recall Ruth's name being mentioned in her will when I first skimmed over it the day she, she passed away. I must make certain. Forgive me, my abruptness." Widow Douglas rose, and hastily scurried out of the parlor.

"Ah, dear Brittany. She has always been a captivating woman. Now, this night, even more so. I never dreamed she would want to aide in the plight to free an enslaved human being. I underestimated her strength. Peter would have been proud. My sagging heart has warmed and tingled, and been given a few extra moments of life. To think I lived long enough to hear dear Brittany breath from her own lips those golden words. *Captivating*. But, Benjamin, none-the-less fragile, and easily crushed. I want you to understand that; for what I am going to divulge to you, I don't want you ever to repeat to Brittany." Senator gazed with serious intent. "And I say this while I still have memory enough left within me.. And while I still have the memory left embedded within me, I wish to tell it to you, and to you, Anthony. You see, I came to know the events that unfolded that dreadful night because Loftus wrote a detailed report, and mailed it to Peter, in order to blackmail him. At the end of the report, Loftus made his intentions very certain. He was going to turn Peter in, unless he agreed to make known everyone connected with the movement. He promised Peter full anonymity in return."

Said doctor Towers, "That didn't leave him with many options. Obviously he never betrayed the movement. But, could he have trusted Loftus to keep his word, if he had?"

"Peter was an honorable man. Always was, as long as I had known him. So it was with this honor he did the only thing he felt best for everyone involved; for if he had given into Loftus' demands, he believed that not only would he have put a noose around our necks, but his own as well."

"Brittany told me he died not too long after the Stantans. An accidental fall from off his carriage that resulted in a broken neck."

"Yes. But, but it was no accident. It was suicide. Peter killed himself, rather than meet Loftus' demands."

"Su-suicide?" Muff, more than doctor Towers, took the news the hardest."

"Forgive me, the harsh way in which I revealed the truth. Yes, Peter committed suicide that august afternoon. But not before mailing Loftus' report to me, along with an explanation as to why he chose suicide. He said it was the only way; that with him dead, the underground would be safe, as well as the people connected with it; and that Brittany, for whom he worshiped so dearly, would be spared the humiliation, and disgrace; that with him dead, Loftus could not make a legitimate case. By the time I received his package in the mail, Peter was already dead."

"He came to me, the day before. 'Muff', he said, 'do me a favor'. I told him I'd do anything he asked. He wanted me to look after Miss Douglas, in case anything should happen to him. I didn't understand what he meant, and he wouldn't go any further. He made me vow I'd look over Miss Douglas, from a distance. I did, vow I would, and I have. Twenty-four hours later he was dead. I didn't know what to make of it. But I remembered my vow, and kept to it. But, but somewhere I failed. 'Twas the nightmares I had every night, that done it, that drove me back to the bottle. Those horrid, horrid images of the Stantans. I couldn't never get 'em—,"

"Images?" Senator interrupted. "Are you saying you *saw* Robert and Marribelle, after they had been murdered? But it was reported Murrell's Gang threw their bodies into the river."

Muff looked out a window facing the Stantan Home. "I never told sheriff Tilman, nor anyone else, the whole truth 'bout that night. Course, he, and everyone else, thought I was drunk, anyway. " Senator and doctor Towers listened intently. "Well, I had waited 'til after Murrell's Gang was clear out of sight, b'fore I entered the Stantan Home. I never exactly knew what to expect. I tried to prepare myself for the worst, but it didn't never come close to what I actually saw. Well, I found 'em, Robert and Marribelle. Rather, I nearly stumbled across them.

They had stripped the Stantans of their clothing, and brutally hacked them to pieces."

"*Hacked.*" Senator felt queasy. He jittered unsteadily.

"There they was, they who had been alive only minutes earlier; now, dissected and piled atop one another, as cruelly as randomly. Hands and feet, arms and legs. They was beheaded too. Their bellies gutted like a fish, and most of their insides cut out and thrown into a separate heap. I couldn't make out whose limb belonged to who; though the hands, the hands, well, I could see by the long, painted fingernails which hands were Marribelle's. It made the gruesome discovery so much more harder to bear. And *blood.* Everywhere blood. Before I realized I was stepping on it, it had soaked through to my feet."

"Oh, Robert. Marribelle." Senator shook his head in disbelief.

"My mind clouded, and I felt more helpless than ever. I had to pull myself together, figure out what to do. There was a chest, off against a side wall. Waren't anything in it; was only just a decoration. 'Twas Marribelle's I knew, 'cause she talked about it often. Said it had been in her family generations. Wasn't easy, but, but I, as tenderly as I could, my hands shook so terribly, I placed both there remains, everything, inside. Don't know how I got the strength to, but I carried it out back of the home, out to the garden. Buried it there. I knew nobody would ever suspect what was there, 'cause Marribelle was alwus planting flowers and such; always had flower beds ready and waiting. I made sure the grave blended in. Then, I returned to the home one last time; to the room they was murdered. I tried wiping away the blood, but it weren't no use. So I took a rug from another room and covered every last trace. I set a table and a couple chairs over it all, and hoped for the best. That is, nobody would go poking their noses under the rug. I don't reckon anyone ever did. I fled afterwards, but didn't make it halfway down the hill before Sheriff Tilman and a group of men spotted me. So I had to think of a story quick. I told them I had seen Murrell running out of the home with a chest under his arm—which was true. But I lied about seeing his gang carrying two bodies out of the mansion. I let Tilman speculate. He put me in the jail overnight. Said he might want to ask more questions. Never did though. By morning I discovered the house was boarded up."

"Yes," Senator reminisced. "My doing. I had townsmen work the whole night boarding up every doorway and window, for safety reasons; but as well to keep the public from finding the tunnel. If anyone had found the tunnel, *well*."

"Twas caved in anyway."

"Oh? Oh," Senator soon realized. "It must have occurred during the mad exodus, in total darkness. My god, the terror they must have experienced. Their bodies pounding against the walls, loosening the dirt, until it finally gave way. How many of them perished under the weight, slowly suffocating as the dirt forced its way down their throats and noses?"

"'Twas only two in there. I, I went back, just this night in fact. First time I been through that tunnel since that night."

"You dug out the dirt?"

"No, Ben. But two innocent children did. Oh, they only thought there was buried treasure down there. All them rumors that'd been floatin' around. Well, they never suspected what the tunnel really was, and they never found treasure. They was the ones that found the skeletons. The only two slaves that never made it out. I know'd who they was right off, when I shined a lantern on 'em. They was the two that planned to get married, soon as they was free. I know'd 'cause Marribelle had given 'em a diamond ring."

"Marribelle was always generous to the slaves."

"I saw it on the woman's finger. What used to be her finger."

"What happened to them? The slaves I talked to never mentioned anyone left behind."

"I didn't put two and two together 'til after you told us 'bout the chaos, after they heard the gunshots. I took a good long look at their skeletons. Their ribs was broken in so many places, well, it 'peared they had been trampled. Even if they had made it outside, they wouldn't have lived long enough to journey much further. They looked to have clung together, in one another's arms. There, they died."

Doctor Towers said, "With all the internal bleeding they must have endured, for however long they lived, it could not have been very comfortable."

"No, Ben. But they was together. I reckon that made it easier, somewhat."

"I should like to see them. Pay my respects. Apologize, for, for my terrible blunder."

"They ain't in the tunnel any longer. I removed their remains only hours ago, and buried them, properly, and together, so they wouldn't never be apart, ever."

"You're a true human being, Anthony. Not many others would have gone to such impassioned lengths. I wish I had known you while you were in the movement."

"Yes, Muff. I, I tend to agree. I've been rather, well hostile to you all night. Asking, demanding things of you; questioning things about you, well, because I've had such distrust of you for so many years. Maybe, maybe after tonight we can put that behind us. Maybe we can get to know one another, all over again."

"I, I don't know what to say, Ben. I said many a harsh word agin you, fer so many years. But especially this night. I reckon jealousy, vindictiveness, unwarranted hatred was the cause. I s'pose now, well like you say, maybe we *can* put it all behind us. Maybe—." The recognizable footsteps of Widow Douglas could be heard descending the stairs.

Senator stopped and listened. "Quiet now, I hear Brittany returning."

Entering, she sighed wearily. "Oh what a fool I've been, to have allowed sis' letter to rest untouched, up in her room; afraid of what was contained inside. But I've read it, finally, twice in fact. It's part will, part apology letter. She apologizes for all the mistakes she has made throughout her entire life, to everyone she has wronged. She makes an apology to you too, Ben, for the way she had treated you while you took care of me. Ben, she wants us to be happy together; she wrote her consent, that we should be married, and live together, forever."

"It seems I owe her an apology as well.."

"There's also something about Ruth, and of Ginny, and even of Jim, if ever he is found. She's set them free, all of them, in this letter."

"Oh!" came a loud cry from the hallway near the library; then a thump. Moments later Franklin walked into the parlor, holding Ruth in his arms.

"Franklin!" exclaimed Ben.

"Ruth!" exclaimed Widow Douglas. "I didn't know you were there."

"I's awful sorry," Franklin said, setting Ruth down upon the couch. "Me an Ruthie, we only jus' came in; we worried 'bout what wuz t' become of us; me 'specially. Ruthie wanted to know. I couldn't hol' her back no longer; I had t' foller her. Mighty strong girl she is. We heard voices, and de fu'st words we made out was yours, sayin' Ruthie was free, and not a slave no more. She fainted she could hardly b'lieve her ears. Here, she's comin' to now."

Ruth sat up and rubbed her eyes.

"Is it all a dream? Is I really free, and Ginny too?"

Widow Douglas sat down beside her. "Yes Ruth, it's all true."

"Oh, bless you Missus!" Her arms twined around Widow Douglas, squeezing tightly. Widow Douglas was tolerant; she hugged Ruth with equal strength.

"I *am* so happy for you Ruth. But it isn't I you should be thanking. Miss Watson set you free. I'll have sis' letter printed in all the papers, this very Monday, so everyone can read her apology, and know she has set Ruth and Ginny free."

Senator interrupted. "There is still the matter of *you*." He pointed towards Franklin. "However, the problem is easily overcome, if you don't mind waiting here a few extra days while Ruth's and Ginny's freedom papers are drawn up and legalized. I'm sure you all would want to leave together."

"Yes, su'. But, them Quakers, ain't de gonna worry?"

"You let me straighten the situation out. They are very understanding people, of whom I've had many pleasant interactions with. They won't mind waiting, not at all."

Ruth, Franklin and Ginny slept in the mansion; which became the first of Widow Douglas' atonements. The second would take place with the freeing of her slaves. "I have money to hire servants," she told herself. "I wish this had transpired long ago."

Ginny, having taken a great interest in Senator, begged him to tuck her in. Saying good night, she asked him why, as a white man, he went to great lengths to treat her kindly.

"Child," Senator gladly explained, "when I look upon your beautiful face, your beautiful skin, it is as though I am looking at myself. In a way, perhaps I am—looking at myself."

CHAPTER 40

On Monday, Tom went with Becky to her home. She wanted to straighten it up, make the place look presentable; but did not want to go alone.

Widow Douglas made good on her promise to have her sister's will printed in the paper; and the town buzzed with the news Miss Watson had freed Jim before she died. Nobody understood why she had done it, for she had taken that secret to her grave; but this stunning revelation put to rest anyone's hopes of collecting a reward. Though, many people believed Jim already dead; drown in the storm while trying to escape.

Reaching the Thatcher residence, Becky turned to Tom; she lightly rubbed his shoulder.

"I'm glad you came with, Tom. I'd 'a' cleaned the house anyway, but company always makes the task that more enjoyable. And, and it also makes it easier for me to go inside. I don't think I can do it alone, now. Maybe later. *Much* later."

All of Tom's life he had dreaded work, and had gone to great pains in order to get out of anything remotely laborious. This time, the boy did not hold to these aversions. Quite oppositely, and much to his surprise, he gladly welcomed the work; any time, doing anything, so long as Becky stood by him.

Said he. "I don't know how much longer we got together. Well, Aunt Polly's been talking with her sister down in Arkansas; she and her husband has got a farm there, and they think it'd be good for me to visit for a spell. Aunt Polly says as much too. Looks like I'm going whether I want to or not."

"How soon?"

"There's a boat, the *Helen Claymont*, Aunt Polly says, due to arrive towards weeks end, or early the next. It's bound for Orleans, but Auntie says its likely to make many stops along the way. If Pikesville is one, that's the boat for me she says. Their farm is only two miles below, and it ain't no trouble to ride—. Oh, Becky! No, not again."

Those mysterious forces, unexplainable evils, mischievous deviltries, again silently crept up behind Becky and took complete control over her entire body, possessing her for the longest time yet. Tom held her, as he had before, until this unknown cancer lifted its stronghold upon Becky. Without speaking about the incident they began straightening the furniture, sweeping up as many cobwebs as they could hunt down, and all the loose and reachable dust they could stomach; for it had the tendency to spurt inside their noses at times, and cause unpleasant reactions. In the middle of this cleaning, Becky heard the front door push open, and slam against the wall. She turned around. Tom, in the other room, rushed out to see what had happened.

"Becky, what—. M—. Mr. Thatcher," Tom stammered in disbelief.

"Pa!" Becky dropped her broom. "You're back."

Judge Thatcher stood, wearily; his head drooping so low as to give the impression it had been partly severed. He leaned up against the door, to support his fatigued, worn out and abused body. His clothes were torn; and where his skin lay exposed, there were various, nasty cuts and infections.

Yawning, as a lion, the man slammed the door shut. Lifting his head above his shoulders he spied Tom and Becky. Surprised to see them, his heart raced; and he awoke, slightly, from his drowsy slumber.

"Becky? Tom? I, I didn't expect t-to see you, here." Judge Thatcher had been able to control his stuttering, now minimally noticeable.

"Pa!" Becky cautiously approached her father.

"Not so close, Becky. I've cuts and bruises. God knows what else. I slipped down a muddy embankment is all, while tracking them. Let me rest a spell. Get washed, perhaps checked by a doctor. Oh, I'm s-so tired. I didn't realize, 'til just now. I could sleep a year, though." Judge Thatcher laid a hand upon his daughter's shoulder, and gently patted it.

"Did you, did you find the men?" Tom asked. "Are they in custody?"

No," Judge Thatcher responded. He walked past both Tom and Becky, towards the stairs. Slowly, and with some difficulty, he ascended.

"No?" Tom pressed the question further. "They got away, then?"

"No."

"Pa, what happened? Can't you talk about it?" Becky did not want to aggravate her father, but she, like Tom, desperately yearned to know the fates of Jed and Sim.

Continuing to climb the stairs, Judge Thatcher spoke softly, though a bit annoyed. "I'd rather not go into all the details. Not now. They, they're dead."

Neither Tom, nor Becky, were prepared for *this* shocking response. They each held a certain pity for the brothers; even as Tom had once been eager to *avenge* Becky's kidnapping, and "do away" with her aggressors, for which he envisioned in his riveting dream. Now, that earlier sentiment rang hollow.

Becky, for whom they had held hostage, and treated poorly, felt sorrow for them as well; for during her time as their prisoner, she began to understand Jed and Sim, understand they were not so much evil as misunderstood.

"Could you tell us anything, Mr. Thatcher?"

"Yes. Anything at all, pa?"

Reaching the second floor, Judge Thatcher painstakingly turned his body, using the bannister for leverage, and peered down.

"I know how you two must feel. I know you m-must be hungering for the news. I'll be brief, and afterwards you both will let me go into my room and sleep; for I have been without it a very good long time."

Judge Thatcher explained how he had met up with Jed and Sim some twenty miles up river; how he had discovered both men behind a group of decaying logs; and how he crept up as close to them as he could, and positioned himself behind a large tree.

"I never t-tracked anyone so easy, as I did them." His tone, one of sorrow. "But, if it hadn't been for my carelessness which resulted in me slipping down the embankment, I might have caught up to them sooner."

Readying himself, Judge Thatcher called out to the men, and ordered them to surrender. One man, however, defiantly raised his long rifle in the direction of the trees Judge Thatcher stood behind.

"I felt compelled to shoot first. I struck him, fatally. After he fell dead upon his rifle, the other man, in a state of horror and panic, picked the dead man up; and for the next few moments slapped and shook him. Then, apparently realizing the man was not going to wake up, this other fellow did a curious thing. He gently laid his dead companion down against the logs and looked towards me. I felt sure he was going to give himself up. Instead he..."

Judge Thatcher explained how the sole survivor had removed a knife from his belt and plunged it into himself; though he had made sure to be delicate about the translation of events.

"This man fell upon the other man, clutched him tightly, and there, he too died. That is all I can tell you. Now, you must allow me time to sleep."

Judge Thatcher did not tell them, nor did he ever confess to anyone, that, while inspecting the dead men, he made a horrific find. At least, from his point of view. Not only had the rifle been unloaded, but the trigger was jammed back, remedying the weapon totally useless.

In his mind, Judge Thatcher had committed murder in cold blood. And while he knew no-one would ever convict him, it did not mend his grieving heart. In an attempt to appease his conscience, he delivered the bodies to the undertaker, where he paid a handsome sum of money so the two men might be buried properly and humanely, and with due respect.

As Judge Thatcher walked stiffly into his bedroom, Tom and Becky were left to speculate which brother had been fatally shot, and ponder why the other had killed himself. Unfortunately, for the children, their curiosity would only intensify; for when Judge Thatcher awoke, many hours later, he could not recall any details of the event; nor could he even remember discussing them with anyone. And by this time, Jed and Sim were forever buried.

Very little remembrance of that day resurfaced in his mind.

The next day, feeling his strength sufficient enough to venture out, Judge Thatcher rode over to Doctor Towers' office, hoping he might be treated for his cuts and bruises. Upon finding it closed, with a note across the glass pane reading—*At Widow Douglas'*—he slowly departed in the direction of her mansion. A postal clerk stopped him before he had made much progress.

"A letter, sir," the young clerk announced, running alongside the carriage. "From Constantinople. Three days old now." Reading it, Judge Thatcher turned the carriage around and headed for home, fast. The letter had been in response to one he sent out just prior to setting out after Jed and Sim, in which he wrote of Becky's safe return. This new letter read...

> *Mrs. Thatcher out of harm's way, and recovering well,*
> *now that she knows her daughter, dearest Rebecca, is safe.*
> *She longs to see her, and hold her. We agree Rebecca's*
> *swift return to Constantinople will do wonders for Mrs.*
> *Thatcher's health. Godspeed!*

Judge Thatcher relayed the information to Becky later that day.

"Your mother needs you. You know that, Becky. In fact, I may return to Constantinople too, permanently. I've given it much thought over the past few—." Judge Thatcher reconsidered his words. "Well, we were a happy, a *happier*, family back in Constantinople, when I was only a judge; nothing higher, or more prominent in stature; and where I could be a good husband and father. I'd like to return to that lifestyle, quickly. First, first we must get you off to your mother. After which, I shall take care of my affairs here, in St. Petersburg, and then, then join you both."

"When will you be taking me back?"

The man contemplated. While doing so, he examined his daughter carefully. "Well, not this very minute; for I know *you* have affairs in which you must straighten out too, eh." He smiled, with an air of understanding. "Besides, I have to see about borrowing a wagon. Tomorrow morning, early. It's the best I can do. It gives you all of today."

"Thank you, pa."

"Oh, and Becky," Judge Thatcher called out to his daughter as she walked out the door, "tell him he's welcome to come by and see you off."

Becky said nothing; she only smiled, brilliantly.

Some hours after daybreak, well longer than Judge Thatcher wanted to remain in St. Petersburg, he slid a large trunk packed with Becky's belongings upon the back of the wagon he had borrowed. Grunting in disdain, he told Becky, "I have a few things to do inside, before we leave. We'll be off soon, very soon."

Her father inside, Becky turned to Tom. He saw in her a deepening emptiness, and thought to quell it; though a conceited part of him wanted to fill it with his own self pity. He bravely held back.

"Becky, I, I didn't know it would be this soon. I thought, I wish, we would have had the whole summer. But it's all so sudden. I don't know how to react, to say goodbye without I've had time to prepare for it. It ain't like all them tall tales I've told, where I didn't need but a few moments to see where the wind lay. This is different."

"I know. I feel it too. But pa is anxious to get home, to Constantinople, to see ma again. And who can blame him? I want to see her too; I miss her so. It's been so long since—."

Awkward quiet. Then—

"Have,. have you got the *nonamous* letter?"

"Right here," Becky replied, patting her dress pocket.

"Your pipe? And arrow-head?"

"Uh-huh. I check every few minutes, to make sure they *are* there. I'm always afraid they'll fall out somewhere, and I'll loose them forever." She lowered her head. "Silly, huh?"

"No! Why—."

More awkward quiet.

"Oh, Tom!" Becky cried out. "If you and I could, *just one last time,* maybe—." Becky turned her head, gradually at first, then, in one violent jerk she froze. Terror seemed to grip her. Tom became alarmed when Becky kept this stare too long. Before he could do anything she shouted, "Hark! Me thinks me sees danger approaching, from the west."

Tom turned, but saw nothing out of the ordinary.

"I don't see—,"

"Oh, *yes.* Pirates! Thousands of them. Black Avenger, dust thou see them *now*?"

"Becky, I..." Becky smiled, hinting her desire. Tom finally understood her motives. "Why, I *do* see them. They're landing. Quick now, step lively. We haven't a moment to loose. We must flee!" They both crept around the carriage, circling it a few times.

"Oh fearless Black Avenger, hast thou a plan of escape?"

"Never fear Guinevere."

"Call me—Joan of Arc," she stated, proudly.

"Joan of Arc?" Tom questioned. Becky nodded. "Well then, fear not *Joan of Arc.* Tis not a pirate as bold or cunning as I, the Black Avenger of the Spanish Main, that could overtake me. Ye are safe whilst in thy protection."

"Oh, I know it; I know it. But keep close watch. They're closing in. We cannot allow capture, else they'll take the treasure map for themselves, and slit our throats."

"Aye. Here now, let us make use of this bridge. Crawl under. They'll ne'er find us."

They both stooped down and crawled under the wagon, and spoke above a whisper.

"They doth approach. I hear the steady reign of hooves."

"Steadfast then, Gu—. Joan. Hold tight. Maketh not a breath." They huddled together.

"I hear them. Closer."

"They grow nigh."

The scene might have been imagined, but their racing heart beats were quite real.

"Oh, Avenger, the footsteps, they seem right overhead."

"Steady."

"They've stopped."

"Steady."

"I can hear the breathing of a thousand horses."

"Stead—,"

"Tom! Becky!" Judge Thatcher's voice boomed. Where are-?" Seeing two shadows illuminate from under the wagon, he knelt down to investigate. "What is going on? Becky?"

"Oh, well. Pirates." Becky turned red with shame.

"Pi-!" The man looked all around, not because he believed there *were* pirates, but rather out of a general and natural reflex. Tom and Becky crawled out.

"Sorry, pa. We got carried away."

"Well, well all is in order. It's time, Becky."

Becky nodded with sad understanding. "Okay."

"Tom, you are welcome to travel along, part of the way. As far as the border."

Tom, thrilled, hopped up on the back. Becky joined him.

As the wagon pulled away from the Thatcher residence, Becky sighed deeply. It had been her home for over a year and a half; she had many fond memories, not soon to be forgotten.

The large crates and trunks provided the two with privacy, which enabled them to be more open and frank in their conversation. Knowing their time grew shorter, Becky had but one last confession to reveal to Tom. Petty, perhaps; but not to her.

"Tom." Becky confessed. "Remember I told you I hadn't any thoughts of you being a coward? Well, that was true, but, I, in the passage, when I believed all was lost, there came a time when I wondered why you hadn't shown up yet."

"That's only natural, and to be expected."

"Maybe, but I had them, and I'm so ashamed, Tom. I *am*. I did think you to be a coward. I was in a weak condition, then. I did not know what I was thinking, or what I was doing. I only tell you now because, well, because we have come so far, and I may never see you again. I wanted to be honest with you. I wanted to tell you. This is something that has really bothered me for some time."

"I understand."

"I hope you do. I really hope you do. I thought, maybe I should keep this from you. I thought maybe that would be the right thing to do. But then I thought, I must tell him. If I don't, I could not have that on my conscience. But I want you to know now, that I was wrong to think such things. I was delirious, and people under that condition do not know what they are doing, or saying. Once I was better, once I had all my faculties again, the thought never crossed my mind about your bravery. I knew you would come. I always knew. And I wanted you to know that. I wanted you to know how much I care about you."

"I, I care about you too, Becky. I do."

"I'm glad you do. It's makes it all the more harder to say goodbye; but we will always have fond memories of the times we did spent together. Cherish them, Tom; cherish them as I do. Promise me."

"I promise."

Though the carriage had crossed the border leading out of St. Petersburg, Tom stayed with Becky a little longer. Time became urgently precious for them, and they made the most of it, together.

When that dreadful moment did arrive, Tom said, "I had better get off now; while there is forest left, for cover. If your pa knew I was still aboard—,"

"Don't say any more. I know; I know, Tom." Tears filled their eyes.

Tom slipped down off the carriage, waving to Becky; she waved back to him, donning her effervescent mega-grin, forcing herself to hold back her tears. He watched her until she disappeared out of sight; she never once relinquished that most pleasant of smiles.

Made in the USA
Middletown, DE
21 September 2017